W9-BUT-673

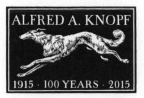

In the Country

In the Country

STORIES

Mia Alvar

ALFRED A. KNOPF
New York   2015

THIS IS A BORZOI BOOK
PUBLISHED BY ALFRED A. KNOPF

Copyright © 2015 by Mia Alvar

www.aaknopf.com

Knopf, Borzoi Books, and the colophon are registered trademarks
of Penguin Random House LLC.

Grateful acknowledgment is made to Hal Leonard Corporation for permission
to reprint an excerpt from "White Rabbit," words and music by Grace Slick,
copyright © 1966 by Irving Music, Inc., copyright renewed. All rights
reserved. Reprinted by permission of Hal Leonard Corporation.

Several stories in this collection first appeared, in different form, in the
following publications: "Legends of the White Lady" in *The Cincinnati
Review*, "The Virgin of Monte Ramon" in *Euphony*, "Shadow Families"
on FiveChapters.com, "The Miracle Worker" in *The Missouri Review*,
and "The Kontrabida" in *One Story*.

Library of Congress Cataloging-in-Publication Data
Alvar, Mia, [date]
[Short stories. Selections]
In the country : stories / Mia Alvar.—First edition.
Pages   cm
ISBN 978-0-385-35281-9 (hardback)
ISBN 978-0-385-35284-0 (eBook)
1. Filipinos—Fiction. I. Title.
PS3601.L863A6 2015
813'.6—dc23
2014036940

Jacket photograph by TanMan/Fototrove/Getty Images
Jacket design by Oliver Munday

Manufactured in the United States of America
First Edition

for Glenn

CONTENTS

In the Country

The Kontrabida

My mother was waiting in front of our house when I rode up in a taxi. "There you are," she said, as if we'd simply lost each other for an hour or two, at a party. I only half-embraced her, afraid she might break if I held too tight. She hadn't been able to collect me from the airport herself. Years ago my father had forbidden her to drive, though I supposed he could do little to prevent it now.

"Let me," she said, reaching for my suitcase. I waved her away. I would no sooner allow my mother to carry my suitcase than allow her to carry me. "Oh, Steve," she protested. "You don't know my strength!" She dropped her arms, flattening the palms against her lap, a habit I remembered well. Throughout my childhood she often looked to be drying her hands on an apron, whether or not she was wearing one.

In the decade since I left she hadn't aged, exactly. To my eyes she seemed not older but *more*. More frail; more tired; softer-spoken; her dark, teaspoon-shaped face cast farther down. Every feature I remembered had settled in her and been more deeply confirmed.

My parents still lived in Mabini Heights, a suburb of Manila and monument to a time when they belonged to the middle class. My father had called himself an import-export business-man before sliding, through the years, down a spiral of unrelated jobs, each more menial than the last, and harder for him to keep. And my mother had been a nurse before he banned her from working outside the house altogether. But if they'd come down in the world, so had Mabini Heights. Ever since my childhood in the seventies, when so much of that middle class fled Marcos and martial law, houses had been left unfinished or carved up for different uses. Squatters set up camp amid the scaffolding and roofless rooms. Families took in boarders or relatives. Our house had changed too: on its right, a gray unpainted cinder-block cell had been added, taking up what used to be a yard. My parents had cemented over the grass and built this *sari-sari* store five years earlier, selling snacks and other odds and ends through a sliding wicket to people on the street. The *sari-sari* compromised what I imagine was the dream of my parents, who grew up poor: a green buffer between the world and *their* world.

The addition seemed to shrink the main house to a toy, its windows tiny and its clay roof something storybook elves might have built. Next to it, I felt gigantic. I hunched my shoulders as I followed my mother inside. I was convinced, walking behind her, that the dishes on the shelves were rattling.

"Papa's in here," said my mother, opening the door to my old bedroom. The blast of cold came as a shock, then a relief. There was an air conditioner now, in the window under which I used to sleep as a child, and my old bed, where my father lay, was pushed into a corner. I saw, from the straw mat rolled up beside him, that my mother had been sleeping on the floor at night. Otherwise the room was clean and bare and quiet as I remembered—same white cinder-block walls, same wood-tiled floors, same smell of mothballs from the same chest of drawers—if all faded a little, like an old photograph. My mother kept a tidy house—a trait we shared—and things probably lasted longer in her care.

Two oxygen tanks stood beside my father's bed. He breathed through a tube. The sight of him brought me back to New York, where I lived, and to the hospital where I worked as a clinical pharmacist. My father no longer resembled me. The short boxer's physique, a bullish muscularity I'd always detested sharing with him, was gone. In fact he no longer resembled anyone in the family; he belonged now to that transnational tribe of the sick and the dying. Without the dentures he'd worn most of his adult life, my father's mouth was a pit, a wrinkled open wound below the nose. What I could see of his eyes, under lids that were three-quarters closed, did not appear to see me back. He looked not only thin but vacuum-dried, desiccated—less a human than the prehistoric remains of one.

He groaned, a low and heavy sound.

"All right, Papa. All right." My mother took a brown dropper bottle from a chair next to the bed. "This used to hold him for a while," she said. "But lately he's complaining round the clock." Steadying his chin, she released a dose of liquid morphine into his mouth, with the dainty caution of a woman ladling hot soup or lighting a church candle. He let out another groan. "Sshhh." She stroked the sides of his face. Even bedridden and in pain, my father had managed to preserve their old arrangement: when he called, she was there to wait on him.

I'd predicted this, and how much I would hate to watch. In my suitcase, I carried an answer. Succorol was the newest therapy for chronic pain on the market in America. White and square, the size of movie ticket stubs, Succorol patches adhered to the skin, releasing opiates much stronger than morphine. Doctors had just started prescribing them to terminal patients in New York. Succorol could take years to reach the Philippines, a country whose premier pharmacy chain boasted LAGING BAGO ANG GAMOT DITO! as its tagline (*We do not sell expired drugs here!*). Still, something kept me from unpacking the patches right then. I did not want my mother to see my hands shaking—to know what I had done to bring them here in the first place, let alone the price I'd pay if anyone found out.

"Is that better, Papa?" My mother returned the morphine to the chair next to a rosary, a spiral notebook, a folded white hand fan. She logged the dose in to the notebook like the nurse she'd once been. I picked up the fan and opened it, rib by wooden rib.

Its lace edge had frayed, but the linen pleats remained bright and clean. I remembered sitting in her lap as a child during Sunday Mass, while she flicked her wrist back and forth to cool me with it.

She'd brought my father to the doctor eight months before, when he had trouble breathing and couldn't finish a meal without hunching over in pain. His belly had grown to the size of a watermelon and, from the veins straining against the skin, nearly as green. When my mother called me in New York and said "liver cancer," I imagined my parents as clearly as if I'd been sitting in the free clinic with them. I saw my father shrug or grunt each time the doctor addressed him, as proud and stubbornly tongue-tied as he always became around people with titles and offices. I saw my mother frown in concentration and move her lips in time with the doctor's, as if that would help her understand. I saw her dab the corners of my father's mouth with the white handkerchief she always carried in her purse.

Because of his age and his refusal, even after this diagnosis, to stop drinking, he never qualified for a transplant. At my mother's request, I wired money into a Philippine National Bank account that I kept open for the family. Whenever someone needed rent or medicine or tuition back home, I sent what I could, having no wife or children of my own to support. In my father's case, I thought about refusing. But it occurred to me a relative might say he could get better care in America. His coming to New York for treatment and staying with me—or, worse, in the hospital where I made my living—was something I'd have wired any sum to avoid.

When chemotherapy did not stop the cancer's spread to his lungs, when radiation did not shrink the masses, my father's doctor began to speak in a code we both understood: *pain management* instead of *treatment;* not *recovery* but *comfort in his last days.* My money turned from doxorubicin and radiotherapy to oxygen tanks, air-conditioning, the dark brown bottle of morphine. Still, I expected my father to survive. For all the years I'd spent wishing him dead, it was my mother's role in the family drama, not his, to suffer. *Esteban has got some heavy hands,* the family always said. *Loretta is a saint.* When she called to tell me "end-stage," my mother may as well have said we'd never lived under a clay roof in Mabini Heights, that I remembered my entire childhood wrong.

I insisted on seeing the inside of the *sari-sari* store before lunch. "Corporate headquarters," said my mother. She pulled aside the screen door that once led from the kitchen onto grass.

Once more, I felt like an ogre in a dollhouse. The vast and open yard of my childhood amounted now to just ten feet from the screen door to the wicket, and barely six across. Sacks of rice, tanks of soy sauce, and bricks of dry glass noodles, stacked against the walls, narrowed it even more. Candy in glass jars, each with its own metal scoop, sat in rows upon the shelves above. Reels of shampoo and detergent hung from the ceiling, dispensing Palmolive or Tide in single-use packets. I thought of the thin, sealed sleeves of Succorol, flanked by dental floss and blister-packed vitamins, in a side pocket of the toiletry bag lodged between my socks and shirts. A complete amateur's attempt at smuggling, which nearly froze my heart nonetheless as I sent my luggage down the airport X-ray belt.

I closed my eyes and tried to breathe. *Sari-sari* meant "assorted" or "sundry," and so the store smelled: like a heady mix of bubble gum and vinegar, salt and soap, floor wax and cologne. My mother switched on a ceiling fan that hung between the fluorescent strip light and the wheels of Tide and Palmolive.

"We should get you another air conditioner," I said. "There's a lot that could melt or spoil in here."

I walked to the far end of the store and ran my palm along the wooden counter. Receipts were impaled on a spike next to a calculator with a roll of printing tape. Behind the scratched Plexiglas wicket, my mother had placed a call bell and a RING FOR SERVICE sign. They'd opened the *sari-sari* five years back, after my father was fired from another job, this time for stealing a crate of Tanduay rum from the restaurant where he'd been waiting tables. "He isn't built to work *under* someone," my mother had said. "It's just not his nature, answering to another man." I said nothing, just sent the money they needed to start. The *sari-sari* gave her a loophole, at least, in his law against her working outside the house.

At the time I hadn't minded so much about the money, which I never expected to see again. But I knew I'd miss the yard, my refuge in the years before I could stand up to my father. When he called my mother a dog or a whore or a foul little cunt who'd ruined his life, she sent me outside. When he seized her by the hair and asked, *What did you say? What did you just say to me?*, she sent me outside. When he struck her face with the underside of our telephone until she wept and begged, first for forgiveness and then for mercy, she sent me outside, into the grass of the yard, where twigs from the acacia tree would have fallen overnight.

In the kitchen, my mother set the table for two. Then she planted a baby monitor at the third chair and tuned it to a grainy black-and-white broadcast of my father, snoring. "This thing saved me," she said. "Now I can keep an eye on him while I work. Or while you and I sit and eat together."

But she hardly sat or ate at all. Throughout lunch she alternated between serving him and serving me. She stood to answer a groan from the sickroom, then heaped my plate with fried rice and beef. She uncapped a bottle of San Miguel for me, then went to feed him a bowl of broth. I spent most of the meal alone with him: my father's screen image and me, facing off across the table.

At this time three days earlier, I was in the hospital, taking inventory of the narcotics cabinet. As I unloaded the most recent shipment of Succorol, I found six more boxes than were counted on the packing slip, a surplus as unlikely as it was expensive. And immediately I imagined my mother, titrating morphine into his mouth by hand, as I re-counted the boxes and rechecked my number against the invoice. I thought of my mother running back and forth between the *sari-sari* and the sickroom, as I typed the lower figure into the inventory log. I thought of her, crying or praying after morphine had ceased to comfort him, as I wheeled the Pyxis in front of the surveillance camera and slipped a month's supply of Succorol into the pockets of my lab coat.

"Bed or bath?" she asked, returning to the kitchen. A pail of water was filled and waiting for me in the bathroom; on the master bed, new sheets. Which did I want first? All that was missing was the *sir*.

The baby monitor groaned on the table. The call bell dinged in the store. My mother glanced from one to the other, torn.

"I've got the store," I volunteered. "You take care of him." Her eyebrows rose, but I said, "What is there to know? I saw price tags on your jars and a cashbox under the counter. I'll print receipts from the calculator, if people want them."

As it turned out, I was no help at all. My first customer wanted shampoo. I pulled too hard on the Palmolive, unspooling hundreds of packets to the floor. My mother had to climb a stepladder to reel them back in. Another customer asked for detergent. I ripped a packet of Tide down the middle, sending a flurry of blue-flecked snow everywhere. My mother swept up after me with a broom. The women barely spoke above a whisper, sometimes covering their mouths to hide bad teeth. *"Ano?"* I asked, over and over. The louder I asked, the softer they answered. The farther they retreated from the wicket, the closer I stooped to read their faces, feeling more like a bully than a shop clerk.

My father's groans, on the other hand, I heard perfectly well. In her trips back and forth from the *sari-sari* to the sickroom, my mother moved the baby monitor to the freezer case, rushing from the store as soon as he called or stirred on-screen. While she was gone, a teenage girl asked me for Sarsi cola. Relieved to understand, I handed her a bottle from the freezer. She giggled, staring, and said something else behind her hands. "... *plastik*" was all I heard. Remembering the jar of plastic straws on the counter and the bottle opener underneath, I uncapped the bottle and added a straw. She giggled and shook her head, asking again for "*plastik.*" I wondered if she meant a plastic shopping bag and searched the store, finding one crumpled on a shelf. Now she was giggling too hard to speak. I felt as confused as in my earliest days as a clinical pharmacy resident in New York—a beginner desperate to impress my superiors, bungling even the basics.

When my mother returned, she spoke to the girl and poured the Sarsi cola into a plastic sleeve, thin as a layer of onionskin. She stored the bottle in a crate that would go back to the factory. How had I forgotten? I'd drunk sodas from plastic sleeves up until the age of twenty-five. And yet the liquid bag I handed over made me think not of my childhood but of some dark, alien version of the waste pouches and IV fluids I'd see at the hospital.

"Relax, *anak.*" Dragging a stool to the center of the store, my mother invited me to sit under the ceiling fan. "You're sweating." She handed me a mango Popsicle from the freezer case. The jaw-cramping sweetness of each bite felt vaguely humiliating as I sat and watched her work.

Unlike me, she had no trouble hearing her customers. No sooner had a face appeared at the wicket than she was reaching for the shoe polish or cooking oil. Her right hand could pop open a bottle cap while her left tore a foil packet from the shampoo reel. To the voice of a young boy, so small I couldn't see him through the wicket, she sold three sheets, for ten centavos apiece, of the grainy, wide-ruled paper on which I'd learned to spell in grade school. It was a way of shopping I had completely forgotten: egg by egg, cigarette by cigarette, people spending what they earned in a day to buy what they would use in the next.

That night I lay in my parents' bedroom. Jet lag and the whir of an electric fan kept me awake. Somewhere above me a gecko made its loud clicking noise, and I was no longer used to the Manila heat. But I refused to sleep any closer to my father, even if it meant losing out on the AC.

Down the hall, he groaned nonstop, as if to say, unless he slept, no one would.

Growing up in this house, I used to hear other noises from him at night. I must have been four or five years old, lying where he did now, the first time a lowing through the wall made me sit up. Until it had echoed once or twice, I didn't know the voice was his. My father sounded more like a flagellant on Good Friday, parading through the streets of Tondo. I thought my mother had found a way to strike back: that he was the one, this time, suffering and forced to beg.

I rushed to the door they'd forgotten to close, and detected my parents' shapes in the dark. He was sitting on the edge of the bed. Naked, but hidden from the waist down by my mother. She knelt, a sheet around her shoulders, wiping the floor with a washcloth. And though she was at his feet, though her shadow rose and fell as she cleaned, as if bowing to a king, my father did not look to be in charge at all. He peeled the lids off his eyes, unsticking his tongue from the roof of his mouth. His skin was waxen with sweat. Stripped and drained, limp and compromised—he could not have hit her, in this state.

Then he saw me in the doorway. "What now?" he said, alert again, his fists starting to lock.

My mother startled. *"Anak!"* She pointed past me, the wet washcloth covering her hand like a bandage. "Get out!"

I ran out to the yard. Not to escape him, but because I knew he'd punish her for every second of my presence there.

This was before I'd learned much about sex; I was too young to be disgusted by it. For a while after that, whenever I heard him groan in the darkness, I didn't know enough to pull my pillow over my ears or run outside in embarrassment. Instead my father's baying, and his stupor afterward, put me under a kind of spell. I'd listen through the cinder-block wall, believing he had fallen out of power, was in pain. Whatever else he might do to my mother, at any other hour, during this shimmering nighttime transaction *he* was the conquered one.

A swarm of aunts, uncles, cousins, and cousins' children descended on the house early the next morning. I passed out all my *pasalubong,* or homecoming gifts: handheld digital games, pencil-and-stationery sets, duty-free liquor, nuts and chocolates I'd stockpiled on layovers in Honolulu and Tokyo. A *balikbayan* knew better than to show up empty-handed.

After the gifts came the inquisition. How cold was it in America, how often did it snow? I kept my lines brief. I had a role to perform: the *balikbayan,* who worked hard and missed home but didn't complain, who'd moved up in New York but wasn't down on Manila. "You get used to the winters," I said. I didn't tell them I loved the snow, was built for the American cold, and felt, upon entering my first job in a thermostat-controlled pharmacy, that I'd come home. What did I miss most about the Philippines? "The food, and Filipinos," I said. "Good thing the nurses always bring me *lumpia* and let me tag along to Sunday Mass." But my days in New York never involved Mass or *lumpia:* outside of work, I spent my free time exercising at the gym, or cleaning my apartment on the twenty-eighth floor of a building made of steel and glass. What about women—was there someone? An American? "The hospital keeps me busy," I said. "No one special enough yet to meet you." I didn't describe the women who sometimes spent the night with me, how they chattered nonstop, intimidated by the tidy home I kept. "Is this an apartment or a lab?" said one, glancing at my countertops. "Are we getting laid here, or embalmed?" asked another, under the tightly tucked bedspread. In every case, I found a reason to stop calling: false modesty, too loud a voice, careless toothpaste spatters around the bathroom sink. Any time a woman opened her mouth and I could imagine myself clapping a hand over it, pinning her to the bed, I knew that my father still breathed somewhere inside of me. I couldn't risk repeating his life.

The questions ended when the karaoke began. Bebot, my cousin's son, had hooked the monitor of my old Commodore computer, outgrown since I first bought it in New York, to a DVD player. When he fed it a karaoke disc, song lyrics and video footage of couples on the beach appeared in green screen. I took on "Kawawang Cowboy" (Pathetic Cowboy), a Tagalog satire of "Rhinestone Cowboy," to show I remembered my Tagalog and to cover my lack of singing talent with silliness. *"A pathetic cowboy,"* I sang. *"I wish I could afford some bubble gum / Instead of dried-up salty Chinese plum. . . ."* The family roared. In New York, the nurses would have shooed us out of any hospital. But here no one worried about disturbing my father, who'd loved karaoke and had a gift for it. In a voice like wine and honey, he used to croon everything from Elvis Presley to classic Tagalog love songs. Even I had to admit that, back then, his signature "Fly Me to the Moon" was charming.

My mother scuttled through our living-room reunion like a servant, pulled in opposite directions by sick groans and the *sari-sari* bell. I thought again of the Succorol, but stayed in my seat. Twice—first in Tagalog, then in English—I had taken a pharmacist's oath to tell the truth and uphold the law. People lost jobs and licenses for less. If our suppliers discovered their mistake, called all their clients and somehow—between time stamps, shift schedules, signatures, and security footage—found me out, I could land in jail, to say nothing of the damage to my name with colleagues and the department head who'd trusted me with inventory to begin with. Deceit of any kind was a foreign country to me. As a child, I'd never so much as shoplifted a comic book, or lied to a teacher, or cheated at a game of cards. This discipline earned me perfect grades in high school, scholarships through college, my first job at a Manila drugstore, a doctor of pharmacy degree from my school's brother university in New York, fast promotions at the hospital. Whenever I saw classmates copy each other's homework or make faces behind the priests' backs, I thought of my father, and how he too must have started small on the path to worse.

I considered hiring a live-in nurse, but my mother was the kind of woman who waited on even the people she'd paid to serve us, back when we could afford them: the laundress, the gardener, the *yaya* who watched me before I started school. Now she did the same for relatives who covered *sari-sari* shifts and friends who visited them. They all ate at our table and helped themselves to free snacks and sodas from the store. A paid nurse would only give her another plate to wash, another chair to pull out.

The next time the bell rang, I followed my mother into the kitchen and through the screen door. Away from my family's relentless yammering, the *sari-sari* felt like a sanctuary again: in but not of the house, and cooler than the crowded living room. My mother helped a customer, then gazed at the baby monitor, perched up on a shelf between jars of Spanish shortbread and tamarind candy.

"*I've got a gun without a bullet and a pocket without money,*" she turned to me and sang, off-key. "You inherited my singing voice, *anak.* Sorry."

"Apologize to your family," I said. "They had to listen to it." From the shelf I picked one of her favorites: *pastillas de leche,* soft mini-logs made with sugar and *carabao*'s milk. My mother had a sweet tooth that didn't match her frame. I set the yellow box on the counter and reached into my pocket.

"Oh, no you don't," she said. "This is on the house."

"Absolutely not," I said.

"We're a Filipino store; we don't accept American dollars."

"Nice try. I exchanged my money at the airport."

"Your money's no good here."

"Stop giving things away for free." I unwrapped one of the *pastillas*, knowing she wouldn't start ahead of me. "That's no way to keep a business afloat. There's my first piece of advice for you."

"It's your second," she said. "Yesterday you said it was too hot in here." She pointed at the whirling blades on the ceiling. "People pay all kinds of money for good business advice, don't they? So I'm not giving anything away for free." She frowned as she bit into a *pastilla*, as if eating required all her concentration.

I took my hand from my pocket, and we crunched for a while without speaking.

"If I ever leave the hospital and open my own pharmacy," I said, "it will be a lot like this." I walked her through my rather old-fashioned vision: tinctures and powders in rows, a mortar and pestle here, a pill counter and weighing scale there.

"Oh, *anak*." I'd become her young son again, pointing at a mansion in Forbes Park or a gown in a shop window, luxuries I vowed to provide her in the future. My mother's eyes filled with tears. "Your pharmacy will be fancier than this. And you could have built it years ago, if you hadn't been busy helping us."

That settled it. Nothing disturbed me more than the sight of her crying. It was time to end her call-button servitude, once and for all. "Ma," I began, "I've given everyone their *pasalubong*, except you."

The baby monitor groaned, bringing her to her feet. "You've given me so much already." She wiped her eyes. "*Pastillas*, free advice . . ." Setting down the call bell and the SERVICE sign, she rushed out, again, to attend to him.

I dropped five hundred pesos into the cashbox and brought the rest of the candy to my relatives in the living room. Once they'd emptied the box, I took it to my room and filled it with the patches of Succorol, then went to the sickroom and closed the door behind me.

My mother was pressing a washcloth to his forehead. "You're a CEO, not a slave," I said. "No more scurrying around. You've got a business to run." I showed her the Succorol and how to use it, peeling a square from its adhesive backing and pressing it to my father's side. "Remove this and apply a new one at the same time tomorrow," I said. "On his back, or arm—anywhere there isn't hair. Rotate or you'll irritate the skin." In my mother's notebook I started a new page and recorded the dose. "So we don't double up," I said. "This isn't Tylenol, if you know what I mean."

We stayed until my father quieted and slept. I closed the yellow box, now full of Succorol, and placed it in the top drawer of the dresser. Before we left the sickroom, she touched my cheek. "You're home," she said. "All the *pasalubong* I need."

In the living room the family had switched from karaoke to a Tagalog movie. Even in green it looked familiar, observing the rules of every melodrama I'd grown up watching: a *bida,* or hero, fought a *kontrabida,* or villain, for the love of a beautiful woman. The oldest films would even cast a pale, fair-haired American as the *bida* and a dusky, slick-mustachioed Spaniard as the *kontrabida.* Between them, the woman spent her time batting her eyelashes or being swept off her feet; peeking out from behind lace fans; fainting or weeping; clutching a handkerchief to her heart or dangling it from the window as a signal; being abducted at night, or rescued from a tower, or carried away on a horse. My relatives talked back to the screen as it played. *Kiss! Kiss!* they insisted, not with any delight or romantic excitement but in a nearly hostile way, heckling the protagonists and the plot to quit stalling and hurry along to the payoff. Even I joined the chorus. When, at last, the *bida* won the woman, we cheered and whistled, again not out of joy so much as a malicious sort of triumph. The script had succumbed, in the end, to our demands.

For three days my father dozed peacefully, waking only when my mother fed him or shifted a bedpan under his haunches. With the Succorol, he never groaned again. At first she ran to check his breathing throughout breakfast and lunch, but by the second day she trusted the baby monitor to show the rise and fall of his chest, his mouth dilating and shrinking. Seeing her relax, I slept better too.

Meanwhile the heat climbed to ninety-three degrees. I woke on my fourth night in the country feeling stained by my own sweat. Next door the air conditioner was humming, and I craved the cold rush that first greeted me there. If I could just stand in that doorway a moment, I might feel better and fall back asleep. I found my way through the dark living room, running my fingertips along the cinder block. The door creaked on my push. I stepped forward into the chill, but didn't enjoy it for long.

My mother turned with a gasp, her eyes wide. Moonlight through the window fell onto the bed and, for the second time in my life, the silhouette of my father, bare-chested, the sheet pulled down to his waist. Her back, bent over him in a ministering pose, straightened up. "*Anak*, don't!" She raised her hand to stop me, mittened by a white washcloth, her body twisting to cover his.

I shut my eyes and the door. My stomach turned. I couldn't go back to their bed now, the place where I'd first walked in on them. Like a child once again, I ran through the living room and kitchen for escape.

The screen door to the *sari-sari* was locked. I shook it, panicked, before remembering the loop hook above the handle. My fingers searched the wall to switch on the light and ceiling fan. I headed for the wicket as if I could flee through it, then climbed and sat on the counter. A mouse darted across the floor to its hiding place behind the freezer. Moths buzzed around the fluorescent strip above me, and another gecko made its clicking sound. It seemed that all the secret forms of life and movement that took place in this house at night had decided to expose themselves to me, and by the time I forced myself back to bed, the sweat on my neck and face had turned cold.

In the morning I heard a man's voice through the wall. I startled, thinking at first that my father had recovered. Then I recognized it, from long-distance phone calls in New York. The doctor. My father was dead.

At his bedside the doctor was removing the buds of a stethoscope from his ears. He gave me a collegial nod. My mother paced across the room. Pins from her hair had scattered at the foot of the bed. ". . . peacefully," Dr. Ramos was saying. "In his sleep." But my father looked far from peaceful. In death his face had gone thuggish again, the underbite and squashed nose giving him as aggressive and paranoid a look as ever. In forty, fifty, sixty years this was how I might die: with my worst impulses petrified on my face.

My mother had stopped pacing but kept rubbing her hands flat against her lap, as if this time she couldn't get them clean. "Loretta?" Dr. Ramos said. Only when he called her name a second time did I notice her head rolling backward, her eyes to their whites. I caught her just before she fainted to the floor.

"I'm sorry" were her first words upon coming to. Her eyes bounced from me to the doctor to my father.

"You're in shock," said Dr. Ramos. "Happens all the time."

I opened the fan on the nightstand and waved it over her face. "Nothing to be sorry about," I said.

And there wasn't. The doctor assumed that my father had passed in a morphine-softened sleep, but now I wondered if he'd gone into cardiac arrest while my mother satisfied some dying wish. Perhaps this would haunt her in the days to come. The hair she usually pinned back hung loose around her face. But I felt calmer than I had the night before; there was no mystery. She'd served him to the end. I should have known she would.

In the basement of the Immaculate Conception Funeral Home, the mortician curved a sponge between his fingers, spackling my father's face with brown grease. An American parlor would never have allowed me downstairs. But Manila wasn't so strict, and I liked to keep a close eye on everyone I paid. The mortician had gone darker than my father's current skin tone, closer to the shade he was before the illness. I wondered if my mother had shown him a photograph.

The funeral directors led us to their Holy Family room. "We asked for the penthouse," I said. They apologized; a service was running long in their Epiphany suite. "Then tell them it's time to leave." My father had relatives coming from all over the archipelago to pay their respects, I explained—from all over the world, in fact. Again they were sorry, throwing in a *sir:* the funeral taking place in Epiphany was a child's. "Did the child pay you in American dollars?" I asked. Doing business in Manila hardened something in me, the same muscle I'd observed in men who stood up in hospital rooms and did all the talking for their families. I focused on the French doors of the penthouse as we skated my father past the displaced mourners and their four-foot coffin.

Our family brought in plates of fried rice, barbecued chicken, pineapple salad in condensed milk, sandwich halves stacked in pyramids. Only the corpse, really, distinguished the wake from any other party. People kissed and caught up. Bebot fiddled with the green Commodore computer. My uncles set up speakers beside the guestbook and blew into the microphones: *Testing, testing, one two three.*

"Loretta, please eat," an aunt was saying. "Next time we see you, you'll be invisible."

My mother accepted a cheese pimiento sandwich. Then the room started to fill with the family's insistent clamor, and I longed for another escape. She looked like she could use that, too. My sandwich-pushing aunt noticed the bare platform around the coffin. "They call this a 'full-service' funeral parlor," she said to me, "but apparently that does not include flowers."

I saw my chance. "The flowers aren't going to buy themselves," I said, approaching my mother's chair. "Shall we?"

She abandoned the sandwich and took my arm. We stepped out onto Araneta Avenue, Manila's funeral district, walking past the parlor, stonemasons, chapels, coffin shops, and rent-a-hearse garages: one after another, like beads on a grim rosary. A rough and glittery dust filled the air, as if crematory ashes had mingled with fumes from the traffic.

We stopped at a flower stand outside the parlor. "How much?" I asked the vendor, pointing at a white spray of carnations and roses that my mother liked. I didn't know what flowers cost. I never bought them in New York—not for promoted colleagues or sick friends, certainly not for women. Flowers reminded me of my father and the hangdog contrition that followed his nights of drinking: the swooping, romantic gestures that came after he'd blackened an eye or broken a bone.

"Five thousand pesos," said the vendor, "plus fifty per letter on the banner."

FONDEST REMEMBRANCES, the display models said. IN LOVING MEMORY.

"I can do two thousand," I said, "banner included."

The vendor shook his head. "This is difficult lettering, sir. The roses are imported."

"That's a pity." I took my mother's arm and headed for the next kiosk.

"Twenty-five hundred with banner," the vendor shouted after us.

I walked on, to keep him guessing for a few paces, before doubling us back. I couldn't have cared less about the cost of flowers. I simply wanted every peddler in the city to know he didn't stand a chance against me.

None of the things I wished to say to my father were printable, so I took my mother's suggestion: REST IN PEACE, YOUR LOVING FAMILY. We strolled the avenue waiting for our banner. "Don't let anyone try that on the *sari-sari*," I said.

"I don't think anyone could," she said. "You still haggle like the best of them."

"What choice do I have? They can read *balikbayan* written on my forehead."

"Ah, no—it's too long to fit there." Her words hung in the air a moment before I realized I should smile. Ten years before, I had arrived in New York with ideas of what I'd miss most about my mother: her cooking, her voice, the smell of rice and detergent in her skin and hair. I did not expect to miss her humor, the small wisecracks that escaped her mouth sometimes, often from behind her fingers, hard to hear.

When we returned for the flowers, my mother reached out as if to carry them. I waved her away as I paid. "This thing is nearly twice your size."

"You underestimate me," she said, pretending to flex her muscles.

After the memorial service, my uncles offered to stay with the body overnight. The last of our relatives were expected in the morning. We would bury my father in the afternoon.

Back in Mabini Heights, my old bedroom was mine again. The air conditioner seemed louder now that I was alone in the room, but I slept easily. I dreamed of winter in New York, walking alone in snow, pulling my collar up against the cold.

I woke in a sweat again. The AC had stopped. I turned the dial, but the vents stayed silent. I flipped the wall switch and got no light.

A brownout. My first since returning to Manila.

Moonlight from the window told me only a few hours had passed. A muffled sound, like crying, came through the wall. I stood, ready to console my mother on the sofa or at the kitchen table. But the living room was empty, the kitchen dark. The only light I saw flickered weakly from the *sari-sari*. Approaching the screen door, I saw a candle burning on the counter. Was she keeping vigil? Praying? I squinted in the shadows.

She certainly wasn't crying. In fact, she was laughing—a strange, sleepy laugh that dominoed through the *sari-sari*. She reached along the counter and picked up a white square. Succorol. I watched her slide it through the wicket. Then she was repeating my instructions, in my accent.

"This isn't Tylenol, if you know what I mean." She drawled the words, like a cowboy trying to speak Tagalog, as if I'd lived in Texas, not New York, for the past ten years. She reached toward the wicket and came back with a fistful of cash.

I turned from the screen to the darkness, as if a film projector behind me had faltered. Her laughter followed me through the living room as I tripped against the furniture and nearly missed the sickroom doorway in the dark. I opened the drawer where we'd stored the yellow box. Six Succorol patches left, of the thirty I'd brought. Five days had passed since I'd arrived, four since I'd given them to her.

My skin itched with the humidity. I grabbed the fan beside my father's bed and flapped it at myself, then felt ridiculous and snapped it shut. Nothing about my mother—not her voice, soft as a lullaby, when I could hear it; not her hands, drying themselves on her lap; not her posture, a constant curtsy—squared with the woman in the *sari-sari*. I had to erase that strange laughter from my mind, the tongue that wet her thumb before it counted out the money.

Returning to the dresser, I fingered the box of Succorol. Would the world end if I indulged this once, crossed another boundary, broke one more rule?

I glanced again over my shoulder before peeling a patch from its backing. I pressed it to my chest as if saluting a flag or anthem. My heart raced under my hand. In the distance, my mother's laughter rose and fell. But nothing changed as I lay back on the cot. It seemed as if the years of virtue had made a fortress of me, a barricade that human appetites and weakness couldn't breach.

Then my bones began to melt. Things happened too quickly, at first, to feel good. The rosary, the notebook, and the fan, unfolding pleat by pleat, rose from the chair and hovered over my father's bed. The doors swayed. I gripped the edges of the cot, feeling control slip from me inch by inch. Only when the melting reached my fingers, loosening their hold, did I begin to enjoy it. Patches flew out of the box and lined up like a filmstrip in the air, each one a panel with a picture in it, and from there every square inside the house became a screen: song lyrics in the baby monitor; my father's face in the green computer. Even the windows and the wicket came alive with scenes of *bida, kontrabida,* and the woman they both claimed. My body sailed up and out of the room like a streamer: through the corridor, the kitchen, the *sari-sari*. Walls and ceilings yielded to me as they would to a ghost. I heard my mother laughing and my father singing "Fly Me to the Moon," the sounds and words escaping through the roof into the stars.

I woke the next morning to find my bedsheets balled on the sickroom floor, the Succorol patch still on my chest. Tearing it off, I wondered if my mother had checked in on me and seen it. In the bathroom I tried to soap off the patch's square footprint, but the adhesive was stubborn. I needed a washcloth to work at the residue.

Rubbing away the evidence, I looked down. As if I'd never seen my own hand before. I stretched my arm out and stared at the white cloth, wrapped around my fingers like a mitten. A bandage.

I rushed from the sink to the doorway of the sickroom, thinking back to the night he died. Here was where the moonlight had shone over the bed. Here was the step I took before seeing them. Here was where she gasped, stopping me in my tracks, and bent to hide his body. My mind shuffled through the kinds of scenes you saw in those trashy Tagalog melodramas: on-screen villains, polishing their guns and planting their poisons; my mother, not ministering to him as she had when I was four years old, but instead waiting for me to fall asleep, kneeling at my father's bedside, removing his shirt and applying a patch to his chest. I pictured her adding another patch and then another, a week's worth, her fingertips blanching his skin briefly at each point of pressure. I could see her laying an ear to his chest. After midnight, when his breath and heartbeat stopped, she must have peeled off the patches, soaked the washcloth, and tackled the sticky residue just as I opened the door for some cold air.

Now I opened the candy box and counted again: five. Only three should have gone to my father on my second, third, and fourth days home; one to me. I'd seen my mother sell one. Of the other twenty that were missing, how many had she sold? Had she sold some in the nights before as well, while I slept? How many would it take to finish off a dying man?

I must have known a drug so powerful could end his life. So what? Didn't I want him gone, hadn't I always? My mother was better off.

But at what cost? I had to ask myself. If she had killed him, I had handed her the weapon. If I'd kept track, a closer eye on the supply, I might have caught it all sooner. What kind of pharmacist lets days go by without taking inventory? Someone incompetent as well as criminal. Like him, in other words.

In spite of what I'd told the staff, my father did not have a vast global fan club traveling to see him. No need to drag the wake on for days, as other Filipino families might for more beloved men: we would bury him later that second day. At the cemetery, a block of earth had been hollowed out for the grave. My aunts cooled themselves with lace fans, or brochures they'd lifted from the funeral parlor and folded into pleats. A priest read from his small black Bible. *The Lord is my shepherd, I shall not want.* In this kind of heat the valley of the shadow of death sounded inviting.

My cousins' children broke flowers from the bouquet set on the coffin. Before the lid was closed and locked for good, I looked for the last time at my father's face, under its sheet of viewing glass. The mortician had not only restored the color but buoyed up the flesh itself, faking fullness in the hollows and droop. I could almost imagine that face moving again, the mouth stretching backward to spit. Nearby a headstone waited, even simpler than the banner on his flowers: ESTEBAN SANDOVAL, SR. 1935–1998. SON · BROTHER · HUSBAND · FATHER. My head ached, and my mouth felt dry; there was a grit behind my eyelids I couldn't blink away.

Now, at his grave, my mother wept into her white handkerchief. She still looked frail, the woman who cleared platters and pulled out chairs, who knelt at my father's feet and mopped up after him. Her tears affected me the way they always had. I swore to stop them; I'd do anything. I reached for her, then froze—afraid, for the first time in all my years consoling her, that I might cry myself. For years there'd been no question of how much she leaned on me, like any mother on her overseas son. It never dawned on me how much I'd leaned on her: to play her part, stick to the script. Her saintliness was an idea I loved more than I had ever hated him. I put my arms around her, making vow after silent vow. I'd never cut corners again, no matter what the value, who the victim; I would never violate any code, professional or otherwise. I would take her with me to New York. I would never leave her again. I'd bury the patches somewhere no one would find them, so long as she could always remain the mother I knew, not some stranger laughing in the dark.

My uncles turned a crank to lower their brother into the ground. They picked up shovels and began to bury him scoop by scoop. My mother passed her fan to me, then her handkerchief. It felt damp in my palm, the cloth worn thin and soft from all its time in the wash. She stepped forward to join her in-laws, struggling with the shovel's weight.

A smell of grass and earth took me back to the yard that once existed in Mabini Heights, and I half-expected an acacia tree to appear beside me, or my mother's voice to call me to dinner through the kitchen screen. I remembered how I used to climb that tree and sling a branch onto my shoulder, aiming sniper-style at the place in the house where my father might be standing. Another time I stabbed a fallen twig into the grass and twisted it, imagining his blood. But I'd fought tooth and nail to rise above that yard. Even in return for all the harm he'd done my mother, to harm him, to be *capable* of harm to him, was to honor what was in my blood. His blood. I trained myself into his opposite: competent, restrained. The hero in an old Tagalog movie did not win by stooping to revenge; there was a pristine, fundamental goodness in his soul that radiated out to crush the villain. Character and destiny—I believed in all of that, I guess.

My mother raised her foot and staked the spade into the

ground. She heaved the dirt into the plot and made a noise, almost a grunt. *You don't know my strength!* Through all the melodramas that my family and I had seen over the years, in which the *bida* and the *kontrabida* crossed their swords over a woman, I never guessed that *she* might be the one to watch.

The Miracle Worker

When Mrs. Mansour first came to the house, I thought she was alone. Naturally I could see only her face; the rest of her had been draped in the traditional black. But there was something modern about her right away, even ignoring the fact that she had arrived without a husband. She wore sunglasses—Chanel, I saw, as she approached—and deep red lipstick.

"Mrs. Sally Riva?" she said, removing the sunglasses.

I nodded. Only my birth certificate had ever called me Salvacion. I reached out to shake her henna-tipped hand, but Mrs. Mansour leaned in further, to kiss me on both cheeks. She smelled pleasantly of tangerine and something stronger, perhaps a spice. Once the outer gate had shut, she parted her *jilbab* to reveal a gold-embroidered bodice and a little daughter. "Here is Aroush," said Mrs. Mansour. The child had been anchored on her hip and concealed by her clothes all along. Mrs. Mansour shifted Aroush's face to show me.

I was stunned. Back home in the Philippines I had been trained to work with all manner of "special" children. But I had never seen any child quite like the five-year-old Aroush. Her head swelled out dramatically at the forehead and crown, like a lightbulb. Faint brown smudges the size of thumbprints dotted her face. Along the left side of her neck grew a pebbly mass of tumors.

"Aroush, this lady is a teacher. *Hello, Teacher.*" Mrs. Mansour held Aroush's hennaed hand and made it wave. Through the rust-colored designs on her skin I could see more of the pebbly tumors.

I led them from the gate down a tile path to the house itself. A year had passed since my husband, Ed, and I had moved from the Philippines to Bahrain, and still I thought of these three stories as "the" house—not "our" house, certainly not "my." Expatriate families like ours were well provided for: a car, a travel allowance, the promise of schooling if we were ever to have a child. Strangest of these provisions, to me, was the house. Too large for two people, it was outfitted with luxuries I never would have chosen: gold leather upholstery, curtains embroidered with camels and date trees, shelves and tables with brass frames and glass surfaces. Plush red carpeting covered every inch of floor except the bathrooms and the kitchen. We wanted for nothing, and none of it was ours.

Having grown up poor and Catholic, with the Beatitudes and tales of the first Filipino workers overseas swirling all around me, I still got nervous at the sight of luxury; I couldn't tell the difference between wealth and obscene, ill-gotten displays of it. In college, before Ed, I had dated a boy who railed against the president for exporting labor to the Middle East. To the editor of the *Metro Manila Herald*, he wrote about "the hidden cost of remittances" and said a peasant was a peasant was a peasant, whether on the rice fields or the oil fields, and that at least the Filipino rice farmer could come home every day and see his family. I thought of that old boyfriend sometimes, when I looked around my home at the life the oil fields had given us. Certainly we lived more like foremen than like farmers.

Mrs. Mansour stopped at a full-length mirror in the foyer. "Look here, little woman," she said to Aroush. She lifted the girl's chin and draped the edge of her *jilbab* around the grotesque little face, so that two veiled heads were facing the mirror. "Who is that?" said Mrs. Mansour. Aroush grunted. I could see this was an established call-and-response between them, one of the few rituals in which a child like Aroush could be expected to react.

In the living room Mrs. Mansour spoke of the cool weather that day, which to me was not cool but merely less hot than usual, and of how much she adored people from my country, most of her household help being Filipino as well. Clearly we would circle for hours around the real purpose of her visit, unless I addressed it myself.

"Mrs. Mansour," I said, "let me begin by telling you that I unfortunately don't speak any Arabic."

"Of course," said Mrs. Mansour. My friend Minnie had already informed her. But the language barrier, it turned out, did not disqualify me. Mrs. Mansour preferred it this way—for, unbelievably, she wanted Aroush to grow up bilingual. *Bilingue* was how she put it: Mrs. Mansour herself had learned French as a schoolgirl in Beirut. She supported Aroush's head against her chest as she spoke. With a clutched handkerchief, she caught a dribble of saliva from Aroush's mouth before it could land on their clothing.

I asked what else she expected out of Aroush's education.

"Mrs. Sally," she replied, "you know of the deaf-blind Helen Keller and her teacher, Annie Sullivan?"

Aroush grunted.

"Teacher, *you* must be Annie Sullivan for my Aroush!"

I had been warned in advance about Mrs. Mansour's illusions. My friend Minnie worked as a maid for the Mansour family. "The child can't hold its own head up," Minnie had said, "but Madame believes it will grow up to write poetry or cure cancer someday." My friend had sucked her teeth, shook her head. "That must be something, no? To be so rich you think you can buy reality?"

"I'll need to know more about your daughter's history," I said.

Aroush had been born at full term, the third of the Mansours' children and the only girl. At first the only trait to mark her as unusual was a largish head. The thumbprints did not appear until she was a year old, the skin growths some months later. The Mansours began keeping Aroush indoors, out of public view. "Often people do not love difference," said Mrs. Mansour. She, on the other hand, surprised herself by how much she cherished Aroush's limitations at first. Aroush was the pliant and portable child every young girl imagined when she played at motherhood: you could dress Aroush and position Aroush and tote Aroush around like a doll. She provided no resistance—a welcome quality, said Mrs. Mansour, after years spent raising boys.

But by the time she turned two, Aroush had yet to grab on to things, roll to her side, sit up, raise her head, make sounds other than grunting or crying, or hit any of the milestones that had come naturally to Mrs. Mansour's sons. Thrusting her tongue by reflex allowed milk and soft foods to fall into her throat and be swallowed, but she had never mastered even an elementary sucking. The Mansours traveled to London, where a battery of tests pointed to a rare, profoundly unlucky combination of cerebral palsy and von Recklinghausen's disease. Her mental age would never advance beyond infancy. Language, of the conventional spoken variety at least, was not in the cards.

"So they said." Mrs. Mansour shrugged. She took Aroush's hand in hers and gazed fondly at the henna.

In any other place, with any other parent, this might have been the time to discuss "realistic expectations." But I was here in Bahrain, with Mrs. Mansour. I thought of Minnie, who cleaned the Mansours' house in Saar six days a week. I thought of my husband, working on the pipeline to Saudi Arabia all afternoon in the desert heat. Mrs. Mansour's hopes put me in a position to mend an injury, correct an imbalance. I took a deep breath, then fed her all the bright teacherly clichés I could muster. I talked of *needs* and *environment* and *response*. "*Education*," I said, "comes from the Latin *ducere*, 'to lead'; and *e-*, 'out of.' 'To lead out of,'" I said. With my hands I made an ushering gesture.

Mrs. Mansour nodded, her eyes misting. Her face seemed familiar yet unreal, as if I had seen her before, but in a dream. As a child in Sunday school I used to read about certain queens in the Bible, women I pictured with dark eyes and crimson mouths, elegant and proud and doomed. Mrs. Mansour looked like that. Her skin, pale and smooth, was made paler still by the black veil that framed it.

"This is never so true as with the special child," I continued. "You lead her out into the world. You lead her out of her own self."

"Oh, yes," said Mrs. Mansour. "I believe this. I believe this for my girl." She looked down at Aroush and smiled. "Teacher, shall we talk about money?"

We settled on an hourly rate of fifty dinars: only fair, we agreed, given my level of specialized study and experience. In truth, I had never been paid so well. Certainly I had never earned money for feeding a fantasy. Mrs. Mansour issued my first check right then, to cover any supplies needed in Aroush's first week. Before leaving she noted the bookshelves in the foyer, crammed tight with Ed's engineering manuals and textbooks I had kept since college. "A house of readers," said Mrs. Mansour, with a nod of approval. "So are we. For me, to buy a car is desireful; to buy a book is needful."

Until she used those words, it hadn't occurred to me to see these books as trophies—but they were, no less than a car, or even a house, would be for other people. I could have sold or given them away back home, but used up precious cargo space to bring them here. It wasn't as if Ed or I ever cracked them, these days. But our parents had cleaned floors to put us through college: these books stood for how far their sacrifice had sent us.

Aroush would come at eight o'clock every morning, like a regular child to regular school.

———

"I just can't imagine Mrs. Mansour with three children," I told my friend Minnie the next day. "She seems too young. Or, more than young: ageless. Her complexion is like bone china." Absently I ran my fingertips along a shawl whose peacock-feather pattern changed from blue to green and back in the light.

We were browsing Abdullah's Gift and Novelty Shop for toys I could use with my new student. It was Minnie's day off. She'd been the Mansours' maid for sixteen years, starting before Aroush's eldest brother was born. "Oysters," Minnie said. "That's her secret. Madame eats one every night, to keep herself beautiful. And her skin cream, from Paris, has caviar in it." Minnie followed me through the store with her hands clasped behind her back. She herself touched nothing, as if to do so would require a special kind of permission not likely to be granted.

I picked up a twin-bell alarm clock and set it to ring.

"What is that for?" Minnie pointed with her chin.

"Testing her response to sound," I said.

"You think there's a problem with her hearing?"

"No. But I'll need to stimulate it if she's ever going to"— I cleared my throat—"acquire language."

"Aroush acquire language! Are we talking about the same child?"

I sighed. "I'm not sure Mrs. Mansour is."

"Well, who are you to argue, at fifty dinars an hour—right?"

The first time we met, Minnie and I had also been shopping, at the Central Market in Manama. I went there in the middle of the day to avoid crowds. A vendor was weighing my bag of prawns when Minnie approached and told me that I looked familiar; hadn't she met me before? "Who is your *amo*?" she asked. (Who was my master, she meant, my employer; whose maid was I?) I explained with a laugh that I was not a maid but an oil wife and that the only house I cleaned was my own. We were both embarrassed—Minnie fearing, of course, that she had offended me. But I didn't care about that. What mortified me was the change in Minnie's aspect when she learned I was—as she saw it—a rich woman; she retreated so quickly from small talk to bows and helpless apologies. She was under five feet tall, and small-boned, like my mother. Servitude had become a habit and posture of her body, in a way that felt painfully familiar: it really could have been my own mother bowing and apologizing to me there, at a fish stall in Manama's Central Market. In Bahrain I often missed my mother—craved her company and pitied her life, more than I ever had back home—and meeting Minnie felt like a reunion in some dream where my own mother thought she recognized me, then didn't.

I told Minnie that anyone could have made the same mistake. Recently I had read, in the *Manama Times*, about the wife of a Philippine ambassador, who was ordered out of the swimming pool at a Dubai country club. "The lifeguard told her only guests—no domestic helpers—were allowed there," I said. "A diplomat's wife! So at least I'm in good company." I would have gone on and on, just to put Minnie at ease.

Finally she did open up, coming back around to the idea of a friendship with me. This was during Ramadan, and Minnie was tired. "Their holy month is hell on me," she said. "Every year I wonder if I'll make it to Eid. Fasting makes them cranky in the daytime, and their breath stinks. Then they run you off your feet at sundown and before dawn." And while they slept off their feast, Minnie would dust, mop, scrub, sweep, and wax the house to perfection as on any other morning.

"You should see it," Minnie said, of the Mansour estate. "Forget *house*. *Palace* is more like it."

Months later Minnie found out that I had a degree in special education. It turned out that the mistress of the house she cleaned was seeking a private teacher for her daughter. "What's 'special' about her?" I asked.

Minnie shuddered at the question. "Let's put it this way,"

she said. "Money doesn't buy everything." Then she described Aroush, who had spent most of her five years in her bedroom, its windows opening onto a terrace where she was taken for fresh air. Only the family and servants like Minnie—who changed the sheets and dusted there daily, and performed a thorough cleaning once a week—were allowed to enter Aroush's bedroom. Likewise, any teacher for Aroush would have to be foreign (that is, not an Arab), because the Mansours did not want word of their daughter's condition to spread within their own community.

At Abdullah's I paid for two bags' worth of plush toys, rattles, blocks, pacifiers, teething rings, and cups with training spouts. I had forty dinars to spare. Minnie checked the tag on the blue-green shawl I had admired earlier. "Forty exactly," she announced with glee. "It's destiny." When I hesitated, she said, "Oh, Sally. Madame won't ask you for a receipt."

I bought the shawl. Outside the store, I draped it around Minnie's shoulders—which were narrow, like my mother's. "It's yours," I said.

Of course, she tried to refuse.

"Consider it your Ramadan bonus," I insisted, tucking the ends of the shawl into Minnie's collar. "From me. And Mrs. Mansour."

For her first day of school Aroush wore a pink dress embroidered with silver thread, hoop earrings, and a stack of filigreed bangles. Two tight braids along the sides of her head followed her ears' shape and coiled at the ends like sea horses.

"*Good morning, Teacher,*" sang Mrs. Mansour, waving Aroush's hand.

They had brought a servant with them this time, a Filipino dressed in black-and-white livery. He carried in Aroush's car seat, a special recliner with support for her neck and head, and a gliding rocker and ottoman for me. I greeted him in Tagalog, but his brief, accented response suggested that we shared neither a hometown nor a dialect. And he seemed loath to socialize in Mrs. Mansour's presence. For my part, I could barely look at the man without an urge to laugh at his ridiculous costume. Minnie had once described her own uniform as "French maid," which at the time had almost made me laugh as well.

Mrs. Mansour spoke gently into Aroush's ear—in English, seemingly for my benefit. "Aroush, listen to Mrs. Sally Riva and learn from her. *Ummi* will return for you in the afternoon." She kissed Aroush and gently passed her to me.

Aroush let out an extended version of her low, atonal grunt, and I learned that this was how she cried. The servant held the front door open for Mrs. Mansour, who stopped and looked back. I saw that her arms, in the sleeves of her *jilbab*, longed to reach out. We both stood there awkwardly, the emptiness as new to her arms as Aroush's weight was to mine. I began to rock and hush Aroush, for both our sakes. Mrs. Mansour smiled and was able, finally, to leave.

I stood in the foyer comforting Aroush until her tears and drool formed a damp spot on the shoulder of my blouse. I grew tired. Despite being smaller than a healthy five-year-old, Aroush felt solid and hefty in my arms. I sat down with her on the new gliding rocker in my living room.

At this time of day, I would normally have been waking up, descending the stairs to make my first cup of coffee. That kind of leisure had troubled me when I first became a housewife, at the age of thirty, the year we came to Bahrain. It felt not only dull but somehow criminal: I'd always worked at some job or other since I was twelve years old. And work was not a matter of choice for Minnie, who sent her wages home to a sick mother and school-age relatives in Manila. In college I had marched with tenant farmers on the Congress Building, and built a campus barricade with striking jeepney drivers, throwing firecrackers at the military helicopters overhead. It felt strange for all that activist fervor on behalf of working people to have gone down the gold-fixtured toilet and matching bidet of this house, once Ed and I moved here.

Aroush's crying faded to a grunt, and then to rattled breathing. I sang her a song of greetings and good mornings that included both her name and mine. She cried again when I stood to install her in her recliner. I imagined Mrs. Mansour and her servants tiptoeing around Aroush because she cried so easily. A common, well-intentioned error. In fact children like Aroush needed more stimulation, not less, than regular ones. I stroked her hair, her thumbprinted cheek, and her knee; I turned on the chair's massage function and sang some more.

Back in Manila, I had chosen my field for reasons I would never share with anyone. It seemed in college that if a girl was not rich, or beautiful enough to marry rich, then there were two honorable ways for her to survive: nursing, or teaching. Weak in science, I would not have made it through nursing school. Yet I had a medical kind of appetite for staring at disorders, at things gone gruesomely wrong in the body, which seemed wasted on ordinary teaching. I was drawn to special education, whose textbooks included pictures of collapsed spines and rock-like formations in the brain. I liked the sound the two words made together and the person I became in other people's eyes when I uttered them. I told stories of afternoons spent coaxing antisocial boys out of bathroom stalls and of violent girls who bit me until the skin broke. "You're brave, Sal," people said. "I wouldn't last a day."

I guided Aroush's hands over a stuffed terry-cloth bear, a satin blanket, a ball with knobs on its rubber surface. A cold tin rattle set her off again. The growths on her hands were buoyant to the touch, the rust-colored henna patterns drawn to perfection despite their uneven canvas. I wondered if the henna artist had special dispensation, like the Mansours' Filipino servants, to enter Aroush's bedroom, or if Mrs. Mansour knew how to paint the vines and flowers there herself.

She arrived at three o'clock sharp to pick up her daughter.

"You must reward every response she shows, to any stimulus at all," I told Mrs. Mansour. To demonstrate, I set the alarm clock one minute ahead and sat silently in front of Aroush, holding her hands, waiting for a reaction. Mrs. Mansour's presence there seemed to require a performance on my part. The clock rang, and Aroush startled at the sound. "Good girl!" I cried, clapping my hands and exaggerating a smile. I kissed her cheek.

"How wonderful," said Mrs. Mansour. She bent down and took Aroush into her arms, murmuring to her in Arabic. "Today, clocks; one day, symphonies. Right, Teacher?"

At fifty dinars an hour, I could hear Minnie saying, who was I to argue? I looked away as Mrs. Mansour covered Aroush with her veil and went to the door. "We will see you tomorrow, Teacher," she said, her eyes misty with hope. "For the meantime, here is our gift to you."

There was a basket on our front step the size of the cradle of Moses, its cellophane wrapping tied with a gold ribbon. Inside were tropical fruits and comfits I hadn't seen since leaving the Philippines: sugar apples, bristly-skinned rambutans, strips of dried mango, shredded coconut preserve. I looked up to protest, but the gate had already clicked shut behind Mrs. Mansour and my little student.

At night I served Ed his dinner of pork and root vegetables. "How was your day?" he asked. My husband was always the first between us to ask how the day had gone—even in Bahrain, where on some days all I had to report was the price of cabbage, or the latest plot twists on *Falcon Crest*. Today I told him about Mrs. Mansour. "She seems to believe her daughter will be an astronaut or artist one day," I said. "This limp, drooling, averbal, severely delayed child."

Ed kept his face close to the bowl as he ate, chewing open-mouthed while his spoon secured more. "Sweetheart, if you had tennis courts in your backyard and a separate wing for the servants, you might lose touch with reality too." Bits of squash and potato landed on his place mat and the surrounding tablecloth. "How much did you say she was paying you?"

"Fifty an hour."

"*Dinars?*"

"Dinars."

"Not bad. Soon I'll be here watching soaps, while you bring home the bacon." Ed winked at me in the manner of people who cannot wink: both eyelids fluttered awkwardly, as if sand had blown into them.

In the Philippines, before marrying Ed, I had warned him that I did not want children; I worked with them, and I had no desire to bring my work home. Ed didn't mind. "I'd make a lousy father anyway," he had said. "I can't imagine sharing you with anyone else." When I gained weight during our first six sedentary months in Bahrain, Ed proclaimed himself a lucky man. "Now there's more of you to love," he said. He was a decent, doting husband, remarkably blind to my deficiencies. His devotion had once offered me an oasis: from gossipy friends and demanding family members, from challenged students and their challenging parents.

But now that we really did live on a desert island, I was finding myself less and less in need of that oasis. Here in Bahrain, where my daily stresses were so few, where television or groceries provided the most taxing strains on my attention, I'd grown more and more aware of what came with Ed's constant, indestructible love. His incompetent winks. His noisy, desperate way of eating. The texture of his skin, baked rough and leathery by this new climate, and its now perpetual film of grease. The odors of sweat and petroleum on his body and in his clothes after a day's work.

I had no right to find such fault with him, of course. Now that I brought in no part of the household income, was losing what looks I ever had, and could rarely even offer interesting conversation, some basic patience and loyalty were the least I could give Ed in exchange for his kindness. I owed him winks in return. I owed him my permission to sit at the dinner table in those damp clothes when he was too exhausted to shower or change. I owed him hums of sympathy when he complained about his job. And I owed him my dutiful, wifely laughter when he ridiculed those who worked with him.

If his day had been pleasant enough, Ed's face would take on a goofy, simian expression at dinner, and he'd wag his head from side to side in imitation of his Indian subordinates. "The new *Bumbai* are so difficult to train," he said now. "First of all, I can't understand a word they're saying. They're like chickens clucking in boiling water. *Vee are vorking as qvickly as vee can, sir.*" If he had suffered a bad day at work, I would also know it by Ed's face: his features would contort with bitterness, and his voice would imitate, instead, the hard, thumping English in which his Arab superiors had scolded him.

I cleared our dinner dishes and arranged some of Mrs. Mansour's fruits in a bowl, placing them at the center of the table. Ed reached before he saw what was inside.

"Surprise," I said.

"What—*atis*? *Santol?*" He peered closer. "Where did you get these, Sal?" He broke open a sugar apple, scooped out one of the inner pods, and began to suck.

"Mrs. Mansour."

"Not bad! Did she have them flown over by private jet? How is it the ants didn't get to them first?"

"I don't know." I was grateful for the fruit, whose fragrance sweetened the kitchen and seemed to absorb my husband's odor. According to Ed, though, it was the Indians who stank. "The pipe will spring a leak one of these days," he liked to say, "and I won't even smell it for all the *Bumbai* around me. The stench of curry armpit will have knocked me out."

I blurred the focus of my eyes until Ed became a set of disembodied sweat stains in front of me: the spots under his arms, the gleaming oily patches on his cheeks and forehead, the tie that grew darker as it looped around his neck. Only by the sounds of him eating the fruit—the slurping of pulp and spitting out of seeds—could I tell that my husband was still there. With my fingernail I punctured the skin of a rambutan to expose the white jelly inside.

On our second morning together I began to train Aroush's eyes. I placed a doll and a flashlight beneath the heavy, floor-length tablecloth in our dining room and carried Aroush under. She began to cry. As I soothed her in the dark, I noticed how much she smelled like her mother—that pleasing scent of tangerine mixed with something stronger. When the moaning stopped I shone the flashlight upon the doll, a few feet in front of us. "Do you see the pretty little doll, Aroush?" I had fallen into the special-needs teacher's habit of narrating each minute as it happened, of repeating myself, of asking questions Aroush could not answer. "Do you see?" I peered around at Aroush's face. Her eyes were as aimless and agitated as ever.

I had been taught that senses were the doorway to skills. In the kitchen I held against Aroush's tongue a pretzel-shaped teether that had spent the night in the refrigerator. She shivered. "Good girl!" I hugged and kissed her. An older, less impaired child I could have rewarded with raisins or candy; Aroush, who had never eaten solid food, I could only praise and love. I exchanged a cold teether for one that had steeped in a pan of warm water since morning. A furrow appeared between Aroush's brows at the change in temperature, and I practically attacked her with cuddling.

By the time her mother arrived, Aroush was in her chair, and I was holding the flashlight two feet from her eyes. "Where is the light, Aroush?" I said, moving the flashlight slowly from side to side. "Do you see it? Aroush, follow the light with your eyes." Again it was I who felt in the spotlight, with Mrs. Mansour there.

She applauded. "Now a flashlight; in time, a telescope. Isn't that right, Teacher?"

"We have lots of work to do," I said carefully, "before we start thinking about telescopes."

Mrs. Mansour gave no indication that she heard me or understood. Lifting Aroush from her chair, she saw a plush rattle on the coffee table. "Toys, Teacher?" she said, with some concern. "Will my girl learn from baby toys?"

I picked up the rattle and shook it. "Auditory stimulation will develop her receptiveness to sound," I said, "which is precedent to the acquisition of language." In my earliest days of teaching I would sometimes hide behind jargon this way, learning quickly that a crowd of syllables could soothe the most anxious parent. It seemed to work on Mrs. Mansour, who smiled again and handed me a velvet pouch.

"Teacher, do you believe in miracles?" she asked.

Inside the pouch I found a choker: pearls as large and heavy as marbles, with a bluish silver tone to them. "In Libya they have built a river where there was no water. A pearl is only sand before it turns to precious stone. Then there is the flood, the burning bush, the tree in our desert that has lived four hundred years on nothing." She took the choker from my hands and reached over to secure the clasp at the nape of my neck. "They say only children can believe such stories. Me? I believe. Like a child, I believe." Her fingertips were cool, and some of their coolness seemed to linger in the pearls at my throat after she had gone.

Minnie came to visit me on her next day off, arriving as I lay Aroush prone on her rubber mat.

"Make yourself at home," I said. "I'm just giving her some

exercise before a nap." I bent and straightened Aroush's knees, then cycled them in the air. Her feet, unlike the rest of her, were normal, even perfect: smooth and plump as any little child's, free of tumors or thumbprints. Her tiny toenails were painted a shade of pink darker than her dress.

Standing at a distance from us, Minnie swiped one of the shelves in my living room with her fingertip, reflexively checking for dust. Again she reminded me, in spite of her own childlessness, of my mother. "I don't know how you do it," she said, looking over at me while I massaged the backs of Aroush's tumored palms, trying to coax her fingers to open and stretch. "My job's no walk in the park, mind you. But at least when I polish the glass, it shines."

I extended Aroush's arms and turned her head from side to side. Minnie disappeared into the kitchen, and I could hear her opening the refrigerator and cupboards. "Please don't bother, Minnie," I called. "Relax and put your feet up." It was her habit during daytime visits to prepare a dinner I could just reheat when Ed came home.

By the time I had put Aroush to sleep Minnie was wiping down my kitchen counters. "Pot's in the fridge," she said. "*Afritada*. Just put it on the stove when Ed's ready to eat."

"You didn't have to do that."

"Is she asleep?"

I nodded. We went into the den to watch television and ate the last of the sugar apples before they could rot. On screen, women with mink coats and feathered hair said evil things to one another.

"We're going on strike," Minnie announced.

"We?"

Some Filipinos had banded together, she explained, wanting the Ministry of Foreign Labor to raise both the minimum wage and the age ceiling for new incoming workers. "They're even calling themselves a union," she said, though the group was loose and informal and, like its members, had little real status in the world it hoped to change.

I thought of how she'd walked into my house and checked the curio shelves for dust. "Minnie, you just spent your day off cooking my husband's dinner," I said. "I can't imagine you on strike."

"You mean you can't imagine me chanting or holding up a picket sign," she said. "But not everybody does that." The union had floated other, subtler strategies. Withholding smiles, for one. It had worked for a group of cashiers in Italy, omitting a personal gesture that appeared nowhere in their job descriptions but nonetheless brought management to its knees. "It's time they felt it," Minnie said—softly, like a timid child learning to speak. "How their lives would be without us. How this piece of sand would sink into the Arabian Gulf!" The rallies I attended in my youth had sounded a lot like that.

Aroush began to cry. I stood up, setting aside my glass and bowl. "I'll just go see if I can get her back to sleep," I said apologetically. "Be right back."

In the living room, Aroush had soiled her diaper. I gathered her embroidered dress gingerly at her waist while changing her. A drop of soupy infant excrement leaked onto the carpet on my way to the trash. By the time I had washed my hands and scrubbed the stain, Minnie was at the doorway with her bag, putting on her shoes. "I just remembered something I promised to do for the church," she said, which sounded like a lie. On most visits she lingered at my house as long as she could, sometimes through dinner. More than likely, I guessed, she hadn't counted on hearing and smelling Aroush on her day off.

"I'm sorry I wasn't a better hostess," I said. It dawned on me that I would have driven Minnie home before, back when I wasn't working for her boss myself.

"You're busy," Minnie said. "It's all right. It's a good woman who works when she doesn't even have to."

I was mesmerized by Minnie's story of the Italian cashiers, their intimate but fierce rebellion. The quietest, most docile worker could, behind her apron or her uniform, be sharpening a blade. I began to imagine all the soft, subtle weapons a worker might employ. Avoiding all eye contact, perhaps, even while saying *yes* to an order; completing one's duties very slowly, as if moving underwater. I paid closer attention: to the man wrapping my fish in brown paper at the Central Market; to the waiter who took my order and Ed's at a restaurant near the Diplomat Hotel. It bothered me to think our life was built upon their backs, that even Ed's crew at the pipeline must have wished for his downfall at some point or another. My instinct, my muscle memory, stood with and for the little guy, still. If the Minnies of the world felt wronged, I was on their side; I'd never owned a skin cream made of caviar in my life.

In college, with my fellow campus troublemakers, I lived by the gospel of solidarity. When the university's expansion threatened to tear down the shacks and displace the residents of a slum outside the campus walls, we slept under tin scraps outside the chancellor's office in protest. When yet another city newspaper was taken over by the government, its writers sacked and replaced by puppets, we tied black gags around our mouths. When former Senator Aquino was gunned down at the Manila airport, we wore shirts spattered with red paint and carried signs that said, WE ARE ALL NINOY. Now, with Minnie's friends plotting revolt, however silent, I caught the fever again. After all, I'd thought of her when I took the job under false pretenses; I'd given Mrs. Mansour undue hope with Minnie's grievances in mind. To act out on the job itself was just the natural next step. How far could I go, for the workers' sake?

I stopped preparing lessons while Aroush napped or consulting my old textbooks. I began to spend that time dusting the shelves, or chopping the vegetables for dinner, or catching up on other housework. When I ran out of chores I watched TV or read my paperbacks, legs stretched along the sofa. I left toys on the floor after Aroush and I had handled them, stopped structuring our afternoons. When housework, books, and even TV bored me, I napped beside her.

My lies grew. At the end of each day, when Mrs. Mansour came, I overstated Aroush's every twitch and reflex, claiming successes that were unlikely. Mrs. Mansour rewarded these tales more handsomely every day. It was her custom to travel to London on weekends to shop for beautiful things; these trips now yielded loot for me and Ed as well. Her gifts fell into the category Mrs. Mansour called *desireful:* boxes of dark chocolate truffles; silk scarves; perfumes with such luxuriant names as Joy, Obsession, Poison; eye shadow kits with brushes the size of matchsticks. She herself had no use for the perfume, she said; she had been blending her own for years, a formula handed down from her mother and grandmother. She would hand it down to Aroush as well, when the time came.

I passed these gifts along to Minnie. (I wanted her to use them, to dress up for karaoke night at the Gulf Hotel, or even go on a date with Mrs. Mansour's Filipino chauffeur. But she too passed them on, to her sisters and nieces in Manila, or to raffles that the church held for charity.) These fancy things, I told myself, were like the riches Robin Hood would redirect to those who worked harder or had less than he. I didn't deserve them, but someone did.

Aloud, Ed mocked the gifts that Mrs. Mansour left for him. "Just what I always needed," he said, smirking at a diamond-encrusted tie clip; or "Time and money sold separately," in response to a box of golf tees made of eighteen-karat gold. But later, through a halfway-open bathroom door, I would see him model the watch or the shirt studs, changing the angle of his arm and chest in the mirror. One morning, when he thought I was asleep, he quietly transferred the contents of his cracked vinyl wallet to a monogrammed money clip, and his keys to a brushed-platinum key ring, both from Mrs. Mansour.

One day Aroush made a small, unprecedented sound, distinct from her usual grunts and moans. I was watering an ivy plant near the living room window and polishing its leaves with a soft cloth.

"Haa," it sounded like, but gentler than a laugh. A sigh.

"Aroush?" I said. I knelt beside her and looked into her eyes. Perhaps I had misheard the sound of one leaf brushing against another, or the spray of the bottle in my hand, or my own breath, as a whisper out of her.

The furrow in her brow smoothed over when I bent down. Her eyes thinned to crescents, with delicate folds around them. I could see each of her widely spaced teeth.

A smile. It went away, but I had seen it.

I felt as shocked as if she'd spoken a full sentence or stood and walked around the room. It was the closest thing to a miracle I had ever witnessed, and I'd done nothing to cause or earn it. Quickly I placed a chair on either side of her head, tying a length of string between them. With more string I hung a rattle, a soft block, and a squeaky toy from the line. I took her wrist and batted the block with her hand. Its inner chimes jingled as it swung and then slowed to a stop.

"Haa," Aroush sighed again, looking—it seemed, for a moment—directly at the block, and *smiling again.*

I lay down beside her and looked up. I shook the string and took in the swinging toys, their jangling sounds, all the colors and textures, at her level. "Good girl," I said. I kissed the soft, downy zone where her temple became her hairline.

The breakthrough energized me. When I fed Aroush her formula and puréed pears, I became determined to teach her to suck. Instead of placing spoonfuls near her throat, as Mrs. Mansour did for easy swallowing, I left them on the middle of her tongue or on the corners of her mouth. Aroush furrowed her brow, made a gagging noise. I dipped a pacifier into the mush and held it to her lower lip. Her mouth stayed open, her tongue slack. Eventually she cried, smelling the food but lacking the skill to obtain it. I relented, feeding her the rest of the meal as she was used to.

For once I didn't feel I was completely lying when Mrs. Mansour arrived. "We had a grand day," I told her. I threw words like *developmental* and *affective* into my report. But Aroush's sigh and smile I kept to myself. To hear Mrs. Mansour say, "Today smiling, tomorrow Shakespeare," or something like that, would have diminished our private milestone in a way I couldn't bear.

That night I dreamed that Aroush was my child. Under a great black cloak I carried her against my body, clutching her henna-patterned hands in mine, and when she sighed or smiled only I knew it. I woke up suddenly and shook my husband's shoulder. "Ed," I whispered, "wake up."

His head sprang from the pillow.

"What if I wanted a child?" I said. A ridiculous thing to ask a sleeping man in the middle of the night, and I knew it.

Naturally, he was disoriented. "Child?"

"Yes. A child."

"But you don't."

"What if I do? What if I changed my mind?" It was an impulse, a cheat, a conversation I could later disown. In the morning I could easily convince him I had been talking in my sleep or that he had been dreaming.

"Sally, whatever you want," he slurred, "you've got." I wondered: was that a yes, his drowsy answer, or a no? Did he mean that I could have anything I wanted, or that I already had it? With a grunt, he turned his face back to the pillow and embraced me so tightly as to bury my face in his armpit and squash my mouth under his shoulder, ending the questions and conversation altogether. *Where do you think you're going?* he used to demand, playfully, in those early days of our courtship, every time I rose from the bed or left his side. Then he would reel me back into his arms. And so it seemed now: as though he'd sensed me moving away from him, and knew even in sleep to grip me closer.

I formed a warm animal attachment to Aroush: to her smooth, square feet, to the clean smell of her scalp when I held her in my lap. As I had predicted, Mrs. Mansour, when she did notice them eventually, took the smile and "Haa" as evidence that in due time her daughter would map the stars or choreograph a ballet. But we were both happy. I had a renewed hope that one day I could bring Aroush to respond to her own name, to hold a ball with both hands, to point to objects when I named them. I felt like a teacher again: not necessarily heroic, but useful.

My textbooks and store-bought toys gave way to the elements. I took Aroush outside into the garden, touching her plump feet to the dry, rough patches of grass. I gave her flowers to smell. We lay down and gazed together at the shapes the clouds made. One day I filled a bowl with ice and another bowl with warm water. I cleaned out an old medicine dropper and found the spray bottle that I used to water the plants. I bathed her hands in the ice water and then in the warm, cheering as she reacted to the change in temperature. I squeezed the medicine dropper onto her palms and wrists. She was mildly ticklish, as I learned from her squint and sigh whenever something brushed her face, and so, playfully, I raised the spray bottle and misted her cheek with it.

Aroush began to scream: a guttural sound, higher-pitched than the moan that told me she was merely upset. She stiffened at the knees and elbows and squeezed her eyes shut. I felt the resistance in her body, the sudden rigid terror. "It's all right, Aroush," I said. "It's just water." Stupidly, I misted her palm. Her screams turned into violent choking noises; her face grew purple.

I dropped the bottle and picked her up, rocking her until my knees hurt.

In the afternoon I watched Mrs. Mansour hoist Aroush onto her hip and drape her with the veil as usual. Accustomed by then to keeping secrets from her, I said nothing about the spray bottle. Parents at the special-needs school in Manila would take offense the moment we asked about a bruise or scratch, hearing only accusation. *Are you a parent?* I'd been asked, more than once. *Then you've got no right. No right!* She might ask why I'd sprayed Aroush in the first place—question my new curriculum, based as it now was not on science but on my own instincts. Why I had inflicted things on Aroush that would have tormented even a regular person.

That night Ed came home angry, having suffered some humiliation at work. "If a *Bumbai* screws up, it's my fault," he said. "Always my fault. None of the credit, all of the blame." Sand sludge had accumulated in one section of the desert pipeline, and acids had eaten away part of the pipe wall. Sections would have to be replaced, at great cost to the company. *"No good! This no good!"* Ed shouted, imitating his Arab bosses.

"Aroush is terrified of spray bottles," I said. "Today I spritzed her with the one I use on the plants, and she started screaming. As if I was torturing her."

"They've got no right," Ed continued. "Dressing me down like a schoolboy. That oil has got my blood in it!"

"A spray bottle. Can you imagine? Is there anything less threatening than that? I can't wrap my head around it."

"I can," he said. I looked up—surprised, though I should not have been, that Ed had listened to me through his own complaints. "What did you expect?" he said. "She comes from a race that cuts off people's body parts for petty crimes."

His face was flushed. I touched his forehead, which was hot with fever. Upset as he seemed, I envied Ed his clarity. I had always been fascinated with kinks in the natural order, with anomalies, but my husband was a man who dealt in diagrams and blueprints. At work Ed drew up flowcharts and predicted outcomes, checking that the pipeline did in real life what he'd said it would on paper. His view of Arabs and Indians, and our place among them, was no different. Could he be right? Was there some brutal form of discipline I didn't know about, involving spray bottles, and why would Aroush need it?

"I'm calling in tomorrow," he said. "Screw them. Let's see how their precious pipe does without me." For the first time that evening I noticed that his voice was hoarse, as if hours of defending himself had worn it out. His nose was congested. A better wife surely would have noticed earlier.

It would be his first missed day of work in the time I'd known him. The next morning I chopped ginger and boiled chicken for Ed's soup while Aroush took her morning nap and played peek-aboo with her while he watched television. "These women!" I could hear him chuckle from the den, where he watched *Dynasty* while I changed Aroush's diaper. "They're something else!" The lid on the pot of rice began to rattle.

"Sorry to interrupt," I said, standing in the doorway of the den with Aroush in my arms. On-screen the wife and ex-wife of the same man were waist-deep in a lily pond, clawing at each other. "Can you keep an eye on Aroush while I get your *lugaw* ready?"

"Where's she going to go?" said Ed.

"Just watch her. Please." He reluctantly followed me into the living room, where I set Aroush down in her recliner. When Ed approached her, as one would a curiosity in a museum, I couldn't help but feel protective. "Don't get too close," I said.

Ed stopped and held his hands up.

I smiled. "I don't want her to catch your cold, that's all."

In the kitchen I added rice to the broth and shredded the

cooked chicken from the bone with a fork. The porridge was close to done when Aroush screamed—the strained, desperate sound I had heard only once before. I dropped the ladle.

In the living room Ed was crouched over Aroush with the spray bottle. Her body had stiffened at the knees and elbows.

"Don't!" I ran and knelt to shield Aroush's body with mine. Mist from the bottle landed on the nape of my neck.

"I wanted to see for myself," he said. I picked Aroush up, her wet cheek against mine, and backed us both away from Ed. He looked like the child who has just learned to throw salt on a garden slug and watch it implode. "You're right—it's uncanny. She's got something against that spray bottle."

I glared at him, rocking Aroush. His eyes were bloodshot, and I could imagine the brain behind them, busy at the work of redrafting. Updating his diagram, based on new data before him. Arrows pointing in directions he had not foreseen; an invisible line along the living room carpet, with him on one side and us on the other. Ed stood, and the spray bottle toppled to its side. I turned from him, shielding Aroush as he walked across the living room. Her skin and dress were damp.

"Sally, you never wanted a child," he said. Sweat trembled on his forehead and above his lip, despite the air-conditioning. "Now, all of a sudden, you want one? I've stopped being enough for you? All because you made this limp, drooling, delayed child smile?"

Of course he had heard me, even in his sleep; why should I be surprised? All my life I had heard wives complain of husbands who paid no attention to them. Why couldn't I appreciate mine? "Go and rest," I said in a voice I hoped sounded calm. "I'll bring you your *lugaw* in a minute."

He went, trailing a sweaty odor behind him. I swayed in place until Aroush's body relaxed against mine. It was Wednesday. In a few hours Mrs. Mansour would pick her up, leaving me alone with Ed in this house for the weekend.

The following Saturday, Aroush was late. By nine o'clock she had yet to arrive. I turned on the television. Had Mrs. Mansour somehow found out what Ed and I had done? *I wanted an Annie Sullivan for my Aroush,* I imagined her saying, her fine, aristocratic face hardened against me, *but now I find you are hurting rather than helping her.* I watered the plants, dusted the shelves, dried the dishes. I configured the toys in the living room, then dismantled the arrangements and started over. Finally, when it was nearly eleven and time for Aroush's morning nap, the gate bell chimed.

A yellow blanket had been thrown over her shoulder and Aroush, but Mrs. Mansour herself was not covered. "We are very sorry to be late, Teacher," she said, hurrying in from the gate. She wore a pale green caftan over trousers, and no veil. Her black hair was gathered in a low ponytail. I saw that she had skipped her makeup, too, from the pallor of her lips and the naked circles around her eyes, which resembled stains. The rest of her skin, from her long neck to her hairline, still had its soft alabaster clarity.

Aroush was already asleep. Mrs. Mansour laid her on the nap mat and sat on an armchair close by, catching her breath. "We rushed so not to be late," she said.

"Would you like some coffee?" I asked. I had never offered Mrs. Mansour coffee before, but I would have offered it to any woman in my house who looked as pale and exhausted as she did that day. "It isn't strong like Arabic coffee. But you are welcome to some."

"Thank you," said Mrs. Mansour. "Yes."

In the kitchen I fixed a tray with two cups of hot water and a jar of the instant Nescafé that Ed and I usually drank. The spoons rattled on the saucers as I brought the tray to the living room. I was strangely shy, like a child heading to the master bedroom on Mother's Day. "It isn't Arabic coffee," I repeated apologetically, setting the tray down in front of her.

"Thank you," said Mrs. Mansour, reaching for the jar and spoon. It appeared that she had drunk instant coffee in the homes of foreigners before. She sipped at great length, closed her eyes, then looked across the coffee table at me and smiled.

Again I felt apologetic, this time for being caught staring. "I'm not used to seeing you without the veil," I explained.

"Nor I." She laughed. "I never veiled until nineteen years old, when I married and came to Bahrain. Now I feel strange without." She touched her hair and looked wistful.

I began to stir my own cup of coffee to direct my eyes elsewhere.

"My staff have gone on strike," said Mrs. Mansour. "Three servants left to do the work of twelve. On the weekend I could not go to London. I have to stay with Aroush. That is why we are so tired."

"You could have called me," I said. I was surprised to learn the union had gone radical after all. I hadn't opened a newspaper or spoken to Minnie in days. All weekend long, it was Ed who had required all my attention and reassurance. Had things changed, he wanted to know, since I started working for Mrs. Mansour? Between him and me? Did I feel that *he* had changed? No, I virtually pleaded with him, nothing had changed; I wanted him to believe, as ever, that I was on his team. "You never wanted a child," he said again, as proof. At first I tried to claim I had never said anything about a child. Then I admitted that I had said it, but hadn't meant it—I had been sleepy and half-dreaming, like him, at the time. All the while I reassured him, I tried not to watch his mouth, forming its receiving O toward the food on his fork, then closing when the food fell back onto his plate with a splash. All the while I tried not to consider what it would mean if I did want a child, but not with him. And all the while I longed for Saturday, the start of the workweek, when he would be back at the pipeline and I would be alone with Aroush.

"I could have watched her for you," I said to Mrs. Mansour. "I would have taken Aroush off your hands this weekend."

"Oh, Teacher, I did not think of it." Mrs. Mansour looked genuinely surprised at the idea. "You are Teacher, not baby nurse." Was I flattered by this distinction, between my work and a servant's?

From her cot Aroush snored once. We both looked over. She stirred but did not open her eyes.

"Teacher, do you believe in tests?"

"Tests?" Again I panicked, thinking of standardized tests, the kind that would evaluate Aroush's progress under my teaching. She'd found me out. And now Mrs. Mansour wanted to measure how much improvement fifty dinars an hour bought. "Of course tests will be important," I said, "to gauge her development in the future. But we don't want to place too much emphasis, too early, on—"

Mrs. Mansour shook her head. "For example, God, He takes away everything that you have. Or oppositely, he give you riches and gold. Tests."

"Oh," I said, "tests from God." I took a sip of coffee. "You think the workers' strike is a test?"

"Not the strike. Aroush," she said. "My husband, he says she is a test. A trial from God, which one day He will reward us for this difficulty. My parents, they think she is *adhab*. A punishment. Pentance, Teacher, in your Book."

Whether she meant *penance,* or *penitence,* or *repentance,* I understood.

Mrs. Mansour said she no longer spoke to her parents. Having a child like Aroush served her right, her father had said, for marrying into the wrong sect, for following her nose to the vulgar smell of oil money, for abandoning her war-torn country to live an easy life of leather floors and marble ceilings in a mansion on the Persian Gulf. "I am happy most days," said Mrs. Mansour. "Most days Aroush, she is my little miracle. But sometimes . . . this weekend, she cried and cried. She would not stop. And I . . ." She paused, then whispered, "I wanted to be in London. In the shops. Away from her." I could hear a hot tremble in her voice. "So maybe it is true. Maybe I am being punished."

"No." I meant this, though my voice rang false. Lately I'd been dreading when Mrs. Mansour might catch me in my lies and scold me, as any boss would a dishonest worker. But she treated me like a god. As a teacher in the Philippines I'd often felt myself at the mercy of mothers; Mrs. Mansour was the first mother I had known to put herself at my mercy. I saw more clearly how much power she had given me, the damage I could do, her dependence on what I chose to say.

"Tell me, Teacher, what kind of mother thinks her daughter is punishment?" Mrs. Mansour turned up her hands. The henna had faded to the slightest of traces. She seemed to be exposing to me some raw layer underneath the jewelry, designer clothes, and potions: her flesh, not an idea. Deceiving Mrs. Mansour had revealed to me a Mrs. Mansour who was not so easy to deceive. And loving her child made it harder still. No better moment to come clean with her than now.

But "you can be forgiven for thinking that" was all I offered. Then I added, softly, "No one ever sat with a howling child and didn't think for a moment she might be in hell."

Mrs. Mansour set her half-finished coffee cup on the tray. "Thank you, Teacher." Her voice had cooled. "You say the perfect words to give me hope always." She stood and bid Aroush and me a good day. By the time she returned for her daughter in the afternoon, she had put on her sunglasses and her veil. Her lipstick and henna had been freshened. Hard to imagine, then, the wan, depleted woman who'd accepted coffee in my living room that morning.

A Filipina maid ended the strike by jumping from the third-story window of her employer's home in Riffa. She had been new to the country, said the *Manama Times,* and so had no local friends to suggest reasons for her suicide. She left no note. The "union" organizers refocused on finding the girl's family and raising the funds to fly her body home for burial. Eleven workers who had walked out of their employers' homes were dismissed for breach of contract. Six went home to the Philippines.

As for Minnie, she had changed her mind at the last minute and gone on working. "I got scared," she said. "It's not just the money. Of course I thought of the people back home, but also: what would I do with myself if I wasn't working? What would I do with my hands? It's for young people, these rallies, this strike."

We were entering a classroom in the Awali neighborhood school, which allowed us to give a memorial service there when the country's only Catholic church, owing to the way the girl had died, would not. It was a kindergarten classroom, with an alphabet scroll above its blackboard and artwork pinned to a clothesline. More Filipinos crowded into it than the girl, twenty years old, had probably known intimately in her lifetime. The union leaders handed each of us a white taper candle, and we passed a flame along until the whole room flickered. Minnie and I glanced at the Xeroxed program and joined in the opening song, a show tune about rainbows. Since none of us had known the girl, the union leaders took it upon themselves to stand and eulogize her, giving us tidbits from the cassettes and posters and other belongings found in the room that she had occupied for less than a month. She was born in Tarlac. An older brother had gone to Hong Kong for work some years before she herself left home. "She loved all American movies," read one of the union leaders from an index card, "and even saved her ticket stub from the time she saw *Blind Date* at the Royal Theater."

The sob was out of my throat before I could swallow it. I dropped the program into Minnie's lap and gave her my candle, then covered my face with both hands and wept like a child. Unable to stop, I stood and rushed down the aisle between rows of Filipinos staring from their tiny chairs, thinking, most likely, that the dead girl and I had been close.

I walked past the doors of other classrooms, trying to find my breath. The school building formed a horseshoe around a grassy playground. I sat down on a swing and pressed the heels of my hands against my eyes. Faintly, I could hear the classroom congregation shuffling to stand and sing another song.

Minnie followed a few moments later and sat on the swing next to mine. We swung together in that slight, noncommittal way, our feet on the ground. She turned herself around, twisting the chains over each other, then lifted her feet to spin them untwisted. "I know how you feel," she said gently. "I think everybody in there is feeling it. *Will I die alone, with no one to mourn me but a bunch of strangers in a classroom? Will anybody even remember who I was?*"

I dried my eyes and murmured some agreement. In fact, I had not been thinking of that at all. In my mind I was seeing only Aroush's tumored hands, the droop of her head. "Can you imagine," I said to Minnie, "if you had to go on living after your life had stopped? If, at a certain age, that was it—the best you'd ever do—the most you'd ever accomplish?"

"I can," said Minnie. I knew she was thinking still of the girl who died. "I was eighteen when I came here. I'm forty now. I've never done much besides clean rich Arabs' houses." Minnie turned to look toward the parking lot, so that even years later I would wonder if I'd heard correctly what came next. "I'll probably die in uniform"—she sighed regretfully—"with a dustrag in one hand and a spray bottle of cleaning fluid in the other."

I squinted, then squeezed my eyes shut. I shook my head. Small, deferential Minnie, who'd backed out of a peaceful strike: she could not be capable of it. I coughed, thinking I might choke, my eyes burning. At the same time, my vision seemed sharper, clearer than before.

Minnie wasn't dead to me after that; in fact what she became was more alive than ever, revealed to me in new textures and colors. I had underestimated her: what looked like a lifetime of toil and taking orders had contained subversions no one, until now, had seen. She'd been silently striking all along; she didn't need my protection. What arrogance, to think I should take up her cause, even the score. I was no smarter than a child, who didn't understand nuances. She was not my mother. (And God only knew, of course, what little mutinies my own mother had waged, in secret: the better life she'd planned for me could not have been enough to get her through her own, every day.)

I had to believe that my friend had suffered, that humiliations I could barely imagine drove her to cruelty. *You've been through a lot,* I could say, *but the child isn't the one who put you through it.* Of course Aroush would be the one to pay the price; Aroush, the only one less powerful than Minnie, the only one who couldn't punish Minnie back. Aroush, who'd done nothing to deserve punishment.

I did not, in that Awali playground, tell Minnie that her suffering was not Aroush's fault, or that her rich employer was a human being too. I drove her home, and then myself. At dinner, I did not tell Ed to spare me his pronouncements about the *Bumbai* and *Arabo.* Their theories had had years to harden; my love for Aroush and sympathy toward Mrs. Mansour couldn't topple them in one day. All I knew to do, and had to do immediately, was right my own mistake.

I invited Mrs. Mansour to spend an afternoon with Aroush and me by the small kidney-shaped pool in our compound. "Parents' Day," I said. The kindergarten classroom, with its finger paintings and bulletin boards, had made me nostalgic for a "real" school. A glimpse into our days together would prepare Mrs. Mansour nicely for the truth. If she could see her daughter's actual education with her own eyes, she would find joy in Aroush as she was, aim for humbler milestones, no less miraculous for being within reach.

Mrs. Mansour had dressed Aroush in a ruffled pink bathing suit and waterproof swim diaper. "Thank you for bringing us here," she said, when I unlocked the gate to the swimming pool. "This is quite a nice vacation."

She was being polite. Surely there was nothing the Astroturf and cement walls had over the boutiques of Bond Street. I eased Aroush's arms into a pair of orange water wings and brought her car seat to the edge of the pool so that her feet touched the surface. Her toenails were painted a dark beet color. I splashed her right foot into the water, then her left, causing her to smile and shiver.

Mrs. Mansour removed her sunglasses and applauded. I took Aroush from her car seat and submerged her to the waist, supporting her against my chest. We faced Mrs. Mansour. I cradled her against one arm and flicked water from my fingers onto her neck and face. She blinked and smiled again. Holding her that close, and smelling the particular warmth of her scalp, I almost lost my nerve, tempted to keep the truth, and the real Aroush, to myself.

"Teacher," Mrs. Mansour called, "when first I see you, I know you are the right one for Aroush. From looking at you—so independent, so *able*—I know you are a modern woman."

I bowed my head. Again my eyes hurt as if they'd been blinded and gained total clarity all at once. The sun winked in a million facets off the water. I could hear every slight movement that Aroush and I made through it.

"This is how I will like my girl to be. Alive in the world. I would like that she understand business, understand computers, understand politics."

The locks at Aroush's hairline had begun to curl from moisture, and I had to speak.

"Mrs. Mansour," I said, "I'm afraid I have not been completely forthright with you."

"Forth right?" she said casually, settling back into her chair.

"Honest," I said. "About your daughter. You know, Mrs. Mansour, that Aroush will never understand business, don't you? That she'll never understand computers, or politics?" A cheat, to ask this way, to suggest that Mrs. Mansour knew the truth despite my lie. So I added, with as much grave certainty as my voice could muster, "She'll always be close to how you see her now."

"Now you are doctor, as well as Teacher," she said, her red lips barely moving to say it. She seemed to freeze in the chair, a statue on a throne, her eyes cold as they locked with mine.

"I was confused," I said, speaking quickly so I wouldn't lose my nerve or her attention. "I thought taking your gifts, your money, would offset some imbalance in the world. Please listen, Mrs. Mansour. Aroush is not Helen Keller, and I'm no Annie Sullivan. She won't write books or cure cancer. But I can teach her to hold objects, to communicate without words, to recognize sounds, even shapes . . ."

Mrs. Mansour cut a terribly elegant figure against the Astroturf. Only her sandaled feet showed at the hem of her *abaya*. I noticed for the first time how exposed I was next to her black-veiled figure: my tan lines, my hips, all the places where the bathing suit dug into my bare flesh. I held Aroush close, as if to hide my flaws behind hers. My need to come clean was of no concern to Mrs. Mansour. I wondered how many teachers had been interviewed before me and passed over, when they chose to break the truth to her from the start. Someone like Mrs. Mansour must have had no problem holding out for what she wanted most.

"Thank you again for bring us to this place," Mrs. Mansour said, with a cheery finality to her voice. "It is like Paradise." A kind of paradise was what she paid me for, after all: the dream of Aroush's bright future. She replaced the sunglasses atop her cheekbones, a warning I understood: that whatever I wished to illuminate, she was happy in the dark. What I had thought of as deception was my duty. If I cared to keep Aroush in my life, *this* was the service I had to keep providing, whether or not I'd thought better of it. And so I held my tongue and treaded water, looking up at where Mrs. Mansour's eyes were hidden from me. From a distance perfect strangers could assume that Mrs. Mansour was my *amo*, and I a servant at her feet.

Legends of the White Lady

If you are beautiful and broke, one place left for you is Asia. Usually when I ran out of money I went to Tokyo—always a face cream or a push-up bra there that could use me. This time, I went to Manila. I'd been there once before, with my roommate Sabine. In cities like these there is a demand for blue eyes and light hair and skin like milk.

Manila's airport is a bit like Tokyo's but noisier, more crowded, its faces a few shades darker. I towered, in both cities, over almost everyone. But while Tokyo could match New York for all its rushing, solitary people, in Manila no one seemed alone but me. At ARRIVALS each brown face would find the cluster of faces it belonged to and merge into a heap of arms and laughter and chatter. Not that I had blended in much better with Sabine there. She was only half Filipina, and five-ten—almost as tall as me.

I looked for a cab and could only get a stretch limousine—the airport's longest person hailing its longest car. On the highway, skinny boys in wifebeaters dodged the traffic, some wearing flip-flops, others barefoot, their shins and calves dark with scabs. They carried trays of gum and cigarettes. When traffic stalled us, some boys lingered at my window, which was mirrored on the outside. They cupped their hands around their faces and squinted. Their eyes roamed, blank; they couldn't see a thing. There were older beggars too, with body parts missing: hands, a leg, an arm.

This was the city where Sabine was born; when I'd first met

her, though, I couldn't guess where she was from. It was a question she had to answer often. "My mother's from the Philippines, my dad is American," she would say, in a practiced manner. "And no, he wasn't 'in the service.'"

Now my driver asked me the same question. "You American, miss?" he said, as he steered through the cars and bodies.

"As apple pie," I said. It sounded more serious than I meant it.

"I can see that, miss. Where in America? Texas?"

"New York."

"Here on vacay?" he asked, just like an American would.

I shook my head. "Work." Then I remembered something. "Look, I've been here before," I told the driver, "and I know we don't go through Quezon City to get to this hotel." Five years ago, the cab ride from the airport had taken three hours and cost eight hundred pesos—about double the time and money that we should have spent, Sabine and I later found out. We looked at a map afterward. The driver had taken us along the edges of greater Manila and through Balete Drive, a long street in Quezon City that was supposedly haunted. While scamming us he told the story of a woman dressed all in white who roamed Balete after dark. She'd been run over by a car, he said, and now she crossed the street when least expected, causing accidents, wanting people to share her end. She favored taxi drivers or men who drove alone. One night after his shift, our cabbie thought he ran her over. He didn't see her in the street until too late, and though he heard a thump and saw a body roll across the windshield, he found no woman and no blemish on his car when he stopped and got out. "But I have proof," he said, rooting in his glove compartment for a length of white lace—allegedly torn from the lady's dress and fished out of his fender hours after the accident.

After that, like a new celebrity or clothing brand, the ghost seemed to be everywhere for me. My first trip to Manila had been packed hour to hour with castings and photo shoots; I didn't sightsee and met only the locals I worked with. The one thing I learned about Manila was this weird and hazy ghost story, which kept on changing shape. Every stylist, every makeup artist knew a different legend of the white lady.

"They say the Japs raped her in World War Two," said one assistant on a swimsuit job, while she slaked my arms and legs with a light-diffusing cream. "Now she wants revenge against all men."

"She stopped a Coca-Cola truck on Balete Drive," said a photographer. "When the driver got out, she was gone. But the leaves of a banana stalk were waving nearby, even though the air was still that night." This was allegory, he explained; Coca-Cola was America, somehow, and banana stalks the tropical Third World.

"She had big bones, and strong white teeth," a hairstylist informed me. "The white lady was a white woman."

I wondered now if the white lady was still popular here or if, like a clothing label or celebrity, her star had faded since my last visit. By the time I left the limousine, sweat had blossomed darkly under my blue cap sleeves. The humidity made a mist over everything; even the car windows were coated with little drops. My skin would probably break out in this kind of heat. The driver charged me three hundred pesos. "Fair and square," he said. "I'll remember you. I'll tell everyone there was this pretty Stateside actress in my cab, who knew her way around Manila."

I laughed, picking up my suitcase and going into the hotel. Aside from that Balete Drive business, I knew nothing about Manila. I was not an actress but a "mannequin," as Sabine liked to refer to us. I was twenty-eight, old enough to know I would never be the Face of My Generation or the Body of My Decade, but not old enough to get it together to do anything else.

The hotel wasn't five-star, but it wasn't bad. There was something holy to it: stark and airy, like a chapel, all lace and dark wood. An effort had been made to save it from the usual peachy wallpapers or gold-framed paintings. A sheer white curtain flared above each single bed. We had stayed here last time as well. "I feel like a princess," I remembered telling Sabine, never having had a canopy bed before. It turned out to be a mosquito net, and Sabine laughed at me. "*Some*one hasn't lived in the developing world," she said.

Sabine was my family, which sounds tragic, but it was true. We didn't know our fathers or speak to our mothers. When I was eighteen and had to get away from my mother, and Sabine was twenty and needed a new roommate, our booker introduced us. Had we looked alike, we might not have been friends; but she was a Winter and I was a Spring, and we were never up for the same jobs. For ten years we lived together, in a two-bedroom above a diner that sent up smells of coffee in the morning and fried potatoes in the afternoon. The only time we ever really closed our bedroom doors was when we brought boys home for the night.

In the hotel room, I unpacked some vanilla candles and lit them one by one. This was how Sabine used to soothe herself in strange places. I picked up a grainy-paged magazine from the hotel nightstand and flipped through. It had no photos or interviews in it, though, and what use did I have for a magazine without photos or interviews? The room began to smell like cake. I lay back on one of the beds. Through the little ring at the top of the mosquito net I saw a cockroach, crawling in a slant across the ceiling. I could feel myself falling asleep, which these days was my default state.

I hadn't worked, or looked for work, in five months. I had never been a morning person to begin with, and after Sabine died, getting up for jobs or castings didn't feel possible. Leaving the house at all didn't feel possible. Depending on what kind of sadness I was having, I lived on either what Sabine and I had called vitamin C_3—coffee, always black with no sugar; cigarettes from the corner bodega; and cocaine from a model friend who dealt on the side and came around one morning a week—or pizza and Chinese food delivery, whose flat boxes and take-out buckets littered the living room tables; the kitchenette counter; even, eventually, my bedroom floor. For a few weeks my booker tried to call and get me back out there. "Alice, I have a possibility in L.A.," he said. "The work would do you good. Can you be ready in an hour?" I deleted every voice mail and returned to bed. Sleep became my needy, whining lover, pulling me back down the minute I tried to go anywhere else. For a model on the wrong side of twenty-five, this was disastrous. We were told, sternly and often, that the difference between the "huge" girls and us struggling dime-a-dozen girls was that the huge knew how to wake up early, booking this job and that while the rest of us, who might be just as pretty, slept. My own mother, by her account, could have been huge—was on the dizzying, starlit verge of huge, when some D-list runway show producer knocked her up and saddled her with me.

In Manila's garment district the next day, I stood outside an office among forty girls, all waiting for our names. Casting calls were nobody's favorite. "Cattle calls," we'd say, or go-sees. We would stand there, sit if we were lucky, and wait an hour or more, usually to hear we weren't right. Sometimes they liked a girl a little but not enough. Or asked us back once, but not a second time. "I didn't realize," one London editor told me, "that you'd got such a very long torso." In Milan a woman told her partner: "There's nothing wrong with her *per se*," and shook her head at me.

A year ago, I would have sized up the girls around me. Usually at least a handful didn't stand a chance. Girls who overdressed, for instance—small and swallowed up in borrowed suits and pumps—or who caked on the makeup, were the clear rookies. You wanted to look chic but clean: a blank, expensive canvas. My uniform was Chloé jeans, a fitted tunic, and canvas slippers I picked up by the dozen in Chinatown. Underneath (and this was key) I wore my flimsiest, most delicate designer underwear. High-end quality was essential, matching less so. Odds were they'd strip you down to really get a look. Jeans were a gamble I took pride in pulling off; my booker liked to say that some girls looked cute enough in denim "but in couture, *shazzam!* They vanish."

A year ago, I'd have looked around for that kind of girl, or wondered if I was one. But now a crowded room of hopefuls felt like home. I showed one girl—Rae was her name—my book and looked at hers. My tear sheets were old, in fashion time. I'd avoided my booker for so long, in fact, that he stopped calling about jobs and started calling about roommates. "We got a new girl in from Czech Republic that needs a place to live," he said. "She's been getting steady work." The following week he had a new girl in from Senegal; the next, Argentina. "Alice," he said, "let's not pretend you can afford that place on your own." This was true. After paying double my old rent for five months, I had almost nothing. A few hundred dollars in my bank account was keeping me, alternately, in vitamin C_3 or in pizza and Chinese. I started signing credit-card "convenience" checks to my landlord. I didn't want a new roommate.

When I returned Rae's book, she made a crack about her morning fight with bronzer that the bronzer won. There were bands of orange at her wrists and elbows where the spray-on stuff had pooled. Seven months ago I might have pitied Rae or hated her. She had extremely narrow hips, and clavicles that could slice cheese. Now I laughed along. When a head with silver hair and smooth young skin that didn't match it poked out of the office door and said, "Alice Anders?" I felt a little sad to leave my new friend.

The silver-haired woman introduced herself as Carmen. She was tiny, barely tall enough to stare into my chest. She flipped through my book quickly. It was always quick, the crinkle and slap of the plastic-sleeved pages. I never could be sure they really saw me. Now, as Carmen and some others eyed me, I filled in their thoughts: *pretty, but then what? All of them are pretty.* People in our business often used the term "It." *Does she have It?* There was a girl Sabine couldn't stand, who for some months was getting every booking in New York, it felt like. Sabine said, "She is full of It." "Dipsh-It," she said about someone else. But she believed—we all did—in "It."

"It" was different for everybody. Sabine was moderately exotic in a way that pleased a range of people. The almond-shaped eyes, the pillowy lips, the skin that coppered easily in summer, could all be played up or down. She once brought home a brown man who claimed he only dated white women; he gave her sapphire earrings and said, "after your eyes"—which were her father's, blue. Another time she brought home a white man who claimed he only dated brown women; this one gave her an original wood-cut etching by Gauguin, and a rare edition of Gauguin's travel diaries too. At go-sees, there was a lilt about Sabine—an upturn to her face that musically matched her voice. Even her name was a little bell. There was a certain lightness to her personality that came with not planning to do this forever. Not wanting any job that much.

I did not have "It." *Sexy* or *pretty* or even *beautiful* weren't It. Those weren't enough. Editors were always asking me, "Where are you from? Utah? Kentucky?"—always wanting some Cinderella story to fit my sunny, corn-fed look. But I was from New York. No one discovered me at a Wendy's in the Bible Belt. My mother had done some catalog work herself, and I signed on with her booker at fifteen.

Years ago a girl in the industry got raped, had her face sliced up beyond recognition and couldn't work anymore. When I heard this story, I had to wonder what else in the world I was good at. I could think of one thing: I was flexible. There was a trick I had been doing since first grade: I would knit my fingers together, lock my elbows, and stretch the ring of my arms to just behind my head. Here I'd pause—for effect; this is as far as most people can go. Then I'd stretch farther, all the way, until my clasped hands were at my tailbone. I would do it slowly the first time, to simulate a lot of effort, then go back and forth faster and faster, until I was snapping my arms from front to back like a metronome. That's what Sabine called the trick when she first saw it, the Metronome. I could turn my toes out until they faced backward, do the splits both ways, and windmill each arm 360 degrees from its shoulder socket. These things would still be possible if my face were ruined—but without a body? I couldn't imagine. I blanked. Sometimes when I thought of what else was out there, I felt there should be more and weirder options. I felt I would do a very fine job of being a vapor, for example, or a silk scarf. I would make a very good wall.

For this go-see, I ridiculously thought of doing the Metronome to distinguish myself from the other girls. Then I remembered how I'd sweated on my way over that morning, the ugly stains under my arms. I stood still and moved only to follow directions. *Turn around, walk, stay just like that, take this off,* and so on—I had been doing this since I was fifteen and was used to it. It was like security at the airport, removing a hat or a pair of glasses. "How old are you?" asked Carmen. "What have you worked on? Where are you from? Oklahoma?"

Every count against me back home worked in my favor here. I was just the right kind of pale. They didn't want somebody cat-eyed and golden, like the Brazilian girls plastered on every bus in New York. They didn't want edge, either. "All-American is what we need," said Carmen. "You're like couture meat-and-potatoes." They took a Polaroid and told me to come back the next day.

I met the real star of this campaign, a local model named Jorge Delgado, for test shots in the morning. He had a broad nose, kind of bullish at the nostrils, and a white scar across his upper lip. Something hadn't healed right. This could have been ugly, or beautiful in a devastating sort of way. In Jorge's case, it was devastating. I told him my name. He said, "A.A.," in a mellow voice, and studied me, as for an exam. There was a hostile energy around him, familiar to anyone who's worked with male models—a kind of radiating arrogance that almost had its own smell. He shook my hand in his warm, dry one, and I felt embarrassed at my sweat. He was shorter than me by a whisper. We stood side by side for the camera and then embraced, crotch to crotch.

The ad was for Liberty Denim, but I didn't wear any. They were men's jeans. I wore a blue gingham bra and panties, like Dorothy Gale Gone Wild. Invisible spray glue kept every band and seam in place. Jorge wore the jeans, and nothing else. The denim was starched and lacquered, so permanently and perfectly creased it could have cut my shins.

"Give me more curve in the back," the photographer said. "Not like that, that's too cute. Too pinup." The photographer moved aside his tripod to demonstrate two poses. "See the difference?" There was more abandon in the second one. "You're the cover of a romance novel," said the stylist, "the laces on your bodice bursting." I lashed my body like a whip, threw my head back and my ass out. "Right there, here we go, perfect." My job was to look at Jorge, Jorge's to look at the camera. "Say it with your eyes," they told him: "with jeans like these, you can get a girl like this." Then his job was to look at me, and mine to close my eyes, ecstatic.

"So where are you from?" he asked, as we shifted positions. "California?"

"New York," I said. "It's OK, no one ever guesses right."

"You're a dying breed," he said, clutching the nape of my neck. "New York is all Brazilians and Danes now."

I leaned back. We both knew how to hold a conversation without moving our lips too much. "Yeah, my booker says I would have been a perfect little waif, in 1950."

"Well, you are perfect," he said. I opened my eyes. No one ever said this, not at work. "Liberty Denim's all about sweet, not edgy, girls. Anyway, those Danish chicks look like aliens to me." For a moment I was flattered, but he wasn't paying me a compliment. He was just describing things, coldly and casually, as he saw them. His hands and body were warm, but the hard denim and his taut muscles seemed to be resisting me.

At night I had to face the tricky question of food. It was important not to eat, of course, but important also not to faint or get lightheaded in the middle of a job. One evening in our early twenties, Sabine and I pretended that our makeup was food. Makeup—boatloads of it, samples swiped from different jobs—was one thing we had plenty of. The colors had names like Mocha Fudge or Maraschino, and we kept them in the refrigerator so they'd last. It was easy to imagine they could do something for hunger. We rolled the lipsticks out of their tubes and sniffed them. I called Sabine by her shade of foundation, Caramel; and she called me by mine, Buttermilk; and we nibbled at each other.

Since room service was pricey and wouldn't cure me of my delivery habit, I went out to eat. The dust was thick and almost glittered in the air. At least the sun had gone down. I passed a wall plastered with ads despite a POST NO BILLS warning. Old posters for Liberty Denim featured Jorge with another girl, looking as he had earlier that day: bare-chested and relaxed. I saw what would happen to me, eventually. While Jorge came across as his flesh-and-blood self, the girl was out of focus, a little blurry, not quite real. And some vandal had systematically spray-painted the girl's face black, on every single poster, so I couldn't see if she resembled me. She had my hair, though: a flossy margarine color.

I knew from Jorge that the girl changed "every season." I was girl number four, and he had a three-year contract. He didn't tell me if we were in the first, second, or third year of his contract, or how many seasons there were in a Manila year.

I went into the first restaurant I saw, which had four tables and a glass-roofed counter, like a canteen. The cashier and four teenage customers stared at me. It was the airport all over again: I felt conspicuously alone. I went up to the glass and examined my safest options. There was a noodle dish with brown cubes of tofu in it; I could pick those out and eat them and throw away the starch. Cucumber slices and julienned carrots floated in a colorless dressing that probably had sugar in it. Closest to the register was a sad-looking tub of pale shredded lettuce and quartered tomatoes. Those would work, I thought. Over my shoulder I heard someone suck their teeth, annoyed. I turned—it was one of the teenagers, her arms folded and her right foot tapping the floor behind me. "Sorry," I said and stepped aside to let her pass. In less time than I'd spent deliberating she got her food and brought it on a tray back to her seat. Her friends, giggling and whispering, said *Amerikano* and the Tagalog word for "white." I only knew it from Sabine, whose relatives had called her that, amazed at how one half of her had made her so distinct from them. The teenagers seemed to be staring at me, challenging my presence there. Laughing at who I happened to be.

I felt rebellious, wanting suddenly to answer those whispers. Give them something to stare at. I turned back to the counter and ordered every murky stew and stir-fry that I couldn't recognize. Loneliness, whenever I felt it, hit me generally as a hole somewhere between my heart and gut, and now I tried to fill it. "Keep it," I told the cashier who tried to hand me change. I remembered the early days of working, when a shoot wrapped for which Sabine or I or one of our friends had starved herself into seeing stars. Relief at finishing the job, an urge to spend the money we'd made, a craving for the grease and salt we'd been denying ourselves—all these things overpowered us, along with a curiosity about who could put away the most. At the table now I force-fed myself squid in its own ink and pork in its own fat. I nearly gagged on a dark pudding that stank of blood. Undressing an egg from its magenta-dyed shell, I felt the tears fall hot and fast out of my eyes into my food. When a sob rose in my throat I stuffed the egg down, barely chewing. It was saltier than a mouthful of seawater. The teenagers had left trails of sauce on their plates, so I soaked up the last puddles of grease on mine with white rice and shoveled everything like coal into the furnace of my mouth. My plates were clean. I felt disgust, and also victory. I had eaten myself sick. I won.

I looked up then from my tray into the window of the restaurant. And there, as if it had just fallen from the sky or risen from the ground, was a dress: white and gauzy, fluttering at the straps and hems, like something by Alberta Ferretti. And there was a body in the dress, a long-limbed woman who turned and walked away just as I caught her eye. She seemed to be alone, and tall for someone local. I abandoned my meal and went after her, not considering how I would find my way back. The alley from the restaurant went straight on like a tunnel for a while. She might have been in a private hurry somewhere, but now and then she would turn and, at the sight of me, speed up. The alley veered left and onto a set of stairs so suddenly that I almost fell. Either the stairs were steep or I descended slowly: I had time to notice that the walls on either side were made of old, crumbling bricks, pocked here and there with holes that could have been from bullets.

At the bottom of the stairs, the black strap of my sandal broke. A flash of white skirt hurried down another long alley. I had to limp to keep my sandal on. I followed the woman around a corner, but then lost her. The street was lit by fancy iron lanterns. Confetti and crepe streamers littered the cobblestones, and workers were sweeping them up with stick brooms. This had to be a tourist spot, I thought. At every other streetlamp was a taxi. The drivers, leaning on their doors and smoking, laughed together. One of them crushed his cigarette under his rubber slipper and nodded at me. "Taxi?" he said. Just below my ribs, I felt the pang that comes with too much movement after too much food. I looked down both ends of the street for any trace of white, but couldn't see anything. I could taste, at the back of my throat, the bilious burning of a meal that wanted to come up. Dragging my loose sandal, I limped to the cab.

Our beach shoot the next day started at 4:00 a.m. so we wouldn't lose the sun. We took a little jet plane, which listed drowsily in the air, to another island. When I undressed, Carmen gave me a look and tapped her stomach. "What's this?" she asked. "I don't remember this."

I sucked it in. "Nothing," I said. A little bloat had happened, from last night's feast of grease and salt. I sucked in some more. "See? Abracadabra," I said and laughed. Carmen relented and laughed too. It was always better not to apologize too much and come off like a new girl, a needy amateur. Better to act flighty and forgivable, like a supermodel.

On the beach it took two hours to pump me up and out in the right places: clouds of mousse to fatten my hair, chicken-cutlet-shaped silicone inserts for my bra. I wore a linen slip and a gold string bikini underneath. But Jorge wore only the product, the Liberty jeans. We lay down where the sand met the water. We were on our sides, propped up on elbows. When I leaned back against Jorge I noticed how blue the sky was and sighed. "Paradise," I said, without thinking much of it.

Jorge laughed and said, inside a loud cough, "Typical."

"What?"

"Oh, it's just . . . *paradise*," he said, in an extremely condescending way. "It's so American."

"You don't know me," I protested. "You know a story you

heard once about some dumb blond girl who's never left the States." I thought of mentioning Sabine, and how we'd traveled to the Philippines before, but then it seemed just like something that blonde would say.

Something tensed between Jorge and me; the energies had changed. But because we were professionals, our faces stayed the same. He kept on looking down at me with that mix of desire and attack. "Listen," he said, "what's the name of this 'paradise' island?"

"No one told me," I said.

"Did you ask? You've been to this country before, right? Name one thing you know, one thing you've learned in your time here."

"I'm only ever here to work." On our previous trip, Sabine always woke up early in the morning and went out into Manila with a canvas hat and Lonely Planet guide. She'd invited me to go with her. But the jet lag had stretched me out like taffy and I just wanted to sleep. Unlike me, she hadn't come for work, just tagged along to visit family and explore the city she hadn't lived in since childhood. "Balete Drive," I said. "I've been to Balete Drive, I know about the ghost woman. She got hit by a car. Or raped in World War Two. People say . . . I know someone who ran her over. He's got the lace to prove it."

This surprised Jorge; he almost broke the pose. "Is that true?" he said.

"The ghost story? Or that I've been?" I felt proud, as if the white lady proved my membership in some club I didn't know existed.

"A guy I grew up with lives on Balete Drive," said Jorge. "The version I know is she borrowed something, and now she wants to give it back. I like that one best. There's no violence in it."

We stayed out for as long as the sun was high. "Here we go. Perfect. Right there," said the photographer. The sand was bright as a blank canvas. As we dressed I felt a little desperate not to be, again that night, the one lonesome person in this city of laughing brown faces. I reached for Jorge's arm. *"Saan tayo?"* I said. Sabine's Lonely Planet had taught me that one.

He smiled—forgiving me, I guess. "Anywhere we want," he said.

We rode a jeepney, it was called, tricked out with streamers and painted in the colors of a carousel. The sides read *Bubble Gum, Candy, Cookie,* and *Lollipop.* "The driver's kids, no question," said Jorge. On my way in, I banged my head hard against the metal entrance; I didn't know to duck. Or maybe jeepneys were made for shorter people. "Manila's dangerous like that," Jorge said, with a laugh. "It ain't Kansas, if you know what I mean." We passed my hotel, the walls of Liberty Denim ads with Jorge and his faceless girl, the little restaurant where I had eaten. In the district of cobblestones and iron lampposts Jorge said, "There was a festival last night, for the Virgin Mary's birthday."

"A parade?" I said.

"Yeah. They bring Mary statues out of all the churches. Girls get all dolled up in their little white dresses to watch."

He took me to a karaoke bar, Crescendo, and dedicated a song to me. *One pill makes you larger and one pill makes you small.* It wasn't the first time I'd been serenaded with that—a tough song to listen to in the first place, and Jorge sang it badly. He swirled an arm above his head, genie-like. *Go ask Alice, I think she'll know. . . .*

I smiled as he returned to our table. "Don't quit your day job."

"Your turn," he said.

I shook my head. "I take a good picture—that's it."

"I don't believe you. What if you didn't take a good picture? What would you do?"

My mind went blank, and hummed like feedback from a microphone. "What would *you* do if you couldn't take pictures?"

"Me? Oh man, what wouldn't I do?" Jorge stretched his arms and laced his fingers behind his head. Looking down at his stomach, he said, "Someday this'll be a keg and not a six-pack. You know? I would love to act."

"No cliché there," I said. In the last few years Sabine had thought about acting, and even landed a few walk-on parts here and there. She would rehearse scenes with me even though I was no good at reading aloud. One scene involved a woman who couldn't work because of a traffic accident and sued the driver for loss of earnings. I looked at "loss of earnings" too quickly and said "loss of earrings." The misreading stuck. Every time we practiced I'd say "earrings" and then "sorry, earnings." I thought, wouldn't it be nice to be able to sue someone for loss of earrings? And get back all the missing earrings you had left in bars or beds or clubs or cabs? "You're kind of an idiot, Alice," Sabine had said, but there was laughter and forgiveness in it.

A fat woman got onstage and started on that song from *Titanic*. Jorge was gazing very intently at the karaoke screen, with its beaches and mountain ranges and lovers walking hand in hand above the neon lyrics. A shadow of stubble had begun on his jaw. "You know, you'd get so much work in New York," I said to him suddenly. For a second I imagined him sharing the apartment with me, taking up the room I had denied the Czech and Argentine and Senegalese girls. "Did you ever think about living there? In my agency the ethnic boys are huge."

"Why would I?" Jorge looked amused. "All the hot American girls come here," he said—and smiled, hotly.

Day three they shot us in a studio. "What happened here?" asked Carmen, frowning up at me. There was a bruised ridge, the size of a baby carrot, in the middle of my forehead, where I'd knocked into the jeepney. She called the photographer over.

I prayed I was less trouble for them to keep than to replace.

It was not completely true that flexibility was my only skill, or that I could do nothing but model. During lean months in New York, I used to go out with some other young pretty people who knew how to dress and laugh. Cafés and bars had us sit near the windows, on their slowest nights, and act like we were having the time of our lives. Some of these places paid us; others let us eat and drink for free; others said they would pay us, then not only *didn't* pay us but even charged us for the food and drinks. I had also worked as a shot girl, cinched into a dirndl or a corset or a sailor dress, depending on the liquor company. I circulated dance floors to peddle sticky-sweet drinks in test tubes or dosage cups. College boys became theatrical when drunk, said things like "You are so hot it *hurts* me," and tipped extra for a body shot or a little pawing—though we were supposed to say no to that. One night a girl saw her boyfriend suck the salt off my neck before downing his tequila. It was true his mouth lingered on me too long. His tongue was oddly cold, and furry in texture, and I said, "Are you checking for a pulse, or what?" I had taken his money and turned away by the time his girlfriend announced herself. She lunged at me from behind, knocking a rainbow of test-tube flavors out of my arms and clawing my neck. The next morning my booker called about a go-see. Sabine helped me sponge foundation over the evidence: a hickey from the drunken kid and fingernail tracks from his jealous girlfriend. "Most action I've had all month," I told Sabine. But that was a bad night. Other nights were better, and the gum of spit and sweat and alcohol washed off easily in the shower.

"She'll be in the background anyway," said the photographer, squinting up at me. "As long as we don't take her profile . . ."

Carmen was annoyed. "If I needed a rhino," she said, "I would've held a go-see at the zoo." Her words buzzed at my forehead and at my stomach, which was flatter today, at least. The photographer directed me to the porch of a fake grass hut on stilts. The studio was lit to look like dawn. I wore a cotton eyelet bedsheet that I gathered at my chest, my hair deliberately tousled.

Jorge stood a few feet in front of the hut. "I'd do this," he told me, picking up last night's conversation as if no time had passed. He gazed at our backdrop.

"Make studio sets?" I said.

He looked insulted. "Live off the land."

The "land" was a Technicolor vista of rice terraces and sky. The photographer shouted to me about Marilyn curves and a time in America when butter was golden. The directions sounded strange to me. Where I came from, everyone was over people like me; they were always looking for the Next Big Thing, and It Girls came in brown and onyx-black. "Peaches and cream," said Carmen, and I loathed them all for loving something so commonplace—even if that commonplace thing was me.

After work, Jorge sped me into his car, which had that cooped-up airplane smell inside. He didn't say where we were going. I recognized the place slowly. Balete Drive reminded me a little of the French Quarter in New Orleans: tall, sturdy-looking trees, large old houses set far back from the traffic, scrollwork on the gates and shutters on the windows. Some of them were walled in. Vines hung down from the trees and brushed over Jorge's windshield as we drove. We stopped at one of the iron gates, which was unlocked. Jorge parked the car next to a motorcycle in the driveway.

I followed him inside to yet another huddle of brown limbs and laughter and chatter. Some men sat at a low table with cigarettes and beer bottles, playing bingo. "*Hoy!*" they shouted when they saw Jorge, and one man—dressed in Jorge's usual work ensemble of jeans and no shirt—jumped to his feet and half-hugged Jorge, half-shook his hand. "Alice, this is my friend Will," said Jorge. Will welcomed me and kissed my hand, then turned and ruffled Jorge's hair. A young woman was curled up on the sofa, bottle-feeding a baby. Jorge murmured something to her, kissing her cheek and stroking the baby's bald head. "Alice, this is Will's sister Rose," he said. Rose just smiled and looked at her baby, swaying with it. I couldn't tell the baby's sex until Jorge took it from her, bringing it up close to me. Two ruby studs glinted in the tiny earlobes. "I'd have a kid. And raise it well," he whispered to me. "I'd do that in a heartbeat." To the room, he announced: "Alice has heard stories about Balete Drive."

Will laughed. "Don't worry. This is my grandmother's place—too shitty for anyone to haunt," he said.

"No, it's great." I didn't know what else to say. Two women materialized from a set of stairs near the back of the living room. They started clearing a round table where it seemed a feast had taken place, balled napkins and broken crab shells on the dishes. Everywhere I turned, expensive-looking objects mingled with crap, reminding me of a fashion editorial I once shot ("How to Mix Low & Luxe"), dressed in three-thousand-dollar coats and Payless shoes. Silk tapestries hung on the wall above dusty orange shag couches. A curio cabinet was empty except for a jade horse and branches of red coral. Jorge's and Will's friends were mismatched, too. Three of them looked young and put-together. I recognized at least one designer shirt. Two others seemed greasy, aging, toothless. We sat on the gritty, unclean floor. The coffee table, when I touched it, had the heft and coldness of real marble.

A friend of Will's—one of the greasy, toothless guys—introduced himself as Piper. The reason for his nickname was a high melodic whistle, which he demonstrated. A gray mouse scurried out from under the curio cabinet to the middle of the floor. The mouse stood on its hind legs while rubbing its front paws together, as if to warm them. Then it returned to all fours and disappeared again under the cabinet. Everyone laughed, and I pretended to—even though I hated rodents, and the evil speed at which they darted out and disappeared.

It was a rodent that got me back to work, one day when I had started a new listen-delete-sleep cycle with my voice mail. "Why don't you come into the office, Alice," my booker was saying. "We need to talk about your career. Are you still in this, or are you out?" I was thinking maybe if I slept long enough, the decision would be made for me, when a mouse darted out from under my bed and disappeared between the white take-out cartons. I was up from the floor and standing on the windowsill faster than you could say "evil." The next voice mail was about my credit card; I caught the main points, which were "past due," and "collection agency." I called my booker back. "In," I said, when he picked up.

The games we played on Balete Drive passed like a dream, without any fixed rules or reason. We used buttons and shells as playing chips. A glass aquarium sat on the table, filled with coins—they kept calling it the betting pool, but no one kept track really of what went in or out. Sometimes coins were taken from the pool to use as bingo chips as well. One by one, the guests went home and the women went upstairs, until only Will, Jorge, and I remained in the living room.

"It's a long drive back," Jorge said. "Alice and I are pretty tired." That was all he needed to say to his old friend. Will gave us some mothball-scented T-shirts to sleep in. At the kitchen sink Jorge and I cleaned our teeth with red toothpaste and our fingers. Rats had made a nest in a vent along the top of the kitchen wall, and I could hear them shrieking. "It's an old house," Jorge said quietly, as if defending it. He spat into the sink and splashed his face with water.

The lights went out.

"Brownout," said Jorge. "Fuck."

Without thinking I kissed him, my eyes not quite adjusted

to the dark, not finding his mouth right away. Our tongues were sweet from the red toothpaste.

In an upstairs room, we took off our clothes slowly. Trying to keep quiet elongated everything. "I have a really long torso," I said, and felt my body lengthening to prove it.

"Your torso's fine," he said.

I started babbling—"George. Can I call you George?"—not wanting to be silly but not wanting, either, to match his intensity or his seriousness. He shushed me with a thumb above my lip—the place where the scar would fall, on him.

I said, "It's just that *whore-hey,* in English, sounds—"

He shushed me again, laughing a little. "I know what it sounds like." We lay down, and he raised my legs up so my toes touched the wall.

In the middle of the night I woke to the whir of a ceiling fan. Electricity had come back to Balete Drive. I got up, found a bathroom at the end of the corridor, and reached for the string hanging from its naked bulb. In the light, I saw the bathroom had no boundaries. A faucet came out of the wall, with a plastic pail, cracked at the rim, under the spout. There was no sink or shower, only a drain in the floor. Two mirrors hung opposite one another: a square one above the toilet tank, and a round one on the back of the bathroom door. I bent down to lift the lid of the toilet seat.

I couldn't sit on a toilet, in a double-mirrored bathroom, without remembering. The night Sabine died, we had gone to a party on Mercer Street, in a fancy apartment whose owner we didn't know. It was a triplex, with spiral staircases and a white grand piano in the living room. Someone called me into a bathroom that had mirrored walls, a mirrored ceiling, and a mirrored floor, on which Sabine lay, unconscious. A fun-house bathroom. As I knelt to her, at least four other versions of me did the same. People assumed—and I did too, at first—that she had overdosed on something. That would have been typical, if a little eighties, of a model. But it was nothing so dramatic as that. I picked her up—how many times had one of us done that, when the other was drunk or sick or sad or just horsing around?—but this felt different, her skin already growing cold, her weight a stranger's weight.

A burst aneurysm, the doctor told me, in the brain. Did I notice the warning signs, they asked: had she complained of blurry vision, feeling weak or numb? "No," I told the doctor truthfully. I didn't say we'd both set out that night to get as sloppy as we could, and even if I were to notice that her pupils had dilated or her speech was slurring, I'd have taken it as a sign that we were right on track. I didn't mention that I'd been sitting in a ghost chair, laughing at a joke told by some guy I was considering sleeping with. Was she a regular cocaine user? Not unless we had money, I said, which wasn't "regular."

Essentially she'd had a stroke, which struck me so much as a thing that happened to old people that I thought, at her hospital bedside, *Are we old?* But it was possible, the doctor said, that she'd been born with this—an inch at most, a weakness on the wall of one of her brain arteries, a thin balloon that after years of growing happened to rupture that night.

It stunned me to lose the person I had known and lived with for a decade to something that was a secret from both of us. We had seen each other through colds and fevers, cleanses and crash diets, STD and pregnancy scares, bad drug trips of the kind some people thought killed her, the mole on her ankle that turned out to be nothing, once she bothered to have it checked out, a lump in my armpit that did have to be excised, as a precaution. She knew that more than one tequila shot made me miserable the next day; I knew that tap water and any less than five hours of sleep made her skin break out like a teenager's. We'd seen more of each other's bodies than of any body we had ever fucked, no question.

Not to mention we *discussed* our bodies, day in and night out: every bone and muscle, every gland and errant hair, was fair game. It's possible that most girls bring these things up now and then with their close friends. But girls who live or die by their metabolisms, whose reactions to caffeine, herbs, or laxatives can mean the difference between shot-girl double shifts and a thousand dollars an hour just to sit there? We were scientific and exhaustive about it. Sabine would not have been amused that her body kept this information from her, after a lifetime spent studying it. But she wasn't around to learn the news. I was the one blindsided. It made me wonder what secrets *my* body was hiding from me, when and where my own flesh would betray me after the years I'd spent getting to know it.

At Sabine's viewing, someone said if she'd survived the stroke she would have never been the same. This way she got to die young, and be burned forever in our hearts and brains as beautiful. Someone else said, *People don't think beauty's an accomplishment. Maybe they're right, but close your eyes for just a moment and imagine this world without beautiful people in it. Is that a world you'd want to live in?*

For a while after her death I was convinced that every stiff neck or cramp, every nauseated feeling, every moment of forgetfulness, was a ruptured aneurysm. If I woke up and sunlight coming through the window felt too bright, I thought, *Is this it? Am I dying?* I still couldn't accept I was alone, I guess—or that I'd always been alone and now I just knew it. No matter how close we had gotten, no matter how well I knew her, there was this fact of death that set Sabine apart from me forever. The trick her body pulled had made me frightened, frankly, of my own body. I wanted, even tried, to forget I had a body altogether.

When I flushed the toilet now, the water cycled in the bowl

slowly and very loudly. The faucet, too, was loud. On the floor next to the plastic pail was a bar of soap, rough as pumice. I washed my hands as quickly as I could. I pushed open the bathroom door and stared again into the square mirror just before switching off the light. Then I heard a rustle in the corridor behind me. Afraid to see another rodent, I closed the toilet lid and sat on top, hugging my knees. My eyes adjusted enough to make out the jut of my cheekbones in the mirror, and a moving silhouette beyond my shoulder.

She was different from the woman I had seen outside the restaurant. This white lady was old. Her hair, long and wild against her shoulders, was the shade of ice. I stood and turned to approach her. At the sleeves and hem of her nightgown, I saw age spots all over her hands and feet. It seemed she had been tall—almost as tall as me, before old age hunched her spine. She was by herself, and not so brown as the women I had seen around the city. I wondered what she would do: turn and flee right then, or run just as I plucked a strand of her frost-white hair as proof? Or would she fade, right in front of me, into the darkness of the empty hallway?

I took another step forward. That was when she screamed and ran straight at me. She jumped my shoulders, and I fell back against the floor. Shouting things in gibberish, or maybe Tagalog, she clawed at me. There was the ringing metal scent of blood, and then I was looking at her liver-spotted fist up close. I didn't see stars so much as lightning in my head, a nerve in my brain flashing brighter than the others.

A light came on from another door along the corridor. *"Lola!"* Jorge's friend Will called from his room, grabbing her shoulders and pulling her from me. He talked in their language until she calmed down, then added in English, "Alice is our friend, it's OK." I touched my nose and looked at the blood on my fingertips. "God, Alice, I'm so sorry," he said. "My *lola* lived through the war. She's so old. I'm sorry."

Lights were turning on one after another now; Will's sister came from her room to see about the commotion as well. "Did we wake her?" Jorge asked about the baby. He didn't know where to look or who to apologize to first. He went into the kitchen and came out with two wet washcloths, one filled with ice. "Where'd she nail you?" he asked. I reached for the part of my face that was still ringing. My cheekbone felt tight, like it was being pushed against, and my nose ached. Jorge dabbed at the blood under my nostrils with the washcloth and placed the bag of ice onto my cheek.

Everyone was quiet for a moment, and then Jorge said, "Alice, meet Will's grandmother. *Lola,* meet Alice Anders."

"There's Manila for you," Will said. "Everybody but their mother under the same roof."

"Everybody *and* their mother," I corrected.

"Exactly," said Will. He whispered to his grandmother and guided her down the hall back to her room.

"She's not all there," Jorge said softly into my ear. "Anyone who doesn't look familiar, she assumes is an intruder. You're not the first."

In the morning I woke inches away from Jorge's scar. It was longer than I had thought, spanning the tip of his nose to his upper lip. I reached up to trace it with my finger, and he opened his eyes. "What is this from?" I whispered.

He drew away from me and sat up, covering his mouth.

"Sorry."

"I had a cleft lip, when I was born." He grinned the plastic kind of grin that twinkles, in a toothpaste ad. *"GrinGivers International made my beam come true!"*

"I did a thing for them once!" I cried.

He looked at me, incredulous. "You're kind of an idiot," he said, without laughter or forgiveness. He yawned, looking at a watch he'd taken off and set on the floor beside us. "We're late for work." Taking my chin between his fingers, he turned my face aside—a bit roughly, I felt. "I'll tell them it's my fault," he said. "I'll explain."

Outside, a heavy white mist hung over Balete Drive. In daylight I saw that the tree branches reached so far up that they made arches over the street. The hanging vines thumped and swished over the windshield. Jorge hummed the Alice song while driving.

In the studio, they were furious. It hadn't looked so bad to me the night before, just a redness in some patches of my face. Nothing a good makeup artist couldn't fix. Now the skin was swelling below my eye. Jorge tried to explain, but what could he do? We were paid to look perfect.

"A lot of girls were up for this job," said Carmen, massaging her temples.

It was the first time since I was eighteen that I'd been sent home with a cancellation fee.

Jorge was speaking rapid-fire Tagalog with a member of the crew when I approached him for the last time. A kind of morning-after shyness kicked in that I hadn't felt earlier, and I handed him my comp card. "If you're ever in New York," I said, "we should hang out. Call my booker." It felt less desperate than saying "Call me." I had an image of him serenading me in the Lower East Side, at another karaoke bar I'd been to, and I liked it.

He glanced at the comp card and then at me, like a client at a go-see trying to remember who I was. I thought, *I should have a new card made up.* This old one had some tacky lingerie shots that I was no longer proud of, and my hair was longer now, with fewer highlights. I hadn't taken measurements in over a year.

"I've never had to leave my country to find work," he said, "but thanks."

———

The front desk of the chapel-like hotel called me a cab. I was glad to see a regular sedan and not another stretch limousine roll into the driveway. Inside I wanted to relax, just let my mind grow blank and stare at the scattered bodies selling candy and cigarettes and garlands, but the driver was another talker.

"He doesn't deserve you," he said, looking at my bruised face in the mirror. "Walk away, is what I tell my daughters. A guy hurts you like that? Walk away."

He had it wrong, but for a second I pitied myself. Tears came to my eyes.

"Bruises or no," said the driver, "you are the most beautiful woman I have ever seen. But where have I seen you before?"

That made me laugh.

"American?" he asked.

I nodded.

"Vacation?"

"No," I said. "Work."

Of course he asked me what work, and I told him. "No kidding!" he said. "Where should I look for you?"

I said, "Liberty Denim."

"*That's* where I've seen you before!" he said. "My daughters will go crazy! Wait till I tell them. They won't believe."

I suppose he *had* seen me before, whoever the previous Liberty Denim girl had been, and would see me again, whichever girl they picked next. "I quit," I said, deciding and believing it right then. "This Manila job was my last."

"Quit? But you're so young! Too young to retire."

I figured I could lie about my age and keep on selling sticky drinks. I could lie about my experience and try to wait tables or tend bar. I wouldn't eat or buy too much. Did the Czech or Argentine or Senegalese girl still need a place to live? Would my mother take me in, now that I'd repaid her failure with my own?

"You'll miss it," the driver said.

"Sure." But I didn't think so. At most, I'd miss hotel rooms:

coming back to sleep in a clean slate every night, every morning my footprints vacuumed out of the carpet.

It took two hours to make it through the midmorning traffic to the airport. The driver heaved my suitcase from his trunk. "If you don't mind, miss," he said. "If it's not too much trouble?" He made a little rectangle with his fingers.

"OK," I said.

"For my girls. They'll go crazy. But I need evidence, or they will not believe."

"OK." I wasn't famous. People didn't ask for photos often, but once in a while they did.

He rummaged in the glove compartment and came back with a disposable camera. I expected him to look into the viewfinder as I smiled. But he hugged me to his side and aimed the lens at arm's length toward our faces, including himself in the frame. Of course! What kind of proof would I offer, on my own? Without him in it, the picture could be anyone's, from anywhere.

I knew by heart how the angle would distort us: the driver's face, closer to the curve of the lens, would look large and bloated, and I'd seem pale and sharp beside him. "One, two, three, cheese," he said, and snapped the plastic button.

I'd been at this work for years. I could imagine almost anything and then become it, visually speaking. For this very last picture, I put aside the all-American sex-heat and became the white lady of Balete Drive, cold and not exactly there. I made like moonlight flooding the camera lens. I receded to a bright puddle and dissolved. *Perfect. Right there. Here we go.* By the time they touched my image—blurred it, altered me—there would be nothing left.

Shadow Families

Every weekend, in Bahrain in the 1980s, we took turns throwing a party. Luz Salonga hosted the first one that September of '86, and as always, we crowded into her kitchen to help. Rowena Cruz soaked rice noodles at the sink. Dulce deLumen made spring roll skins from scratch, painting batter onto the pan with a brush. Rosario Ledesma threaded sweet pork onto thin bamboo sticks. Over the clatter of dishes and the crackle of oil and the smells of vinegar, soy sauce, garlic, and fermented fish settling on our clothes and skin, we laughed about children and gossiped about marriage, the noise as much a comfort to us as the food itself.

Soon our teenagers came downstairs, whining of boredom. We lent them the car keys and sent them off to the shopping mall for an hour or two. They returned with rented Betamax tapes and watched them upstairs: episodes of *Top of the Pops,* movies that the Ministry of Culture had cleaned up beforehand. (There was no lobster dinner in *Flashdance,* so far as our teens knew; no montage of oily limbs in leotards.) Flor Bautista's son Rommel had hair on his chin already; Fe Zaldivar's daughter Mary was starting to fill out her blouses. We felt we could do worse than raise them on this small Islamic desert island, where some women veiled from head to toe, where cleavage and crotches were blurry bands on-screen.

Meanwhile the babies, as we'd forever call our younger children, tore through the house with their dolls and robots, trucks and ponies. Our "Catholic accidents," Rita Espiritu liked to say—she was the vulgar one. We'd given birth to them here on the island, in our late thirties and early forties. The teens, who acted more like junior aunts and uncles to them than older siblings, had helped us name them: Jason and Vanessa, Stephanie and Bruce, names they'd accuse us of mispronouncing almost as soon as they could speak. Our babies learned math from Irish nuns and played soccer with Bahraini children and changed their accents at will. "Watch her bob that head from side to side like a *Bumbai*," said Paz Evora of her daughter Ashley, whose best friends at school were Indians. At noon and sundown, when the muezzin's voice piped from the mosques, our babies ran to the windows. *Allahu akbar!* they sang, as if they knew what it meant.

As for our husbands, they retreated to a room where smoking was allowed and, implicitly, women and children were not. They turned on the television and spread the Sports pages of the *Manama Times* between them. A horse track in Riffa held races every week, but gambling there was *haraam*, of course. And so our husbands made their secret bets indoors, on the same notepads where we wrote the grocery lists. Now and then a great male chorus erupted from the den, hooting at wins, groaning at losses, ribbing one another for bad calls. They waxed authoritative about odds and breeds, trifectas and photo finishes. For speed and grace, said Domingo Cruz, no horse could match the white Arabian stallion whose genetics had not changed in four thousand years. Efren Espiritu talked up the sleeper potential of mixed breeds, which combined their parents' best traits and evolved out of their worst. This was our husbands' surging, primal release from the neckties and briefcases and paper-stacked desks that bound them through the week. The wagers, the beer, and the sizzling pork bits they ate with their fingers broke just about every law sacred to their Arab superiors. Men who'd seemed pummeled into defeat by the office, us wives, "bills to pay and mouths to feed," relatives back home in the Philippines who took them for millionaires; men from whom we looked away in embarrassment on weeknights, when they sat on the sofa picking trouser-sock lint from between their toes; these same men became brash and young again, every Thursday afternoon in their improvised gambling dens.

In the evening we came together to eat and to sing into the Minus One, a double-cassette stereo system that let us dial down a song's vocal track and step in for Tony Bennett or Stevie Wonder. Holding printed lyric booklets (this was before karaoke gave us words on a screen), we crooned into the microphone: "Feelings," "My Way," "Three Times a Lady." Sometimes Vilma Bustamante's husband changed the lyrics to suit the occasion and Xeroxed them for all to follow. "Mañana (Is Soon Enough for Me)" became "Manama (Is Good Enough for Me)," to welcome a family who'd just arrived on the island. "I Made It Through the Rain" became "I Made It Through Bahrain," for a family on its way elsewhere.

Outside the walls of Luz Salonga's house, beyond the fence around her yard, past her street and the gate to our compound, lay the oil fields and refinery that employed most of our husbands. We lived and worked in Bahrain at the pleasure of a people who mystified us. Everything we knew about the Arabs one day could be voided by what we learned the next. Luz Salonga, the most religious one of us, admired their devotion. "I see them kneeling by the highway at all times of day," she said, "while I can barely sell the kids on bedtime prayers." But the Arabs that Fe Zaldivar knew worshiped only sports cars and gold jewelry, mansions and shopping trips to London. To Dulce deLumen, who worked in an emergency room, *Arab* meant incompetent and backward. "The best of their doctors couldn't heal a paper cut," she said. But Rosario Ledesma didn't think a country could get this rich, and have all of Asia at its feet, without some special brand of intelligence. Every morning Vilma Bustamante passed their marble palaces in Saar. Every afternoon Paz Evora drove by crumbling concrete villages in A'ali. It didn't matter that our own community had its kings and hobos, geniuses and fools, heathens and believers; this didn't keep us from wanting a more perfect knowledge of our hosts, a clearer definition. We'd arrived on their island like the itinerant father in the fairy tale about a beauty and a beast, our houses fully furnished by some unseen master. Would he reveal himself to be a prince or monster? We decided early to behave ourselves rather than find out. In their shops and on their streets, we wore hems no higher than the knee, sleeves no shorter than the elbow, necklines that would please a nun. We lived like villagers at the foot of a volcano, hoping never to offend the gods who governed our harvest and our wealth.

We were the lucky ones, and we knew it. Flor Bautista, a nurse, delivered babies at the state hospital. Vilma Bustamante taught English at a girls' school. Paz Evora was a social worker, Lourdes Ocampo an accountant. The rest of us, despite the advanced degrees we'd collected and the résumés we'd built back home, spent our days baking cakes and hanging curtains now, carpooling and grocery shopping, even reading Harlequins or watching soaps while our diplomas gathered dust in file drawers. We'd married engineers, doctors, diplomats, and executives, who earned enough these days to keep us at home.

Other women had come from our country to clean floors or mind rich people's children. Other men had come from our country to pump gas or bus tables, drive cabs or repair the pipeline to Saudi Arabia. These *katulong*—"helpers," as we called them—were often younger but always aging faster than we were, their skin leathering from the desert sun, their spines hunching over brooms and basins, their lungs fried by bleach and petroleum vapors. They lived not with spouses or children but with each other, five or six *katulong* to a flat. Or else they lived with employers, who kept their passports and work contracts under lock and key. These shy and sunburned servants couldn't host us in their homes if they wanted to.

And so we welcomed them, every Thursday, to eat and sing with us. When they arrived, in jeans and T-shirts our teens had outgrown, we all but hoisted them onto our shoulders. We lifted their feet onto Moroccan poufs or camel-saddle ottomans. We refused the housemaids' help in our sweltering kitchens. We sent the bachelors to watch TV and swig Black Label with our husbands.

Sometimes we tried to match the helpers up. We seated Dolly, a janitress, next to Bongbong, a gardener. "Doesn't Dolly sing like a bird?" we said, or "Have you heard Bongbong impersonate his *amo*?" We found them pen pals in Manila, snapping photographs and drafting letters for them. We owed them a chance at the life we enjoyed. At night we sent them home with leftovers. "The children would rather eat *machboos* anyway," we insisted. Before bed, we prayed for them. The helpers came from farming provinces, like our fathers. They spoke Tagalog with country accents, like our mothers. Our parents too had fled droughts and typhoons in their youth, hoping for steady servant work in Manila. Helping these helpers, who'd traveled even farther, felt like home.

In October we met Baby, the island's newest *katulong*. She'd come to clean offices at the Gulf Bank, and moved in with five other women who worked there too. When her flatmates brought Baby along to our next party, we expected someone just like them: another sweet, humble church mouse, who'd somehow strike us as child and granny all at once.

We guessed wrong. Before we ever saw Baby, we heard the

click of her high heels on the deLumens' doorstep. And before we said hello, we smelled her perfume, a striking mix of cinnamon and roses.

She was taller than her flatmates, taller than us, taller than most of our husbands and even some of our teenagers, whom we'd raised on fresh vegetables and fortified milk. Her heels added more height still. She had the fair skin and narrow nose we'd all tried for as young girls in Manila, before we understood that creams and clothespins wouldn't help. Her hair, the improbable color of Sunkist soda, followed the slant of her jaw, longest at the chin and shortest at the nape, with bangs that stood in front like stiff feathers.

"Pasok!" we cried, but Baby wasn't waiting for permission. She peered past us to the living room, as if entering a shop instead of a home. By the time we said *"Kumusta?"* her long legs had made it halfway down the corridor. We hadn't known that shoes like hers existed, with their translucent heels and straps: from a distance she appeared to walk on air, with just the balls of her bare feet. When at last she turned to us, we felt like saleswomen who'd kept her from browsing the shelves in peace.

"Hi," Baby said in English. Her voice was low and rough, as if the pipes had rusted.

Dulce deLumen invited her to the buffet table. *"Thanks-no,"* she said in English. There was a gap, wide enough to fit a skeleton key, between her two front teeth. These jutted so far out she couldn't close her lips without pouting.

Did she have a rough journey? we asked in Tagalog. Baby shook her head. *"When I'm on the plane, I sleep the whole hours,"* she said, again in English.

Was she finding Bahrain too hot? *"Not so,"* she said.

What did she think of her new employer? *"She's OK also."* (Although we knew from her flatmates that their boss at the Gulf Bank was a man.)

All very common errors, for someone in the helper class. Why wouldn't Baby just relax and speak Tagalog? "She says she forgot it already," said her flatmate Girlie. How this could have happened to someone who'd just arrived on the island, none of us knew.

"She'll come around," said Fe Zaldivar. We too had landed vowing to stick to English—to impress others, to practice, to avoid embarrassing our children. Although the teens still found plenty to ridicule in our accents, nuns in convent school had at least taught us to pronounce our *f*'s and *v*'s correctly, to know our verb tenses and distinguish genders, to translate *naman* differently depending on the context. But at these parties we spoke Tagalog even to the babies, who barely understood it, for the same reason we served *pancit* and not *shawarma*. Between Arab bosses and Indian subordinates, British traffic laws and American television, we craved familiar flavors and the sound of a language we knew well.

Why would she refuse our food? we wondered, glancing at Baby from the buffet. One look at her bony arms and tiny waist told us she had no need to "reduce." She sat on an armchair in the corner, drumming her knee with dagger-shaped fingernails.

"No amount of 'English' can disguise a voice like that," said Lourdes Ocampo.

"Or hide such teeth," agreed Rosario Ledesma.

"She opened her mouth," said Rita Espiritu, "and suddenly I was back at the Quiapo wet market, haggling with the *tindera* over milkfish."

"Maybe that's why she tries not to say too much?" said Rowena Cruz, who had a soft heart and a breathless angel's voice. "Maybe she's ashamed of those roots."

So we tried harder. We filled a plate for Baby in case she changed her mind. We tried to forge some bonds at our expense.

"Baby, I'd kill for skin like yours," said Paz Evora, pointing at the rough brown patches on her own cheeks. "These were supposed to fade after I gave birth, but never did. I blame this climate."

"What a beautiful color," said Vilma Bustamante, gazing at Baby's hair while fingering her own split ends. "Is it hard work, to keep a cut like that? It's all I can do to pluck my grays out once a month." Baby had to bleach it first, the flatmates told us later, before coating the hair with orange.

"Just like Cinderella's," said Fe Zaldivar, pointing her cracked, unpolished toes at Baby's shoes. "I can't last an hour on anything higher than two inches. Just say the word if yours start hurting, I've got spare *tsinelas* here somewhere."

During the Minus One hour we seated Dodong, a gas station attendant, next to Baby. But when he offered her the microphone, she shook her head and waved it off, her bangles clinking wrist to elbow like ice cubes in a cocktail glass. No one could get anywhere with her. Even Lourdes Ocampo, our gold-medal gossip, struggled for the single tidbit Baby gave us of her life that day: that she came from Olongapo City, on Subic Bay, some seventy miles northwest of Manila.

Over the next few weeks the Gulf Bank janitresses—Dolly, Girlie, Tiny, Missy, and Pinkie—drew us a portrait of their vain, eccentric new flatmate. "Our very own Madame Marcos," they called her, someone we couldn't imagine scrubbing a toilet or pushing a mop. Baby never cooked, they said. But her beauty regimen often disappeared such staples from the kitchen as eggs, sugar, milk, and mayonnaise, which she whipped into plasters that hardened on her face and stunk up the flat. She soaked her lace panties by hand, their bright dyes staining the bathroom sink. She took long bubble baths that left the tub with a frothy residue, like the inside of a drained milk shake glass. At night, she colonized the living room, following exercise videos at the very hour her flatmates hoped to catch *Dallas*.

Baby's father, we learned, was an American seaman who'd been stationed at Subic during the Korean War. Her mother had worked as a hospitality girl outside the navy base. (We whispered these occupational euphemisms, curling our fingers in quotation marks: *"hostess," "hospitality girl," "guest relations officer."*) As a child, Baby did meet her father on one or two of his liberties in Olongapo. "But once the war was over," said Dolly, "he went home to his wife and kids in America. New Jersey, I think it was." *Isn't that the way?* we all said. Baby's origins put an American twist on a story we'd all heard before. As children in the Philippines, we hardly knew a family that didn't have its second, secret, "shadow" family. Husbands left the provinces for Manila, wives left the Philippines for the Middle East, and all that parting from loved ones to provide for them got lonely. Years ago, Paz Evora had received phone calls from her father's pregnant mistress. Vilma Bustamante met a shadow nephew, fully grown, at her own brother's funeral. Lourdes Ocampo even began as a shadow daughter, though of course she didn't advertise it.

Girlie, who shared a room with her, told us Baby's scent was Opium by Yves Saint Laurent. The bottle, with its red lid and bamboo-leaf pattern, sat on Baby's window ledge, along with her mirror and makeup and assorted relics of her father: an anchor pin, an eagle patch, a fading snapshot of a freckled sailor in T-shirt and canvas cap. Here, before this little shrine, was where she liked to pluck her eyebrows and glue on her fingernails. "It's like the gulf between Bahrain and Saudi," said Girlie, of the four-foot space between her side of the room and Baby's. On *her* window ledge, Girlie liked to pray the rosary, keep a Bible open to the day's scripture, and write home to her mother in Pangasinan.

Her flatmates never saw Baby pray, day or night. And because she slept till noon on Fridays, Baby never joined us at Our Lady of the Pillar, the island's only Catholic church. "Friday's when she gets her hair done," Missy said, during coffee hour. The Pillar was the other place we gathered every weekend, like clockwork. We had our babies baptized there, by Indian priests, in banana-silk gowns we'd ordered from Manila. We forced our teens to sit through Bible Study, ignoring their fake colds or periods and complaints. In this adopted Muslim country, we worshiped with a vengeance. We fanned our sweating faces with the service bulletins through the scorching open-air Masses. What was a little desert heat, we figured, next to the fires that consumed Joan of Arc, the hair shirt under Saint Cecilia's wedding gown, the martyrdom of Agnes?

Every Thursday party ended like this: after the horse races and food and Minus One, our husbands drove the helpers home. "Door-to-door service!" the housemaid Minnie called it. It was the least we could do for the men and women who didn't own cars and rode the public bus to work on weekdays. And they couldn't thank us enough. "That's one less Pakistani next to me this week," said Dolly, holding her nose. They praised our professional men for stooping to such a menial favor. "Engineer *na*, chauffeur *pa*," said Pinkie.

Only Baby never thanked us. She seemed to take each ride as her birthright, her long legs striding to claim the passenger seat before any of her flatmates could.

One Thursday, after Flor Bautista stepped out of the living room, Baby began to laugh. Her low and rusty cackle startled us. We'd never seen her so much as crack a smile before. And there was something foul in it, a vulgar quality that made us drop our eyes into our laps. We crossed our legs, as if this would restore the room to decency. Then she stood up, bracelets and earrings jangling, and laughed her way to the bathroom.

We turned to the *katulong*, who dropped their eyes too. "It's the silliest thing," her flatmate Tiny finally confessed. We could still hear Baby cackling through the bathroom door. "When Fidel Bautista drove us home last Thursday, Baby claimed that he had . . . *stared* at her." Tiny tucked her chin to show us "where," mortified.

Who, in recent time, could we accuse of staring at *our* breasts? The babies, three-four years ago, before we'd weaned them onto solid food?

"Poor Fidel," said Pinkie. "All he did was open the car door."

"Baby said something like 'Wanna take a picture?'" Missy added. "I never saw a brown man turn so red before."

At this time Flor came back from the kitchen, and we changed the subject.

That night, as an experiment, we put Baby in Pirmin Ocampo's car. And when he came home, Pirmin swore: never again.

"What's the matter?" joked Lourdes Ocampo. "Couldn't you keep up with her English?"

But Pirmin didn't laugh. During the ride, he said, Girlie had mentioned a faulty light switch in the bedroom she and Baby shared. Pirmin, an electrical engineer, offered to take a look. "*You* wanna come to my *room?*" Baby said, her first words to him all night. Before Pirmin knew what was happening, Baby wagged her finger at him and cackled. *Bad boy, Pirmin Ocampo! Very bad boy!* Pirmin's voice cracked in the retelling. "So much for trying to help!" he wailed to his wife.

Next we gave the job to Rosario Ledesma's husband. And like clockwork, another accusation came the following Thursday, this time out of Baby's own mouth. "That one—so fast with the hands!" she said, jerking her chin after Vic Ledesma. He'd hurried past her into the gambling den. The charge appeared to tickle rather than offend her. We sat and waited, through her wretched laughter, for specifics. But "If you're gonna touch, *touch*" was all she added. "Don't pretend you want a cigarette."

Rosario later cornered Vic Ledesma, who winced. "I didn't want to waste your time with something so absurd," he said. "We were in the car, and I reached over to the glove box for a smoke. Right then was when she crossed her legs. So naturally, my hand brushed her knee by accident! And she started howling like I made a dirty joke."

The thought of Fidel Bautista, Pirmin Ocampo, and Vic Ledesma as lusty wolves was enough to make us choke on our *adobo*. We'd met our husbands in high school, in college, at our first jobs. "Before his balls had fully dropped," as Rita Espiritu put it. They'd waited for us, more or less patiently, when we were virgins who imagined sex as the great typhoon that would destroy our grades, our futures, and our reputations. They studied business and engineering so they'd never have to work the soil or serve a master. Our mothers' sad, hard lives had taught us just how much a man's good looks and silky voice were worth. Our fathers never wore a suit or wedding ring between them. "Mine chased skirts instead of looking for a job," said Paz Evora. "Mine drank away what he could win at *jueteng*," said Fe Zaldivar. "Mine was a dog," said Vilma Bustamante, "who couldn't learn how to sit or stay."

Now we had something better than lovers. We had companions. Providers. Sex with these men hadn't ended, but it was quiet, civil, and grown-up, a world away from dirt floors or one-room tenements. "No 'Lullaby of the Straw Mat' for my kids," said Rita Espiritu. "I fell asleep hearing all my brothers and sisters being conceived." Now, even as the babies played outside and the teens turned up their Walkmans, even with the carpets underneath us and the air conditioners above, we locked the master bedroom doors and pursed our lips together so no one would hear us shout. Our husbands apologized for their receding hairlines, their potbellies, the sweat and petrol odors that lingered on their skin. *Let me shower first.* We hoped to hide our stretch marks and cesarean scars. *Hang on and I'll close the light.* Dentures, for the teeth that rotted in our early twenties, floated in cups on our nightstands. Rico Salonga talked to Luz as he would to his mother. *Are you tired? Feeling up to it?* Dulce deLumen steered Nestor like a hospital patient. *Careful not to aggravate your back.*

Once in a while we did see flashes of lust, like signals from a far planet. Ver Bustamante couldn't keep his hands off Vilma when she wore the *abaya* a student had given her. *Searching for me in all that fabric drove him crazy.* Paz Evora's husband was roughest in bed on days he'd argued with his Arab boss. *Let's pray Alfonso gets this promotion, or I'll be sore all week.* But mostly they were tender if not inventive lovers. And if they sometimes took us before we were ready, if they sometimes shrank from us before we felt a thing, if they fell asleep faster than we could get started, we remembered their long hours and hard days, the work that gave us beds and private rooms in the first place.

"So he's a gentleman," we told Flor Bautista, imagining Fidel's bifocals and bald pate as he circled his car to open Baby's door. "Would you expect any less of him? It's just wasted on *her.*"

"Only *she* would take Pirmin's help as a proposition," we told Lourdes Ocampo.

"Can you blame Vic," we asked Rosario Ledesma, "for needing to relieve some stress around that woman?"

Our husbands found themselves in a pickle then. On the one hand we still insisted on their duty as gentlemen. "Cuckoo or not," Rowena said to Domingo Cruz, "I can't put her on a bus while all the other helpers get a ride." On the other hand, any man who drove Baby home risked more than just her allegations. Even the least jealous wife among us couldn't resist questioning her designated driver afterward.

"Did Baby flirt with you on the ride to Adliya?" Fe asked Jose Zaldivar.

"Do you find Baby beautiful?" Paz asked Alfonso Evora.

"Would you consider it," Vilma asked Ver Bustamante, "in a different life?"

Bringing Home Baby, as our husbands called it, became the final penalty for the man who scored lowest at the races.

November brought us cooler days, and we started to gather out-doors. Our children dove for coins in the neighborhood swimming pools. Our teens bobbed like buoys in the waters off the public beach. We couldn't turn Baby away from these parties any more than we could send her home on a public bus afterward. We decided to get used to her, the way a village grows to tolerate its fool. "Here comes Baby," we'd say, at the late-arriving clink of bracelets and gust of Opium. "You know Baby," we'd say, when her long, painted talons waved away our food. We chalked up any tales of driver-side lechery to Baby just being Baby again. In any case, we'd get a break from her soon enough. By early December we'd booked our plane tickets home to the Philippines.

We liked to spend Christmas and New Year's in Manila, keeping the children out of school for two extra weeks to make the trip worthwhile. Our husbands joined us for part of this, but the helpers, of course, stayed on-island all year long. Before the holiday, we gathered at Fe Zaldivar's house to collect the letters, gifts, and envelopes of cash they wanted to send home.

"And you, Baby?" asked Rowena Cruz. "Anything we can deliver to your family?"

Baby was sitting near the door, tapping her fingernails against her cheek. Without leaning forward, she scanned the denim vests, the tennis shoes, the designer logos the *katulong* had steam-ironed onto cheap clothes: Members Only, Benetton, a Lacoste crocodile facing left.

"Thanks-no," she said.

"Strange," said Rosario Ledesma, as we cooked up the year's last fiesta in the kitchen, "to travel so far and have no thought of your loved ones back home."

"Maybe she has no loved ones back home," Rowena Cruz allowed.

"But *everyone* needs help back home," snapped Luz Salonga.

"You could be an orphan or an only child and still do better by the Philippines than blowing all your pay on jewelry and press-on nails."

"Still," said Vilma Bustamante, "it's not as if I'm dying to deliver packages to go-go bars."

We agreed we'd have to draw straws for any mission to Olongapo City.

In exchange for our courier services, the helpers would check on our husbands while we were gone. If they felt inspired to brew some *nilaga*, dust some shelves, or even do a little laundry when they stopped by, so much the better. Meanwhile, in the Philippines, we rode bumpy buses from Manila and swaying boats to outer islands. We arrived at tin shacks, where Totoy's mother or Tiny's brother spoke to us in dialects we didn't know. Our brains, grasping for what foreign words we had in store, could only give us *shukran* and *inshallah*—phrase-book Arabic that didn't serve us here.

The holiday melted away; it always did. We returned in January, some of us with our mothers in tow. We gave them guest bedrooms, allowances, rides to the mall. And one by one, before the Feast of the Conversion, they wanted to go home. "Your sister's sick," said Dulce deLumen's mother. "Your brother lost another job," said Paz Evora's. Someone in the Philippines always needed them more than we did. *I see you're doing just fine on your own.* Bahrain's empty streets spooked them; the air con gave them goose bumps.

And so our Thursday parties resumed. We re-created the hams and rice cakes we'd eaten over Christmas and added new cassettes to our Minus One collections. Our husbands reopened their gambling dens. The babies destroyed the last of their new board games and stuffed animals. The teens discovered compact discs and shut themselves up in their rooms to play Depeche

Mode and the Beastie Boys on repeat. Amid all our hostessing and gathering, we didn't notice, right away, who was missing. We heard it from the helpers first.

"Baby's found a place of her own," announced her former roommate, Girlie.

"She drives herself to work now," Dolly added, "instead of taking the bus."

Later that week, at a traffic light, Lourdes Ocampo stopped and saw a black Saab to her left. Sunlight glanced off its windows, and a pair of dark glasses hid the driver's eyes. But there was no mistaking the orange hair, said Lourdes, or the long pale fingers on the steering wheel.

No one knew where the money came from. Baby didn't seem to be scrimping in other areas. Flor Bautista saw her buy a Persian rug in Adliya, while Vilma Bustamante spotted her leaving a pricey hair salon downtown. At the Suq, Rita Espiritu came across Baby trying on the nose chains and slave bracelets we'd refused to let our daughters wear.

"She must be moonlighting, then?" said Rowena Cruz, our constant Pollyanna. "Before her night shift at the bank? Maybe she's been cleaning houses, or watching someone's kids for extra cash."

Whatever its source, Baby did not come explain her new windfall to us. She avoided our parties in February—even after her former flatmates accosted her at the time clock, even after Luz Salonga approached her in the parking lot outside Jawad's Cold Store. She may as well have donned a *niqab* for all we saw and understood of her new life.

By March, we'd all come to the same conclusion.

"What a disgrace," said Luz Salonga.

"I suppose that cleaning offices on its own," said Dulce deLumen, "can't keep you in jewelry and perfume for long."

"She joined the family business after all," said Rita Espiritu, who didn't mean the U.S. Navy.

Perhaps a Bahraini banker had eyed her shape while she vacuumed his office one night. Perhaps a British investor had copped a feel in the elevator. Perhaps Baby herself, her feet and shoulders aching more than usual one day, had wondered if this country of pearls and oil and gold, white yachts and ice-cold shopping complexes, might offer richer rewards for other exertions. In any case, something nudged her back into her mother's line of work, the seedy industry that claimed so many girls back home. We'd wanted to believe this island didn't deal in all of that, but our husbands called us naïve. "What do you think the lobby of the Two Seas Hotel is for?" they said. "Those girls aren't wearing housemaid uniforms."

"Imagine," said Fe Zaldivar, "coming all the way to the Middle East to do what she could've done in Olongapo."

"It's one thing to do it *there*," said Rosario Ledesma. "People lump us all together here." This was true, and mostly worked in our favor. Now and then the sheikh himself declared his love for Filipinos, our cheerful, hardworking, and obedient tribe. And sometimes Bahraini women mistook us for their maids while shopping. *That'll teach me to dress better*, we'd joke, when the helpers couldn't hear.

Come March, Baby had stopped going to work.

"Her time card's missing from the rack," said Girlie. A new Bangladeshi girl took over Baby's floors. We stopped seeing her in the Suq or at Jawad's. At most we'd find her in traffic, driving her black Saab behind dark glasses, like a film star who wished to elude the public.

"Where did we go wrong?" said Flor Bautista, as if she'd lost control of her own child. And we did feel that responsible for Baby. Back when we lived in Manila, our own country cousins had come to work for us as maids or *yaya*, supporting their children while they helped raise ours, hoping to climb into the middle class within a generation or two. If our rising tide lifted all boats, what did Baby's descent mean for us? If she could fall so fast from "maintenance" work to "hospitality," just how far up *did* we live from the slop sink and the soil?

By spring Bongbong the gardener had proposed to Dolly the janitress, the happy coda to a match we'd orchestrated in September. We saw our chance to rescue Baby, if we acted fast. We bought *barong Tagalog*s for Bongbong and his groomsmen, a stiff *piña* gown for Dolly, bouquets and lavender dresses for the bridesmaids. Dolly chose her flatmates for attendants: Girlie, Tiny, Missy, Pinkie, and, at our urging, the woman who'd briefly lived and worked with them—Baby. What better showcase than a wedding, of the life that honest, decent work created? Didn't every girl, no matter how loose or eccentric, want the gown and cake in the end? We defied Baby to hear Mendelssohn's march or see the gold rings on their satin pillow and continue on her wayward path.

Of course, Baby said "Thanks-no" to the lavender dress. She didn't respond as a regular guest either. But we refused to give up. The next time Lourdes Ocampo saw the black Saab in traffic, she followed Baby home. As it turned out, "home" for Baby was not some run-down workers' village, but a small white bungalow near our own compound. Not far from the Evoras and deLumens—no former *katulong* we knew lived there.

"She got out wearing a black *abaya*," said Lourdes, who'd idled her engine nearby. "Of all things."

To see her new Muslim garb for ourselves—and really just to get poor Dolly her RSVP, we swore—we started following Baby too. Rosario Ledesma saw the *abaya*, but noted that Baby stopped short of covering her orange hair. "When she gathered up the hem to walk," said Rosario, "I could still see the high heels underneath." Dulce deLumen went so far as to knock on Baby's door, but the shades were drawn, and Baby didn't answer.

"She's found favor with an Arab," Lourdes concluded.

No one had a better theory. Baby had receded from us, a hidden harem of one. What Rita Espiritu called her "family business" didn't explain the *abaya*, after all. It was true we'd never seen anyone, least of all an Arab, with her, but Lourdes countered that a man who could afford such a mistress could afford to keep her in a second home. "If you were his wife," she said, "could *you* stand to have Baby around?"

This new hypothesis troubled us more than the first. If losing Baby to her mother's profession made us nervous, as if one of our children had joined a bad crowd, losing Baby to a world of mosques and *abayas* and possible polygamy set off a more desperate alarm, as if one of our children had woken with a fever and was speaking in tongues. Without friends or her job at the Gulf Bank, what defense would Baby have against her new local benefactor? A few of our husbands' embassy ties could help, if only she'd let them.

But Dolly's wedding day arrived without any word from Baby. As Luz Salonga played the organ, we listened for high heels along the nave. As Father Almeida swung incense around the altar, we waited for the smell of Opium to pierce the smoke. As Dolly and Bongbong knelt, accepting a silk cord and pouch of coins from their sponsors, we still saw no sign of Baby. Soon the priest was blessing man and wife. Dolly turned, giggling at her new last name. "What a shame *she* isn't seeing this," said Rowena Cruz.

We turned to watch Dolly and Bongbong recess past the pews. Before them, the church doors swung open, and the afternoon sun brightened the dim narthex, as if God Himself were easing and illuminating their path.

But it wasn't God at all. It was Baby who'd opened the doors and entered, wearing the black *abaya* we'd all seen or heard about by now. She turned sideways to nod at the newlyweds as they exited. And that was how she showed us.

Her shape had changed. The once slim, flat waistline had "popped," as they say, tenting the black crepe out in front of her.

We looked to the altar, but Father Almeida had gone into the sacristy. We turned to our husbands, who only dropped their heads. Some of our teenagers trained the video cameras on her. We covered our babies' eyes. "Take them to the car now," we said, and the men complied.

We filed out of the pews and circled her shyly, as if we were the maids and she the bride. Lourdes Ocampo guessed her to be six months along. But who could say for sure? Her proportions had never matched ours.

"I think she is farther gone than that," said Luz Salonga.

Lourdes addressed her first. "We had no idea, Baby." An admission of failure, from a woman we'd always relied on for the scoop.

"I suppose congratulations are in order," said Dulce deLumen.

"If we can help in any way . . ." Rowena Cruz began.

That word *help* did relax us. We knew how to help an expectant mother. "Come to the reception, Baby," said Paz Evora. "We've cooked enough at my place to feed an army! And we love to do it. Anytime we can feed you or the little one, just say the word."

"Don't dream of buying any toys or clothes," said Fe Zaldivar. "We've got more in boxes than our babies can use. Brand-new."

"The teens would love to babysit," said Vilma Bustamante, whether or not she believed this.

In the dim church, our words seemed to get through to Baby, or at least spook her. A hint of fear, like a trapped animal's, flashed in her eyes. This encouraged us. We gathered up the nerve to start offering the kind of help she truly needed.

"We'll throw another party," Luz Salonga said, stepping forward, "when the child is baptized. The child will be baptized, Baby? Here in our church?"

"And attend Sunday school with our babies?" said Lourdes Ocampo.

"Of course *you'll* be her first teacher," said Fe Zaldivar. "Children look to their mothers above all. My first pregnancy, I took the opportunity to . . . examine my life. It wasn't just *my* life anymore—do you know what I mean, Baby?"

"Cars and jewelry are one thing, Baby," said Rosario Ledesma. "But a child needs a family, a—"

"Father?" Baby interrupted.

Rosario was going to say *community.* "Sure," she said. "A father, while we're on the subject."

"She has that."

"Oh, Baby," said Luz Salonga gently. "Of course she does, strictly speaking. But that's not all we mean by *father.* Who will teach the child and raise her? Who'll provide for her?"

"Who provided my house?" said Baby. "Who provided my car?"

Lourdes Ocampo decided to level with her. "Baby, we worry about you." She grasped a fold of Baby's cloak between her thumb and finger, like the edge of a curtain. "Do you know what you're getting into? One day you wear their clothes, the next you're a slave to a stranger's way of life. Are you prepared to convert? To raise your child as one of them? To *lose* your child, if things don't work out?"

Baby knit her eyebrows in confusion. Then, as Lourdes released the *abaya,* she understood. A smile twitched at the corners of her mouth, threatening to expose the gap between her teeth. "Ah! If only!" Baby said. "I wore this because he wanted me to keep it secret first. Now it's the only thing fitting me. That's the only reason. If he's an Arab, then I'm rich!"

It was our turn to be confused, and Baby's sloppy English didn't help; the syntax almost taunted us. "He isn't, then?" Rowena Cruz said weakly.

"If he's an Arab, he can have a second wife," said Baby. "They're allowed, isn't it?" This much she knew.

"I just don't follow," said Vilma Bustamante coldly. "The English you insist on speaking is difficult to understand."

Baby smiled, and then obliged her, with simple words that no one could misread. "He's a Catholic, like you. A *kababayan*. If he's here, I'll point to him. But you sent him out with the kids."

She'd been saving up the news. That much was clear, as Baby threw her head back and let the coarse, full-throated cackle rip. "What did you think? While you were cooking in your kitchen, while you were shopping in the mall, while you were in the Philippines—where did you think he was?"

The stone walls echoed with her laughter. When she recovered, she stared ahead at the altar. We didn't try to catch her eye just then, or ask who *you* and *he* were.

"I think you'd better leave," said Luz Salonga.

Baby tilted her head, returning the soft, pitying gaze Luz had given her just minutes earlier. "This is not your house," she said, and stayed where she was.

We marched past the pews, tearing down the ribbons and flowers. Baby stood in the nave like a statue as we stormed out of the Pillar. Even stranding her there didn't satisfy us as it might have in the old days. She had her own car now, courtesy of a man who'd once drawn straws against driving her home. So she claimed.

Outside, we flung rice at Dolly and Bongbong and scolded the *katulong*. We felt they should have known. "A little warning," said Dulce deLumen, "and we wouldn't have let her ruin Dolly's day." We drove quickly to Paz Evora's house to get the reception over with.

A faction of us dismissed the charges out of hand. Flor, for one, didn't even mention it to Fidel Bautista. Driving away from the church, she remembered how Vic Ledesma and Pirmin Ocampo and her own husband had been punished for the simple favor of getting a *katulong* home. She didn't believe this latest delusional claim for a second. Paz did tell Alfonso Evora, but not because she bought it. "How could Baby tell such trashy lies in church?" she whispered, as they opened their home to the guests. "After all the times we reached out and welcomed her! After all the help we offered." Lourdes Ocampo and Rita Espiritu laughed it off with their husbands, the wave of Pirmin's hand and the shake of Efren's head erasing any doubts they might have briefly entertained.

Some of us, by the time Minus One began, couldn't help but speculate. "If it's true," said Vilma Bustamante, "just for the sake of argument, if it *was* someone's husband—whose?"

Maybe Domingo Cruz, said Dulce deLumen; Rowena could be oblivious sometimes.

Maybe Jose Zaldivar, said Luz Salonga; he only pretended to be so busy and so religious.

Not Efren Espiritu, said Rosario Ledesma. Rita would have his head or his something-else on a platter and he knew it.

Our husbands remained our allies, as we rated our friends' marriages, proud of how our own stacked up.

But later, on the drive home, Baby's words floated back to Dulce deLumen. *Where did you think he was?* By the time her children were dozing in the backseat, Vilma Bustamante thought of the Christmases and summers spent four thousand miles away from Ver, the spaces between aerograms, phone calls, sentimental cassettes she'd recorded of the children's voices and mailed back to Bahrain. Pop music blasted from the foam Walkman ears on Luz Salonga's daughter. *Where would I be without you?* Luz could hear, the lines of a love song turned sinister.

After she'd tucked in her little one, Fe questioned Jose Zaldivar, her brain tormented with the math of dates and alibis. "Absolutely not!" said her husband, slamming their bedroom door closed. "Good God. Never."

Domingo Cruz turned off the bedside lamp beside a hysterical Rowena. "I won't dignify this nonsense with an answer."

For Rosario, *no* was enough. "She had me there for a second," she said, kissing Vic Ledesma good night, sorry to have doubted him for even that long. But others couldn't shake their suspicions.

Dulce woke Nestor deLumen in the middle of the night in tears. "If this were true, which it is not," said an exasperated Nestor, "could you blame us? Who decided that a wife and mother's not a woman anymore? Would it kill you to wear a little perfume, make some effort?" Rico Salonga confessed to a horrified Luz that, although he'd been a faithful man, he didn't see the big deal about mistresses, so long as wife and kids were well provided for. Vilma pulled it out of Ver Bustamante that several Christmases ago, while she and the children were in Manila, he'd consoled one of the *katulong* in their living room. "Minnie was homesick and couldn't stop crying," he said. An arm around her shoulders turned into a kiss, a shamefaced mutual apology, and nothing more. They'd recognized their one-time error and religiously avoided one another since. "As for this Baby," Ver said (he was the one crying now), "I barely know what she looks like. Please believe me."

We quarreled ourselves hoarse. Some of us grew so sure of a past betrayal we felt it like a poison in our gut. Fe demanded details on the fling Jose Zaldivar would not admit to: "When did it start? Last Christmas? On a night you drove her home? Did you do it here, in our bed? Just tell me if you're still seeing her. Are there others?" Dulce accused Nestor deLumen of practical stupidities: "Ever hear of a condom? The Pill? What kind of idiot knocks another woman up, with everyone you've got depending on you, here and back home?" Luz banished Rico Salonga to the sofa. Vilma Bustamante threatened revenge. Rowena Cruz threatened to tell the children. Dulce deLumen even threatened divorce.

The heat had been rising through all of May, and for those of us who feared the worst, our simplest indoor chores—laundry, balancing the checkbook—felt no safer than minesweeping. Vilma

Bustamante tiptoed through her own home, glancing over her shoulder, alert for lipstick stains and crumpled receipts. "Men stray," said Dulce deLumen's mother over the phone one night. "It's a fact of nature." What did we expect? That they could live on aerograms and cassettes alone?

Finally, Rowena Cruz led some of us—Dulce, Fe, Luz, and Vilma—in a march to Baby's house. "Woman to woman, we're begging you," Rowena shouted at the window shades. "We haven't eaten and we haven't slept. Put us out of our misery, Baby, and tell us who did this." We watched the door, like cops on a stakeout. Rowena of all people might have kicked it down, if it hadn't given so easily on her push.

Inside we found the same thick carpets and sleek furniture that had greeted us in our own homes when we first arrived. We stepped carefully through the rooms, cringing when the floorboards creaked. The bathroom smelled of mint shampoo but contained none of Baby's trademark trinkets or cosmetics. "Baby," we called, finding a black *abaya* on the closet floor. "Baby?" we called, louder, as we traipsed through every room a second time, in case we'd missed her. After a while, we stopped expecting a response.

That Friday our little ones marched up the church aisle to receive their First Communion. As the priest made the Sign of the Cross over their veils and *barong Tagalogs*, Rowena Cruz's army of truth seekers learned that they had stormed Baby's house a few hours too late.

"She's out of your hair now," whispered Rita Espiritu from her pew. "She won't bother anyone here again."

For Rita—along with Flor, Lourdes, Paz, and Rosario—had remembered that the Arabs had their own solution to the Baby problem. And—for her own good, for our suffering friends and the very sanity of our beloved circle—they'd deployed it. A British obstetrician, one of Flor Bautista's colleagues, had accompanied them a few days earlier to visit Baby. *I've seen women in your predicament give birth in handcuffs,* warned the doctor, *just before they went to jail.* Baby was advised to catch the next plane to Manila. *This is Bahrain,* Lourdes Ocampo reminded her, *not Olongapo City.* Even the so-called playground of the Gulf had no room for an unwed mother. *You're in enough trouble as it is,* Flor Bautista said. Without a job, Baby had already jeopardized her status on the island once over. "*Repatriation,*" said Rosario Ledesma peacefully. *It's got a nicer ring to it than "prison," don't you think?* Money was quickly pooled for a plane ticket. At the consulate, Efren Espiritu managed to smooth over the snag of Baby's expired work visa.

Those of us just learning of this mission stared, with jaws ajar, as our First Communicants filed back from the altar. We should have known the only law that could contain her was the one that ruled us all. And we did start to feel better, as our friends predicted. Knowing Baby had left the island balmed our hearts, unclenched our muscles. That this all happened during Ramadan renewed our awe and obligation toward our hosts. "The Arabs are fasting," we reminded the children when the Mass was over. "Show them your respect." They crouched into the footwells of our cars to crunch their Jordan almonds and chocolate eggs in secret.

We never did find out who had betrayed his wife with Baby. Or if indeed she'd faked the scandal, just to watch us squirm. In any case, our husbands went to work the next day and the next, loosening their ties at night and dumping their briefcases on the sofa, as they always had. We schooled our growing teens in deodorant and maxi pads. We helped the little ones with end-of-year quizzes and construction-paper crafts. Our families would expect us home in a few weeks, not far from where we knew that Baby, by the end of summer, would give birth.

———

We reunited in the fall and saw each other often, though our parties didn't happen every Thursday as before. In Baby's wake we shrank a little from routine, from rituals that might invite disruption. We were a little warier, too, of the *katulong* who came to our houses to share our food and accept our hand-me-downs. For the first time they seemed capable of harming us. And yet none of them "pulled a Baby" on us, as Lourdes Ocampo termed it, that year. In fact, they acted shyer and more self-effacing than before, as if atoning on behalf of Baby, ashamed that one of their own had wronged us so, afraid we might suspect them of such wickedness. By the time Dolly and Bongbong announced that they were expecting their first child, all was well. They even named Paz and Alfonso Evora as the godparents.

Some of our husbands walked a narrower line after the Baby scandal. Vilma Bustamante joked that if she'd known her house would turn into this wonderland of flowers, cards, candy, balloons, and jewelry, she might have hired someone like Baby to shake things up years ago. And some husbands swung in the opposite direction. It served Dulce right, Nestor deLumen believed, for taking him for granted, that she was not so certain of him anymore. He came home later and drank more, realizing for the first time in their marriage that he could.

Our babies started to complain about us calling them our babies. This upset us less than knowing they'd grow older still—old enough to understand that we would always call them babies, old enough to ignore anything we said altogether.

That year Hope Espiritu and Arvin Ledesma graduated from high school. Faith Salonga was admitted to Columbia University in New York, while Joseph Ocampo barely eked his way into his mother's alma mater in the Philippines. These were always moments of reflection for us: the larger world brought in, the reminder that we'd all move from this island sometime, our success gauged by how far our children had surpassed us. "When do you leave?" they asked each other, when acceptances arrived from Baltimore or London or Sydney. The question was not *if*, not "Will you go?" for we'd assumed that all along. The island was a way station, never a home.

Over the years we toasted each other and scattered to Amsterdam, Chicago, Jackson Heights, Vancouver. For a time, we had to tell all our new acquaintances what Bahrain was. *A small desert island off the coast of Saudi Arabia.* Then came the nineties, and a war that put this strange hot chapter of our lives on the map. Two decades later, we watched from living rooms in Toronto and Dallas and Honolulu as the Pearl Monument, once a fixture in our lives, the roundabout through which we drove our children to the park or ice cream shop, was razed to the ground, its white fragments like the shattered bones of a whale.

Our children grew into jobs and families of their own. They married so often outside the community it no longer surprised us. Poor Chad Bustamante even had to convince his parents, when he proposed to a Filipina, that he'd done so out of love, not duty. Some had children without marrying at all. When we met our hybrid grandchildren, with their hyphenated names, we almost wept at their beauty. We couldn't stop touching their hair or trying in vain to name the color of their mesmerizing eyes. In school they learned Spanish, French, Arabic, Mandarin, or Hindi. "'Tagalog School' is not really a thing," said Heather Bautista, who couldn't well instruct her kids in things she barely remembered herself. "Anyway," our children reminded us, "it's not as if they can use it in more than one country." We almost mentioned the Filipino who bused our table in Germany and the Filipina who cleaned our cabin on a cruise ship to Alaska, but this wasn't what they meant, and we knew it.

Some of our marriages didn't last all that transnational drift. Over the years we heard that Dulce deLumen was now Nestor's ex-wife, and that Fe Zaldivar had become a stepmother. And somewhere outside Palo Alto, Flor Bautista lived alone—happily, so far as we knew. We never thought we'd leave our husbands or take up with other women's, like villainesses in some soap opera. But some of us formed shadow families of our own, after all. We boarded buses, crossed whole continents on trains, or watched the lights of our old cities shrink as we climbed into the sky. We moved into apartments whose leaks and leases we would have to handle on our own; we lay awake in single beds, sensing that we'd snipped a cord not just from home but from the law of gravity itself, and if we tumbled off the planet altogether no one, for a while, might know.

What all this did was get us thinking again, for the first time in years, about Baby, the woman who had once been enemy and outcast to us. Now we were outcasts, of a certain sort, as well. Time had toppled our pillars of domestic and family life without her help. It might be overstating things to say we've walked a mile in Baby's high-heeled shoes; we had advantages she didn't, after all, to ease our lonely exile from the land of perfect wife- and motherhood. But now we do know something, do we not, of what it is to be the woman other women hope not to become? The world's so big, it has exploded our old ideas, and we're not the people who condemned her then. We've wondered if she too has changed. Whenever we hear *Baby,* a not-uncommon name in Echo Park or Cabbagetown or Daly City, we turn to check for that familiar pair of slender legs, that orange head of hair.

Now that her husband has grown old and frail and needs such care as she once gave their children, Vilma Bustamante wonders if, after he dies, Baby and her child might turn up, claiming a connection. We have all imagined it: a click of heels across the parlor floor, a scent of Opium overwhelming the condolence wreaths. She would be older now. Her child, like all of ours, would be grown up. Would he or she look fair, like the American half of her, or would we see our husband's features right away? Our guesses as to what the years have been for Baby vary, like the paths we've taken around the globe. Not all of us believe she wound up in Olongapo for good. Luz Salonga has pictured her repenting, like a modern Magdalene, her flame-red hair under a wimple. Rowena Cruz believes the nursery, not the nunnery, redeemed her, and that Baby found her calling as a mother. Paz Evora would like to think that Baby went to school and on to a career. We know these images have more to do with our own obsessions than with any Baby that existed or exists. We know the likelihood of seeing her this way is slim. And still we picture it, every so often: this rare reunion with our distant past, the chance to look at her again and maybe recognize our selves.

The Virgin of Monte Ramon

Annelise was my neighbor, if you measured the distance in steps. I lived on a quiet hill in the town of Monte Ramon. She lived in the ravine below, among squatters in tin-roofed shacks who drank from the same narrow creek where they bathed. My mother's house, a *casita* in the Spanish Colonial style, had guest rooms, well-manicured hibiscus shrubs, and wrought-iron gates the servants needed keys to enter. These servants—a maid, a gardener, and a laundress—came from the ravine. One March afternoon, my mother fired the laundress. "The poor get so lazy in old age," she complained—and Annelise's mother came to fill the vacancy.

So before I met Annelise, I met her mother. When she arrived, the new laundress stooped—to greet me closely, or so I assumed at first. She had on what we call a duster, the kind of sack-shaped dress ordained for housework. Her veiny, brittle-looking shins could have belonged to a much older woman. And the stoop I had assumed was for my benefit turned out to be her usual way of standing. To greet our new servant, my mother floated down the stairs wearing pearls and a shiny robe. She smiled, her teeth as white as when she was sixteen and crowned Miss Monte Ramon, the favorite local beauty. What teeth the laundress had were rotten. And unlike the laundress, who walked with a haste that suggested there were too few hours in the day to earn a living, my mother was not given much to walking at all, but could more often be found reclining: prone on our dark velvet sofa, or taking siesta upstairs, where only her gentleman guests were allowed to disturb her.

I was always conscious of the ways people moved through the world, because of my own condition. Where others have legs, I have only the beginnings of legs; below that, a semblance of ankles; and finally two misshapen knobs, smooth as stones worked over by water. I got around in an old manual wheelchair that once belonged to my grandfather. The reason for my handicap was neither accident nor illness. No: when I was very young, my mother told me of its mystical and far stranger origin.

My mother's father, Daniel Wilson, was an American GI who came to Monte Ramon in 1944. Our town had been invaded by the Japanese, and my grandfather was among the troops sent out to liberate us. As a soldier he helped evacuate the wooden statue of the Virgin of Monte Ramon—the gilt, gem-encrusted patroness of our town—from her church into the nearby mountains. This was to keep her safe from wartime desecration; yet strangely it was those carrying her who felt protected as they ventured deep into the forests and mountain trails. She became known, after that journey, as Our Lady of Safety.

At the height of the liberation, during a battle in the forest, my grandfather happened upon an Axis land mine and lost both his legs. America flew him home and nursed him at a veterans' hospital as the war was ending. Once healed, Daniel Wilson traveled back to help rebuild Monte Ramon and seek out a girl he'd met during his first visit. He arrived just in time for what became the very first Festival of the Virgin. Pilgrims came from all over the Philippines to make offerings to Our Lady, now salvaged from her mountain hideaway and safely reensconced in her church. Daniel spotted his girl (who would become my grandmother) in a parade, waving from a float of beauty queens. She descended from the float and placed a garland of *sampaguita* around his neck. One year later, they had my mother.

I never met this American grandfather, who died in 1963. But just before she gave birth to me, my mother had a vision. The deceased Daniel Wilson spoke to her, dressed in camouflage and lying in the forest where he'd lost his legs. *Although I am dead,* Daniel told my mother, *I shall live on through my grandson.* He told my mother to name me after him, *her* father, not after the boyfriend who would end up deserting her. Daniel Wilson would not reveal specifics, but said I would be different from other children and remind my mother every day of the family's legacy of pride and courage. And so I arrived: with a telltale lightness to my skin, and the vague buds of feet and toes that never quite articulated themselves.

My mother told this story often when she was not too tired. Its ending left her eyes lacquered with tears. She would gaze tenderly at her parents' wedding portrait: a fair-haired soldier in a wheelchair, Purple Heart pinned neatly to his uniform, and a Filipina bride standing behind him, her white-gloved hand on his shoulder. My mother saw no need to replace Daniel Wilson, Sr.'s old wheelchair for an electric model. "What was good enough for a man like Dad is good enough for us," she said. (He was always Dad or Daddy to her—never Papa, or Tatay.) "Who needs a Motorette when you've got an heirloom like this? And who needs an ordinary father when you've got such a *grand* father?" My mother smiled at her own pun. As it happened, my "ordinary" father had left us soon after my birth, and was said to be living these days in Manila.

I tried to hold the stalwart image of Daniel Wilson, Sr., in my thoughts each morning when I went to school. My books were bound by a leather strap, which I would grasp between my teeth, while my arms pumped at the steel rings of my grandfather's old wheelchair. When I was younger, my schoolmates could be violently, unimaginatively cruel: there was a day they shoved me to the ground and ran away with my chair, leaving me to crawl hand over stump about a quarter mile until I found it. Sometimes they hobbled on their knees, in amputee fashion, beside me. They were often caught, of course, and punished by the priests; and so they soon discovered ways of mocking me that didn't risk lashings or demerits. Recently they'd christened me Manny—to rhyme with my nickname, Danny, but also short for *mananang-gal.* The *manananggal,* a mythical vampire, could detach from her own legs and fly her torso freely into the night, feasting with a forked tongue on the wombs of unsuspecting women. Whenever those other boys aped me or called me Manny, I thought of medals and uniforms, of the Bataan Death March, of my grandfather bleeding in a nameless wood. Did I think it would be a cakewalk, the road to glory? Was it easy for Daniel Wilson, Sr., to risk life and limb for the freedoms of his Little Brown Brothers? Of course not! "Christian children bear their burdens," a priest once said to me, "and suffering burnishes our lives to a high radiance."

Daniel Wilson, Sr., also helped me to endure the sordid claims that schoolmates made about my mother. Once, in grade five, I stood up to my tormentors, informing them that I was descended from an American war hero. "You'd all be speaking Nippongo now if it weren't for my grandfather," I said to the other boys. I told them of my mother's vision and how my birth had confirmed it. My classmates' jaws fell open. The school yard turned so quiet I was certain I had put the insults to rest at last. But then from someone's mouth there came a sound like a balloon deflating, and everyone began to laugh and slap their knees harder than ever. "How precious!" "That is rich!" "What a grand inheritance!" "The baby's got his mother's eyes, and his *lolo*'s stumps!" Then a boy named Luis Amador said: "That's a good theory, Manny. But I've got a better one. You didn't get this handicap from your grandfather. You got it from your mother—who earns her living on her knees!" To what seemed like a million voices cheering, Luis genuflected and bobbed his head like a chicken in a coop.

It was true my mother had friends in Monte Ramon's finest men: engineers; police officers; even, on one occasion, the mayor. These guests showed their gratitude to my mother in various ways. Bright flowers adorned our mantel every week. After a brownout, our lights were among the first in town to be restored. A priest from my own school gave her a *payneta* comb, carved from coconut wood into the shape of a lady's fan. "Oh, Father," my mother breathed, fingering the comb's scalloped edges, "you are *too* generous." She coiled her hair—cola-colored hair with streaks of copper in it—above her nape, and secured it with the comb. Even the dentist offered us his services for free—a welcome gift, as my teeth ached often from the weight of my books and other belongings. Countless men in Monte Ramon were good to my mother. I refused to believe, however, that she could somehow be degrading herself in the exchange. In her own words, my mother repaid her friends with "company and comfort—that's all," and I did not consider it my province as a son to challenge her.

I suppose that there were reasons, as many as the hills in our town of Monte Ramon, to doubt my mother's stories; and reasons, as variegated as the stones that sparkled on our Virgin's robes, to doubt my mother herself. But what were reasons in the face of faith? I believed her—honoring, as the commandment taught me, both my mother and that greater, universal parent Himself.

In the month of March, every year since 1947, the town held a fiesta to honor our Virgin. Pilgrims flooded Monte Ramon to pay her homage, and men carried the statue of Our Lady from her church into the mountains and back again in a parade that commemorated her odyssey to safety during the war. Vendors sold roasted cashews and jars of coconut caramel along the streets.

The church stood between my school, General Douglas MacArthur Preparatory, and our sister school, the Academy of Our Lady of Safety. Tradition held that when the boys of "Doug Prep" and the girls of "Safety" were thirteen, we met and prepared to escort each other in the March parade. Half a school year's preparation led up to this, and the Safety girls arrived at our campus on a bright Tuesday in October. My classmates kept their hands in their pockets and their eyes on their shoes. The nuns and priests who had taught us Comportment told us now to introduce ourselves and make small talk. In my wheelchair, I sat apart from everyone.

"What's the matter with you, Manny?" Ruben Delacruz called out to me. "Haven't you been taught that a gentleman stands up in the presence of ladies?" His friends ate that one up. Ruben was our unofficial school prince, blessed with a screen-idol smile and a supernatural ease in everything from basketball to elocution. He was also the son of our one and only Dr. Delacruz, a man beloved in Monte Ramon. Dr. Delacruz ministered to a scraped knee with the same gentle attention as to a severe pneumonia. Every few years, when my back became afflicted with a pressure ulcer, Dr. Delacruz gave me antibiotics and applied the saltwater rinses with his own hands. An outbreak of influenza in the town, two years before, had Dr. Delacruz making house calls even to the grimiest parts of the ravine, with no concern for his own safety. It was these qualities that earned him the nickname the Messiah of Monte Ramon.

Dr. Delacruz's late wife was said to have died giving birth to Ruben. Other boys—like Renato Cazar, whose mother had succumbed to cancer; and Vince Santiago, whose father had run off to Cebu with a younger woman—were teased and shunned for their family situation, as if being half-orphaned was a disease anyone could catch. And other boys—like Oscar Padilla, whose father was a lawyer to accused criminals, and Nemecio Ferrer, whose father was a debt collector—seemed stained by their parents' work and clientele. Having both misfortunes would have surely doomed any other boy, but not Ruben. Somehow he'd fixed it early on so no one dared mention Dr. Delacruz's patients or the late Mrs. Delacruz's death to him; in fact, in Ruben's case, his father's work and mother's absence seemed only to heighten the air of specialness that hung about him always.

"Give Manny a zero in Comportment, Father O'Connor," said Pedro Katigbak, though not loudly enough for Father O'Connor to hear. I stared down into my school trousers. The laundress had pressed a crisp, straight crease down each leg, long past the point where it mattered.

The girls, on their patch of campus green, paid little attention to us boys. In their pinafores and Peter Pan collars, they had formed a circle, singing:

> *Negrita of the mountain,*
> *what kind of food do you eat?*
> *What kind of dress do you wear?*

I remembered hearing "Negrita's Song" in primary school, when we learned about mountain tribes like the Batak and the Aeta. The nuns took notice and put a stop to the chanting. Then some of my classmates, led by the brave Ruben Delacruz, started to approach the girls, and I saw Annelise for the first time.

Though a schoolgirl in uniform herself, she was unlike the others. She did not blush or chat with her classmates, or glance at us from the corners of her eyes every so often. Instead, she was reading a book. Anyone who was not a child was tall to me, but this girl, in particular, loomed. Her cinnamon-dark complexion stood out against the regulation white, and tight, spongy curls bloomed from her head, unpinned and unribboned. As if she sensed me looking, she glanced up and directly at me, displaying a blunt wide nose my mother would have called "native."

After some secret chatter the girls brought their new boy acquaintances to Annelise. "How do you do, Negrita?" Ruben said, extending his hand as for a formal introduction. "Tell me: what kind of food do you eat, up there in the mountains?" Other boys followed suit, so that the insults of "Negrita's Song" could seem from far away like small talk. The girls grew red holding in their laughter. Before long both boys and girls had crowded around her. There was no response from our teachers, this time; they mistook the huddle for a social success, and smiled in our direction.

I had longed for the day when my schoolmates would find a new target, a victim other than me. Now that she was here—a girl, who seemed unfazed by the teasing—I felt none of the relief I'd expected. I felt only shame at my own school-yard weakness, and a deep curiosity about this girl they called the Negrita.

A few days later, when Annelise came to our doorstep, she struck the brass knocker despite the key her mother had lent her. I was midway through my daily push-ups, which I did against the arm-rests of my chair to keep the steering muscles strong. I wiped away the sweat above my lip and caught my breath as I wheeled myself to the front door.

Her feet were dusty in their rubber *tsinelas*. She was not in uniform but in a shapeless duster like the ones her mother wore. Only when I looked up did I recognize the cloud of curls and the dark *indio* face from school. Annelise, for her part, did not seem to remember me. Blunt and bold as she looked, her first words to me were polite. "Evening, sir," she said. My mother would have approved: she liked when people understood that ours was an English-speaking household. "Your *labandera* cannot come today. I'm her daughter, Annelise." Her voice was as forceful and as flat as a wooden spoon against a table. It was not a voice that would sing sweetly to you, or tell tales. "If you show me where the clothes are, I can start now." I let Annelise into the house. Beside me, she trailed the powder-clean scent of fresh laundry.

A narrow stone paving led from our back door to the grass and the house's outer wall. Clotheslines hung in between. Annelise surveyed the plastic basins, the steel sink and faucet, and the folded ironing board. She seemed accustomed to breezing into strangers' houses to do the wash. She turned on the faucet, testing the water temperature with her fingers.

"Is your mother sick?" I called out, over the sound of water striking a basin.

Annelise seemed surprised that I should ask. "No. She just gave birth to a son." She unfurled some lacy garment of my mother's, scanning the front and back for stains.

Had I known that our laundress was expecting a child? She stooped and wore such tentlike clothes, it was odd to think of her in such terms at all. I suddenly realized with horror that, among the other laundry, Annelise would soon be scrubbing my briefs. I wheeled myself over the cracked, loosening cement and reached for my laundry basket. "These are clean," I said, balancing the basket on my lap and using my other arm to retreat toward the house.

Annelise gave me a puzzled look, then shrugged and wiped her hands on her duster. "She was pregnant when she started here," she said, as if she'd read my earlier thoughts. "You didn't know what she looked like not pregnant."

"Can I bring you anything?" I asked.

Most servants apologized shyly for so much as breathing or taking up space in a room. Annelise looked up from the wash and said, "Do you have a radio?"

I brought a small transistor from my room and set it on the windowsill between our yard and the kitchen.

"Thanks." She smiled. "We don't have one at home." Drying her hands on her duster again, Annelise tuned the dial to a *radionovela*. The characters of *Pusong Sinugatan* (Wounded Heart) included Joe, an American soldier, and Reyna, a Manila debutante, who met fatefully in 1944. "A pair of star-crossed *magkasintahan*," the announcer called them. The radio was old and full of static. Shampoo jingles alternated with bombs and air-raid sirens. "After a word from our sponsors," said the announcer, "we'll find out what the Japs have done to Reyna's beloved papa!" Annelise plunged her shining brown arms into the suds, unaware that I was listening along.

Our first coed Catechism took place at the Academy of Our Lady. The girls played with their skirt hems and pencil cases as we arrived. My classmates filled the spare desks along one wall of the room, leaving me only the space behind the very last row to park my chair. I spotted Annelise up front. Her curls hovered over a composition book. Sister Carol rapped her desk with a ruler to quiet us, and Father O'Connor said something about miracles.

Sister Carol directed us to a passage in Luke. "Annelise Moreno," she called, for a first reader. The laundress's daughter stood.

"A woman with a hemorrhage of twelve years' duration," Annelise began, "incurable at any doctor's hands, came up behind Jesus and touched the tassel on his cloak."

There was a murmur on the girls' side of the room, and some of Annelise's classmates giggled softly into their hands.

"Immediately her bleeding stopped," continued Annelise. "Jesus asked, 'Who touched me?'"

Two girls in the row before me turned to each other. "How fitting," said one. "*She* should touch that cloak!"

"Hemorrhage girl!" whispered the other. They giggled and then mumbled something else I couldn't catch.

"Everyone disclaimed doing it, while Peter said—" Annelise began, then stopped and slammed her Bible shut. She whirled to face my corner of the room. I startled, briefly convinced that she was glaring at me. "Rose and Gemma, if you have something to say," she called, "say it loud and to my face. Don't cover your mouths. Let's hear it." Her voice was hot and full of challenge. The two girls in front of me crossed their legs and laced their fingers, then glanced at each other, wide-eyed.

"Miss Moreno!" Sister Carol rapped her ruler against the desk. "Were you not instructed to read a passage from the Bible?"

"I was, Sister Carol," said Annelise, without lowering her voice.

"Then tell me, please: why do I seem to be hearing other words out of your mouth?"

"I'm sorry, ma'am. Those words were meant for Rose and Gemma."

"I see. As a reminder, Miss Moreno, that teachers, not students, are in charge of classroom discipline, you may remain standing at your desk until I invite you to have a seat. Let's have someone better able to follow instructions read where you left off."

Annelise didn't argue, but didn't seem ashamed either, as she placed her hands at her sides and stood straight in her place. There was more giggling and murmuring. The pleats of her pinafore were perfectly ironed, but a single crease slanted down the back of her blouse. One fallen strand of her frizzled hair hung on to the wrinkle, stubbornly. I didn't realize, till Annelise's replacement began to read in a calm, dull voice, that Annelise's had set my heart racing. I'd never heard a child speak to adults with such boldness, or stand almost with pride while being disciplined.

At the end of our lesson, after Sister Carol allowed Annelise to sit again, Father O'Connor brought out an offertory basket full of paper slips, which he shook gently. "It's time to partner up for the fiesta," he said. "Gentlemen, when I call you, please step forward and draw your lady's name out of the hat."

Students shifted in their seats. I believe it was fate that brought Annelise and me together, for Father O'Connor announced, as if on a whim, "Let's start at the *end* of the alphabet today, and go backward from there." He glanced at the roll. I had inherited my surname, like my handicap, from my grandfather, and—ever since Joel Zamora's family had moved to Manila—always came last on the list. "Danny Wilson, Jr.," said Father O'Connor.

Faces turned as Sister Carol helped widen an aisle for me. I rolled awkwardly to the front of the room. At each spin my wheels struck the legs of another girl's desk, a sound that seemed to ring into the hallways. "Watch your step, Manny," Ruben whispered. "You wouldn't want to stub your toe." The girls—each praying silently, I knew, for anyone but the class cripple—turned away as I passed, and fiddled with their girlish things: a gilt-edged Bible, mechanical pencils, a blue heart-shaped eraser whose left lobe was blackened and rubbed flat with use.

But I had a silent prayer of my own. I glanced at Annelise's curls, and imagined their powdery scent, just before Father O'Connor lowered the basket before me. Was it Father O'Connor, or another priest, who had taught us to pray with pure and total trust that our prayers would be answered? I closed my eyes and reached for her name.

We took recess outside. Annelise and I stayed close to the hedges separating the high school from the little girls' playground.

"How is your mother?" I asked.

"She'll be ready to work again next week."

"I didn't mean—"

Annelise laughed. "She's doing better," she said. "My little brother kept refusing her nipple, at first. Like a spoiled little prince! But good old Dr. Delacruz brought us some formula."

Annelise glided easily from Dr. Delacruz to her next subject and then the next, treating them all as casually as she had her mother's nipple. You would presume from her tone that we had known each other for years.

"You seem different from the girls here," I admitted. Then, fearing I'd insulted her: "Sorry."

"I am," she said. "I'm the 'scholarship girl.' The nuns took me on as their charity case." She smiled and looked at me expectantly. "And you? Which 'boy' are you?"

It was not so easy to name my status. How should I explain the fine house, and the servants who were sometimes paid in bowls or jewels to maintain it? What title bridged the space between light skin and no legs, between a white hero for a grandfather and a half-white mother whose doings were whispered of in town? Which "boy" did all these things, combined, make me?

"I'm not the Delacruz boy," I finally said.

Annelise nodded. As if their ears had pricked at the sound of Ruben's name, some of her classmates approached, and made a show of holding their noses. "You stink, Negrita," they said. "Stinks to be poor, eh?" Annelise turned away. She faced me and held the handles of my chair, her knees touching my trousers, so that we made a nearly self-enclosed unit on the grass. Her movement made a rustling sound like plastic bags.

"What's in your diaper?" they asked. "We think Negrita needs a diaper change."

My mother once fired a maid who, she said, filled the house with a wretched odor. "The poor live in a Dark Age of superstition," said my mother at the time. "I won't have her trailing her animal smells into my house."

"In one ear and out the other," said Annelise, looking down at me. "You don't let the things they say affect you, do you?"

"No," I lied.

Later that week Sister Grace and Father Johnson excused us from a joint Physical Education class, where the other pairs would learn a folk dance called the *kuratsa*. Annelise and I watched from the sidelines of the Doug Prep gymnasium. "It isn't fair that you won't dance in the fiesta, because of me," I said. "I'm sorry."

"You say this word a lot," she said.

"Sorry?"

"There you go again." Annelise grinned. "I used to be like that too. Shy, and 'sorry' about everything. Anyway, does that seem like a good time to you?" She turned to where our classmates were shuffling along, two by two, some looking like they wanted the gym floor to swallow them. "I wish we had our own radio, though."

"I listened to *Pusong Sinugatan* last night," I offered. I didn't mention that I'd missed Annelise's company just as soon as my class left Safety's campus, that I'd wished almost immediately to go back to the Catechism lesson and the recess, or that I'd tuned in to the radio as a way, alone in my room, to conjure her. I didn't talk about searching my Bible at home to reread Luke's story of the bleeding woman. *Daughter, faith has cured you. Go in peace.*

"Well?" said Annelise. "Catch me up, then."

I told her how, after the program had been following their separate paths for days, Joe finally laid eyes on Reyna at a dance. It wasn't love at first sight—not for Reyna, anyway. Joe had to fight through a thicket of other suitors to say hello. Those suitors had only one thing in mind—so said the narrator—but Reyna was too blind to see it, or to notice Joe. It surprised me how easily I fell to talking about these people, like an old village gossip. As if they were neighbors and lived on our same hill in Monte Ramon.

Annelise sighed. "She'll come around."

I was sorry that she couldn't listen at home. Before I knew

what I was doing, I said, "You're welcome to borrow it, Annelise. The radio. Next time you or your mother come . . ."

"That's kind of you," she said, "but we'd need electricity for that."

I felt sorry again, but now I knew not to say so.

"Thanks anyway." Annelise reached over as if to touch me, but gripped the armrest of my chair instead, helping herself up and excusing herself to the lavatory. As she crossed in front of me she smelled different, this time, from the laundry powder she had used to do our wash. She tossed her hair behind her, sending a damp and loamy scent in my direction. It reminded me of our garden after a very heavy rain, the grass and hibiscus buds gone slick and overripe under the weather.

Because we couldn't do the *kuratsa*, Annelise and I were in charge of serving punch and cake at a dance—a kind of rehearsal for the March performance. The Safety girls wore fancy dresses to this event, with flowers on their shoulders and waists and hems. The boys arrived in white *barong Tagalog*—sheer dress shirts of banana silk thread or pineapple fiber, embroidered at the placket and worn loose over the undershirts we'd tucked into the waistbands of our trousers. I wore the same *barong* I'd worn at my Confirmation the year before, a plain linen one left behind by one of my mother's visitors, still large on me. My classmates raised their eyebrows at the frayed sleeves, buttoning nearly at my fingertips. Ruben, whose *barong* seemed to have gold thread in it, called me *Lolo* as I filled his punch cup. I watched the clock and waited for Annelise.

An hour passed, and then another. She did not come. Three hours into the dance, there was still no one at the refreshments table but me.

A few girls from Annelise's class approached. "Your Negrita girlfriend's on the rag," said a petite, snub-nosed one, taking a cup of punch from my hand. "She's a freak of nature. Her rags go on for weeks and weeks and she can barely stand for pain. She's bleeding her guts out right now."

Sharp words, turning this girl's tiny voice and delicate face ugly. I looked away. I knew so little of what female bodies did in secret. Women's privacy, I'd been taught, was sacred. The second story of our house, my mother's zone, was forbidden to me and difficult, in any case, for me to access. Sometimes, when I passed the foot of the stairs, I'd catch a gust of perfumed air or a flash of eastern sunlight as a guest opened my mother's door and then closed it behind him. Ruben once smuggled a medical textbook of his father's to school and showed his friends a page headed "Female Reproductive System." Excluded from their circle, I glimpsed only something like a symbol of Aries, that ram's head with great curlicued horns. These subjects felt as far from me as my mother's quarters, closed and quiet at the top of the stairs that I could never climb.

"Maybe Danny's mother can get Annelise some medical help," Jacinto Cortez said. "Doesn't Danny's mother know Dr. Delacruz?"

Ruben Delacruz balled his fists. "Did you say something?" he said, staring Jacinto down and away from the table. When the gymnasium began to empty and Annelise still had not appeared, I wheeled my way home.

In Annelise's absence, boys and girls alike went back to teasing me. After dismissal that Monday, Pedro Katigbak clutched his heart and forehead like a girl. "Help!" he falsettoed. "I'm bleeding to death! Oh, how can I stop this bleeding?" He placed a hand between his legs and made as if to faint.

Rizal Rojas lumbered over on his knees. "I am Manny-*manananggal*," he said. "*I* can save you, Negrita." He knelt at Pedro's standing legs and looked up. "Negrita, let me drink your blood! I'm a womb-eating vampire, after all—and look! I'm the perfect height! Somebody get me a straw!"

The girls howled in squeamish, scandalized delight. Ruben Delacruz clapped his hands. "Well done," he said. I tried to picture myself as an actual *manananggal*, flying my half-body high above the school-yard laughter. This little piece of vaudeville wasn't the worst they'd inflicted on me, in my school career, but I felt new and unaccustomed to it. In the short time I'd spent with Annelise, I had forgotten what it was to be lonely.

After school, a group of students followed me home on their knees. They went as far as the gate and then abandoned me, knowing that our gardener would shoo them off with a giant pair of pruning shears. Once they had gone, I started to wheel myself past the front yard to the house, then stopped. Annelise lived down the other side of the hill, on the banks of the ravine dotted with squatters' shacks. Without pausing to consider why, I turned my wheelchair and pumped past the houses on our street, then coursed down the yellow grass to the ravine.

It took some doing: each rut in the hill's soil bumped me forward. I pressed my weight back to gain some balance. The slope seemed to grow steeper the further I rolled. I hooked an arm behind me, the wooden backrest in the bend of my elbow, while steering forward with the other hand. The grass gave way to rocks and mud, which clung to my wheels at every turn. Every few years, during the wet season, mudslides swept some houses clean off this bank into the creek. I feared toppling forward and landing in the water with my chair overturned, its dirt-caked wheels spinning.

By the time I reached the first shack, the air had thickened, with an overwhelming stench of smoke and urine and spoiled milk. The shacks were patched together from cardboard and plywood and other scraps, raised by stilts, and roofed with corrugated tin. Clotheslines joined one shack to the next like crude telephone wires. An old woman, her lips puckered inward where the teeth had fallen out, stood in front of the first shack. Some children kicked around a metal can beside her. When they saw me, they stopped and gathered to stare.

I recognized Annelise in their large bottomless eyes. Perhaps all the ravine's children learned to look at people this way. Suddenly I remembered what was said about the squatters: that their kind would dive into canals and landfills, scavenging scraps to sell or use or eat. What would they do with me, an outsider in a school uniform, with a steel chair and books hanging from his mouth? I resolved to give them anything they wanted, so long as I could see Annelise and make it back up the hill, using my bare hands if I had to. Like a dog who'd just fetched for its master, I released my books into my lap.

"I am looking for Annelise Moreno," I told the children. "Do you know where she lives?" One boy, wearing a shirt but no pants, pointed down the row of houses. A small girl said she'd show the way if I let her push me. I agreed, blinking away another vision of my chair upended in the ravine. My wheels sank slightly into the earth and caught every so often on rocks within it. But my young guide pushed with surprising force. She left me beside a woman yanking clothes off a line. "Over there," said the woman, jerking her head to the next shack. "Girl kept us up all night with her moaning and crying!"

I tapped lightly on the side of the house. Instead of a door, a faded green tarp covered a gap between the tin walls. Because of the stilts, I could not go inside even if I were someone who entered other people's houses uninvited.

When the tarp lifted, none other than the famous Dr. Delacruz emerged from the doorway, with his kind eyes and waves of gray hair. "*Anak,*" he said, surprised to see me there.

"Doctor?" I said, then explained: "Annelise and I are partners. For the fiesta. And her mother . . . works for mine."

"But how on earth did you . . . ?" The doctor looked from my wheelchair to the hilltop, in the direction of my house.

Annelise's mother, our laundress, lifted one side of the tarp and looked out, her arms cradling an infant. I could hear groans from behind the tarp.

"*Anak,*" the laundress said, looking frightened, as if I'd come to scold her.

"Who's out there?" I heard Annelise call from inside. "Danny?" I was not prepared for the smell that came from beyond the tarp, magnified since the gymnasium to something like raw meat and burning sugar. But I was even less prepared for the wail that Annelise let out just then, a sound of pain so mighty that it seemed the walls and tin roof might not hold it.

"Let's go, *anak,*" said Dr. Delacruz. "The medicine might take some time to work. Right now your friend's not in a state for visitors." He wheeled me around and pushed me through the dirt, where Annelise's smells gave way to the surrounding air of mud and smoke.

The doctor brought me up the hill and home. "And here I thought *I* was the only one from town who visits the ravine," he said, kneeling to clean the mud off my wheelchair before we entered the *sala.*

"I'd never visited before," I said. "I haven't known Annelise long."

Inside, he sat down on the sofa next to me. "How are the fiesta preparations coming?"

He was so kind I didn't feel the need to lie. "Annelise can't learn the dance everyone's learning, thanks to me." I told him how my day had gone, the new *manananggal* insult, the children hobbling home beside me on their knees. I didn't mention Ruben, but the doctor winced anyway, as if my suffering were his fault. He stayed and listened until my mother came down from the bedroom with the electrician, who nodded quickly at the doctor as he hurried out.

When Dr. Delacruz greeted my mother, she barely nodded in return. On other days the doctor would bring food to us—

leche flan, a macaroni salad—or send his cook to deliver them, but when my mother saw he had nothing like that on offer this time, she went back upstairs. We heard water running. Of all the men who visited our house, only Dr. Delacruz never followed my mother up the stairs. And for all his kindness and attention, my mother was as cold and distant with the doctor as she was warm and inviting with almost all other men. Sometimes she refused to greet or come down to see him at all. Instead, he'd sit with me, flipping through comic books Ruben had already read and thrown away, or asking how my day had gone, how I was feeling.

"What will you and your mother eat tonight?" the doctor asked, after she'd gone.

"Whatever Marivic prepares." My mother had taught me always to present to the world that we had plenty, in the way of food and help.

"Are you sure?" asked Dr. Delacruz. "I can send Celia over with something after I get home."

"No need," I said, repeating words I'd heard my mother say to him before. "We have enough to feed a village. Thank you, Dr. Delacruz."

We said good night.

With the doctor's help, I got better at navigating the slope between my house and the squatters' colony. On my third visit, I saw we weren't Annelise's only guests. Squatters had gathered at the steps of her shack, holding buckets of water. I recognized the old woman with the sunken mouth, as well as the young girl who'd pushed my wheelchair, among the others forming a passageway from the ladder and the tarp.

"This is good news," said Dr. Delacruz. He rested his palm on the back of my chair. "It means your friend is doing better."

Annelise was descending the bamboo steps and walking across the dirt. The squatters dipped their fingers into buckets and sprinkled her with water. Young children splashed her with glee. She trained her gaze a few paces before her, as if balancing a basket on her head. She stopped at my chair. "It's a tradition," she said, with a flicker of embarrassment upon her face, slight as the mist of water on her arms and cheeks, and evaporating as quickly. "They don't let girls bathe in the creek during our time of month. So when it's over, they do this. I hate it, but that's life in the ravine."

I thought of the maid that my mother had let go because of her smell. Once again I was at the foot of those stairs, catching perfumed air and sunlight from a momentary crack in the doorway. "You can use our house, Annelise," I said, without thinking. As soon as I'd offered it, I knew it wouldn't be easy. My mother wouldn't abide it. She would have to be upstairs with a guest, or think that Annelise had come to do the wash again in her mother's place. But I wanted to give Annelise something, since I had nothing for her pain.

Dr. Delacruz patted my shoulder. "Annelise, your partner is a gentleman," he said. "I might have to fight him for the title of Messiah of Monte Ramon." He scraped some dirt from my left wheel with the tip of his shoe.

Dr. Delacruz helped us accomplish it. A few weeks later, the next time Annelise was banned from the creek, and girls at school said vicious things about her smell, Dr. Delacruz brought her up the hill to my house. "How many times will she send you to do her job for her?" my mother asked about the *labandera*, adding that she'd expect a discount for less experienced hands. Once we knew that my mother was occupied upstairs, Dr. Delacruz and I would take over the wash. We scrubbed and wrung, while Annelise finished her bath and then rested on the sofa with a hot water bottle, her face clenched against the pain. As soon as we heard my mother's door open upstairs, we switched places with Annelise.

Around this time, so much of which I spent with the doctor

in the *labahan* behind our house, an idle wish began. "Pass me that bleach, *anak*," said Dr. Delacruz, and for the first time in my life I paused over the word. Adults called us *anak* or "son" or "my child" all the time, but Dr. Delacruz said it with such soft regard as to sound literal. I began to imagine him as my father, living in this house, or any house, with me, married to my mother. A pipe dream—or was it? Now that Annelise had introduced me to her *radionovela*, I saw exchanges between Dr. Delacruz and my mother in a new light. This was courtship, from another angle. In *Pusong Sinugatan*, Reyna ended up in the arms of the one suitor she'd tried the hardest to fight off. And Joe had been admired by every woman about town except the one he loved most, which only strengthened his resolve to win her. He waited patiently, persisted for as long as he had to. Likewise, perhaps the reason Dr. Delacruz never remarried all these years since his wife's death was that he only wanted to marry my mother. My imagination, once ignited, went wild. If Dr. Delacruz married my mother, she'd have all the comfort and company she needed in him. All the men who passed me by in the *sala* without so much as a second look would step aside. Why else would Dr. Delacruz spend so much time with me, and in our house? Even granting how many people in Monte Ramon he cared for, why should my life, and my mother's, be of such special concern to him?

The fiesta was approaching. Church bells rang and cannons fired throughout our school days now, rousing us in the morning and distracting us from classroom lectures. Both were being fine-tuned for the ceremonies.

Annelise decided that she and I would bring our petitions to the Virgin early. During fiesta month, she reasoned, the Virgin fielded so many requests for love or health or babies or luck that we ought to lay our concerns at her feet before the others overwhelmed her. We set out with votive candles, a box of matches, and bananas from a tree outside my mother's house.

They kept the four-hundred-year-old statue behind glass in the church, but a plaster replica of her stood on a roofed pedestal outside. The Virgin's nose was fine and strong, her mouth tiny, her eyes bold. Annelise lay her palm on the Virgin's robe, which was brocaded with gold paint.

She had a theory about praying. "You must be specific," Annelise told me. "Vague prayers end badly. There was a man who traveled up here from Manila and asked the Virgin for money. No specifics, just money. On his way home children threw worthless coins at him. They thought he was a beggar in his raggedy clothes. Well, he prayed for money, and he got it! The Virgin needs *specifics*." She set her votive down before the statue.

I lit my own candle, and then a prayer came to me as easily as the tune of a familiar song. I prayed for Dr. Delacruz to become my father. I prayed that he would win my mother's heart at last, with all the gifts and dishes he brought us and the amount of time and care he lavished on me. I prayed that she would come around, as Reyna had with Joe in *Pusong Sinugatan*, to the one suitor she had overlooked. I asked the Virgin for a soap-operatic surprise that would change my life. Was this specific enough? Annelise was crossing herself already; I had no time to revise. We ate two of the bananas and placed the rest beside the candles. We looked up at the Virgin's face as if to read her answer, but her weathered plaster expression remained still.

Finally the day of the fiesta came. Bright streamers laced the avenues, which filled with tourists escaping the Manila heat, as well as pilgrims from beyond the capital. On the day of the parade, my classmates and I went to Safety to fetch our partners. Annelise had tucked sprigs of baby's breath into her thick hair and wore a light blue dress—left behind at the convent, she said, by a Safety alumna. As we headed from the campus to the church, Annelise smelled powdery and immaculate. She seemed well. I could not help but think that some specific prayer of hers had been answered.

Six townsmen, Dr. Delacruz among them, took the Virgin down from her glass case in the church and perched her on a wooden boat. The real Virgin was both darker and brighter than the plaster decoy to whom Annelise and I had prayed. Wood grain striped her varnished cheeks, and the jewels in her robe were real. Garlands of *sampaguita* dangled from the boat's rim. Parishioners loaded the hull with offerings of mangoes, bananas, pineapples, and coconuts. As they brought the Virgin of Monte Ramon into the streets, her crown trapped and seemed to magnify the sunlight. A throng of pilgrims followed close behind, holding candles. The flame-specked worshipers appeared from far away like a train extending the Virgin's gown.

Behind the pilgrims glided the elaborate float of Miss Monte Ramon and her ladies-in-waiting. College boys in stiff white *barongs* escorted these reigning beauty queens of our town. The speakers on their float warbled a folk song in praise of the *sampaguita* flower. Our group marched behind, boys on the left, girls on the right. The pace of a parade suited me. I wasn't struggling to catch up with anyone, and the spectators seemed too deep in the pageant queens' thrall to stare at me or point fingers. Behind us, the elementary school children sang about the wonders of Monte Ramon, from its hills to its Virgin to its local sweets.

After the parade, Annelise and I bought *suman* and unraveled its leaves to bite into the sweet, sticky rice packed inside. We vowed to taste everything along Monte Ramon's main street. Halfway through our mission, Annelise complained of an upset stomach. We laughed at our foolishness and called ourselves *takaw mata,* more greed in the eyes than room in the belly. We made our way down the littered street, feeling full.

Then Annelise said she had to sit down. As I looked for the nearest bench, she held her middle and doubled over in the street. Her eyes grew listless. I could only catch her wrist as she fell.

"Help," I called. Some passersby rushed over. What happened? they were asking, but I didn't have an answer. "That's Annelise, my neighbor," a voice behind us said. "Her faulty machinery does that to her." A crowd gathered as Annelise whimpered on the pavement. Help came in the form of the wooden boat that had just carried the Virgin back from the mountains into town. Dr. Delacruz set Annelise down on this makeshift stretcher, and she curled her body to fit inside. The marchers brought her to the town hospital. By the time she reached the emergency room, the skirts of her borrowed dress were soaked in blood.

Two days later I was allowed to see her in the recovery ward. I had my radio with me. Annelise sat upright on her bed, sipping from a can of pineapple nectar. A bag dripped fluid through a plastic tube into her arm.

"They made *bunot* of me," she said, sweeping a hand over her body.

Bunot was coconut husk stripped of its inner meat, dried out and used to polish floors.

"I had the wrong cells growing in the wrong places. So they took out all my equipment. It would've been of no use to me anyway."

A vision of a ram's head hovered at the edge of my sight.

"Would you like to see it?" she said. "My crown of thorns?" She folded down the bedsheet and gathered up the hem of her hospital gown, exposing a swatch of gauzed flesh below her navel. Peeled aside, the bandage revealed a length of dark, scab-colored sutures, crisscrossed like barbed wire. The shadow of raised pink skin around them looked to be weeping.

My head did not know what my hand was up to. I watched,

separate, as my fingers rose and reached out—for what? To point, or touch her scar, like a doubting Thomas? But Annelise reached out her own hand and caught mine.

"Show me yours," she said. I'd never heard her whisper until then, or known her voice to tremble. Still, her grip was tight. I knew what she had asked to see, without her having to explain: *my* wound, my absence, the feature no one but my mother and Dr. Delacruz had seen. I could not show her without undressing. It terrified me, but I placed my other hand on my belt buckle. Annelise stared without blinking as I showed her first my right side, then my left. My head grew light; there was a drained feeling at my chest, as if my heart had stopped beating. I could still see her scar and was imagining the feel of knives and needles on my own flesh, and wondered if this—the cold sweat above my lip, the difficulty breathing—was how Annelise had felt in the street after the parade.

Then, instantly, we seemed to remember who we were, and to be ashamed. Annelise replaced the bandage and the sheet. While I got back into my trousers she switched on the transistor radio, finding *Pusong Sinugatan*. Ignacio, one of Joe's unscrupulous rivals for Reyna's affections, had exposed the priest who had married Joe and Reyna as a fake and was therefore trying once again to win Reyna back from her American love. In the meantime, General MacArthur had begun his humiliating retreat from Corregidor and out of the country. Joe despaired of ever seeing his sweetheart again. Then the station interrupted the episode for a weather advisory. The rainy season would arrive any day now. In other news, the Pope would soon induct Jaime Sin, the Archbishop of Manila, into the College of Cardinals. "Cardinal Sin!" laughed the announcer. Annelise fell asleep, and I was sitting a safe distance away from her at sundown, when Dr. Delacruz came into the room. "It's late, *anak*," he said to me. "Let's get you home to your mother."

Dr. Delacruz and I rode in a silence that felt tender and familiar, fetching food from his own kitchen along the way. "Your friend will be much better now, *anak*," he said. "She's suffered for three years, and now she won't suffer anymore." He paused. "Not unless she decides she wants children." At our gate he unloaded the wheelchair from his trunk. With care and confidence, he lifted me from the passenger seat and set me down in my chair. It took me a moment to unclasp my arms from his neck.

The doctor handed me a plastic bag with a Tupperware container inside, still refrigerator-cold. He carried my books in one arm and pushed my chair with the other, using my keys to unlock the garden gate and front door.

My mother had just come downstairs from a bath, her hair wrapped in a towel. She looked weary, the lines and hollows of her face sharper than usual. I remembered then that she could become grumpy and delicate around holidays and festivals— times of year that even her most devoted guests spent with their wives and children.

She turned and stared at the doctor, without greeting.

"Danny and I just got back from the hospital," he said. He pointed to the dish in my lap. "We brought you some *dinuguan*."

The dish was a fiesta tradition: a stew of pig innards cooked in pig's blood that followed the roasting of *lechon*. "Thank you," said my mother, "for thinking of the help. They'll eat this when they're working late."

Dr. Delacruz looked down at the floor.

"As for Danny and I," she continued, as I knew she would, "we've got these sensitive American taste buds—no *dinuguan* for us."

I felt sure that he knew the truth, but was too gallant to expose my mother. She stepped aside—a cue for me to wheel toward the kitchen and refrigerate our dinner.

After Dr. Delacruz and the last of the servants had gone, I reheated the *dinuguan* on our stove. I was hungrier than I had realized, and the mud-colored gravy sated me as no meal had for some time. It seemed my mother hadn't eaten all day, either. In her haste a splash of *dinuguan* landed on her robe. She barely paused between the mouthfuls to wipe it off, her napkin leaving a dark smear. I saw my mother in a sad new light. She looked as much like a child as she'd sounded, earlier, pretending for Dr. Delacruz's sake that *dinuguan* offended our American palates. By this time I was so certain our lives were about to change that the house seemed already occupied with other people, watching as we slurped dark innards from my mother's fading china and sharing in this ritual that had once been our secret.

The rains began gently enough that I could still visit Annelise after school each day. In the hospital, the week she remained under observation, we passed the late afternoons reading or listening to the radio. I finally confessed to her my hopes regarding Dr. Delacruz and my mother, and we laughed, imagining how Ruben Delacruz would suffer, then learn to tolerate me as a brother. We daydreamed about Dr. Delacruz's big house, which had room enough to board the servants, meaning Annelise could live under the same roof, and move out of the ravine with her mother and her little brother.

Each time Dr. Delacruz spoke to me or brought me home, my sense of imminence grew. I found myself recalling all the moments he had entered our house or tended to me when I was ill, finding signs I might have been too young to recognize before. Had he always said *"anak"* to me, and always with such tenderness? One evening after I'd visited Annelise, Dr. Delacruz took me home as usual, and we found my mother in a miserable state. She was sitting on the floor in our *sala*. The gardener and the maid were standing over her, surrounded by some things dragged from her room: a mahogany trunk inlaid with mother-of-pearl, and a mirrored vanity tray cluttered with brushes and bottles. Her shiny robe had loosened, revealing a swath of pale freckled skin at her chest.

"What do you mean, you cannot take it? This is French perfume, very expensive," my mother was telling the maid. Payday had arrived, it seemed, and my mother once again lacked cash to give the servants outright. The maid, a girl so young she still wore her hair in two braids, looked at her feet, but kept her hands clasped behind her back, resolved not to accept my mother's half-empty bottle. The gardener held an ivory nesting doll in one hand but seemed to be waiting, however meekly, for more.

Dr. Delacruz approached them from behind my chair.

"Where have you been?" my mother demanded—whether of me or of Dr. Delacruz I wasn't sure. The doctor whispered to the servants, handing each of them a sheaf of peso notes from his pocket. After the gardener set the doll gently upon our coffee table, both servants hurried past me and out of the house.

In my concern for Annelise I had forgotten how lonely and fragile my mother could become during fiesta season. "I was visiting my friend," I said, "at the hospital."

"The *labandera*'s daughter?" My mother laughed. "The squatter child with the 'feminine problems'? You be careful of squatters, *anak*. People from the ravine see a boy with a big house, a nice garden, and—"

"That's enough," interrupted Dr. Delacruz. "Danny has been a great friend to Annelise."

"And so have you!" she replied. "Another outcast only the Messiah of Monte Ramon could love! You think I don't know how you've been encouraging my son, bringing her here to use our water and foul up our house? I can smell her from upstairs!"

Despite my shame at getting caught, I thought of Reyna and

Joe again, the turning point in *Pusong Sinugatan* when they were on the verge of love but didn't know it yet. They too had shouted at each other, seemed ready to come to blows, just moments before their first kiss.

"Look at this house." My mother pointed to the ceiling. A leak from her upstairs bathtub had made a growing stain in the plaster, damp and beginning to smell like mold. "My phone's been cut off, too. But I suppose I have to be a *labandera*'s daughter to expect help!"

"Was he a phantom that just paid your servants?" said Dr. Delacruz. "I've been getting your son home every day. I've brought you food—"

"Oh, the servants' *dinuguan* has nothing to do with this!"

"The servants!" Dr. Delacruz laughed. "That's right, it's the servants who eat the *dinuguan*. Because your 'delicate American stomach' can't handle native grub. You know, it's all this make-believe that's the problem. It's not the house that needs fixing."

My mother huffed air out of her mouth, dismissing him.

"*Anak*," said the doctor, kneeling suddenly to address me, "I've always wanted to help you. There are prosthetics we could try, or better chairs. But your mother says no to all that."

"Because this chair is an heirloom," said my mother, "and Danny is proud of his grandfather."

Dr. Delacruz ignored her. "*Anak*, your mother was sick in the mornings while she was expecting you. So sick she came to me for help."

My mother's eyes grew wide.

There was a German pill, said Dr. Delacruz, which women in both Europe and America had taken for my mother's symptoms. "It calmed their nausea and helped them sleep."

I was confused. Their union was taking a long time and veering in a direction I hadn't foreseen. I scrambled to reword my prayers to the Virgin, to be more specific, to make sure she understood my exact fantasy. But it was difficult to pray—or hear my thoughts at all, for that matter—in our living room that evening. The skin of my mother's face seemed to have tightened to the bone, and turned nearly as white.

By the time she was expecting me, Dr. Delacruz continued, Westerners had lost interest in the miracle pill. Large shipments were made to pharmacies in Manila when it would no longer sell in Europe and America. My mother, in her suffering, begged Dr. Delacruz for a prescription. That was all she needed; with it, her American father could obtain any Western drug she wanted, even ones not readily available in Monte Ramon.

"I should have taken more time," said the doctor, "done more research. But after my own wife's death, I simply couldn't stand by and watch a pregnant woman suffer without taking action. So I wrote the prescription. The day you were born, I saw my mistake."

My mother looked pale and stunned, as if we had been robbed and found ourselves in a *sala* emptied of its sofa, its cabinet, its sepia portrait of my grandparents.

"It's my everlasting penance," said Dr. Delacruz. "If there's anything you want or need, Danny, I'll do my best for you. And for your mother, too. I can't forgive myself. But I can't lie to you either, *anak*. These fairy stories that her father's war heroism begat a son with no legs . . . Even children deserve to know the truth." He stood up. "You poor boy," he added, in a voice laden with regret, and left the house.

His words and his departure sent me reeling, as if I'd been pushed downhill to the ravine at high speed, losing all control, nothing below to catch or save me. The idea I'd been polishing like a precious stone slipped from my hands. And with it, all ideas that had carried and sustained me through the years seemed to be crumbling too. If I'd been wrong about Dr. Delacruz and my grandfather, it seemed possible I might be wrong about my mother. It seemed possible for the first time that the defects of our bodies—mine, Annelise's, anyone's—were errors of nature, caused and cured by science, nothing more.

"Don't believe him," said my mother, falling to her knees in the doctor's place. "Who is he? I am your *mother;* believe *me.*" All this kneeling was starting to remind me, perversely, of the children who mocked me at school. There was nothing left for us to do, my mother said, but pray. She threw herself forward, weeping on the empty fabric of my trousers. She crossed herself and gazed tearfully at her parents' wedding portrait, looking for a moment to be praying to them.

But I didn't feel like praying. My palms simply refused to meet. They went, instead, to the wheels of my chair and pulled, retreating from my mother. I turned my back to her—a first. "Danny," I heard her call as I pushed myself to the foot of the stairs. I could hear her calling still as I pitched myself onto the steps and started climbing like a crab, on my knuckles and the heels of my hands, up to the forbidden room.

And what did I find there? Only the light, which had seemed otherworldly when it streamed down through the seldom-opened door, but which came from the sun—the same plain sun that shone on all Monte Ramon, no more than that. Only a bed that took up most of the room. A chest of drawers, clothes draped on the backs of chairs, and trinkets cluttered on surfaces—no big secret to settle my confusion. Still, I searched. I opened the drawers, rummaged through the silks and laces, pulled aside the wardrobe doors where dresses fell from their hangers, tore the lids off boxes and capsized them so that chains and beads and buttons clattered to the floor. I would have flipped the mattress if I'd had the strength, or torn the framed photographs off the walls if I were tall enough. By the time I reached the vanity, whose mirror was just low enough to show me my reflection— and my mother, coming through the doorway, weeping—I was not afraid to pull at it, and watch it crash to pieces on the floor.

In a *radionovela* I'd have found a key, a clue that would unlock a season's worth of mysteries. I found only my own shame and exhaustion. The room looked like a thief or vandal had attacked it. I felt sorry for disturbing all my mother's belongings, which she'd expressly made off-limits to me, and for denying her the trusting, dutiful son she'd always had. But something had been taken from me, too. Adults I had relied on to explain the world and my life to me—especially when children made that world and life so hostile—had kept the truth from me, then wrecked the fantasy that had replaced it. I turned back toward the stairs. I did not wish to look at another adult now, let alone console my mother. I wanted consolation for myself, and knew only one source for it.

As the school year ended, the monsoons began in earnest. Rain fell so hard and fast it struck up fat white stars along the ground. It became difficult to see in front of us. Still, on the last day of school, I insisted on seeing Annelise home. My chair gave us some trouble down the hill. Along the ravine, children were laughing in the storm, shirtless or bare-legged or naked altogether. Their rubber *tsinelas* clapped along the mud. Below them, the creek collected raindrops with a sound like frying oil. Some of these children might soon lose their houses. Annelise might have to sleep, as she sometimes did, in the Safety convent.

I noticed as the children played that they were trying not to slip and fall. The care they took had slowed their movements into a kind of dance. I turned to Annelise, who said, "The rain has crippled everyone," and laughed. I laughed too. She curtsied to me, and I bowed my head: a joke, the first movements of the *kuratsa* we'd watched for months and never had to do ourselves. She promenaded around me, her arms outstretched, and I moved my wheels to turn with her. It wasn't easy. But for one brief moment, in the rain and mud, I saw a world where everyone was struggling in the body he or she'd been given. That world and struggle seemed bearable to me, and even beautiful.

Some squatters had dismantled their homes and were carrying the scraps to higher ground. Others stayed put and held up as hats what used to be their walls. Our cold, drenched uniforms clung to our skin. A mighty stench was rising from the creek. And soon the rain made it impossible to dance, even as a joke. Annelise gripped the handles of my chair and plowed it through the dirt toward a shining, solitary scrap of tin that we claimed as ours.

Esmeralda

That morning you are woken by an airplane, humming so close overhead it seems to want to take you with it. The clock says five—an hour ahead of your alarm. You've lived close to two airports for almost two decades. You're used to planes. They even show up in your dreams. In last night's dream, you died; your body crumbled into ash. Before you could learn what came next, before you could see where your *soul* went, a machine—some giant vacuum cleaner, which in real life was this plane—came down to sweep you off the earth like dust.

After today, you'll never hear a plane in the same way again. But you don't know that yet.

The boy whose bedroom you sleep in is now a man. He moved out long ago. His mother, Doris, keeps his room the way it was when he lived here: school pennant, baseball trophies, dark plaid bedspread. You pay low rent, and have agreed to leave this room and sleep out on the sofa when the son visits. (He never does.)

You know you won't fall back asleep, so you switch on the lamp. Because the years of work have given you a bad back, bad knees, and bad feet, you like to pray in bed. A wooden Christ Child and Virgin Mary live inside the nightstand drawer. You lay them on the pillow next to you like shrunken lovers, wrap a rosary around your wrist. You interlace your fingers, shut your eyes, and squeeze your lips against your thumbs as if kissing His feet.

The God that you imagine looks like Father Brennan, the man who baptized you: tall and Irish, with white hair and kind blue eyes, shooting a basketball in black vestments on the parish playground. The Virgin is one of the nuns who ran the adjoining schoolhouse: a spinster with a downy chin, her veil a habit. Old and sacred words, they taught you. You would not invent your own any more than you would try to build your own cathedral. *In the name of the Father, and of the Son, and of the Holy Spirit.* Bead by bead, you whisper the same words Saint Peter spoke in Rome, the same words spoken today by all believers in São Paulo and Boston and Limerick and Cebu:

> *He rose again from the dead.*
> *Lead us not into temptation, but deliver us from evil.*
> *Blessed art thou among women and blessed is the fruit of*
>   *thy womb.*
> *As it was in the beginning, is now, and ever shall be, world*
>   *without end.*

You pray by heart the way you'd plow a field of soil, the way you push a mop across a floor. One foot before the other. After looping your way around the rosary, you coil it in its pouch. You tuck Mary and the *Santo Niño* back into their drawer, thanking them for the strength to rise another day, on two aching feet.

"Like the gypsy," John said, the night he asked your name.

You weren't listening. *"Eee, Ess, Em, Eee,"* you started spelling in reply, as you changed the trash bag from the can beside his desk.

"Mine's John. Not quite as fancy as yours." He held out his hand.

"Please to meet you." You stared at the freckles on his long, pale fingers. When he didn't pull them back, you wiped your latex glove, still damp from the dustrag, on your uniform. Then, embarrassed, you snapped off your glove and tossed it in the mother trash bag hanging from your cleaning cart. His hand was moist and smooth. The hand of a man who studied numbers on a screen and now and then picked up the phone.

He had the kind blue eyes of a priest. His hair was white (though he had all of it), his face almost as pale, but pink in sunburned places. On his desk, three computer screens folded outward like a panel painting at church. A woman with gold hair and green eyes, probably his wife, smiled in a frame beside his keyboard.

This new night job had just begun. You were still learning the floor, along whose windowed edges sat men like John, who had their own offices. These men stayed later than the ones who worked in open rows along the middle of the floor. You'd notice, over time, that John stayed latest out of everyone.

Since Doris is still asleep, you hold off on the vacuuming and step into the kind of fall morning that really does remind you of a big apple, bright and crisp. You buy skim milk and grapefruits, whole wheat bread and liquid eggs that pour out of a juice box and have less cholesterol. Nineteen years of Tuesdays you have shopped and cleaned for Doris. Longer than her son lived in the room you rent for two hundred a month. On Wednesdays you clean the apartment under you, for the Italian landlord and his wife, whose children you have watched grow up and have their own. Thursdays you are in the city early, cleaning Mrs. Helen Miller's loft downtown. And Fridays you clean uptown, for the Ronson family, who own a brownstone top to bottom. Saturdays your fingers smell like pine oil from polishing the wood pews of the same old church that found you Doris and her extra room, those nineteen years ago. And in between you've cleaned for other people, one-time deals—after a party, or before somebody sells or rents out their apartment, or as a gift from one friend to another—never saying no to an assignment. Nineteen years of cash in envelopes, from people who never asked to see your papers as long as you had references and kept their sinks and toilets spotless.

The other day you pulled a knot of Doris's white hair from the shower drain, trying to remember when those knots were brown.

Now that you're no longer hiding, you have one job on the books, at night, in the tower where John works.

The living room TV is on when you get home. "Good morning," you call out, unloading bags onto the kitchen counter. Doris doesn't answer through the wall. She likes to do Pilates—counting bends and raises, panting—to the news.

Putting the milk away, you hear a sob.

"Doris?"

She isn't doing leg raises. You find her on the sofa, eyeballs red, fist covering her nose and mouth.

"Did Matthew call?" you ask. Over the years, her son has said things on the phone to make her cry.

She shakes her head and reaches for your hand. "Oh, Es." Her other hand points at the TV screen. A city building, gashed along the side and bleeding smoke. You almost fail to recognize it. You never see it from this angle anymore: the air, the view on postcards and souvenir mugs.

A pipe or boiler must have burst, you think, watching the ugly crooked mouth cough flame. You think, *A man in coveralls will lose his job today.* There's an Albanian gentleman whose name you know only because it's stitched across his shirt. *Valdrin.* You never speak to one another. He bows as you pass him in the staff lounge; he blows kisses as you leave the elevator.

You're wrong. They show a plane, show it and show it, flying straight into the tower's face and tearing through the glass.

"What if this happened late at night?" says Doris. "Es, thank God you're here."

She weeps as you two watch, again, the black speck pierce the glass, the smoke spill from the wound.

Trying to count floors, you stand. "I have to go."

"What? Absolutely not."

"I'll clean when I come back."

"Forget about that. Jesus! What I mean is, you're not going anywhere."

"I have to see about . . . my job."

But Doris will not hear of it. "No one's working now. Not your boss and not your boss's boss. You've been spared, don't you see? You're staying here. End of story."

"OK." You sit. "I'll get your coffee, then." You stand and go into the kitchen, think. You pour Doris's coffee and bring her the cup. "I have to try to call my boss, at least."

In Matthew's room, you lock the door. You change into your panty hose and uniform, as if it's afternoon. Beside the bedroom door, you hold your shoes, a pair of hard white clogs a nurse friend from your church suggested for your troubled feet, and listen to the wall. As soon as you hear Doris go into the bathroom, you tiptoe through the kitchen. You grab your bag and jacket from the closet by the door, race downstairs, and slip into your clogs outside.

A book sat open on John's desk, the next time you walked in.

"Aha!" he said. "There she is." He pointed at the page and read aloud. *"La Esmeralda. Formidable name! She's an enchantress."*

You thought about hiding inside the cart, between the toilet paper rolls.

He stood and came around his desk, still reading. *"Your parents never found that name for you at the baptismal font."* He closed the book and smiled. "Where did they find it, Esmeralda?"

"Not there," you said, pointing your chin at the book. (Your parents would have used a book that size for kindling.) "They liked the sound of it. Or liked somebody with the name, maybe."

John wanted to know, if you didn't mind saying, where you were from.

"So I was right," he said, when you told him. "My wife's nurses are Filipina."

"Your wife is a doctor?"

"No." He looked down. Darkness, like the shadow from an airplane overhead, passed over his face. "A patient."

"Oh." The woman with green eyes and gold hair, smiling next to his keyboard, looked healthy, but you didn't say that.

Before John—and this is terrible to say; you'd never say it, but—the lives of Americans with money were not very interesting to you. Even the troubled ones, their troubles did not seem so hard. You'd ask, "How are you?" and they'd heave a sigh, winding up to tell you some sob story: how much they worked, who had it in for them, the things they'd wished for and were not getting. *Try hunger. Try losing your house,* a voice inside you, that would never leave your mouth of course, wanted to say.

But John's trouble—that moved you. Enough to ask, "Your wife is sick? What kind of sick?"

"The kind you don't come back from," John said. She'd been sick for fifteen years. The photograph beside his keyboard was how he preferred to remember her. Before nerve cells inside her brain began to die, before the tremors started, before her muscles stiffened and her spine curled in. Back when she could walk without losing her balance, back when she could eat and use the bathroom on her own, without John's help, and then a Filipina nurse, and then a second one for nighttime. Before she started to talk slowly, like the voice in a cassette recorder on low battery, and then stopped talking altogether. Back when she still knew who John, her husband, was.

"I'm sorry."

"I am too," he said. "It started fast, and now it's ending slowly. When you love someone you never think a time will come when they're a stranger." He looked and must have felt alone. But the photo that you kept at home, on Matthew's nightstand, was your brother's baby portrait. Long before the lies, the cruelties, the face scarred up beyond recognition.

John's family was Irish, and he grew up in a harbor town where his brothers still lived. "All five of them," he said. "All fire-fighters, like our father. Or policemen, like our uncle."

"You are not a fire- or policeman," you said.

John shook his head. "Did you ever hear of a family where the finance guy's the rebel? Me, and my cousin Sean, the priest. Plus we're the only two who didn't have kids. No sons to raise into cops or firefighters, either. I guess I never grew up dreaming I'd be some hero. No, I just looked across the bay at this skyline and thought, *I'll work there someday.* Plus"—he tapped his wedding ring against the picture frame—"*she* wanted to work in publish-ing. No better place for that than in this city. And we decided that if one of us was gonna work in books, the other better work in money."

He asked after your family. You told him that your parents raised coconuts, coaxed copra oil from them, sold gallon cans of it to men who came in boats once a month. That you had just one brother. "Pepe."

He said, "You're not a farmer."

"No. I'm not."

"Are you and Pepe close?"

The first time Doris asked you this, you shook your head. *Almost nine thousand miles.* She laughed. "I don't mean close on a *map*," she said. "I know he's far away. I mean, how *distant* are you? Your relationship." This threw you. How "distant" could the blood, running through your own veins, be? "So you *are* close," Doris said. You learned to keep it simple with Americans who asked you after that. *Yes, very close.*

But here, with John, you answered like some old and lonely bag lady, whose cart was filled with stories, waiting for an audience.

"I never had a doll when I was small," you said. "So Pepe—I

was ten when he was born—was like my parents' gift to me. He had the whitest skin. Almost as white as yours. And he didn't know anything! He have to be protected all the time. One day I'm cleaning eggs: he took one from the basket and bit it. Like an apple. I heard a scream and I see Pepe there, with blood and yolk and shells and dirt and feathers in his mouth."

You yammered on. About the dreams you had for Pepe. A boy that fair could finish school, grow up to star in movies, run for office. Being a girl—a poor and dark one, no less—you wouldn't dare dream these things for yourself. You left school at thirteen, to help with the coconuts and Pepe's chances.

John looked so much like priests you'd known, there might as well have been a penance grille between you. Is that another reason you said all this to a stranger?

"Even seven, eight years old," you told John, "Pepe slept with his knees up, his fist like this on his mouth, like he still wanted to suck his thumb."

"I was not my brothers' doll," said John, with a laugh. "Their football, maybe."

Main Street looks different early in the morning. The jade pendants and roast ducks have not shown up yet in the Chinese shop windows. A strip of orange tape is stretched across the top of the stairs you would have taken to catch the train.

A nearby cop confirms. No service. Not today.

But there has got to be a way into the city. There was a way nineteen years ago, wasn't there? When the Guzman family brought you with them from Manila to New York, only to send you back? *I wish we could afford to keep you, Esmeralda,* Mrs. Guzman said, once she had learned just how expensive New York was. *People in this city do it for themselves.* She handed you a one-way ticket back to Manila and the number of a good family there who needed a maid. You found a way to stay then, and you will now. In your bag you hook your thumb into the chaplet, whose gold-plate knobs have been rubbed black from years of prayer.

You turn and walk south underneath the rusty, quiet elevated tracks.

City people pride themselves on walking everywhere. "We're more like Europe than like the rest of America that way," Doris has said. John says his brothers live inside their cars (an insult). *My nieces can't go ten blocks in the city without whining.* What's wrong with cars? you'd like to know. Your clogs crunch over pebbles, twigs, and broken glass. Your feet are rioting already, every pain you've been contending with for years fired up. The pinpricks—quick and sharp along your arches—started at six-teen, the year you left your family's farm for Manila, to nanny and clean house for a city cousin who had married well. The bruise between your third and fourth left toes—a swollen nerve, your nurse friend tells you, but to you it feels round, like a pebble in a horse's hoof—grew the year that cousin moved to Qatar and bequeathed you, like a car or a perfectly good table, to the Guz-mans. The L-shaped tendon from your right shin to the instep has been sore for six years, as long as you've had your green card. Since meeting John, you've noticed both your big-toe knuckles have gone numb.

Farther down the avenue, the Chinese characters turn into spoken Spanish in the streets. Small children in blue uniforms stream out of school, canceled today. At first they laugh and bab-ble, as kids do when they get a taste of freedom. Then some look up at their teachers, smell their parents' fear.

"Why aren't you at work?" says one girl to the father who's arrived to pick her up.

You know some words in Spanish; you know *trabajar* and *nunca* and *mañana*.

One boy starts to cry. You think of *carabao* back home, who'd snort and stamp and know to head inland before a storm. One girl drifts from her class to join the crowd a block away. They're gathered at the window of an electronics store, watching the news, again and again, on screen after screen after screen.

Only because you know a bit of Spanish do you catch the words *la segunda torre.* You would not, less than two miles back, have understood these whispers in Mandarin or Cantonese.

"Otro avión," they're saying.

"Ocurrió otra vez."

Often, when you came in, he'd be reading. His screens would have gone dark, with white and red and green and blue windows that grew in size as they flew closer—meaning he hadn't touched the keys in a while, and his computer was asleep. And he didn't like just any book. He liked them thick as cement bricks, and probably as heavy: books to prop a steel door open. With tiny print on thin pages that crackled as he turned them. When a colleague knocked, John moved his mouse to send the flying windows away and hid the book under his desk, next to his shoes.

Or else he'd be typing away: an e-mail in a white window, so many lines of words that looked like they could add up to a thick book of their own. He'd click his way out of them when a colleague came, the way he'd hide his book.

He was writing to his family, his wife's family, the doctors, lawyers, all the people needing answers about her, and what he planned to do. "It takes me so long to say things," he said. "I don't know why. The irony is, *she* was all about the phone. She always said she could take care of something in a two-minute call that I'd spend an hour e-mailing about. She thought I was long-winded. She'd look over my shoulder and say, *No one's gonna read all that.* She thought most everyone was long-winded, including God and Tolstoy. I'm the crusty old one—I like novels long enough to age you while you read them. *Ninety-nine percent of books should have been thirty-three percent shorter,* she would say. She quantified a lot of things. Sometimes we wondered if the wrong one of us ended up in books and the wrong one in money."

You bowed your head while changing out his garbage bag, his wife's picture like an altar you'd just passed.

"Wow. That's a lot I spewed out, Esmeralda. Let's talk about you. You must e-mail all the time. With your family so far?"

You shook your head. "I don't have a computer," you said, thinking with pride of all the ones you've bought for people in your village. "I type too slow. My mother doesn't know how to e-mail."

"You get home to her much?" he asked, which set you off again. You, Esmeralda, whom nuns and priests and parents always praised for being *such a quiet child*. Doris likes to say, *Nineteen years under one roof and that is news to me*, whenever she learns anything about you.

"I always thought that once we bought the land," you started, "I'd go home for good."

But once those 1.6 hectares were all paid for, the dirt floor needed wood; the tin walls needed cinder blocks. Of course, a house that sturdy should also have faucets and a flush toilet. And even when the house was finished, there was always family to think about. Pepe ran off, but others came to need things in his place. Cousins had babies, who grew up to go to private school and college. Aunts and uncles got sick, needing medicine. And when they died, it cost money to bury them. Then there was the larger family: the village, and they knew about you too. The church could use a new roof after Typhoon Vera tore it off. Who else would pay for it? Who else could they depend upon? Not the sweet plantation daughters who ended up dancing go-go at Manila bars. Not the men who gave up looking for jobs in the capital and hunted scraps from garbage dumps instead.

"A trip home costs a lot of money," you told John, "and time off work. My family needs some things more than I need a vacation."

"And your brother, what does he do?" John asked.

You thought about it. "He gets into trouble."

"What kind of trouble?"

"All the kinds."

You told him about Pepe in grade four, sniffing glue and paint thinners with older friends. About his disappearance from the farm at twelve, and his return, months later, with a motorcycle. How he'd paid for it, no one could tell. About the accident on that motorcycle that scarred his face for good. About the botched electronics-store robbery that landed him in jail.

"He's at the farm every few months," you said. "He stays one day, a week, two weeks before he disappears again. If I stopped sending anything, who knows when my mother would see him?"

"I'm sorry." John gave you the same eyes Doris did, when she asked if you got tired of supporting all those people. *Doesn't it get heavy, Esmeralda—the weight of the world?*

You shrugged. "I think having no one to lean on you is worse."

Sometimes it did get heavy, sure. But then, you did get to go home, each week on Sunday, to the one House and one Father who were never far away. Each day, His Book reminded you— chapter by chapter, verse by verse—what joy it was to serve, to bear another's load. Those loads weren't heavier than a crown of thorns, were they? No heavier than a cross.

They've closed the bridge's westbound lane. Everyone else is streaming east out of the city, as far from the smoke as they can get. Not all of them move fast. Some stop at the pink cables and snap pictures. Even if you had a camera with you, you wouldn't need to. You will not forget the way the towers look today. Like chimneys of a house the sea has swallowed.

At the river, cops are waving west the only cars allowed into the city: ambulances and their own.

But there has got to be a way into the city.

Desperate, you remember a man you once overheard, in a

deli, talking to his friend. The man had sworn off all American women. "They're just so *hard* on you," he said. "The foreign girls appreciate what we can do for them."

His friend had doubts about finding a wife abroad.

"Just try it, man. I like FilipinaFinder-dot-com. Or World-WideWed. Be careful, though. A lot of them these days are *business* women, if you catch my drift."

He meant that some women would play a man—or many men, that is—for fools. They made a job of visiting and being visited, their schedules all booked up with fiancés who paid their passage back and forth to different cities, meeting future in-laws who would plan and go to weddings where the bride didn't show up.

"They always say they're nursing students," said the expert. "What's nicer than a nurse, right?"

I was right, John had said. *My wife's nurses are Filipina.*

You look down at the clogs your friend at church swears by, and at your pale blue skirt. On any other day, you wouldn't dare. You wouldn't cross the street. You wouldn't stand at the plaza's edge, or wave at the ambulance approaching the mouth of the bridge.

May God forgive you, Esmeralda.

It slows. An EMT rolls down the passenger window.

"Elmhurst, right?" he says. He nods at your shoes and blue uniform, sees what he wants to see.

You nod back once.

"There's room for one more in the back."

John must have gone to a meeting, or the men's room, the night your dustrag came too close and moved his mouse an inch or so across his desk. This happened sometimes, and not just with John. The screens woke from their floating windows and filled up again with numbers. Or sometimes, in John's case, words. An e-mail he had yet to send, in its white window. You didn't read them—weren't supposed to, didn't want to, and would never have, that night, except your eye caught on the one word you could not ignore.

Your name.

Esmeralda—when's the last time you heard such a chintzy, soapy, froufrou name? Ridiculous.

You froze, looked at the door. You kept your gloved hands, with their Windex bottle and their dustrag, where they were, and moved your eyes down quickly, in case he came back.

. . . Thanks for taking time with me the other night. Not sure (don't want to imagine) where I'd be without someone to talk to about this, and I'm hoping—trying—not to need much more than to talk about it.

It comes down to the vow, right? In sickness and in health. Not "in health, and some amount of sickness I can bear."

Even the setup's a bad soap opera: "I met someone" (even the words sound pitiful to me, a married-man cliché). And of all people, the woman who cleans my office every night. Who even HAS a name like Esmeralda anymore? Esmeralda— when's the last time you heard such a chintzy, soapy, froufrou name? Ridiculous. And yet. I met her, I went home, I turned the bookshelves upside down to find *The Hunchback of Notre Dame,* to keep the name in my head. To have something to say to her the next day.

I can't remember the last time I stayed up late to read a book, the last time I cared what happened next. But now I sneak them in at work, an addict. I still read to Anne—she would have wanted that, I think—but not those long old books. I started off with those, to tease her. And I thought, superstitiously, that more pages would keep her alive longer. Then it got to where I couldn't tell if she could hear the words, take any of it in. I know *I* stopped hearing them. Now I read her magazines and children's books. Is that sick, am I trying to get rid of her, without knowing it?

Meanwhile I bring *Hunchback* to the office, wait for openings to read it to the cleaning lady.

This woman—Esmeralda—has a story. Sad one. No money, very little love. Some luck, I'll give her that—some priest took pity on her the day she was supposed to go back to the Philippines, gave her a job cleaning his church on Barclay Street. But if you add it up—all the shit she's eaten, from the dirt floor she was born on to the village that's been leaching off her all these years, I think she wins, between us, despite Anne. But I feel happy hearing it from her. Is that fucked up? I hear about her hopeless junkie brother and my heart feels lighter, knowing someone else out there loves someone who doesn't exist anymore, though he's there, the same and not the same. It's not just that—not just, her story's like my story and "we get each other." It's that I'm thinking about stories, other people's, in a way I haven't since before Anne got so sick. I ride the elevator, look at passengers, consider lives outside of my own misery for once. I pity Esmeralda, and other people—I hear Anne's voice: *that's patronizing*—but it's a refreshing alternative to pitying myself. I watch her—Esmeralda, cleaning windows—and she's opened something, let some air and light into the sickroom.

There's the animal part of it too. No doubt about it. You've spent your life proving it can be turned off, kept under control—no sympathy from you on this front, I get that. But it must be said, so you don't think I'm making high-minded excuses. It's about sex, for sure—but also survival. I keep thinking about being close to someone who's *not dying.*

We're all dying, I can hear you saying. Maybe.

Remember being young, in summer, our first jobs—how dusk, the 5 or 6 or 7 p.m. hour—used to feel? The best part of the day—possibility, freedom—starting. Fifteen years now it's meant something else for me: getting ready to go home to Anne, the beginning of another long night. Now Esmeralda comes in, between 5 and 6, and part of me is punching out of my shift at the Y again, at quitting time.

I think of Anne, of who she was, of who we were to each other—two best friends in love—and I can't see her saying, "Don't. You signed a piece of paper." Too dickish? Too convenient? Does every lowlife think of his situation as the one technicality? The person I would ask about this can't answer now. Lucky you . . .

You panicked. Turned away from the screen and started dusting, anything—a file cabinet, even the wall, then looked over your shoulder, like a fugitive. You wish you'd knocked his coffee down, the picture frame, instead. Those things could go back to their places. But this screen, this window—you couldn't put it back. You heard the words inside your brain, even when you shut your eyes. Embarrassment, a slippery disgust slid through you, as if you'd seen a naked photograph he meant to hide. Or found some private trash inside his bin. You sprayed the screens and wiped, as if Windexing the words away.

And the screens did darken; the little windows floated back. It worked!

When John returned, you made sure to be far from his computer.

"Es!" he cried. You could have fainted.

Confusion, like an illness, tied you up inside. You vowed never to come near the lip of his desk again. Seeing your name, yourself, in his words, as he saw you—*froufrou, dirt floor, cleaning lady, of all people*—you winced. And yet, these words too: *happy, air and light, the best part of the day*. For weeks you couldn't clean his office without flushing at the cheeks, feeling a mist above your lip. What kind of schoolgirl silliness was this? You cursed him for it. Called up every dirty word you'd ever learned from fights or movies, here or in the Philippines. *Fuckshitjerkoffthedevilsonofawhore!*

You started to save him for last, hoping he might have left by the time you came to his door. But he was there, almost always. Calling out, "There she is!" Calling you Es.

Along the empty bridge, the driver turns his sirens off. You've taken the third seat, next to a woman wearing scrubs. The man to her right wears your clogs, in black. You sit Manila jeepney-style, six knees in a row—as if you're riding home from Nepa-Q-Mart once again, your cousins' children on your lap, the week's meat thawing at your feet, while strangers pass their fare through you up to the driver. Except there's a neat, unoccupied gurney in front of you. Static and the voice of a dispatcher come through the driver's radio, but you can't listen.

You twist the chaplet on your thumb, catching your finger on the first knob. *I believe in God, the Father Almighty . . .* You close your eyes and move your lips. On any other morning, traffic might have taken you through all fifty Hail Marys, but the streets are empty now. You've just begun the third Sorrowful Mystery when you open your eyes to the back windows of the van, which is already racing south past the courthouse where you took your oath.

Doris had told you of an amnesty five years before, signed by the President. And though you feared it was a hoax, a way to smoke illegals from their hiding holes, she helped you fill out the forms and get your card. REGISTERED ALIEN. Five years later, you rolled all ten of your fingers through black ink and filled ten squares with your ten prints. The lines that cut across the rings told you how many years had passed since you arrived from

Manila with the Guzmans. The oath itself took five minutes.
Your mind, so trained by prayer, has held on to every word.

>*I absolutely and entirely renounce and abjure all alle-*
>*giance and fidelity to any foreign prince.*
>*I will support and defend the Constitution.*
>*I will bear true faith and allegiance to the same.*

Afterward, some students at a table outside the clerk's door
registered you, right then, to vote.

A couple, coming out of City Hall, asked you to photograph
them. They weren't young, but the white daisies that the bride
clutched in her hand were. A few of them she'd plucked and
pinned into her hair. The air had dust and August grit in it, but
on that day to you it was confetti. Every pigeon in the park looked
like a dove.

"Our witness had to get back to the office," said the bride.
"Will *you* celebrate with us?"

You'd barely answered when she took your hand. "I found our
wedding party, hon!" she told the groom, and ran. Your other
hand grabbed Doris's. Cars honked, but in a friendly way, at the
jaywalking four of you. "Congratulations," people on the sidewalk slowed to say.

At a bar close to the water, the newlyweds ordered lemon
pound cake—*the icing's white,* they said with a shrug—and
champagne.

"Which one of you's the bride?" flirted the bartender, pop-
ping the cork.

"I am." She pointed at herself. "But pour Esmeralda's first.
Today she's an American."

The golden fizz filled your glass to the lip. He poured the
bride's, then Doris's, and then the groom's. The newlyweds
insisted he, the bartender, drink too.

"Cheers," said Doris.

"To love," said the groom, winking at his bride.

"*Mabuhay,*" said the bartender, winking at you. "Merlita taught me that. She cleans this place at night."

It went, as they say, straight to your head: cold bubbles starbursting from your tongue and throat to your brain and your eyes, ringing the room with light.

"Now tell me it's still 'a piece of paper,'" said the bride to her groom. "Tell me you don't feel different."

"I do," he said. "It feels like . . . solid ground, where there was water. Right?" He put an arm around her.

"Drink to that," said Doris, so you did.

"And you," the groom asked, "what will you do first, as a full-fledged Yankee?"

The bride: "Besides get drunk with three other Americans."

"She's looking for a real job," Doris said.

"In an office," you said.

You meant the kind of job you did get, nine weeks later, cleaning offices in a city building where thousands worked. But the husband said, "Trust me. It's overrated." .

"I want to send a postcard home and write an arrow," you said. "*See that building? That's where Esmeralda works.*"

They drank to you.

The newlyweds stood halfway through the second bottle and settled the bill. "We need to relieve the babysitter," they said. "But will you stay and finish this for us? Promise you will."

"No need to ask me twice," said Doris.

"All the best to you two," said the bride. Her eyes glassed up with tears. She squeezed your hand, and Doris's.

Doris swiveled her barstool to you. "You know they think we are a *we,* don't you?"

You swiveled back to where the newlyweds had gone. You didn't get it. Then you got it, blushed, and thought you ought to chase the bride and let her know the truth. But you'd drank more that afternoon than ever, couldn't feel your feet to stand.

You opened your mouth to protest, but all that came out was a hiccup.

Doris giggled. So did you; you couldn't stop. You raised your glasses, clinked, and sipped again.

"Congratulations, Esmeralda," Doris said. "Now you'll get jury duty like the rest of us." But she beamed with pride.

You hiccuped, laughed some more, and then you kissed her, on the lips, just long enough to smell the powdery perfume and see the feather-colored down along her cheek. You thought of angels. Thanks to Doris, you were here. She was wearing lipstick for the occasion, and when you turned back to the bar mirror, so were you. The kiss was brief and sweet and overpuckered, like the one between two Dutch boys in a Delft figurine you dusted once. A souvenir. It said, below the boys' feet, AMSTERDAM.

"America!" you shouted at the mirror. That set you both off giggling again.

Today, seeing the park outside of City Hall get smaller from the ambulance, you think that when you see John next, you'll tell him this story. You will insist on what that bride insisted on. Demand that you and he stop hiding, walk out into the sunlight and the traffic and the pigeons and the parks together. "I am good at oaths," you will tell him. *So help me God.*

For weeks his smile, his chirpy greetings, shamed you. *There she is!* One day you'd had it. Maybe the piece of paper had turned you more American after all. Americans loved bringing secrets out. Discomfort didn't kill them. One day you turned to him, hands on your hips.

"It's wrong no matter what."

"I beg your pardon?"

"It's wrong no matter what. No need to ask your cousin who's a priest, because you know already."

You had heard, in many houses, wives beg their husbands for

the truth after seeing something they weren't supposed to see. You must have sounded like them now, confronting him.

"I don't know what you mean," said John. His eyes jumped sideways to the screen. The husbands in those houses gave themselves away like this, too.

"You made a vow; that means always."

"Es," said John, "I really have no clue what you are saying." He stared at you.

You could have said, *Oh never mind;* or said something in broken English. You once wrote off a week's pay from Helen Miller, because you couldn't bear to shame her for her slipping mind. With your own money you replaced the Ronsons' crystal tray, to keep their clumsy daughter out of trouble. And yet, something stopped you from protecting John.

"I saw my name on your computer."

"You had no right to look there," he said, sounding like those caught husbands again, "but I have nothing to hide. Please, be my guest." He rolled his chair wheels back. "Show me what you saw."

"I know it's not there now." You went to him, cloth and Windex still in hand. "I was here, doing my job." You mimed dusting around his files and keyboard. "I moved this thing by accident."

He didn't deny it then.

"It's wrong no matter what, John."

He'd said your name so often. This, your first time saying his, felt like stepping off a high ledge without looking.

He placed his long fingers on the keyboard. "I know that," he said. "I agree."

"It's wrong no matter what." Your voice had lowered into someone else's.

He looked so sad, so tortured by what he knew to be the right thing. Would Doris, Pepe, anyone you knew—even yourself, a day before—have ever guessed you'd be the one to touch him first? You remembered sitting in the church, years before, not knowing what came next but hoping for some kindness. You placed a hand on his shoulder. You felt a shaking from inside him—not a lot, not a "tremor," but enough to make you think he needed more warmth, another hand, which you then placed on his other shoulder. You waited, then stepped forward. His hands descended on your hips. He dropped his forehead to the highest button on your dress, above your breasts—bone against flat bone. His short breaths blew the fabric back and forth.

And yes, if you'd stopped there, it might have been a hug, no more—an awkward hug, between two people, not quite friends. If either of you had moved any faster, any sooner, you'd have fled the scene, spooked like a horse. But John's hand went so slowly from your hip, down to your knee, under your skirt. Any rougher and you might believe it all happened against your will. You looked through the window at squares of light in other buildings, tiny other people, tiny desks and chairs. His hand shifted against you, inches up and inches down, till sounds came out of your throat. You leaned back, seeing pores in the foam ceiling tiles before you closed your eyes.

Next to the churchyard, where he parks, the driver of the ambulance stops you. "Hey wait."

You almost run, prepared to force your way into the building before he can ask for your ID. He doesn't. He just tosses you a hard hat and paper mask before he walks off, putting on his own.

You smell, right then, the burning. Sharper than all other fires you have known. You put the hat and mask on and keep walking. Flames crackle from a broken car window, its alarm whooping. You haven't seen a car aflame since Manila in the early eighties, the riot town the Guzmans were escaping. Two nurses pass, a coughing man outstretched between them, his big arms hanging on their small shoulders. The cops and firefighters move so fast. You realize you're searching for a pair of blue eyes, wondering if John's brothers are here too, working, trying to find him. If this had happened late at night, would John search the faces of these nurses in blue? Their pale uniforms really do match yours. Only the skirt sets you apart. You couldn't sit down on the curb, as one nurse does now in her blue scrub pants, and weep into your knees.

The worst typhoon your village ever saw began while you were in a tree. The tallest one on the plantation (Mahentoy, you called it, after the giant in a folktale) let you see as far as the bay on one side and the next village on the other. You were looking for your father. You didn't know that he had hitched his way already to Manila, where the taxis needed drivers and cafés needed busboys regardless of the weather; or that you would not see him again. You thought there was still time to tell him that a Red Cross tent inland had food and water.

"Come down, Esme," you heard your mother say. Pepe wasn't with her.

You shimmied down. The water, when you landed, reached your knees.

"Where's the baby?"

"Darna brought him to the tent this morning."

But you'd already seen Darna, your neighbor, from high up in the tree, head inland with *her* children—three of them, all her own, and no more. Your mother trusted people who had never wished her well.

"All right." You walked her to the flooded main road and put her on a rescue boat. Then you turned, the water thigh-high now, and ran back to the house.

"Esme!" your mother called. "You'll drown."

The wind whipped at your face; the water slowed your legs down like a dream of running. The house was far enough away you had a chance to look at it, still standing, and feel proud of your papa, whose own hands built it, while scraps of other houses were sailing through the storm. One tin sheet could have sliced you clear in half, but missed. Falling coconuts hit the water with louder splatters than their sound on soil. You ducked. And underwater, it was dark and quiet. You could move faster. You swam until your fingers touched the door.

You prayed for love, not just acceptance, of God's will: even if that meant finding Pepe already bloated with floodwater. Farm girls saw their share of death, both animal and human: stillbirths, yellow fever, malnutrition. And who could blame God, anyway? Looking down on perfect Pepe, how could He not want him back in heaven for Himself?

Inside the house, the water nearly reached your ribs. And there you found him, floating in the wooden trough that had become his cradle. He cooed and gurgled, reaching for his toes. Not a scratch on him.

John was the closest you had ever come to an addiction. As a young girl, you never even longed for sweets. Each morning you sipped coffee next to Doris, but you never *needed* it. Smoking and drinking struck you as a man's vices, and a waste of money besides. Gambling, too. But nights with John—the stars in your brain, the beggar that sex made of your body—gave you a taste of it, that life, those forces that held Pepe at their mercy.

You walked into the walls of houses you'd cleaned for years. You broke a vase that had belonged to Helen Miller's mother. "Esmeralda! What's with you?" said Mrs. Miller. She docked you for it, as if money could replace a priceless thing. *I'm sorry, ma'am.* You went into his office that same night. Watched his reflection grow taller behind you as you wiped the windows. As he trapped you in his arms and closed his mouth over your ear.

If this was anything like what Pepe had felt, you couldn't blame him. You could understand almost everything your brother had done over the years, the lengths he went to for his appetites. But Pepe, at this time, was trying to change. He'd checked himself into a rehab center in the north: the Farm, residents called it, which caused confusion for you and your mother on the phone, between discussing home and Pepe's rehab. The men there lived like soldiers. Their commander was a former *shabu* addict, who'd found God in jail, was now a priest, and lived by the old proverb about idle hands. His soldiers rose at dawn, cleaned the grounds, made and mended their own clothes, and cooked food that they had grown or raised themselves. Only after chores and Mass and meetings could they spend one hour every evening on the one leisure activity allowed: wood carving. They learned to shape blocks of *kamagong* wood: first into planks, then into spheres. The men who mastered those would build the planks into a cross, the beads into a rosary. The veterans learned figures—Mary and the saints, and, finally, to put all previous skills together, a crucifix with Christ on it. Pepe sent his handiwork across the ocean to your nightstand drawer. The priest did not like to rank residents, but Pepe thought he noticed his quick mastery of figure after figure, saw him linger on his work for longer than he did on other men's.

On the phone, in these months, Pepe spoke with all the fire, all the fever, of the new convert. He seemed to know what you were up to, in spirit if not form.

"Women your age forget what God expects of them," he said. "Once they're past childbearing and still not married, they stop guarding their virtue."

He used words like *fornication* and *adultery,* words you hadn't heard spoken this way since your days in the one-room parish schoolhouse. You almost felt his spittle through the phone line, landing on your sinful cheek. He said he had thought about becoming a priest.

Now you know you should have praised him more. Should have told him how much you looked forward to a crucifix made by his hands. But at that time you had your own urges to answer to. Sometimes you stopped listening, didn't write him back. You fell asleep on the train home, too tired even to pray for him before bed.

You're right, Pepe, you should have said.

In another time, another country, villagers would have stoned you to death.

You did not expect to see shoes in the street, high heels that women kicked off as they ran. You think of hallways inside dark apartments, shoes and neckties and discarded bras forming a trail into the bedroom, sounds of muffled laughter and unbuckling, people so distracted by excitement sometimes they forget to shut the door. In those apartments, you've been trained to help and be of use no matter what.

And so, along your way, you stoop and start collecting them. The shoes, computer parts, and paper. As if this wave of people walking toward you has just left the party: you are here to clean up after. This much you know how to do. Your left arm gathers what your right turns up: shoe, shoe, battered keyboard, paper, paper, paper. Where will you bring them, Esmeralda? The wastebasket on the corner? People might want them back. EARNINGS REPORT, one paper says—no doubt something important. Some of these shoes cost more than your rent. And some are not in bad condition. Nicked and dusty, perhaps a bit charred at the heels. You can restore them, bring them to the lost and found. Those nice men at reception held an umbrella for you for two days when you forgot it.

So much turns up that you unzip your tote to carry it. It's possible that you look crazy, heading straight toward disaster, scavenging for scraps, but you don't care. The heaps grow higher the closer you get. One shoe, a patent leather pump, gives you more trouble than the others. You pull harder, then drop it. It's too hot. Your fingertips have swiped into the dust a shiny band of leather that reflects your face. Something inside the shoe has weighed it down. Your eyes move, slowly as the cold blood in your veins, from the shank, over the slender, melted heel, to the ankle. A woman's ankle, dressed in nylon panty hose like yours.

You cross yourself. Start digging through the rubble. You'll bear any sight—a bone, a face—to close her lids for her, in case she left this world with her eyes open.

One night you fell asleep inside John's office and woke up at two.

"Did I snore?"

"A little," he said. "I'm sure I did too."

In the basement, you didn't know enough to skip the time clock, go straight home, pretend that punching out had slipped your mind. Someone like Pepe would have known. Instead, as you had done five nights a week for six months straight, you fed your time card to the clock and listened to it bite.

Thirteen days later, the supervisor's call almost went to voice mail. You were coming back from the Laundromat with Doris's clothes.

"I'm doing payroll and your card says two-thirteen," the supervisor said. "Which means you either took too long to do your floors, or tried to steal time from the company. Which is it?"

She had a pretty accent. *Stealing time,* you thought: how strange, to imagine you could hold minutes in your hand and hide them in your pocket. Had Pepe thought of such a scheme yet? *Time is money.* People said that.

"Which is it, Esmeralda? Are you slow, or do you steal?"

You tried to think: which was the worse disgrace, in your profession? Neither one was true. You could turn the foulest six-stall ladies' room into a lab, in minutes flat. You'd never lifted so much as a slice of bread from someone's pantry.

"I can't hear you, Esmeralda."

By the age of twelve or thirteen, Pepe could spin great yarns of where he'd been and when. He hid things under the wooden floor slats. He sent lists of books and supplies he needed money for, long after he had stopped going to school.

Because you'd met this supervisor only once, barely remembered what she looked like—someone else had trained you—the woman you imagined on the other end had gold hair and green eyes. John's wife, *her* time—you'd stolen that. Ashamed, you chose the other lie.

"I have problem with my feet, ma'am," you told her. Broken English in a broken voice. You, Esmeralda, who'd never griped to an employer in your life—even when you stayed late and earned nothing extra.

"I suggest you get them checked, then. There are doctors just for feet, in the big city. Now that you have medical, you can. Not many cleaning jobs around that give you medical, are there, Esmeralda? That's why there's always applications on my desk."

"Of course," you said.

"I hope the doctor helps you, Esmeralda. But if you can't continue due to problems with your feet, I need to know. You understand—don't you?"

"Of course."

She went on. Words like *unacceptable.* Like *verbal warning.*

So you checked yourself in to your own kind of rehab. That night, when John turned his chair to look at you, you headed for the window, far from him. The glass squeaked as you rubbed at fingerprints that weren't there.

"Es?"

"My boss. She could have fired me," you said. Your night reflection faced you, checkered by the squares of light from other offices.

"That's my fault," John said. "I should have woken you. It won't happen again."

"No." A line from *Annie,* which the Ronson children loved, came back to you. Miss Hannigan putting her girls to work until the orphanage shone *like the top of the Chrysler Building.* It takes a cruel master to keep cities clean. "It can't happen again."

"Es—"

"You know already," you said, "all the reasons we must stop."

For many nights his eyes still followed you. To work, with your head down, while being looked at in this way, took more resolve than anything you'd ever given up for Lent. More will than your first graveyard shift. Your hands shook, as you pushed the vacuum down the corridor, and headaches almost split your skull in half. In time, though, he gave up. In three weeks you were back to nods. *Hello* and *thank you.* In another three weeks you were nothing but two workers, in one tower.

When the splintering happens—or the splinterings, a million pieces cracking into millions more—when the clouds come pouring through the street, you stare at them for longer than you should.

Your mouth and nostrils burn. A thousand knifepoints prick your skin. Something like sand rattles your hat. But you keep looking till the dust chalks up your eyes.

And then you close them.

The world grows quiet inside you, and outside time, slow as the center of a storm. You hear only your breath against the mask, the way John must have heard his on your dress, that night.

You clutch the shoes and papers to your chest like things you love. As if they're what you came to save. The bodies running past you, left and right, are a commotion you're not part of. You're prepared to let the monster swallow you.

And now you know why saints crave suffering, invite all kinds of pain so they can feel in some small way what Christ, whom they love, felt.

The flood had risen to your neck when you carried Pepe out of the house. So many of the trees had fallen. Those that hadn't yet were bowing to the ground as if to tell the wind, *You win.* You sat the baby on your shoulders and marched forward as the water reached your chin.

And then you heard the fibers come apart. Mahentoy, that old giant you had scaled to canvass for your father, started breaking at its base, and just missed you before falling like judgment's sword. It cleaved your home in half, where, not a minute earlier, you'd found Pepe. You ducked and ran, underwater, for both your lives.

Now two arms grab you by the ribs, knocking your breath out. You are yanked back into time and through the ash on someone else's feet, your own dangling. You cough, either from his grip around your lungs or from the soot that's gathered in them. Your hearing's back. And now it's clear this roar is bigger than those typhoon sounds from home. The breaking trees; the thunder in the sky; the helicopter's gun-like patter as it dipped to drop food sacks beside the rescue tent you reached with Pepe, by some miracle; the wave that rose fifty feet high and almost ate your hometown—those are smaller, even taken all together, than this roar, this day.

Your rescuer slams you into an iron fence. His badge is on your shoulder blade, his back a shield against the hail.

The world grows dark. You wonder if you've fainted, but you're fine. You're conscious. Night has, in fact, descended on this morning.

"Come on," the voice over your shoulder says. His hand and flashlight lead you down a set of stairs. He has you stand against a wall. Something like a cloud climbs up your windpipe. When the flashlight shines into your face, you think your eyeballs might ignite.

After Pepe crashed his motorcycle, he woke up remembering some Good Samaritan who'd held his head in her lap and pulled the bits of gravel from his face. She left him when the ambulance arrived. *My angel,* Pepe said, *my ghost.* He could not forget her voice or her fingertips.

"You'll be all right down here." With that, your savior's flashlight, and the portion of his black sleeve you can see, are gone.

You know you're not alone. The coughs and sobs and choking sounds of others echo off the station walls. They find your hands and lead you up the platform in the dark.

"He's gone," your mother said.

The rehab farm had released Pepe with a certificate and a kit of wood-carving tools. You'd bought him an apartment in the city, two hours from the plantation. But Pepe never showed to get his key. The rehab priest discovered money missing from his vault. Weeks later Pepe called your mother from Manila.

"He went to see about a business venture there," your mother said, "with friends."

"And you allowed it?" you said. "Don't you know what *business venture* means with Pepe?"

"He said replacement parts for small electronics. You don't think it sounds legit?"

"Do you?"

Your mother isn't half as dumb as she pretends. "You think I could have stopped him?" she said. "You wouldn't think so, not if you'd been here these years. He was a child when you last saw him. He might weigh next to nothing now, but there's no making him do anything."

That week, the lies you'd told the supervisor came true. Your feet clanged with such misery at work, you might as well have been stepping on glass. The bleach and toilet paper felt like bricks you had to push uphill. Even friends at church noticed a limp. That nurse you knew told you to toss your Keds for clogs that got her through her double shifts. You did. They didn't help.

John waited by his door that Tuesday night. "You've looked so tired," he said. "Can I help?"

You stepped back, fearing he might reach for you.

"I know I'm not supposed to care," he said, steering you to the sofa. "Or act on caring, anyway. You don't have to tell me why you're sad, either. I have an idea, though: you rest here. I'll clean the office."

You almost laughed. "I don't think so." And yet the leather felt so cool against your back. Your eyelids sank watching him take the handles of your cart.

Twelve minutes later, you woke with your feet up. John had finished at the window. He stared at the buildings.

"No one builds castles or cathedrals anymore," he said. "I read that skyscrapers are how cities show off, in our time."

The next night he was standing by the door again. The next night you removed your shoes. Each time, you fell asleep and woke to John dusting his cabinets or replacing his trash. These naps never lasted more than twenty minutes, but calmed you more than your own bed at night. You lay there—Esmeralda, daughter of the dirt, born to toil in God's name till your hands or heart gave out—reclining like an infant or a queen, a hundred levels aboveground. Priests had promised you this kind of peace in heaven.

You shall feast on the fruits of your labor, and your works shall follow you.

One of those nights you dreamed about your work. The office floor had thickened into soil, and you were pulling the cleaning cart behind you by your teeth. As the cart grew heavier, you turned and saw Pepe, dropping his woodwork and tools and motorcycle and replacement parts for small electronics into your garbage bag. Your heart rejoiced: you hadn't seen Pepe in years, and here he was. Visiting you! How did he find you? Still, it dawned on you in this dream that you had to keep walking and could not stop. And Pepe could not follow, only wave good-bye and shrink behind you as you carted his burdens away. You woke in tears, sitting straight up and swiveling your legs as if you'd just remembered an appointment. John was on his knees, dusting the table by the sofa. His gloved hands caught your stockinged feet before they hit the floor.

"Are you all right, Es?"

You shook your head. "I have a problem with my feet."

He nodded. He didn't speak, only pressed his thumbs along your instep. You were silent too, letting the sore bones and stiff muscles speak for you. You looked up at the cratered ceiling tiles and closed your eyes. His forehead touched your knees, bone against flat bone.

"I missed you," he said afterward—his suit, your uniform, stretched across the table like ghost bodies.

Months after he'd disappeared, Pepe turned up again at the rehab farm. *Relapse,* said the once-addicted priest, *is just part of the process.* His rule for returning men was *three strikes and you're out.*

Emerging from the darkness underground a few blocks north, you hobble to the river, coughing clouds of dust. On the grass a rescue worker tears a white sheet from a gurney into strips. Red tears rain down his face. You think again of saints. You collapse to your knees, a park bench for your prie-dieu.

You'll catch your breath here, that's all. Before you head back south. John's tower stands, without its twin, still smoking in the distance. He's still there. You're sure of it.

Why shouldn't you expect a miracle? You found Pepe, fine and floating in his cradle, didn't you? What could have killed him didn't, because you were there.

But Pepe was a child, and without sin, some voice reminds

you. God's book does not mince words about what happens to a man who does what John has done, what a woman like you deserves.

Is today a judgment, then?

God doesn't say.

And so you offer what you would have offered on the day you were prepared to find your brother dead.

Take me.

You'll walk into this river, wash away your sins. And if he lives, you'll see to it yourself that he lives right. You'll walk into this river and you won't come out.

You know that bargains aren't prayers. This kind of pagan trade isn't what Jesus meant by *sacrifice*. Today, though, you'll try anything.

And when you hear the second rumbling, you don't run. When smoke, the second night in one bright hour, again snuffs out the morning, you kneel and wait, elbows on the slats, hands clasped at your brow, stubborn as a statue while the glass and dust and paper coat the town.

You've come this far. Why wouldn't you go back for him? You came into this world with few advantages, but faith is wealth, and you, Esmeralda, are rich with it.

For one whole year you both avoided the word *love*.

For one whole year you never talked about the future.

What you discussed, what kept you listening to each other all those hours in his office, was the past.

"I almost didn't stay here in this city," you told John.

"Get out of here," he said. By then you knew what this expression meant.

You were playing the game that lovers play, when lovers can't believe their luck. What if John had worked for that firm and not this one? What if the cleaning company had sent you to a mid-

town building? You never would have met. And farther back in
time, and farther: what if John became a fireman or cop, like his
brothers? What if you never left the Philippines?

"It's true," you said. "Mrs. Guzman, the one who brought me,
couldn't keep me. She said she didn't know that living in this city
was so hard. She bought me a plane ticket and called up a family
she knew in Manila."

You told John about shopping for souvenirs at the airport.
The T-shirts: so expensive. Snow globes you shook to watch the
salt-shaped crumbs fall on the mini-skyline. People on the farm
would ask about the snow—what would you tell them? That you
hadn't stayed long enough to see it? You looked at yellow-taxi
postcards, bright red apple magnets. People would ask about
the skyscrapers. Had you ever climbed to the top of one? What
would you say?

"I kept thinking of this rhyme that day," you said to John.
"The Guzman kids liked it."

Because John's head was in your lap, your hand combing his
white hair, you sang it.

> *If I were a spoon as high as the sky,*
> *I'd scoop up the clouds that go slip-sliding by.*
> *I'd take them inside and give them to Cook*
> *to see if they taste just as good as they look.*

"I never learned that one." John smiled. "How would the sky
taste, do you think? If we got close enough?"

"Soft but crunchy," you said. (You had wondered too.) "And
good for breakfast; just a little makes you full."

You told him somehow you weren't finished with the city.
Something kept you here. The city wasn't done with you.

"It's brave, what you decided," John said. "When you think
about it."

"But I wasn't thinking, not at all." You laughed. "Is it brave, or crazy? If I was thinking, I'd go home. I had no job. I had no place to live."

The job that brought you to him, to this building, was still eighteen years away that day. There would be lucky accidents and Doris and a change of laws and many other rooms to tidy in between. But as it happened, when you backtracked through the gate, and spent some of your last bills on a taxi back into the city, on a crisp, clear day like this one, you came very close to him and didn't know it. You just didn't know exactly where to go.

As far as towers went, you hadn't even been in this land long enough to know the difference between *tall* and *high*.

"I want to see the highest building in this town," you told the driver.

So he brought you here.

Old Girl

Dad

The old girl's husband—fifty-one years old, the 165-pound champion (as he likes to put it) of a triple-bypass surgery—tells her on March 1, 1983: "I had an idea, Mommy."

Mommy is what the old girl's husband calls her. And *idea* is a generous word for *whim* or *flight of fancy*, the kind of ill-considered impulse he'll have often and won't quit till he's pulled it off (he almost always does, if barely) or failed (more rarely, but with flying colors). Not *scheme* or *plan*—God knows the old girl's husband can't be bothered with anything like a *plan*.

"It just came to me," he says. "I thought I'd run the marathon this year!" As if the race has been, in previous years, an option he just didn't exercise. Such glee in his voice. As if of course the old girl will see it as he does. The best idea in the history of ideas.

Right now they live in Chestnut Hill, in Newton, Massachusetts. So when her husband says "the marathon" he means *the* marathon: Boston, mother of all. Not counting Greece, of course—original but defunct. Not with his colleagues, either—men his age or older, with wives and kids and coronary issues of their own—but with his students. Young, fit Kennedys-in-training—with, the old girl guesses, egos to match or trump her husband's. They run it every year, they told him during office hours, which the old girl's husband holds not in an office but at the Bow and Arrow Pub, in Harvard Square. How had he lived on Commonwealth Avenue for two years and never caught the bug, they asked, on Patriots' Day? They must have talked about Pheidippides, poor messenger, croaking at Athens, just before (the old girl imagines) her husband slammed his pint down on the sticky bar declaring, "Goddamn it, count me in."

What kind of race has the old girl's husband ever run, in his life? The electoral kind. The skills that once won him *those* races—the glad-handing, the tippling with rice farmers in the north and the fasting with Muslim pineapple canners in the south, the all-nighters, the stump speeches, the bouncing of babies while flirting with their mothers—would hardly get him through this one. Athletes turned in early, didn't they? They didn't smoke or drink, avoided fatty foods. And never mind the hours of training, the miles of *preparation*—never her husband's strong suit. The old girl's husband thinks of preparation as a kind of joke. The hero, in his myths about himself, is always slightly unprepared for his adventures. She's known this since they met. They were both nine years old. He told her he'd snuck into a grade five classroom and stayed. *I don't really know fractions, but no one said no.* The old girl can already hear (six weeks from now—too soon, by any measure) his loud, braggy revisions: "I didn't even own a pair of decent rubber shoes!" And just before that, who will stand at the abandoned finish line, while the street sweepers check their watches? Who'll hold the water or the smelling salts, wiping the sweat or vomit, tending to him like a nurse except a nurse gets paid, picking up the *pieces*, in a word, when all his grandstanding comes back to bite him?

The old girl, that's who.

"Dad," the old girl says—*Dad* is what the old girl calls her husband—"that's about twenty-six miles, I think." She knows. Twenty-six point two, to be exact. But delivery matters, in this marriage. *Impossible, insane,* or even *not a good idea* would just cause a digging-in of heels and land her in the camp of killjoys and naysayers, never a chorus he heeds. *I think, perhaps,* or *Is it possible that* are the better notes to strike.

"Twenty-six?" the old girl's husband says, with his trademark puffery. "Is that all?"

Assumption

She only ever spent a year in the Manila convent school whose students called themselves old girls, but that was long enough for her to see herself as an Old Girl always. Her husband, who escorted old girl after old girl to debuts and dances in his youth, hated the term. *You sound like mares the farmer doesn't have the heart to shoot.* Some old girls agreed. Ines Arroyo, on all fours in the locker room, neighed while Margarita Lopez spanked her rump through the red plaid pleats. *Giddyap, old girl!*

And yet, what better name for them was there than *old girls*? As they jumped rope, memorized irregular French *verbes*, spiked and served at warball, drew shapes with compasses and protractors, sewed scenes of cottages and shepherdesses in little hoops, the one constant theme they were meant to meditate on was their future as wives and mothers. Old girls, like the Virgin Queen herself, were as pure and openhearted as children, but ready at the same time to shoulder children of their own, and households, when the time (not far off) came.

And they learned all this, of course, from nuns. Old girls themselves: aging maidens, ancient yet suspended forever at a specific point in childhood. Those sisters, who taught the old girl everything from home ec to geometry, loved her. *Modest, humble, soft-spoken,* they wrote on her report cards. *Pious, simple.* A girl who saw the point in outlines and index cards.

The woman answering the Boston Athletic Association phone scolds the old girl as if she were the opposite. "You're much too late, sweetheart. What did you think? A marathon's not something we just *take up*." The old girl hangs up, thanking her.

Doing her husband's homework for him—it's a habit, at this point. The old girl didn't even mean to start. In school he was the kind of C student—*gifted but needs to focus, waste of great potential*—whose alleged inborn genius was never put to the test by trying. *Relax, Mommy,* he teases, whenever he sees her gathering data, making a nest of what she knows. *There won't be a test on this.* Won't there? There always is. *Life* is a test, she wants to tell him, and those who study well can lick it.

"Registration's closed, Dad," the old girl tells him at dinner. "Even if you made the deadline, you'd have had to run what they call a sub-three by September." Hard, fast rules: how can he argue? He was four years too young to run for President, in 1969—finding his youth (people had called him Wonder Boy) a liability, for once. He'd had to wait, another skill he didn't have in spades. And by the time the wait was over, the Philippines was under martial law—a welcome reprieve, thought the old girl at first, from campaigns altogether.

"We'll find a way," the old girl's husband tells her cheerfully. He thinks like a Manila politician, still. As if they can bribe someone at the BAA. "We'll grease the wheel somehow."

Town

For all her husband's sudden interest in Boston, the old girl is the one, between the two of them, who loves it here. This town's the high point, to her mind, of a beloved northeastern triangle—from Philadelphia, where she rode out Manila's war years at the school that produced Grace Kelly; to New York, where she studied college French and math.

Not that America didn't shock her, at first. At Ravenhill, students talked back. Mount Saint Vincent daughters disobeyed their fathers. But much about America agreed with her. *When a 'kano says lunch at one o'clock, it's one o'clock,* she wrote the man who would become her husband; by high school they were exchanging letters. *I'm learning, when I speak, to—as they say in New York—"cut to the chase."* In the summers, when she went back to Manila, he'd tease her. *What an egghead,* he would tell her, for consenting to attend school all year round:

Some weekends, now, the old girl takes one of her children on the Amtrak down the Northeast Corridor. She loves even that phrase, imagining the country as a big house and its best cities as rooms along the main hallway. They've visited the Empire State Building and the Liberty Bell; had dinner with the nuns who taught her linear algebra and Stendhal; met her former classmates' kids in Rye or Greenwich.

But Boston and its suburbs, she loves most of all. Especially— the old girl doesn't care how corny or obvious it is—in fall, when the hills start to blush along the Charles River like a McIntosh apple. Winter, too, comes close: the Frog Pond frozen for skaters, the snow sugaring the red-brick houses just so. When he got his fellowships to teach at Harvard and MIT, they linked into a four-mile cluster of Filipino expat households stretching from the Jesuit priests at Boston College to the nurses at Brigham and Women's Hospital. *Manilachusetts,* some have called it. They're the ones who found the old girl and her husband their own red-brick colonial on Commonwealth, piped with white shutters and white columns and a white banister around the second-floor balcony, as if designed to hold a memory of snow even in August, when they came, in 1980. And—no use denying it—his name means something different in Manilachusetts than it does in Manila. *Hero. Freedom fighter. Prisoner of conscience.* Some still even call her husband *Senator* in greeting, as if no time has passed since 1972, unlike the fair-weather friends who started taking the long way around their house on Times Street, in Quezon City, and kept their children from her children, as if bad political luck were a communicable disease, which of course it is.

The old girl's husband, on the other hand, is restless here. She's known this for a while.

Whenever they're enjoying Boston—the best of Boston—home comes up, for him. The worst of home. At Fenway Park, for their son's birthday: "It's so damn *civilized* here," he complained. "In Manila, they'd have oversold the seats. Some *gago* would yell 'Fire!' to clear the stadium, and there'd be a huge stampede." He laughed, as if stampedes were charming, something that deserved his nostalgia. On Brattle Street, the rare nights they met to watch a film together, leaving the kids at home: "Remember how you wore your raincoat at the one movie theater in Concepcion? Because of all the fleas?"

Training

The two Akitas—Yoshi and Miki, gifts from a Tokyo congressman—accompany the old girl's husband on his first jog. He doesn't like to be alone. Yoshi and Miki aren't running dogs, any more than his canvas slip-ons are running shoes. The most pampered and, at the same time, most neglected dogs she's ever known, they've been raised as her husband might have raised their children, if she weren't around. Reward biscuits have made them flabby. They're jumpy, flesh trembling beneath the white and fox-red fur, because they never know when their next walk will come. The old girl's husband bathes them with too much of their eldest daughter's Gee, Your Hair Smells Terrific shampoo. But he doesn't plan for who might feed them when he flies to speak in Managua or Los Angeles or Kuala Lumpur.

He hasn't thought, either, about who'll drop off Kit, their youngest, at school, now that he's out jogging in the mornings.

That's been his one job, in the mushroom-colored Chevrolet Caprice he has all to himself. (She and the children share a blue Dodge Diplomat.) "I can't train earlier," he tells her (he doesn't like the dark); and later's not an option: once he's on campus, he wants to stay till evening. (The same reason he's exempt from picking Kit up in the afternoon.) *If you had to find parking in Harvard Square, Mommy, you'd understand.*

The old girl makes the best of it. For twenty-eight years she's been adjusting to his ideas. No fair to violate a silent but long-standing contract now. Didn't she upend her life, at twenty-two, based on a line—a single line—from one of his letters? *I'll see you when we're both home.* He'd gone to Korea during the war. She'd planned, all senior year, to move to New York, get her JD, live with her college roommate. But he'd never, in their years of growing up in close proximity, of running into one another at baptisms and weddings and wakes, mentioned the next time. And the moment he did, didn't the old girl cancel her job, and Fordham Law, and the Upper West Side studio she was supposed to share with Mary Ann; and return to Manila?

After the wedding, didn't she agree to skip the Pangasinan beach honeymoon they'd booked? Didn't she follow him instead to Washington, D.C., and spend most of four months alone in a rented Arlington apartment while he did research in Langley?

And when he ran for mayor and won, didn't she—Manila-born, Manhattan-bred—pick up and move to that country town that always made her feel half-drugged and half-asleep? Into a house that creaked and tilted like a ghost ship all the time, under the feet of villagers who entered as they pleased, roaming the halls, demanding rice or milk, the bathroom or the telephone? He wouldn't let her strip the walls or fix the floor, which was always giving Bitbit—just learning how to crawl—splinters. *It's all some of our constituents can do to keep a roof over their heads. Can't show them up in their own town.* He didn't want curtains at the dining room window, where townsfolk liked to watch them eat. *Even seeing us fight is good. Lets them know we're just like them.* And fight they did. About the time the old girl washed her hands after shaking a peasant's: *You think Bitbit will remember a cold she had as an infant? That man's* grandchildren *will never forget how you insulted him. Never.* About the old girl driving to Manila for Bitbit's checkups: *There are plenty of good doctors here.* About her visits to Clark Air Base at sunset—when the village electricity shut off, every single day, till sunrise—to dine with American friends. He won that one. She tried cracking Flaubert and Proust at home by candlelight, but country heat and boredom made her a stupid reader. For the first time in her life the old girl needed soap operas: the bold strokes, plot twists spectacular enough to pierce through her haze. Running out of radio batteries became the great crisis of her young wife- and motherhood. When the voice of the *Pusong Sinugatan* narrator warbled, as if he too were half-drugged, half-asleep, she thought she might go mad.

The old girl's husband is in luck. He knows someone. A colleague at the K School, who's run the marathon the past five years, has to travel to Berlin this April. "He says his number's mine on the condition that I run a seven-minute mile." The old girl's husband laughs. "Better start calling me Tim Brown, just in case." As if that's all the training it takes.

Drive

In Chestnut Hill, the old girl's husband has a recurring nightmare. He shoots upright, glazed with sweat. *I dreamed I'd been hit.* He grabs his chest, panting.

He never dreamed this in Manila, or in Concepcion, or anywhere they've lived—just here, in their master bedroom in the house on Commonwealth.

The first time, the old girl worried that it was his heart. A real-life chest pain, manifesting in his dreams as a bullet. Assassination, for the old girl's husband, was once a sort of pet obsession. He'd bring it up even as a small-town mayor. Girls who never grew up around congressmen and senators might find this morbid and death-wishy, but the old girl remembers how her father, uncles, and grandfathers all had the same casual bravado about the topic. As if everyone who was *any*one had to be ready for that. Back then, she did not really think it possible for her husband to die that way. He seemed too full of himself, not serious enough. His bulletproof vest, the armored car in which he rode through the sleepy streets of Concepcion, struck her as excess, like an alarm system on a toy house.

But in Boston, it's a drunk driver he dreams of. "Some college frat boy, coming from a party," he says, looking terrified.

"Since when do frat boys scare you?" The old girl brings him a face towel and a glass of water. At Ateneo, he was an Upsilon Sigma Phi brother himself.

But the old girl understands. The banality of dying in a car, because of someone's carelessness, is what terrifies her husband. Oblivion. Obscurity. That he should meet his end because somebody failed to think of him, rather than thinking too much of him. "Did they ask after me?" he wanted to know, throughout his years in prison. "Does anyone remember my name?"

"You've read too much Filipino history," the old girl tells him now. A steady diet of priests on garrotes, of patriots falling to Spanish Guardia Civil rifles, has warped him. Between the two times he cheated death—sentenced to a firing squad in Manila; then furloughed to Dallas for emergency heart surgery—there's no question which one he'd pick. "You've got to mix it up a bit," she tells him. "Go look at Kit's U.S. history book. Those heroes died of old age. Some weren't even heroes till old age, if I remember right."

Newlyweds

Speaking of omens, in Manila, at the wedding, they released a dove from its gold cage. It thought better of flying away, alighting on the old girl's head instead. "*Loko mo,* that's a good sign," said her father, as the old girl tried to shoo it off, grateful to have a veil and gloves on. "It means power, victory."

"Just like we thought," her mother said. "The groom's going to be President one day."

"It landed on the bride's head," a niece said. "Doesn't that mean *she*'ll be President?"

Everyone laughed, and no one harder than the old girl herself—the quiet, simple bride who'd just dropped out of law school for her MRS degree.

"So it did," said the priest. "But *she* and *he* are one now."

He was the old girl's first, and only.

Something about their wedding night recalled their first meeting, at nine years old. He kept exclaiming, "Wowowie!" or "Yehey!" in bed, as if her body was the county fair, and he a child delighted to find so many wonders in one place. Thank God. What would the old girl have done with a suave or more serious lover?

She has never worried about other women. If she had to guess, she thinks there may have been flings, enough to keep up with his Congress buddies, the way men smoke cigars at baptisms or drink Johnnie Black because *men do.* But never a real love affair. He seems too restless, too easily distracted, to maintain a mistress. Pity the half-dressed nymph who tries to stroke his shoulders, coax him back to bed while he's glued to Ted Koppel's *Nightline.*

Campaigning

Wives she has known exact all kinds of things from their politician husbands in exchange for another year, another term, one
more campaign. Cars, swimming pools, a house. A vacation,
another baby, no more babies. And the holy grail of Congressbride or Senate-wife concessions: the promise that this campaign
will be the last. *Where is the mountaintop, and why does it keep
moving?* they wonder. *When can we rest a little, pitch a tent,
enjoy the view?* Those questions, thinks the old girl, only give
a brand-new Congressbride "high blood." The sooner she can
learn that, for her husband, the climb *is* the mountaintop, the
campaign nearly as sweet as the office itself, the easier her life
will be. *By* idea *he means* decision, she told a young, naïve Congressbride once. *He's not asking for your opinion but your help.*

Follow-through is not these men's problem. Their problem is
forethought.

But not, it should be said, fore*talk*. While the other mara-
thoners eat, sleep, and breathe the marathon, the old girl's husband is busy *talking* the marathon. "The men's field is deep this
year," he tells the kids at dinner, as if he's followed a shallower
men's field for years. "You've got Greg, for instance, wanting to
redeem himself from the disaster of 'eighty-one . . ." Greg and
Bill and Budd and Tom and Benji—as if he's known these guys
for years, as if they're friends. And who knows? If he meets them,
someday, they might be.

He can talk, the old girl's husband—*susmariosep*, how he
can talk! Give him an audience—of one or one million, passive
or ill-tempered or smitten or skeptical, it doesn't matter—he'll
go all day. The old girl sometimes tunes out during his daily
speechifying—runs through grocery lists, the children's schedules, a convent-school memory here, a question for her weekly
phone call with her mother there—and when she tunes back

in, contrite over what seems a longer-than-respectful span of time for a wife not to listen to her husband, he won't have even noticed; the old girl's husband will *still be talking*.

After she turns off the TV and sends Kit to bed, the old girl smells McDonald's grease from the study. He must have convinced Bitbit or Ben to take him to the drive-thru after dinner. Through the rustle of wax paper she can hear her husband on the phone.

"I'll wear the flag," he says. "Either Bitbit will sew a cape out of it for me, or else I'll find blue shoes, red socks, a yellow headband. What I'm asking is, beyond the photo, isn't there a number twenty-six somewhere in our history that I can use? Some patriot that Spain locked up for twenty-six years? Twenty-six POWs tortured by the Japanese? Twenty-six international human-rights protocols violated since 1972? A symbol would be nice, beyond *He ran the marathon*. The more recent the better. Find that for me, would you?"

Bitbit

Bitbit, her eldest daughter, is twenty-seven. Bitbit's beau proposed to her before the family left Manila. Now, in Boston, more than eight thousand miles from him, she's wearing her mother's engagement ring. Her sisters have thrown *Brides* magazine and Emily Post's *Etiquette* and the Tiffany Blue Book at her. They've dragged Bitbit to Newbury Street to try on gowns. But Bitbit doesn't care for all that. She only wants to stay home, flipping through her parents' wedding album.

She shadows her mother everywhere, as she has from the beginning. *Little Mommy*, her father calls her sometimes. Everyone else has called her this Tagalog word for "hand-carried belongings" since she was small, always at the old girl's side and in her image. Privately, the old girl also named her for the way their hearts seemed to sync up (she could swear she felt it), toward the end of that D.C. honeymoon, a comforting call-and-response between her full-grown throb and her daughter's tiny, growing pulse: *Beat-beat. Beat-beat. Beat-beat.*

Gear

He didn't pick an easy season to start running. March in New England: blizzards one day, sun-starved coeds airing out their eyelet dresses and sandals in the slush the next. The old girl passes them along Massachusetts Avenue on her way to buy her husband the proper clothes. She doesn't know what's proper, but she knows it can't be Ateneo Blue Eagles shorts over long underwear. It never occurs to the old girl's husband that people might laugh at him, which must be the secret of people who are never laughed at for long.

Not wanting judgment from someone like the BAA receptionist, the old girl spies on what the other customers—all of them men—are buying and grabs the same for her man: knit cap, gloves, muffler, tracksuit with stripes down the legs and across the chest—and then a second pair of gloves, to replace the ones her husband will surely lose.

"Women's is this way," says the salesclerk, at her shoulder, startling her.

I'm here for my husband, she's said, in other contexts. *He's the politician.* But he's not "the runner" yet; in fact he's only slightly more a runner than the old girl is. So she lets the clerk show her a corner table, with a few leggings and sweatshirts, braided headbands and neon wristbands, fanned across its surface. A sports bra stretched across a headless mannequin like taupe armor. "Know what size you are?" The old girl looks around before whispering, "Medium," but no one in the store cares. "And are you satisfied with your current pair of running shoes?" The old girl's not sure if this clerk really believes she is a runner, or pretends to believe that to sell more. But she doesn't correct her. There are no women's sneakers, only a pair of gray New Balances she buys in both her husband's size and hers (men's minus two, the clerk suggests). And then she buys the children some.

Ringing her up, the clerk asks, "Have you read the Bible yet?" Out from under the register comes a book entitled—rather hippie-dippily, the old girl thinks—*Running & Being.* "It'll change your whole way of training."

On her way back to the station, she sees runners everywhere. Have there always been so many? She notes what they're wearing, wondering how soon she might have to go back to buy him a hooded sweatshirt, a pair of sweatpants, a lanyard for his keys. She starts to read *Running & Being* on the T. Scanning the chapter titles—a few she would expect, like "Training" and "Racing," and airy-fairier ones like "Living," "Discovering"—she flips to the one, ironically four chapters in—called "Beginning." *Can tomorrow be the first day of the rest of our life?* What if the other passengers think, between this book and the bags at her feet, that *she* is the runner; that she'll shed this trench coat and these rain boots when she gets home, baring her neon spandex like some secret fitness superhero? *Let them,* she finds herself thinking. She doesn't mind.

Parlor Talk

It is not exactly true that—as the old girl has written the family back home—she has no servants in Newton. There's a maid. One maid, Tweety, shared by five different Manilachusetts families. The old girl has her Tuesdays. On Sundays, Tweety goes to Chinatown to fulfill all five families' requests for *patis* and mung bean noodles in one trip.

It took some getting used to, having no one but the old girl and Bitbit to cook and clean in Tweety's absence. There were years on Times Street when she had one *yaya* per child. They slept in the old girl's house, knew the old girl's rules and preferences. *Right hand* doesn't begin to cover it. With them the old girl felt multiarmed like an Indian deity, invincible.

One thing no maid ever did—in Chestnut Hill, or Concepcion, or Manila—was serve the old girl's husband and his guests in the parlor. That, everyone knows, is a job for the wife. Highborn and well-schooled though she may be, only the old girl can pass through, a ghost carrying a tray. Rice cakes, if it's Manila; *pan de sal* or buttery pastries and *pitsi-pitsi*. Or something savory, like squid balls on bamboo sticks. In Boston, pretzels or club crackers, nuts, crudités, and cheese. The old girl knows which congressman and which professor has a taste for what.

She never expects more of him than how her own father behaved around her mother, reaching for the biscuit or the cup without a glance in her direction. And most men follow his lead.

But some have been jumpy, suspicious of her. The Huk captains her husband had over in Tarlac were tense and wary, never out of their fatigues. They held their coffee cups in their laps without sipping. Didn't touch the food, eternally afraid of betrayal.

And in America, some men feel guilty enough to take her presence on themselves. Not in some weighty way, just long enough to log that she's been seen. Something along the lines of *You'd better figure out your stance on that, buddy,* or *She won't vote for you.* They cock their heads at the old girl, lightening the mood, some cupping hands beside their mouths to feign a secret from her. It seemed gallant, at first—the old girl's husband is a lot of things, but rarely that—until she understood the joke. That a woman, a wife, could have serious political opinions at all. As if the old girl would ever *not* vote for her own husband, they seem to be implying. One of the Akitas could walk into the parlor, sniffing for crumbs, and they'd make the same joke. *Better figure it out, buddy, or Yoshi here will never vote for you.*

Fuel

Over the years, the old girl and her husband's dialogue about food has (as he gently puts it himself, when his political opinion—or even, once, his party—changes) "evolved."

In the late fifties and sixties she was still the bride who raised an eyebrow, shook her head when he reached for the fifth beer or the second dessert. Peking duck and rich white chocolate were his weaknesses. A young and pretty wife who kept those in check for you was, back then, no less a status symbol than the armored car or bulletproof vest.

The old girl did not think, in 1975, almost three years into his prison term, that that same beer- and Peking-duck- and white-chocolate-loving man could be serious about a hunger strike. When he floated it—his protest against a military trial for civilian crimes he didn't commit, or weren't even crimes when he supposedly committed them, before martial law—the old girl said, "Whatever you think is best, Dad." That's how little she believed he would go through with it. Even when he did begin, she waited for him to grow bored, plan his next dramatic gesture. Until she saw him on the twelfth day, looking positively Caravaggian. His breath—cold, sepulchral—sent a shudder through her. The hunger strike inflicted, in one month, all the aging the former cub reporter, baby mayor, Wonder Boy had previously skipped over. When it came to food, after that, all the old girl cared about was that he regain some of his lost weight and color in his cheeks. He could eat Peking duck for breakfast as far as she was concerned.

Then she saw him clutch his chest and search for breath after

Christmas 1979. *Indigestion,* she thought at first. The shock of pork stew and pineapple ham after so much bland prison cuisine. But seeing his face grow gray and damp, like uncooked clay, she called in the guard. *Angina pectoris:* a dirty, vaguely genital-sounding diagnosis. She begged him to get triple-bypassed in the States. Not Manila—who would put it past the President and First Lady to arrange "mysterious causes" on her husband's operating table? "Cabbage surgery," the Dallas surgeon called it—for coronary artery bypass graft, "and also for the kind of diet you'll be on afterwards, the rest of your life." His voice, so reassuring; that word *cabbage*—the old girl had visions of a sweetly ordinary life ahead, slapping his hand away from the butter or the gravy. But the cabbage diet lasted about as long as his vow not to bad-mouth the regime abroad. About as long as the daily breathing exercises he abandoned, saying he'd rather suffocate than watch that spirometer ball go up and down its plastic piston, over and over. Before his stitches healed he started booking speeches in New York, Columbus, Ithaca. *A pact with the devil is no pact at all.*

Now with the marathon approaching, in a decade when everyone's counting calories and cholesterol, the old girl serves up skinless chicken breasts, steamed broccoli, brown rice.

"What's with the prison food, Mommy?" says her husband.

"If you want to be a marathoner, start eating like one," she says.

"All of us?" says Toyang, their second to youngest. "*We're* not running the marathon."

"Yes, all of us," the old girl says. "Dad could use our support. Unless you want to do your own cooking—in that case, by all means, eat what you like."

Miki

Something's wrong. The old girl knows it after she drops Kit off one Tuesday: "Kung Liligaya Ka" (If You'll Be Happy) is blaring from the master bedroom. She follows a trail of gray puddles through the hallway and up the stairs, to Imelda Papin's melancholy voice:

> *If you'll be happy in the arms of someone else,*
> *and if her love is paradise to you,*
> *who am I to argue with what you desire?*
> *It's enough that you loved me once.*

He lies on their bed, still in his sweaty workout clothes, his sneakers muddying the down comforter. He's locked in an embrace with Yoshi, whose nose is resting on his shoulder. Humming gloomily with Imelda Papin, he now and then chimes in on a word—*forever, tears, apart.* He could hear something a million times and not have memorized it.

"We lost her, Mommy," says the old girl's husband. He buries his face into Yoshi's fur, and the pillow. Miki has disappeared, distracted by a squirrel on the Common. After bathing them last night, the old girl's husband didn't bother to put their collars back on. "I was in a rush this morning. Knew I had an early meeting before class. Now, I can't go anywhere."

The old girl doesn't ask whether he's done anything about Miki besides mope. Instead, she unties his shoelaces. *I'll take care of it.* She convinces him to get into the shower, sets out a sweater and trousers for him. *No need to miss your meeting.* She finds a photo of Miki and makes a MISSING poster. $200 REWARD. Her husband drops her at the copy shop in Back Bay before heading off to Cambridge.

She tells him she'll catch the T home after posting copies all around the Common. But the sun's out, glinting off what's left of the snow. It's not too cold. In the sneakers she bought in Cambridge, bouncier and gentler on the feet than the flattest loafers she owns, she walks herself home.

Popsy

The old girl can imagine one of them, out of the seven, as a marathoner outright: Popsy, her second oldest.

Popsy moves fast. Popsy commutes each day to East Cambridge in what the old girl's husband still calls *rubber shoes,* on top of scrunched tube socks and panty hose. Two pairs of leather pumps—one black, one brown—wait in a steel file cabinet in Popsy's office.

She's their only breadwinner these days. How competent Popsy looks, with her briefcase and pencil skirts and pearls! Her personality—*pamparampam,* they call it, like the trumpet fanfare that feels like it should announce her arrival in any room—seems built for shoulder pads.

They call her Popsy for the sweet ice Popsicles she loved as a child. But she's grown into the fatherly sound of it, too. More than her dad—the visiting professor in jeans and polo shirts and sneakers, a suit only for speeches, off on Mondays and Fridays, nothing scheduled before eleven—Popsy wears provider clothes and keeps provider hours. Home by six-thirty or seven in her suit, her insteps aching. She devours what the old girl makes for dinner, while Bitbit, "little Mommy," pulls out Popsy's chair and clears her plate; the old girl's first- and second-born reenacting some domestic dinner scene from a 1950s TV show. Whatever Dad earns on a speech goes right back into the Movement for a Free Philippines, but Popsy has the family-man instinct toward "blowouts" and *pasalubong* on payday. Those Fenway seats for Ben's twenty-second. The IBM in her father's study, installed in secret and festooned with a big red gift bow while her father was in Singapore. They can hear him, from downstairs, typing on it with two fingers—slowly, torturously, until Bitbit or the old girl would rather seize his yellow notepads and type for him than hear more. (All old girls had to pass stenography in high school. An insurance policy in case they—God forbid—never married.)

Ben

Like any other race—even Kit, at seven, stumped for him during the sham 1978 campaign—it's a family affair. The old girl splits the course map up six ways, assigns each child a station. Her husband will need the water and, more than that, the company. Bitbit at the Dairy Queen in Framingham (he'll beg for a fudge caramel sundae; she'll cave). Popsy in West Natick. Ben at the Wellesley gate, easy to spot amid the wall of screaming girls. Effervescent Kit will boost him up right at the drop into Newton Lower Falls, after the mile-fifteen mark. The old girl will stand at the same spot where he'll see the Citgo sign. And Toyang, if she can be convinced to come at all, can simply meet them at the finish.

As for the after-party, a politician's wife can plan one in her sleep. With Bitbit she's drafted a rich and heavy Patriots' Day menu. One afternoon of Sam Adams, baked beans and johnny-cakes, Boston cream pie, and shooters of New England clam chowder, after a marathon, won't kill him. They've invited everyone they know in Manilachusetts. To the kids' (except for Kit's) dismay, there'll be a "program": the young standing to perform for their elders' amusement. The old girl asks her son, Ben, to memorize Longfellow's "Paul Revere's Ride," and recite it to his father, who'll have just commemorated it on foot.

It's easy to forget that, besides Kit, who's in sixth grade, her children are adults in their twenties. Something about Dad's prison term froze their little family in 1972. They live together on Comm Ave to make up for lost time. She sometimes imagines coming to Boston years ago, if they'd had the savvy to skip town before Proclamation 1081. The kids would have been seventeen, fourteen, twelve, ten, and one. *Make Way for Ducklings* might have been Kit's favorite book. Their childhood memories would include baseball at Fenway, swan boat rides in the Public Garden, school trips to the Isabella Stewart Gardner Museum.

As it happened, Ben was twelve—the *balbas* just beginning to darken his chin, the pimples, the voice breaking before it deepened—when his father was taken away. The one time she feared not being up to mothering. Her only son, losing his father just as he was becoming a man: a cruel joke. Even as practical and ready for the worst as she was.

Ben's turned out fine—upstanding, trustworthy. Some might even say boring. Sons of friends have acted out with smoother upbringings. Now he studies part-time at BC, classes called Operational Leadership or Managerial Perspectives, though her son seems more accountant than CEO. Even the way he smokes (out on the front stoop, at the old girl's request) appears as quiet and methodical as watering the plants. In his free time he's been combing the rare and antiquarian bookstores on Beacon Street and Harrison Avenue for crumbling editions of *Tales of a Wayside Inn,* Browning's *Dramatic Idylls,* Herodotus. Learning the Longfellow will be a piece of cake for him. He's reading up on where historians disagree with "Paul Revere's Ride," facts he'll share with the guests while his father, full on chowder and exhausted from the race, tries not to fall asleep. Ben's a fact hoarder, as the old girl was. She hears him practicing upstairs.

> *That was all! And yet, through the gloom and the light,*
> *The fate of a nation was riding that night;*
> *And the spark struck out by that steed, in his flight,*
> *Kindled the land into flame with its heat.*

"Come on," his younger sister Kit, a ham and gifted mimic, says. "Put some feeling into it. And say *Reveah* and *spahk,* like the locals do. *Listen, my children, and you shall heah.*"

Trouble

The old girl never saw the talk show air. She only knew he had to get a haircut for TV, because she'd scheduled it. That day, another Senate wife, during dismissal at Ateneo, said, "Your husband—what a troublemaker, eh?" By then the old girl hardly even heard that shiver in their throats when people talked about her troublemaker husband.

A busy week: the old girl had Ben's Confirmation party to plan. Even if she asked her husband what he'd done, he'd been pulling moves like that for months. By this time people in their circle had discussed martial law long enough to channel their anxiety into domestic jokes. To bratty children: *Daddy's going to lay the martial law on you.* About philandering husbands: *What will he do once there's a curfew?* She knew not to expect him for dinner; he'd be at some caucus meeting at the Hilton. When the phone rang early the next morning, she teased: "Really, Dad? Tariffs and customs codes took all night? All *Friday* night?" But the operator cut in, to announce a call from Camp Crame detention center, monitored and recorded.

When his voice came through, it did sound slurred, hungover. *Mommy?*

What on earth had he said on TV?

Forget it. I've done worse. Or else, they think I have.

Ticking

Was he behind those Plaza bombings, one year earlier? She's never asked, not to this day. There are degrees of being "behind" something, anyway. He *didn't* throw the hand grenades onto the podium, where all the major candidates in his party were standing. He *couldn't* have killed those people. He was with the old girl, celebrating his goddaughter's *despedida de soltera.*

His party fingered the President; the President fingered him. But her husband's appetite for theater ended where someone— on his side, no less—might actually get hurt. Didn't it?

Now and then one memory floats back to the old girl: the way her husband checked his watch during the *despedida* party. The old girl's husband never checks his watch, a wedding gift. He wears it out of respect to the grandfather who gave it to him. But when he wants to know the time, he asks her. She, who only sometimes wears a watch, then has to search the room for a clock, all because her husband can't be bothered to look at his own wrist. An annoying tic, but so consistent she has wondered, sometimes, if perhaps he never properly learned to tell time in school. But that night, he raised his wrist to read it for a good few seconds, before going back to his conversation. Five or so minutes later, someone interrupted the toasts to say there'd been a bombing at the rally. She remembers the commotion. People at the party who had planned to join the rally later, or had come from it. People at the rally who'd sent regrets to this same *despedida.* The old girl's husband acted as the others did: alarm, confusion, anger. She has no reason to connect the watch to the grenades in any way. Why should she?

Runaway

"My heart is broken," says the old girl's husband, about Miki. "I can't trust myself outside with Yoshi. If we lose him, too, I'll be destroyed."

This means the old girl, in addition to Kit's drop-off, is in charge of walking Yoshi now. She takes him west on Commonwealth, in the direction of the firehouse, with Wellesley in the distance. Her husband will take this route in the opposite direction, just after the halfway point. It's quiet in the morning—hard to imagine the screaming crowd of spectators at all. Right now the old girl, and a handful of runners, are the only ones out.

Her husband met some students at the Charles River this morning, wasting no time in filling the void left by Yoshi and Miki. Later this week he'll hit the Harvard Club treadmills with a colleague in Boston. But the runners passing her now seem like loners, who took up running in order to win some time back for themselves.

In 1973, four months after his arrest, her extroverted, contact-hungry husband found himself in even deeper trouble. He'd been smuggling papers out of the camp, sometimes through the old girl and Bitbit, some of which ended up printed in the *Bangkok Post* and elsewhere. Whenever he recalls his punishment for it—*solitary*—she sees how much closer he came to dying then than during any hunger strike or heart attack. The handcuffs, the blindfold, the helicopter's guttering under his feet. The cell with no windows, only a neon tube that flickered harsh and bright. The dry bread, and the water he refused for fear of poison. Without his clothes or books or glasses, without the sound or smell of other life, without a place for him to go except into his own mind, his memory, he made lists. He started with his friends, then enemies: whom to reward and whom to punish once he made it out. And then lists for their own sake: milestones from childhood, classmates' names, teachers. Places and famous people, clothes he'd worn. Skills—would he remember how to fox-trot, or play mah-jongg, if he ever saw the real world again?

For three months, in Manila, no one would tell the old girl where he was.

And then in April, as abruptly as they'd taken him, he was back.

When he saw her, he wept. Not some stoic pallbearer's solitary macho tear, either. A full, blubbering breakdown. To speak, to say her name, took him a few tries.

Yoshi barks, straining at the leash. *Miki?* the old girl thinks, seeing a flash of white and fox-red fur streak past the reservoir. "Miki?" she says aloud, speeding up, letting Yoshi pull her. They jog down Beacon Street all the way to the cemetery, where the old girl lets Yoshi off his leash to sniff at shrubs, to search behind the tombstones, and finally to sit in the shade of a walnut tree. Miki, if indeed it was Miki, is nowhere to be found. Is it the ghost of Miki they've just seen, perhaps run over the day Dad lost her? Then it seems possible to the old girl that Miki just wasn't cut out for family life. That she was just biding her time with them in Chestnut Hill until she saw a chance, that morning in the Common, to break free. And now that Miki's nowhere in sight—again—the old girl and Yoshi make their way, flushed and panting, home.

"I wish I could have traded places with you, Dad," the old girl said, the day he wept about his solitary confinement. She meant it. A month by herself in the green slopes of the Sierra Madre would not have broken her, she doesn't think, as it did him. What would have? What could they use against her? Her children? Religion? Movies always depict the lover as the bait that brings any hero to his knees. But real life wasn't like that. The old girl and her husband have already both survived without each other.

Armor

By the time her husband was imprisoned, no one wore a girdle anymore. And no woman she knew missed them—except for the old girl, during the frisks. On Sunday mornings, young, indifferent fingers, palpating every scar and ripple, then shunting her into the amphitheater. She thought of farmers poking animals upon the auction block, searching for defects to bargain on. *Giddyap, old girl!* She longed for that lost barrier, the sausage-tight elastic, the hook-and-eye trail down her spine, the bra cups peaked like two *salakot* hats, and almost as hard—*something* to protect her flesh from all this easy access.

Only that time of month offered reprieve. Their hands, grazing the sanitary-napkin belt, the bridle holding up the old girl's cotton saddle, would stop there and go no farther.

Toyang

When the old girl's husband hurts himself, three weeks into his training, she thinks he's saying *black guys.* "The goddamn black guys got me," he wails. He was running with a priest friend in Franklin Park. In Dorchester. *Where Boston hides the black people,* their daughter Toyang has said. Manilachusetts wives have warned the old girl about riots in Mattapan, muggings in Roxbury, empty trash-filled lots on Dudley Street, burned-out buildings on Blue Hill Avenue. But in the living room, where he's collapsed on the sofa, there's no blood, no bruising.

"What happened?"

Black *ice.* He and the priest had just passed the Franklin Park Zoo when he stepped toe-first into a frozen puddle and turned his left ankle. He holds it, grimacing, with his shoes still on. "Oh,

God. It hurts," he moans as the old girl gently unties his shoe-laces, as if she's reinjuring him.

Has he taken any aspirin or iced his ankle? No. The old girl helps him to the sofa, props his foot upon the coffee table under three throw pillows.

Toyang comes downstairs then. "What is it now?" she asks. Always more withdrawn than the others, Toyang now, in Boston, needs a disclaimer on her like the kind you see on overhead plane storage: ITEMS MAY HAVE SHIFTED IN TRANSIT.

"Dad hurt his ankle. Go put some ice in a Ziploc, would you?"

"I think it might be broken," moans the old girl's husband.

His drama never lands well with Toyang, who stays where she is. The old girl always tries to model the opinion she'd like the kids to have about their father, even when she doesn't privately share it herself. Except Toyang rarely buys it. Toyang has wondered how "a quote-unquote 'Christian Socialist' can fall asleep so often during Sunday Mass." For one of her Boston College classes, Toyang once wrote an essay calling the Movement for a Free Philippines "a coalition not 'of the people' but mostly of the rich—the displaced Filipino elite, wanting back their slice of pie." The old girl had to beg her not to show it to her father or submit it to the BC *Eagle*. When the old girl moves him to their bedroom, saying, "I'm so sorry, Dad. I wish I could trade places with you," she can hear Toyang saying, underbreath, "So she wouldn't have to hear you whining."

Old Boy

The priest who married them had told them it would happen. That they would change, and grow—and even, if they stuck together long enough, start to see themselves in each other, the way some masters morph into their dogs.

After his return from solitary, they spent Saturdays together in the conjugal cabins. He was—she never told him, never would tell anyone—more of a lover there than ever in real life. No more "Wowowie!" or "Yehey!" but he noticed her in ways he hadn't until now. The hives anxiety gave her. The welts a toddler Kit, her nails improperly clipped by the *yaya*, left on her arm. He lingered on each inch, as if news of the outside world might be found in her flesh. And being weaker, from the weight loss, he was not so focused on the finish.

One Easter Sunday, a decade ago almost to the day now, he asked the old girl for a Bible, and a crucifix. *I think this cell could use one.* Jesus had visited his dreams and scolded him, for running too hard after power and away from faith. This from the man who'd once said, "Put in a good word for me, would you?" when he saw her at the rosary. Or, when he had to miss Mass, "Tell Him I owe Him one for all the yeas on rural redistricting tonight." Once, during a fight, he called her Mother Superior.

But this new Dad wrote her a poem—not a good one, but the only one he ever wrote—on their nineteenth anniversary.

What had started as his closing statement to the military court, this new Dad was expanding into a book.

Valium

After they learn her husband's ligaments are stretched, not torn; after she gives him ice and aspirin, and rubs Tiger Balm into his ankle, and wraps an Ace bandage around it; after she moves his foot through exercises he'll never practice on his own; and he still complains of pain, she offers him the pills. A Manilachusetts doctor keeps a Valium prescription current for her, just in case. She's taken drugs—other than aspirin, that is—exactly six times in her life: five times in childbirth, and once in February 1973, when he was in solitary and no one was telling her. She remembers Valium flattening her in a useful way, helping her to focus on tasks rather than outcomes, removing the past and future, so there was nothing like regret, or fear. The present—leached of color, dulled a little—became manageable. She needed that. She needed things not to be sharp or bright.

He sleeps so deeply on the Valium that his snoring keeps her up, and wakes her early the next morning. In the living room, she tries to read. She brings *Running & Being* to the sofa and dips into the "Healing" chapter. *I am a runner-doctor with a defective constitution.* She finds nothing helpful. *At one time or another, something in every section of me has gone awry.*

Could she have done a better job protecting Dad from Dad? He's worse off now than he'd have been without his hopes up. He never takes illness and injury as helpful messages, the body hinting *Easy there, you've bitten off more than you can chew.* To him they're little mutinies, his own cells betraying him. This never fails to put him in an existential funk.

She's restless. Has she let herself believe that the marathon would root him here somehow, make him *of Boston*, blur away the Philippines and all the races he can't run there? Outside the window, dawn—earlier and earlier with each day—has bathed Comm Ave in a shy light. In their bedroom, he's still snoring. Quietly she finds the knit cap, gloves, and track jacket in his drawer. Downstairs, she laces up her shoes.

What's gotten into her? Last year, Popsy brought home Jane Fonda's book and videotape, along with spandex leggings and sports bras, for the girls to follow. Popsy and Kit lasted a few more minutes than Bitbit and the old girl, who collapsed almost immediately in giggles on the living room floor, and Toyang, who passed on the activity altogether. The most the old girl's ever exercised is dodgeball, hula hoops—games that no one plays outside the school yard.

Kit

Kit and the old girl argue now and then about why she can wear gold studs but nothing dangling from her earlobes, why she cannot grow or paint her nails, why lip gloss is fine sometimes but never lipstick. Her birthday and Christmas wish lists are written in an alien preteen code the old girl can't always decipher. *Hair crimper. Caboodles.* Kit's the one the old girl thinks might have been better off in Manila, under the nuns: she's always spent too much time in front of mirrors, but now she doesn't even care if you walk in on her. She'll smile and primp and pose as if you're not there. She's always been a ham, and talked about being an actress, but now she stars in school plays and tries to master every accent. *Quinzee Mahket,* the old girl hears her enunciate from the bathroom. *Brawd stripes, bright stahs.*

The Bug

She tried to talk him out of running, back in 1978, when the President announced new parliament elections and let her husband campaign from his cell. *He thinks I don't have the stones to take him up on it. Ha! You can take the man out of politics . . .* The old girl said she was worried about his health, and about palace shenanigans. In truth, he'd been out of the game so long. Losing this race, she felt, might crush her husband even more than health issues, or anything the President might do. As usual, though, his "idea" was already a decision; he was asking not for opinions but for help. So she campaigned hard, and liked it. She liked the name of his new party, LABAN, which meant "to fight" and stood for *Lakas ng Bayan,* "People Power": hopeful and aggressive, smart and macho all at once. She liked the gallantry that poor villagers showed her: tricycle rides from one stump to the next; umbrellas or, in a pinch, plastic bags to shield her from the rain; a hundred hand fans flapping to dry off her wet dress. She liked the noise that people made, at an appointed time, all the way from Taft Avenue to the Diliman campus: whistles and car horns and church bells making a ruckus till dawn. The old girl understood a little more—she who had never touched a serious drug in her life, who enjoyed solitude and craved quiet: the high of gathering and getting loud together, making a righteous kind of trouble.

And so it was the old girl, longtime realist to his idealist, who never was so shocked as he could be when people did him wrong—it was *she* who had to be consoled, when the palace-appointed ballot counters announced the tally, and the President, in the thirteenth year of his term, announced that his New Society had swept the vote again.

"Oh, Mommy," said her husband, "you of all people didn't expect 'free and fair,' did you?" How stupid she felt then! Even *he*'d seen it coming. "You've caught the bug, Mommy! Only took you twenty-four years." He found it cute—kissing her temples, jaw, and collarbone, on down to more.

The old girl's husband likes to say that if she ever ran against him for office, he wouldn't stand a chance. "First off, *she's* the rich one," he'll say, with a thumb in her direction. (That's how he'd always defended himself, as well, against those "man of the people" opponents who called him a rich wolf in tattered shearling. *You've got me mixed up with my wife, and if you think I hold those purse strings, you're more confused than I thought.*) He has said things like this in the parlor, while she pours him coffee and passes the tray.

No one, in their marriage, can be called rich now. Between lawyers and doctors and houses and five tuitions, they don't, as a twosome, have much beyond what the old girl's parents set aside for them, which anyway no one will see until her parents die.

Also, she's the smart one. People laugh at that, before they catch themselves. How could the quiet one be smarter than the genius who can mouth off on a book after skimming its first page?

"And she'd get more from the White House," he says. "She's more cosmopolitan than I am. She's practically American."

On their twenty-fifth wedding anniversary—silver ice buckets, silver picture frames, silver candlesticks—he'd pressed a note into the old girl's palm, written on a torn-out page of his prison Bible. *Your eminence, only you can lead our exodus through the desert.*

The old girl almost dropped it, like a burning torch. In his cell, during their visits, he'd started talking in a fuzzy way about letting go of his presidential dreams. "Don't want to turn into some Filipino Ahab, obsessed with spearing Malacañang Palace," he said, and the old girl wondered if he'd really read all of *Moby-Dick* in jail. "It's not the only way to help people, is it?"

"Of course not," said the old girl, trying not to sound too excited.

You loved being a reporter.

You loved running my father's hacienda.

Maybe you'll publish this book, and travel the world to talk about it.

Then, during the luncheon (no doves this time), when the band and dancing started, he said, "Did you give it to him?"

"What? To whom?"

"The note. The one I asked you to give the cardinal."

Relief. Embarrassment. The old girl started laughing.

Mommy, what did you think?

She'd caught the bug, and now her head was too big to fit inside the church door.

"Don't you worry, Dad. The cardinal will get your note!" The old girl dropped her head against his shoulder for the rest of the song. It was "Earth Angel."

Glory

By Easter Sunday, the old girl's husband still can't jog more than a few blocks without wincing. *This isn't good, Mommy.* The old girl senses his self-doubt, but keeps a poker face. At times like this, it's crucial not to spook him with overenthusiasm. She must be careful as a bike rider on a steep downhill. No sudden movements. A few things she could say:

You've trained so hard. (Who cares if this is true?) *No one can take that away from you. We're proud of you already.*

The rest of us eat better now, and get some exercise ourselves.

Bitbit and I have planned the best marathon-viewing party in Manilachusetts. Maybe on our balcony you'll get inspired for next year.

"Whatever you decide," she says instead, "I'm here to help."

And so her husband strikes a compromise. He rounds up four colleagues—casual joggers his age—to band together, under Tim Brown's name, and run the race relay-style with him.

Well, it's something. It's not quitting, but it'll be easier on his heart and on the old girl.

He has just one request of his new team. He wants the leg in Newton, at Mile 20.

"My family lives right there," the old girl hears him saying on the phone. "Spitting distance. They'll want to see me from our balcony."

Then: "If things get rough for me, I'll need to be close to home for moral support, or worse—to have somewhere to be laid up."

His Harvard colleagues must be smart enough to see it. Her husband wants that last incline in Newton known as Heartbreak Hill, and then the finish line. He wants the glory.

As Kit says, "Hahtbreak Hill, Dad? That's hahd coah."

"You're all invited here after the race," the old girl hears him saying. "My wife will cook enough to feed a whole Olympic village."

In Brookline that evening, the old girl buys a potted laurel tree. Bitbit will use its leaves to string together a garland to hang around his neck, and a crown.

Speaking Engagements

He never mentions Atatürk anymore, or Syngman Rhee, or Singapore's Prime Minister Lee Kuan Yew. Strongmen, who he once believed could do great things in a poor country so long as people had more to eat than they remembered having before. But in America, he knows, that dog won't hunt. Now he's shelved all dictators, like action figures he's outgrown. When he brings up Franco, and Juan Perón, and the shah, it's in cautionary tales: men on the wrong side of history, bad bets.

This shift began in jail, of course. He read Thoreau in his cell. He read Gandhi's *Satyagraha in South Africa*. Since the film came out he's been watching Ben Kingsley on repeat, laying himself down before the police horses.

She sits in most of these audiences, clapping along, telepathically feeding him lines from the speeches she typed. The man who once confessed a soft spot for Sun Tzu, now *a champion of nonviolent resistance*. The man who once quoted *The Prince* by heart, now *the inspiration to all freedom-loving people of the world*. The man who made no secret of his plan, in 1969, to style himself as the President's loudest critic (*hit him hard when and wherever I can; the only way to keep my name in print till I can run against him*), now the man at the podium claiming no ambition greater than to fight for his beloved Filipinos even if it ruins him.

How much he loves the Filipinos—that part is not a line, not a lie. He loves them all: poor or vulgar, greedy or corrupt. He loves the death-row inmates at the New Bilibid Prison, the prostitutes in Ermita with their tragic teeth, the karaoke gangsters who start knife fights over songs they've claimed as their exclusive turf. "You've got to hand it to them," the old girl's husband will say, about pickpockets in Makati who can slit a purse seam silently, or snatch a pair of earrings that the owner won't miss until her bleeding earlobes itch, "they're nothing if not good at what they do."

He even smiles, sometimes, about the First Lady, who's visited him in the States, once at the old girl's house. *She went on and on about how much the Reagans love her, how she put the Philippines on the map. Well, I can't argue with that.* He keeps a gold cross the First Lady gave him before he left Manila, emblem of the cozy and unwholesome bond between them. He shakes his head over the President's latest convoluted proclamation. *But he does get people to believe this legalistic mumbo jumbo, doesn't he?* As if they were two unruly children run amok in Malacañang Palace—*minds of their own; what can you do?*—not powers that be who jailed him for eight years.

At times he sounds less like a hero than like a long-suffering wife: the Philippines might be this or that, but the Philippines can't help it. And neither can he: the Philippines is his.

Before the audience leaves, the moderators of these speeches almost always point the old girl out. *They say behind every great man,* and all that. She stands and bows and smiles and waves.

Proposal

When they pick up his bib—the one thing she can't do without him—it's pep talk time.

"Spring's right around the corner," says the old girl. Copley Square glitters, still slushy from the last storm. "These trees will start turning for you by race day."

"Once you turn onto Boylston, you'll have a few blocks to go—that's it! The kids will all be at the finish, waiting for you, calling you their hero." The old girl's even giving herself chills.

"Bitbit's already sewn the letters on your shirt. Strangers will be chanting your name."

Her husband smiles a gloomy smile. "They'll probably mispronounce it."

"So?" They stand above the barren, icy ditch—a babbling fountain in the summertime. "You'll know who they're talking about."

He says nothing.

"Right here you'll get your medal. Popsy's going to take the pictures—not that any of us will ever forget it. Imagine the people back home. 'Harvard *na,* marathon *pa!*' they'll say."

The old girl's husband shakes his head. "I'm thinking I should not run at all."

"Why would you say that?"

"You were right. I'm no spring chicken anymore. A little arrogant to think I could just take this up."

She never said that. After twenty-eight years, it seems, she didn't have to.

"You're not so old," the old girl says, not wanting to discourage him from a dream by now she's bought into. *You've caught the bug!*

"Training takes up too much time," he's saying. "We have more important things to think about right now."

Inside, she feels herself adjusting, one more time. *Don't worry, Dad. We'll still watch from our balcony. Better for your foot to heal.* So he took the long way around to her point of view: so what?

The bronze statue of Copley, with his palette and paintbrushes; the church behind them; and the tint of the dusk sky take her back, all of a sudden, to Manila. Another walk after another dinner with their families—their early dates, if you could call them dates, had mostly been just that. Around this time of day, on one walk, they sat beneath the statue of Rajah Sulayman, with the church behind them and Manila Bay before. He simply asked, "How do you feel about October?" Counting on assumptions that had already passed between them. And she said, "As long as it's not *late* October, too close to All Souls' Day. When death is on people's minds."

"Things are bad back home," her husband says now. "Maybe worse since martial law was, quote-unquote, 'lifted.' More debt, more deaths . . ."

She doesn't mean to tune out, let her mind wander, but as he goes on about successors and juntas and the President's dialysis machine, she can't help it. She's wondering which of his colleagues will jockey for the Heartbreak Hill spot now. She's remembering the year she left New York for good, for Manila— daydreaming, as her law professors droned about property taxes and civil procedure, of the American future she'd forfeited. *It's morning in New York,* she'd think. Mary Ann's alarm clock would be going off; the old girl would be boiling coffee for the both of them. Her not-yet husband, back from Korea, teased her about having an American accent. Come to think of it, he always brought up America jealously. *I don't suppose that's a problem in America,* he said, about the stench wafting from the bay toward Malate Church. As if America were some rival suitor. And in a way, it was. When he asked, "How about October?" she didn't hesitate over some other man she'd rather marry, but flashed instead to New York in the fall, its leaves on fire, and the bachelorette rent she had planned to split with Mary Ann. A life of purer solitude than she has known: she could have been (and happily) the spinster teacher, the aging nun. Back then not every bride-to-be in Manila wore a ring, but he produced one, saying that after so much time in America he thought she'd expect it. She's remembering he had to place it on her pinkie finger— that's how small he thought she was. She's thinking how a marathon is like a marriage: the long haul, the ups and downs, the tests of endurance and faith, the humbling, undiscovered country. Even entering with eyes wide open (and who, of everyone she's known, has ever been more pragmatic than the old girl?) guaranteed nothing, only injuries you couldn't predict, potholes and pitfalls and dark hours no sane person would sign up for willingly.

When she tunes back in, he's still talking. "If I really thought the opposition could get it together by May, on their own, that'd be one thing."

She stares at Copley Square's ash-colored slush, dripping lampposts, ice-glazed trees.

"This is what deserves my energy, and all my focus, now. I'm going back, Mommy."

She doesn't feel it as a gut punch, not really. She can't be too surprised. No one who knows him can honestly imagine he'd be happy here forever, at chalkboards and podiums, in a tweed jacket and suede elbow patches. So why is she struggling, a bit, to breathe? *Old girl, you idiot.* She met him almost half a century ago, and still she hasn't learned.

Finish

Four months later, the old girl wants a word—sometimes she finds them, in German or Japanese, words that capture something Tagalog and English don't—for *preemptive* nostalgia. She's longed for this life in Boston all three of the years she's been living it. This town, this house, this bed where they wake early on the morning of his flight out of Logan Airport.

"Mommy," the old girl's husband says, "what's going to happen?"

But he knows what. At best, no sooner will he touch down

in Manila than he'll be cuffed and sent back to prison, for who knows how long.

At worst—well, he's been talking about that for as long as they've been married, as long as he's been in the public service.

They can't shoot me; they're afraid to make a hero of me. He has said that.

Then, in the same breath: *Who would Rizal be without the firing squad? Just a brown man in coattails and a bowler hat, homesick in Madrid, yakking away about revolution this and independence that. I don't want to be another sad, ranting, exiled old-timer.*

It's not a crystal ball he wants—just a little reassurance.

"You're going to get on that plane," says the old girl, "and we're going to follow you."

A Contract Overseas

When I was in high school, long ago, my brother Andoy used to drop me off and pick me up from campus in a Cadillac. It wasn't his, of course, any more than the rented uniform I wore was mine. And certainly we weren't fooling anyone: not the neighbors in our *barangay,* not the nuns who'd given me a scholarship to their convent school in San Lorenzo. The car belonged to the family my brother worked for, as a live-in chauffeur. Each morning, Andoy woke before they did, put on his gloves and trousers in the dark, and drove from the suburbs to the slums to collect me. He'd already be muddling through traffic on EDSA Boulevard by the time I rose and got into my own X-shaped necktie and schoolgirl pleats.

Our mother was the one who washed and starched and pressed my uniform each night, as if that would fool the sugar heiresses and Senate daughters at my school into mistaking me for one of their own. Andoy knew better. Every morning, in the car, he gave me money for the school canteen and ate the bag lunch our mother had packed. He paid the dentist who filled my cavities and the orthodontist who straightened my teeth. On weekends we saw movies or played records on our father's old phonograph, so when my classmates squealed over Leif Garrett or the Osmond Brothers, I'd know enough to squeal along.

I graduated in 1976, the same year that Andoy was fired from his driving job. His employer's daughter, Ligaya, had just turned eighteen, and she and Andoy had been caught "celebrating" her birthday in the backseat of her father's car. With Andoy unemployed and my mother scraping to feed us, I couldn't go straight to college, even with a scholarship. We both spent the next twelve months mopping floors and stocking shelves to scare up rent and some tuition. I didn't see an end in sight till Andoy told me, in May of 1977, that he'd found a better job.

"This time I want an Eldorado convertible," I said. We'd just stepped off the jeepney on Salapi Road, whose pavement ended half a mile or so before our *barangay* began. Along with his old job, of course, we'd lost our access to the Cadillac. It depressed me to be riding jeepneys again, sardined thigh to thigh with strangers in a steel caravan painted up in circus colors, sometimes so crowded that brave young boys sat on the roof or hung on to the jeepney's sides, the plastic-tarp "windows" flapping against them. After air-conditioning and leather seats, music from a cassette player, and my brother for a white-gloved chauffeur, it felt uncivilized to me to pass warm coins and damp bills forward to the driver, who even when we shouted *para!* sometimes barely slowed enough to let us jump from the doorless rear exit.

So I was thrilled to hear another family had hired him. "Where?" I asked, imagining another garage, another suburb of Manila. The aftermud of a typhoon sucked at our shoes as we walked home.

He said, "Saudi Arabia."

I took this as a joke. "Now *that's* a uniform," I said. Peter O'Toole on a camel, in white robes and a head rope, was pretty much my whole idea of the Middle East.

"I'm serious." He slowed his steps along the creek that flowed through our *barangay*. We called it that: the Creek. In fact it was an open sewage canal, wide enough to fit a pedicab and five or so feet deep, bringing the runoff from our houses through the next village and into the San Juan River. We threw our garbage in the Creek. We joked about what else wound up in there: unlucky cats lured by the fish-bone smell, tainted syringes, worse. No

threat could crush a child's tantrum faster than holding a toy—
or, better yet, the squalling brat herself—above the Creek. After
a flood, eggshells and beer-can tabs and bottle shards clung to
the Creek's banks, as if even trash hoped to escape. But the
Creek did serve a purpose, outside of waste disposal: with everyone holding their breath and hustling past the stench as fast as
they could, it was the one place in the *barangay* to have a private
conversation.

"You're gonna be a college girl," said Andoy. "The textbooks
will be heavier, and so will the tuition." Driving taxis and limou-
sines in Riyadh, he said, would pay him six times what he earned
in Manila. He'd recoup his airfare and work visa fees in time,
with some left over to send us, and save up for the driving school
for rich expats he'd open when he returned home for good.

"But I'll apply for scholarships," I said, panicking at the
thought of Manila without my brother in it. "A year from now, I'll
have enough to start part-time. If I can find a job in the library
and cafeteria—and tutor, too, at night—"

"And study when?" He laughed, exposing a hole near the
back of his mouth that still startled me. Years before, Andoy's
two right upper molars had rotted and fallen out. "Promise me
you'll take just one job, and save the wages for pocket money. Bus
fare, if you want."

We didn't talk about his other reasons. Along with my textbooks and tuition, Andoy's girlfriend, Ligaya, would be growing
heavier too. She was already nineteen weeks heavier, to be exact,
with Andoy's twins.

"What exactly will you do in Saudi?" I asked.

"I told you—same as here," said Andoy, "but for Arabs. Rich
ones."

"But what will *you* do," I said, pointing at him, "in a place
like Saudi?" This was still a few years before everybody's father,
uncle, nephew, son began to leave the Philippines for the Middle
East, but already we'd heard stories, from the earliest recruits:

men who'd gone to jail for looking at a woman the wrong way, unmarried sweethearts who couldn't walk side by side in public, secret sex rooms that charged by the hour and were routinely raided by the police. Here in Manila, the decade of halter tops and hot pants suited Andoy just fine. The night before, he'd nuzzled up to Ligaya and caught her shoulder straps between his teeth. "Spaghetti for dinner," Andoy said, "my favorite." How would he get by in a country where women veiled themselves from head to toe in black?

"I'm going to be a father now," he said. "Saudi's the best place for me."

Before Ligaya, there was Rose; before Rose, there were Vangie, Monica, and Teresita. "She's the one," Andoy would declare each time, clutching his chest as if Cupid had hit the bull's-eye. He knelt at their windows with our father's guitar, crooning till the neighbors complained. *I offer you no wealth or high ambition,* went one of his favorite Tagalog ballads, *beyond the promise of my everlasting love.*

"You sang that to Rose," I said, after one serenade. "And to Vangie, and Aurora, and Belen."

Andoy laughed, flashing that gap behind his teeth—the one flaw, people said, in his otherwise good looks. Looks he'd reportedly inherited from our father, along with the musical gift that had him strumming those *kundiman* by ear. "You'll understand," he told me, "when you fall in love."

That closed the discussion. Love was unknown territory to me: I couldn't challenge him on it any more than I could question what he said about our father, who had taken off for good before my birth; or what our mother told us of life in Manila during the war. I had to take them at their word.

"She puts the sun to shame," he'd say. "I looked at her and every part of me was ringing."

Even more than beauty, what really made my brother weak was danger, obstacles—the chance to break a rule or cross a line or overcome some hideous odds for love. Vangie had a boyfriend. Aurora was engaged. His best friend already had an eye on Rose. Teresita was a decade and a half his senior; Belen lived in another province.

"I can't have her and I *have* to have her," he'd said most recently, after falling for the boss's daughter.

I said, "You've been listening to too many *radionovelas* with Ma."

In convent school I'd known a few girls like Ligaya, girls whose parents had some money but didn't quite play golf in Forbes Park. (Her father owned some fancy cars, as Andoy put it, but his wife was always on his case to sell one.) Ligaya was stunning, even by my brother's standards: rosy and pouty, long and slim but round where it counted, with skin like a steamed pork bun. Pregnancy seemed only to exaggerate those looks. Her hair had grown, with mermaid luster, to her waist. Even her growing belly didn't so much mar her figure as match it, curve for curve. This new look, of course, appalled Ligaya's parents, who had thought that firing Andoy would put an end to the affair. Seeing, in the flesh, how much she'd disobeyed them left them no choice but to kick her out.

So Ligaya came to live with us. When she arrived, with her matching crocodile trunk and train case, she burst into tears. "It's a swamp," she sobbed. "I'm going to live in a swamp."

It *was* a swamp; we didn't need Ligaya to tell us that. Every day my mother washed what clothes we owned and hung them from the banister to dry. Water trickling from the sleeves and hems kept the floor wet. Steam issued from the iron my mother used on the dried clothes, and from the rice she cooked at lunch and dinner, and from the pots of water that we boiled when it flowed brown or orange from our faucets. All that moisture gave the house a smell, so constant we'd forgotten it, of mold.

Nine years before, a "slum upgrade" had turned the scrap shacks of our *barangay* into two-story homes, one room below and one above. We had electricity and plumbing now, concrete blocks instead of tin-and-plywood walls, furniture and some appliances, a bathroom with a faucet and flush toilet at the foot of the stairs. Since then the First Lady, who'd led this initiative herself, had moved on to concert halls and galleries. The crown jewel of the planned upgrade—a concrete promenade to cover up the open Creek—never materialized. And like all the neighbors' houses, ours deteriorated faster than it had improved. Rust had spread its scabs over the bathroom floor and walls. The vent built into the wall above the kitchenette to air out cooking smells became a nest for rats, who chewed through the wire mesh and made a racket with their shrieking every night.

We did feel sorry enough to give Ligaya the upstairs room. Having shared the bed there for nine years, my mother and I moved to the sofa and a straw mat on the ground floor. After she had settled in, Ligaya told us "too much up-and-down" could harm the twins. This meant that someone had to bring her meals upstairs to her and bus the dishes after. And *someone* was my mother. Ligaya saw her as a slave, which enraged me. (I must have felt I was the only one who had the right to treat my mother like a slave.) Ligaya couldn't quite adjust to life without a gardener, a housemaid, or a nanny (not to mention a chauffeur). Of course, she didn't feel that climbing up and down the stairs to walk outside, take the jeepney to Makati, and visit all the shops she could no longer afford to patronize, like a mourner visiting a grave, would harm the twins.

As for my mother, she was too used to taking orders to push back, at least not right away. For six years now, ever since the trouser factory where she once worked had closed, she'd been calling herself a traveling seamstress, making "house calls" after church each morning in some nearby, nicer towns. But most houses there had help already. If she didn't happen on a garden party or a child-care crisis that could use an extra hand right then and there, the best she could hope for was a guilt-plagued housewife who could give her pity money. When I was thirteen, still accompanying her on these rounds, I saw people draw their shades as we approached, my mother's sewing basket of no more use to them than a bundle on some hobo's stick.

After that, I had a terror of becoming her, the multipurpose servant a few lucky scraps away from living on the street. I refused to serve Ligaya hand and foot. At the same time, I remembered enough from the jungle kingdom of high school not to fight with someone like Ligaya and insist she pull her weight. Instead, watching them both while I did homework on the sofa, I pretended they were strangers, who had little to do with me. I imagined I was a reporter on assignment, paid to watch and cover subjects in a house that wasn't mine. *Servant work has turned,* I scribbled in a notebook, looking at my mother, *from what she once did for a living to who she is for life.* I had no doubt that both my living and my life would be different. *She holds a grudge against the world,* I wrote of Ligaya, *for defaulting on its promises to beautiful women.* It didn't occur to me that I'd been counting on similar promises, made to smart girls who studied hard.

In Riyadh, my brother shared a flat with nine men—Filipino gardeners or servants or drivers like him, or men helping to build the pipeline from Saudi's oil wells to refineries offshore. The desert sun tanned him in no time, as it had his friends. *We all could pass for Moros now,* he wrote home, on an aerogram as thin as onionskin.

When he called for the first time, from a pay phone in a downtown hotel, I told him that I liked having a sister for a change. "Why didn't we think of replacing you sooner?" I'd never lied this way for anybody's sake before. I must have wanted him to feel, five thousand miles away, that he was working toward a good cause. *School,* I wrote, because I knew he'd eat it up, *has it all over the real world.*

I'd started college that June. When I arrived on campus, among freshmen who had come at sixteen and would leave by twenty, I felt of a different species altogether: *discipula laboranda plebeia,* the ancient, part-time scholarship girl. I was only one year older, but would age faster than them still, paying *tingi* or "retail"-style for a few credits each semester, the way my mother bought garlic by the clove or shampoo by the foil sachet. My classmates didn't look down on me so much as fail to see me altogether, as I stamped their books and served their lunches, as constant and inconsequential to their landscape as the statue in front of their student union.

This life-size, concrete man on a pedestal was supposed to be a Katipunero, or rebel from the 1896 uprising against Spain. He held a red flag in his right hand and a *bolo* knife in his left, his open mouth a cry to arms. But I saw him more as a security guard: watching for intruders, waving his *bolo* to keep girls like me out of the student union, that exclusive realm of monthly club dues and "activities" that didn't earn a grade or paycheck.

My partial scholarship was in journalism. I'd never cared for newspapers, but I disliked children and sick people even more. (Teaching and nursing were my other scholarship options.) It had been five years since the President declared martial law, and rules had been cemented about who could print what, and where. One famous editor had said that finding decent Filipino reporters was easier in prison or abroad than in a newsroom in Manila. (No one heard from him again.) But I cared less about press freedom than I cared about myself. If media posts kept opening whenever "real" journalists offended Marcos, that left more for me. I would have followed any marching orders that led out of the *barangay*.

Of course, I knew enough to keep these bleak and bitter motives to myself.

Two months after my brother left, a man came to our door in denim (not just jeans, but a vest and jacket too) and gold-framed aviator glasses. His hair was like a soldier's: short, cropped close enough to show his scalp; his tennis shoes and T-shirt so white they hurt my eyes.

"Your *carabao*," he called himself: our water buffalo, our beast of burden. His skin was not quite *carabao*-dark, but close. And rather than a plow or produce cart, he'd brought a woven straw box full of envelopes from men he knew in Saudi. "Something smells delicious, Tita," he told my mother. She plated up some rice and fish for him.

He told us his name and parents' province, what job had brought him to Saudi and how long ago. My mother fixed her eyes on him, as if by staring deep enough she'd locate Andoy there. "We have good times, considering," he said. His shared flat in Riyadh, for instance, overlooked the public plaza known as Chop Chop Square. "Who needs TV when you've got ringside tickets to that?" He raised his arms to show us how the executioner would wield his sword over the accused. We must have cringed; he cut the demonstration short. He cleared his throat and left it at "You know Pinoys. Easily entertained." He reached into his neckband to reveal a gold cross on a chain, purchased in secret from an Indian dealer. "It's a crime to wear it there," he said, stroking his neck as if thinking of Chop Chop Square again. "But I feel safer with it on than not." He tucked it back into his shirt.

Ligaya glowed around him, a sudden charming hostess. "I'd offer you some San Miguel," she said, "if we had any. You miss the taste, I bet." His visit was the most time I had seen her spend downstairs with us. She even smiled and thanked my mother for the food.

I puffed up too, made jokes to get my own kind of attention. "Make sure my brother knows that *beer* is all she meant," I said, "when she offered you what you can't get in Saudi." He laughed.

Before leaving, the *carabao* gave us Andoy's envelope. He didn't blink when I turned from the table to count what was inside it. He must have hoped, when it was his turn to send money home, that his own wife or sister would do the same. Standing from the meal, he rubbed his stomach. "I'll need two seats on my flight back to Saudi," he joked, "if everyone I see today feeds me like this."

After that, they came every two months, on leave between their own contracts. They worked with Andoy or lived with him; they had socialized at parties in the workers' village or worshiped together at a secret Mass held in a basement. Each time, my mother set a place at the table; Ligaya glowed and flirted; I joked around and counted money; the *carabao* ate and told stories and complained, before leaving, about needing two plane seats for his return to Saudi. Each time they wore the uniform I came to call the Saudi suit: the aviators, the white T-shirt and spotless sneakers, the gull-shaped Levi's stitch on their back pockets as they turned toward their next delivery. Ray-Ban, Adidas, Jockey—"Stateside" brands, about as far from Peter O'Toole's *thob* and head rope as I could have imagined. They even smelled the same: like cigarette smoke and crumpled cash. Through them, Andoy remitted half his pay to us, while he lived on a quarter and saved the rest for his return.

Ligaya gave birth in September. Standing in for my brother, I stared at her flushed and puffy face; her plastic cap and sweat-soaked gown; her swollen ankles as they thrashed against steel stirrups that, in my eyes, might as well have had a ball and chain and gang of fellow prisoners attached. I pitied her, and every woman in the ward that day—not just the wailing ones in labor but the nurses at their service and the twin girls who emerged, all smeared in blood and fury, from between Ligaya's legs.

My mother's hope—that babies would smooth out Ligaya's nature; that nursing, cradling, bathing, and swaddling them would calm their mother, too—turned out to be in vain. Ligaya had a new and longer catalog of gripes now. "They refuse to drink," she sobbed, jamming the bottles to their infant mouths. She mourned the changes they had wreaked upon her figure. "They're here to stay," she wailed, in underwear, tracing the stretch marks on her waist and hips.

The twins inherited Ligaya's lungs and her talent for misery. They screamed whether we put them down or picked them up, whether we spoke to or sang to or ignored them. Illness and infections plagued them: thrush, clogged noses, pinkeye, diarrhea. I chased their mucus and secretions, wiping noses, backsides; wetting washcloths to dislodge dried crusts. "This is *Sisyphean*," I said, kneeling to scrub the floor or furniture. As if anyone understood. As if my fancy new college-speak could elevate me from the muck.

In May, another *carabao* with dark skin, military hair, aviators, and denim came to our door. Our mother was boiling rice at the stove. "Save some for me," the *carabao* called through the screen; and there was no mistaking Andoy's voice.

I ran to him, the textbook falling from my lap, and Andoy dropped his suitcases. "You reek like a *carabao*, too," I said, my cheek against the smoke-and-money smell of his shoulder.

Our mother couldn't speak. She touched his face, confirming him the way a blind man would. "It's gone," she finally said, when her fingers reached his hair.

Ligaya played indifferent, unlidding the rice and cooing to her babies. When she turned, she held them out like puppets.

241

"We're not supposed to talk to strangers," she squeaked for them. *"Who are you?"*

Andoy grinned. His daughters, who had fussed and squirmed all day, blinked silently at him, docile as dolls. "I'll show you who I am," he said, taking them into his right arm and winging his left around Ligaya. With a dip, he planted the kind of kiss on her I'd seen in pictures of American victory parades after the war.

"Idiot!" Ligaya yelped, smiling.

He'd brought gifts home from Saudi: gold earrings for Ligaya and the twins, a rug for the upstairs room, a brass coffeepot with a swan-shaped spout. But more came after. From the electronic bazaar in Quiapo, he bought me a digital wristwatch and a typewriter with its own carrying case. Between deliveries to other families of *carabao*, he found my mother an electric cooker that could steam rice without her supervision. By the weekend, we had a color TV set. Neighbors came to watch *John and Marsha* on our sofa. Our mother made *adobo* and pineapple ham, while Ligaya served up the San Miguel and Johnnie Walker Black she'd always wanted to offer the other *carabao*.

Afterward, Andoy and I walked out to dump the chicken bones and paper plates into the Creek. "Do all the *carabao* party like this when they come home?" I said. "What will you have left?"

"Left for what? What am I working for if not my girls?" He put an arm around my shoulder and lowered his voice. "Actually, I've been meaning to tell you something."

The last time I'd heard him whisper, in this keyed-up and conspiring way, it was to tell me he had fallen for Ligaya. "You can't be serious. In *Saudi*?" I groaned. "You're a father now, you said yourself!"

"Not that!" He laughed. "Although you could say I got lucky."

He'd driven, many times, a man named Abdul Ghaffar Al-Thunayan from the airport to his palace in Al Nasiriyah. When his limousine broke down one day, with Al-Thunayan in the back, Andoy was worried. Al-Thunayan, who sat on the Ministry of Oil and had ties to the royal House of Saud, was an important customer. Displeasing him would not go over well with Andoy's boss. But Andoy peeked under the limo's hood, tightened the battery cables, and fiddled with the spark plugs till the engine purred again.

His passenger took notice. "I have great passion for cars," Al-Thunayan said, as Andoy dropped him off. "I like my Corniche convertible, but Maserati is also excellent."

A week later Andoy's boss told him he was free. Al-Thunayan had bought him out of his driving contract and moved him west, into the servants' wing of his mansion in Jeddah. My brother took over for a retiring Indian chauffeur, but he would also occupy a new post, as personal custodian of Al-Thunayan's luxury car collection.

Needless to say, he would be earning more. "Enough for you to go full-time," said Andoy. "No more *tingi*-style education. Have fun, be a college kid, get involved in some campus life, all right? That's an order."

How my brother knew from *full-time student* and *campus life*—things I'd barely dreamed about myself—I had no clue.

When we got back inside, he chased Ligaya up the stairs. She giggled as they closed the door, and then the phonograph drowned out their voices. The twin I carried stopped her gurgling long enough to smile at me. Her sister fell asleep in my mother's lap. This kind of peace seemed possible in our house, the month Andoy was home.

In June, I quit my cafeteria job and gave up all but two shifts at the library. These were the new terms of what my brother called the Abdul Ghaffar Al-Thunayan Scholarship. I flailed, that first day of the semester, at doing as the campus natives did: their slow and easy amble through the grass was harder than it looked, and sitting on the quad, against a tree, made my spine ache. I went and studied them from a bench instead. A boy, reading the campus daily newspaper on the other end of the bench, reached across to clamp his hand on my knee. I froze in fear. *This must be flirting,* I thought, despairing that only "college kids" who lived the "campus life" knew how to handle it.

The boy just smiled, pointing his chin at my knee. My leg had been bouncing nervously against the bench since I'd sat down. "Sorry," I said. He nodded and went back to reading. I was too embarrassed to move again till after he stood, leaving his paper behind.

I picked it up, scanning headlines about an Independence Day earthquake, the ongoing trial of former Senator Aquino, a teenage housemaid named Rosy Lacaba. The second page contained instructions, below the masthead, for prospective student reporters.

Why hadn't I thought of it before? The perfect solution—a necessary notch on my résumé that still fulfilled Andoy's mandate for Life Outside the Classroom.

The next day, per instructions, I brought a steno notebook and ballpoint pen to the campus daily's headquarters, on the fourth floor of the student union. *Don't blame me,* I thought, looking up as I passed the Katipunero on his pedestal. *This wasn't my idea.*

But Room 401 was locked. I checked the paper again, not knowing yet what I'd later find out: that its editors and reporters no longer met in the student union, that they had gone underground after running afoul of both the university chancellor and the national Office of the Press Secretary too many times. I didn't know the paper met in secret now, in the off-campus apartments of its alumni, who believed that any savvy would-be journalist should easily sniff out as much.

I did hear voices, though, and followed them to the other end of the hall. There, under a cloud of smoke, twelve boys were sitting on the floor, around a braided rug. They seemed dressed for some other time and climate, in plaid wool pants, velvet jack-

ets with large buttons and thick piping, floppy printed cravats.
A podium in the corner held a plaster bust of José Rizal; in the
opposite corner, a second podium held a thick unabridged dictio-
nary, open to the middle.

"If I wanted to eat chop suey, I'd go to Señor Woo's," said one
boy in a top hat, flinging a typed manuscript onto the floor. "It'd
be more satisfying, too. Is this a story? Is it enough to take old
sermons and pop songs, comic books and teaching manuals, and
call it a story?"

Another boy held up his hand, in its fraying fingerless glove.
"What other way is there to write about this country?" he replied.
"Three hundred years under Spain, via Acapulco. Thirty years
under the Americans and three under the Japanese. A history
of fragments and confusion—'chop suey' is the only style that
captures it."

A third boy argued one could write *about* confusion without
actually *confusing* the reader. A fourth insisted that old standards of clarity in prose no longer had relevance to how we live
today. "Is that what fiction's after, then—real life today?" said a
fifth. "That's not why *I* read stories. If I just wanted facts shoved
in my face, I'd go and read the campus paper."

By now I knew I'd come to the wrong place and backed away.
A shrill bell rang, and a sixth boy pulled a brass chain from the
pocket of his tweed jacket. "We're out of time," he said.

They were still split down the middle: six of them for publish-
ing the story, six against. A rolled-up manuscript was tossed in
my direction, and all twelve faces turned. "What do *you* think?"
asked the timekeeper, looking at me as he shut off the alarm and
wound the dial.

Now that they had seen me, I was too proud to retreat. As
far out of my depth as I was, I stooped to skim the first few
pages at my feet, which took me on a kind of romp—through
artifacts and documents that stood, it seemed, for the history of
the Philippines. Lines translated from a Spanish *zarzuela*. Menu

items, such as stewed prunes and "college pudding," served on the 1901 USS *Thomas* voyage from San Francisco to Manila Bay. I couldn't tell if these fragments were real or fabricated, or some combination of both. The author, whose name was blacked out in the top-left corner with a marker, had what I could only call a casual relationship with grammar, chronology, punctuation, historical accuracy, and most other courtesies a reader might expect.

I didn't care much for the story, but I had the urge to mimic them, these boys, adopt their earnest style of arguing the way I'd tried to sit and walk the campus like a full-timer. "It *is* a mess," I told them, "but what's wrong with that? Whoever wrote this took away the narrator and left some room for me. I'm not a child. Why hand the story to me on a platter? Why shouldn't it be up to us to piece together our own history?"

With that, somehow, I passed. The tie was broken, and the boys moved aside to make space for me. We spent a half hour on each of three remaining stories, the seconds ticking like a toy heart in the tweed pocket of the boy to my left. I sat and watched and chimed in now and then, feeling like an interloper at some mad tea party. Even when I told them I had landed there by accident, from the journalism department, they just congratulated and welcomed me to what they called the dark side.

And that was how I joined the campus fiction journal: as a sort of challenge to myself, a game. The magazine was called *The Katipunero*, like the statue outside. I'd seen it before in the library, where every three months I would bring its newest issue out onto the periodicals shelf. The heavy, lead-gray cover, textured to resemble slate. The loopy calligraphy of its letterpress title. *The Katipunero* was like that: all preciousness and pretense. Those Victorian getups; those boys, who also called themselves Katipuneros and wrote fiction of their own in their spare time, though everyone knew that, after graduating, they would forsake such things to join their fathers' banks and firms. Outside of class they didn't need to work for money; instead they spent their spare time analyzing paragraph breaks and "pee oh vee" as if the cure for cancer depended on it. A kind of smirking fascination brought me back to the student union every week, to pick up new submissions from the tray next to José Rizal and read them on the jeepney home, at lunch, even on the grass; to type rejection slips and bring them to the campus post office; to bring pieces I liked to the editors' attention; to offer my two cents at the weekly meeting.

The Katipuneros stayed up late to pull off an issue each quarter. Afterward they spent the university's money and some of their own to throw a launch party. I passed out flyers that most students threw away behind my back, hung posters that would disappear beneath other posters the next day, sound-tested microphones in the cafés where student authors read their work aloud. I drank a lot and smoked a little at these parties, feeling as the only girl that I had to keep up. ("Most girls prefer poetry or journalism to us," one of the Katipuneros told me, when I asked if there'd ever been a Katipunera before.) After the cafés closed, they spilled into the dormitories to prolong such life-and-death debates as whether literature had social duties, as Salvador Lopez believed, or whether art's only obligation was to art itself, as Jose Garcia Villa did. I even lost my virginity to one of the editors, behind the common-room sofa in his dorm, after the others had gone home or fallen asleep.

Faking my way among the Katipuneros also gave me an escape from the *barangay*. At home my mother, sick of slaving for Ligaya, had started to stick up for herself. But Ligaya wouldn't go down without a fight, and every day after Andoy's visit from Saudi, I witnessed one.

"You should have thought of that before," my mother said, hearing Ligaya complain of morning sickness.

"Before what?"

My mother eyed Ligaya's belly. "Andoy's had a million girl-friends. You think you're the first? You're just the first to get your-self in trouble."

"My*self* in trouble!" Ligaya almost choked. "Of course. I did this to *myself.* So I could get my hooks into the son of an unemployed seamstress."

Another time, Ligaya alleged our home was unsafe for children. "We live in a death trap," she said, once the twins were crawling. They were always slipping on the wet floor, or picking up dust bunnies and trying to eat them.

"Nothing's wrong with this place, if you *watch* your kids," said my mother. "I brought two children up here."

"I wouldn't brag about your children's *upbringing* if I were you."

"Now my children weren't brought up right? A girl in college, and a son, who'll go as far as Saudi to support his wife and kids?"

"His wife! His *wife!*" Ligaya howled, as if she'd heard a punch line, holding her still-ringless hand against her ribs.

They bickered in that same style about money, about Andoy, about child rearing and housekeeping. Eventually my mother would turn on the TV to drown out Ligaya's voice. At full volume, the soap operas bled into their arguments, so that sometimes I could hardly tell whether a plate had shattered in my own house or an actress on the screen had flung it. The noise would set the babies wailing. Ligaya stormed upstairs and slammed the door (or had the evil landlord on TV slammed it?). Music blared from the phonograph, angering the babies even more.

I feared catching their rages, like the infections that bounced back and forth between my nieces. When Ligaya gave birth to a third daughter, in February, I nearly moved into the student union. "Off to work," I'd say and make tracks as soon as the bickering began. Each time I passed the Katipunero, he looked less like a hostile guard and more like my redeemer. The brass plaque beneath him contained an old Tagalog word for *freedom,* and he stood for mine.

By March most students cleared the campus for vacation—except the Katipuneros, who insisted on a summer issue; and me, who still had credits to make up from my part-time days. With fewer writers around to contribute, we had to lift our policy against publishing staff work. The managing editor wrote a story called "McKinley Road," in which a wealthy businessman left his wife, children, and mansion for a secretary. In the copy editor's story, "Keys to the City," evil typewriters rose up against and killed the leading lights of Philippine literature, one by one. An associate editor wrote about a seventeenth-century Colettine nun with supernatural powers. And one of my fellow readers wrote about a colony of fruit bats fleeing the destruction of their home forest for a new place to live.

These were good stories, and reading them, I had to admit that the Katipuneros were more than spoiled blowhards. The literary magazines and novels they read instead of studying for class; their half-hour critiques; their drunken post-midnight debates about whether, for instance, the English language, as a souvenir of American imperialism, could ever be the basis of a truly national literary tradition or whether Filipino literature had a future only in the local vernacular—all of that had added up to something, which was their own art, or the not-unpromising beginnings of it. The Katipuneros exceeded their own standard for student work. And their devotion to a magazine that turned no profit, whose readership nobody measured, their passionate arguments over what belonged in it, was not a game. They'd given themselves over to exactly what Andoy had wished on me: an enterprise without a practical end. They were amateurs, in the classic sense of the word: they did it all for love.

It came to me that next to them *I* was the dilettante. I didn't sit around in a top hat or a velvet jacket, but I drank their whiskey and passed judgment on their craft, all the while never trying to make something of my own.

But if I were to write myself, then what about? I knew nothing about businessmen and secretaries, evil typewriters or supernatural nuns or fruit bats in the forest—and those were just the ideas that were taken. Pausing before the plaster Katipunero outside the student union again, I felt gloomy, as unwelcome in his world as ever. But for the first time, I looked at his face and fist and bare feet up close. Till then I'd had him sewn up with ideas about wealthy full-time students; I'd never taken stock of his disheveled, common clothes. The Katipunero, I realized, was poor. The muscles showing through his torn *camisa de chino* belonged not to some fop who sat in classrooms and cafés all day but to a peasant "son of sweat," who'd plowed and planted, dug and hoed since he could stand.

Of course he rose above those circumstances to become a founding hero of the nation. Anyone who'd taken grade-school civics or read the plaque at his feet could tell you that. But now I wondered about others like him—the majority of sons of sweat, who didn't end up making history. I couldn't write *their* stories— not exactly, having never seen a farm or country field in all my life. But I knew something about city peasants—Manila sons of sweat like Andoy, whose experiences came to me in letters and cassette tapes, conversations on the phone or with the *carabao*. Before I knew what I was doing, I had found a bench beside the student union and started writing in my notebook:

In Riyadh he shared a flat with nine men—gardeners, servants, or drivers like him, or construction workers on the pipeline being built from Saudi's oil wells to refineries offshore. I could pass for a Moro now, he wrote home on an aerogram as thin as onionskin, about the way the desert sun had darkened him.

I skipped my afternoon classes, gliding through campus, landing on a grassy quad here and a flight of stone steps there to add a paragraph or sentence. At home, my mother begged me to consider the electric bill as I wrote by the kitchenette bulb through the night. I barely ate or slept for two days. If someone had predicted, a year earlier, that my brother would inspire me one day to write fiction, *for fun*, I would not have believed them. Now it felt both new and fated to me, a thing I didn't know I'd always meant to do.

The words came easily, at first. It made me happier than I'd ever been to sketch out scenes in my notebook and type them up. "Aren't *you* in a good mood," said Ligaya, and then: "Did a man finally notice you, by some miracle?"

And then I read my draft again, stacking the masterwork in my head up against the mess I'd made on the page, and sank into despair. "Whoever he is, he's not worth it," said my mother, as I moaned and wallowed facedown on the sofa. That night the same pages I had filled in a manic fever were torn into shreds, floating in the Creek.

The summer passed like this. From the clouds of inspiration to the gutters of dejection and self-loathing and back again, over and over. My grades, meanwhile, slipped in only one direction. By the time I failed a term paper in psychology, after ditching class to write the day it was assigned, I decided that my problem was I hadn't read enough. And the hole in my apprenticeship was too wide to close in my free time. I resolved, like a determined suitor, to get serious. In the middle of my sixth semester in college, I dropped my journalism major and took up English literature with a special focus on creative writing.

"Shifty?" asked my mother.

"Shift*ee*," I said, the registrar's term for students who switched majors. "It happens all the time. The average student changes twice or more before graduation." I admitted that the switch would set me back a few semesters.

"How much longer?" said my mother.

"How much more money is the question," said Ligaya.

I couldn't blame them. What would I want next? A room on campus? A semester abroad?

Rather than sell Andoy on my craziness, I released him. *I'm going part-time again,* I wrote to Jeddah. *I'll pay my own way, take another decade to finish if I have to.*

He called as soon as he received my letter. "It says here it just hit you," he said. "One day you knew."

"It's true." I knew how cracked this made me sound.

"Now it keeps you up at night. You feel *awake* for the first time. Like you'd been sleepwalking through life before."

Instead of answering, I pictured him in Al-Thunayan's servant quarters, standing by the phone, untangling the cord. Everything appeared to be a shade of desert sand—the walls, the carpet, and the telephone; a yellow pencil, dented by different teeth; a yellow notepad filled with scribbled messages. Squares of yellow light checkered the hall from the doorways of the shared bedrooms off it. There'd be a smell of instant noodles and dirty laundry, as in boys' dormitories I had visited; and from opposite ends of the hallway, the sounds of a communal TV and a running toilet.

"Congratulations!" he said.

"Congratulations?"

"Now you know what it's like."

"To change my major?"

"To fall in love." Andoy laughed. "I always wondered who it would be. What boy could keep up with the toughest girl I know? I should have guessed: it wouldn't be *someone* for you. At least not a living someone. It would be Shakespeare, and José Rizal, and the Katipunero outside the student union."

I cringed. "It sounds ridiculous," I said. "Forget it."

"No!" said Andoy. "Listen. I'm no scholar, but love I know about. That's *my* major."

"I'll never get a decent job." His optimism had me arguing against myself.

"Relax! Love's a miracle, not a disaster. Who said it would be easy, or convenient? But if you can't sacrifice everything for love, what else is there?"

"It'll take more time."

"And money—yes, love does." He laughed again. "You'll learn *that* quick."

He did have one condition. "I want to meet this new love of yours," said Andoy. Anything I wrote, he said, I was to send him a copy.

In Jeddah, Andoy told me, every Filipino line cook and janitor seemed to know about Abdul Ghaffar Al-Thunayan. Some saw him as an almost mythical creature: the fair, generous master, rare as a genie or an oasis in the Rub' al-Khali desert. Al-Thunayan fed his servants well, paid them on time, let them hang on to their own passports and work permits. And for all his wealth, Al-Thunayan chose to have just one wife, Alia, and treated her like the princess that she, by blood, actually was.

At his new job, when he wasn't driving Al-Thunayan's family, my brother washed and waxed the cars, dusted and vacuumed their insides, balmed the leather seats with oil. Privately, he christened each one with a Filipino name. He called this BMW Dolphy; that Jaguar, Imelda. He kept the keys to every car and the code to the garage's security alarm. Family or friends who wished to borrow cars from Al-Thunayan—from oil associate to minor prince—went through Andoy first.

Best of all, Al-Thunayan let him "exercise" each car as he saw fit. My brother drove to the coast at dusk to watch the sky change colors over the Red Sea. Or he took the other servants downtown on their days off, to eat fast food and hear the Filipino waiters hoot in admiration. "A Rolls-Royce with anaconda-skin seats!" he said. "My friends can't pick their jaws up off the floor."

I drank these details in, writing one Andoy-inspired character after another. When I mailed him all my drafts, as promised, Andoy was tickled by the attention. "I guess I'm going to be famous after all," he said. That year he answered more of my questions about his life in Saudi Arabia than would fit onto the page.

Other readers (I took my first fiction workshop that semester) were more critical. I couldn't just record Andoy's experiences, my classmates said. Good fortune like my brother's did not make for a story. Where was the conflict? The danger? *Fiction needs trouble, or else it's just* description, wrote my professor in the margin of one draft, underlining "trouble" twice.

"Does Al-Thunayan have a temper?" I asked my brother.

"Not that I've seen."

"But every prince has got his warts," I insisted, quoting that same professor. "What does Al-Thunayan do if a servant makes a mistake?"

"I want to help you," Andoy said. "But he's a good man, and he hires good people. You'll have to make up your own trouble. It is *fiction*, isn't it?"

I tried. I wrote about what might happen to my fictional chauffeur if vandals keyed a Bentley under his watch, or stole the stereo. I wrote about the chauffeur's friends nicking the gold-flecked paint by accident, or staining the anaconda leather with their jars of black-market *siddique*. Goofy scenarios, but they did give me some confidence in my own imagination. I began to see that Andoy's luck could last in real life while I embellished it with fictional disasters. I stopped searching for the hidden dangers in his tapes and letters home.

So when his trouble really started, I missed it. I didn't notice the shift, as he continued to invoke her in his letters, from

Al-Thunayan's wife to *Madame* to *Alia.* If I thought of her at all, I thought of a black veil, nothing more. He'd praised too many legs and lips over the years for me to recognize, in this case, desire for what he couldn't see. By the time I reopened the letters and replayed the tapes, by the time I realized the warts I should have looked out for were his, not Al-Thunayan's, it was much too late.

The eyes of Al-Thunayan's wife are hard to describe.

I know Madame is nearby from the clinking sound of jewelry on her wrists and ankles.

When I drive Alia into town, the car afterwards smells like honey and roses.

My twin nieces could identify a pair of jeans and aviator glasses before their second birthday. "Cow!" they cried from their play-pen that May, pointing to our screen door. Their infant pronunciation of *carabao* had stuck.

It was Andoy, their own father, at the door. They held their palms out to him, a trick we'd taught them to amuse the *carabao*.

"How *is* my brother, Cow?" I said, as he met his baby daughter. The twins, who recognized his uniform more than his face, kept saying "Cow" and play-begging to him, a sight that gave me such sad visions of a litter suckling at some giant teat that I had to joke around to keep from crying. "We hear they're treating him like dirt out there. He must be wasting away."

In fact, Andoy had put on weight. His cheeks looked fuller, with a flush to them, like he'd been jogging in the sun. "He's miserable," said Andoy, grinning. "The one thing keeping him alive is his kid sister, who he swears will be a famous writer someday. He'll retire rich, off her."

Andoy wanted to make his deliveries first thing in the morning. By the time I woke up, he'd already come back from the bank, dressed in his denim and white shoes. He beckoned me to help. At the kitchen table, he went down a list of names and riyal contributions, converting them on a calculator into pesos, which I doled into envelopes. We matched cassette tapes, photographs, and cards to the amounts and put them in a straw *tampipi* box. Then we took the jeepney: from Antipolo to Santa Rosa; from Marikina to Laguna; from tin shantytowns to houses with clay roofs and living room pianos in neighborhoods so tony I could hardly believe the people there relied, as we did, on a son or brother overseas. Aging mothers squinted hard at Andoy, as if they could blur their own sons into being. Wives and girlfriends perked up in his presence. Children gaped at the stranger they were told to kiss because "he knows your father," and I even recognized myself, in teens who surfaced from their textbooks long enough to crack a joke and count the money. Like all the *carabao* I'd met, my brother sat and ate more than he wanted, fed them Saudi trivia they'd likely heard before. I saw what an essential trade was taking place. My brother's health and cheerfulness told them their own beloved boys were well. And he would bring their rosy performances of family life back to his friends in Jeddah. Walking through each *barangay* with him, into the swarm of children shouting *Carabao!*; seeing people through each screen door rise, when he appeared, in hope and recognition; I finally understood the purpose of the Saudi suit. I'd always thought it heavy for Manila, not to mention a billboard for thieves. But men so silent and invisible overseas must have loved this guarantee of *being seen* at home.

After our final stop, Andoy wanted to buy presents for the children. We picked up roller skates and tricycles in Quiapo, toys for children older than his own. "You know the twins don't even know how to use a spoon and fork yet," I protested.

"I miss a lot of firsts," he said. "At least this way I'll leave them with the right equipment." His ideas for his girls, their childhood—much like *campus life* and *full-time course load* for me—seemed to have originated somewhere far outside the lives of anyone we knew. The movies, maybe.

I fell asleep on our way home. Andoy held my hand as I dismounted, woozy, from the jeepney. Then he helped the women after me, standing like a footman in the road. I couldn't stop myself from thinking that he'd turned, the way our mother had years ago, into a servant for life.

"We need a Cadillac next time to get to all those houses," I said, remembering the days he used to chauffeur me to convent school. "Being a *carabao* is more exhausting than it looks."

"It's not so bad." My brother slowed his steps along the Creek, our old signal to talk in private, where the others wouldn't hear.

"Make it quick," I said. "The Creek smells extra ripe tonight." I was so used to his good news by then that I added, "Let me guess. Al-Thunayan adopted you? Or bought you a Cadillac of your own?"

Andoy laughed and shook his head. Then he said, "What I told you about love is true. It's never easy or convenient." His smile faded. He closed his eyes and inhaled deeply, as if the dust and garbage smells of our neighborhood, the mud and sewage, were precious memories he wanted to preserve.

He and Alia, the wife of his Saudi employer, hadn't planned it. And when they felt it, they tried to suppress it. "But it took over us," my brother said. A fragile conspiracy among the other house servants gave them time alone together. "Not that it ever feels like enough."

"You're in love?" I said stupidly, my voice and hands shaking.

"I'll still provide for all my girls," said Andoy. "I'll still come home to see you every chance I get. This won't change anything."

But I couldn't believe that. Not after all the *carabao* stories I'd heard over the years. My brother's love affair broke more Saudi laws than I could count.

"You said yourself how lucky you've been there," I said. "Your *amo* treats you well. And now you want to test that luck? For what?"

"If you knew her, you wouldn't need to ask."

"Why don't you introduce us, then? Invite her to the *barangay* for tea. I'll tour her along the Creek. Show her where we keep our pet rats." I had an urge to smack him, but didn't. "What were you thinking?"

He shook his head again. "I had to stop thinking." He'd lain awake too many nights, he said, thinking: about the religious police, about the lashings men he knew endured in prison, about the public plaza with its granite tiles and chessboard-size drain. Risks he chose to take, for love.

When we got home I didn't breathe a word of Andoy's trouble to my mother, who was chopping onions by the stove; or to Ligaya, who was folding washcloths while her babies cooed and gurgled in their pen. I didn't speak of it that night or the rest of the month, even to Andoy. As long as I didn't mention his dalliance aloud, even after he left Manila for the third time, I believed I could contain his story, leave it unfinished at the point where he had told me he was in love and reassured me everything would be all right. I could just will this craziness with Alia to run its course, like all his love affairs.

For months, it worked. The envelopes arrived, on schedule, through the *carabao*. Andoy called home and wrote, made plans for the future with us while carrying on five thousand miles away with Alia, like any man who had a ship in more than one port.

We kept hearing from him until November. Then a month passed without word from him. At Christmas, we received no phone call or black-market greeting card, the kind he used to buy from an Indian grocer who kept a secret stash under the register. We didn't hear from him on New Year's Eve, the start of a new decade, when the children, as they did each year after using up their store-bought firecrackers, hurled matches into the Creek until a bright hedge of fire blazed through the *barangay*. I'd done this as a child myself, never once considering the danger. Even the youngest of us, I think, got the symbolism: new beginnings, our village cauterizing itself clean of all the past year's garbage.

But that year, the year Andoy went silent, the flames only looked like hell to me, and smelled like what they were: a gutter of filthy gases burning.

By late January, Ligaya and my mother were frantic, and I was channeling my fears into the only place I could. In my stories, Andoy had injured his hand or voice or mouth; he'd argued with a *carabao* who got revenge by "losing" his *balikbayan* envelope; Al-Thunayan had assigned him, as his most trusted servant, to an emergency top secret project in the desert where contact with the outside world wasn't possible. I made up one fat chance after another to explain his silence. I'd written my brother so often into danger, willing his real life to look more like fiction; the least I could do was try to write him out of it.

I was at home alone, typing away at one such story, when I heard knocking at our door and saw a pair of jeans and aviator glasses through the screen.

Andoy used to dream aloud of turning our mother into the kind of woman who watched game shows and soap operas all day, lifting her fingers only to sip cocktails or eat cake. "She'll get too lazy to talk," he said. "We'll have to hang a whistle from her neck to call the servants with."

We stretched the joke out. "Her hands will fatten up," I said. "We'll have to cut off all the rings you bought her. Melt them down into one ring, that barely fits her pinkie." It tickled us to even think of her, our servant mother, at rest.

And yet, in a perverse way, in that first year of a new decade, Andoy's dream came true. My mother did retire to the sofa. Clutching one of Andoy's old bandannas, she watched TV for hours, bursting into tears at times I least expected: scenes where estranged soap-opera lovers reunited, moments when game-show contestants hit the jackpot.

In that same year Ligaya's parents called, offering forgiveness and a place for her and the three children to live. But she surprised me too, by staying with my mother in our *barangay*. I thought their bickering would flare up again in no time, but it never really did. Instead, leaving the twins with a neighbor, Ligaya strapped the baby to her back and traced my mother's daily route: to church, then house to house with a sewing basket and an offer to work at almost anything.

As far as they knew, Andoy was a victim, pure and simple. I told them (when they raised the inevitable questions, and asked me how much I knew) a tale of treachery and blackmail, with details lifted out of Genesis. I cast my brother as the decent Joseph, his lover as the wife of Potiphar, tugging at his clothes. I told them Andoy fled her advances, but not before she'd seized a work glove and the sooty rag he used to clean the cars. *Your servant has insulted me,* this Alia told her husband, waving the false evidence like a pair of flags.

And I, holding the truth inside me, returned to the dutiful path of the old scholarship girl. Around the time the envelopes stopped coming, I asked for my old jobs back at the library and cafeteria. "We miss you," said one Katipunero as I stamped his book. He'd read some of my stories months before, shy as I still was about sharing them, and encouraged me to keep at it. "Come join us when your shift is done," said another, as I served him lunch. He'd once promised to make room in the fall issue for me, if I had something good. I made all sorts of plans to see them, but got too busy. Most of them graduated later that year, replaced by younger boys I didn't know. Whenever I walked past the student union, I avoided my old statue's eyes. *Everybody has to grow up sometime,* I told him. Soon I was majoring in journalism again. A professor offered meals, a room, and fieldwork credits in exchange for my transcribing shelves of interviews she'd taped with politicians since the sixties. So I moved my books and clothes and typewriter to her town house close to campus. Once a week I still took the jeepney home to Salapi Road, to stock the fridge and pay some bills. This started as my private penance for deceiving them, Ligaya and my mother. But over time it just felt like a load that someone had to carry. They were "my" girls now.

Rejoining the ranks of the older, part-time scholar—early to class and early to work, always bypassing the student union—didn't leave spare time for much, least of all something as frivolous as fiction. Except, of course, that I couldn't sleep. At night, after class and work and studying, I lay awake, while my landlady professor snored next door. The guilt of lying to my family, and the grief of missing Andoy, did not exactly add up to a good night's rest. And so I passed the time by writing.

It was always Andoy, or a version of him, that I wrote about. The same imagined brother that sustained me once we stopped hearing from the real one. This fictional Andoy called me from a pay phone in Bahrain, where friendly Filipino workers sheltered him and Alia after a bold, elaborate escape from Saudi. *She left her cousins at the Suq and met our van on an unmarked road.* This Andoy sent a tape from Abu Dhabi, saying he and Alia had bought new passports and work visas from an expert forger. *Expensive, but love always is.* This Andoy wrote home on an aerogram postmarked from Dubai, where he'd secured janitorial work at a hotel. *If you work hard—and cheap enough, I've found—most bosses will keep any secret.* Things didn't always end well for this Andoy, either. In one draft, the strain of all that hiding broke him. In another, Alia Al-Thunayan saw love wasn't much to live on after all, and grew to hate the man who'd plucked her from the comfort of her husband's palace. I even had Andoy arrested, sent to prison, and deported by a Saudi judge back to Manila, never to see Alia again.

These Andoys went by other names, or none at all; but they had one thing, their survival, in common. At times I thought so long and deeply about other ways it might have gone for my brother that I almost sensed him, present in the room, with me. I never could get used to the "withdrawal," as some *Katipunero* staffers called it: the rude comedown from having lived so thoroughly inside a story it felt real. But these stories weren't. I could spend my whole life writing, version upon version, none of which would turn the man in jeans and aviators at our door into Andoy. That *carabao* would still arrive, not two months into 1980, prop the glasses on his head, and tell me, "You look like him." This man would still open his palms to me, to show he had no envelope on him. What he had brought was news: that Andoy's body had been found, alongside Alia's, inside a destroyed Porsche that belonged to her husband, his employer. He'd lost control of the car after swerving off the road to avoid a collision. An accident— on a routine, if secret, drive between lovers, ending in a fate not far from what they might have suffered anyway, if anyone had found out what they were up to. Fiction didn't have a prayer over facts like that. And yet, I felt it would have pleased Andoy to know that I still wrote. I could picture him, reading my words somewhere, chuckling at my attempts to save some version of his life. Who could say, then, that I had an altogether lousy or inadequate imagination? My brother got to live forever, in a sense.

In the Country

1971

She called the strike on a Monday, the busiest day of the week. As strikes go, hers was poetry. Eighty nurses, their brown hands clasped around the Self-Sacrifice statue on the lawn outside of City Hospital. The chairman of the board's white face, turning even whiter when he came out of his car and saw them. Milagros could have lived on that rush forever.

That morning, June 21, their cause was a simple one. At City Hospital, the native nurses, like Milagros, earned less than the American ones. Forty centavos to the peso, if you did the math; less, in some cases, if you weighed education and experience, skill and seniority. When she learned this, months before, Milagros had simply asked her own boss for a raise. *I think you'll agree from my performance reviews that I deserve one.* Her boss liked her well enough to talk to *her* boss, who talked to her boss's boss. A message of hand-tied sympathy came down. "I know it looks bad," said Milagros's boss. "But we're talking two different standards of living. Take transportation. You ride the jeepney to work, correct? Four pesos round trip? Americans love their cars, and they're too tall to stoop under the jeep entrance. Gas costs a fortune these days, and what about Christmastime? You're where you need to be; they fly seven thousand miles or more."

The math made some sense. But then Milagros went home, to the apartment whose rent she'd helped pay since she was old enough to work, and shouldered all on her own since college; the apartment she shared with her mother, who washed clothes for a living, and her brothers, and their wives and children. Her mother said, "You have a job." (Her own brothers should be so lucky.) "Don't waste your time wanting somebody else's slice of pie. Be happy." Good advice, for anyone in this life. But the numbers nagged, like a stitch in Milagros's side. What if she *wanted* to drive a car to work? Travel at Christmastime? Live in a place of her own?

She started small, with crumbs of gossip. "I heard," she whispered to a colleague, as they washed their hands together at a scrub sink, "Peggy Ryan pulled in twenty thousand pesos last year, even without a master's. Know anything about it?" She stepped lightly around her co-workers' squeamishness: about money, about Americans, about advanced degrees.

The story bled from nurse to nurse like dye. They met for lunch at a *carinderia* around the corner from City Hospital.

"I'll just talk to my supervisor," said one nurse. "Can't we all?"

"I tried that," said Milagros. "They don't listen to one woman, by herself."

So they voted, three to one, to start a union, with Milagros at its helm. Together they wrote memos, scheduled meetings, made jokes at the negotiation table. *The greenest American does better than I, because I am brown.* The chairman of the board liked that one. The chairman was *fond of* Milagros, he said. *Impressed with* Milagros. The chairman laughed Milagros and her little union right out of the conference room.

Milagros Sandoval, Registered Nurse, twenty-two years old, had no road map from there. Her mother was a laundress. Her father had hopped farm to farm for work. Growing up, Milagros learned to keep her head down, her boat steady. In college she had never joined a single protest. Maoists or Marxists, Young Patriots or Christian Socialists or Democratic Youth, were only obstacles on her campus course from class to job to library. All those long-haired, picketing boys and girls—that was how she thought of them, as children, next to her—blocked her path and made her late; their chants on land reform and U.S. bases sounded like nursery rhymes, like games for kids who never had to work. In 1969, her senior year, those kids accused the President of bribing and bullying his way to a second term, news that felt as far from Milagros as Armstrong's moon landing. She couldn't call those classmates for advice now. They had not exchanged numbers at graduation, and probably they would not even know her name.

But she was a quick study: Milagros Sandoval hated nothing in the world more than feeling like a beginner. She learned how to pitch nonbelievers who didn't want to cause trouble. Buzzwords—*worth* and *equal work*—set the air crackling. When in mid-June yet another meeting went south, and ended with the chairman patting Milagros on her white cap, the union voted on its best last resort.

Refusal to negotiate in good faith, she keyed into a borrowed typewriter that night.

On strike until an agreement is reached.

It was not about the country yet, though hand grenades at Plaza Miranda two months later would send gurney after blood-soaked gurney into City Hospital. A year later still, strikes would be against the law altogether.

June 21 came before all that. June 21 was about these nurses, the value of one human's sweat against another's. And yet Milagros felt her world grow a few sizes, while the city, street, and small apartment where she grew up shrank. Until the union she'd thought no further than her own degree, her own job, her first proud payday, when she brought home eggs, bread, beer, and chocolate to her mother and her unemployed brothers.

Family, those waiting at home, turned out to be a sticking point, when union meetings lasted late into the night.

"My children need me," said the older, married nurses.

"The union needs you too," said Milagros.

"My children will forget what I look like," they said.

"But this is how you want your children to remember you." To Milagros it was a beautiful thought: the rules suspended for a time, toddlers subsisting on Cheez Whiz sandwiches and staying up late to watch their mothers on TV. Even Gloria Gambito, whose husband didn't want her working in the first place, dared to bring her three-year-old daughter to the picket line, a STRIKE '71 T-shirt reaching her ankles.

Jaime Reyes, a reporter for the *Metro Manila Herald*, came to City Hospital on the twenty-second. On his way to Ermita, to the Congress Building, a tip had reached him from the hospital. When he introduced himself—"Jaime Reyes," he said; "call me Jim"—Milagros was holding too many things. A picket sign, a clipboard, a megaphone. She moved to shake his hand and dropped the picket sign. Not on purpose, not like a lady in bygone days dropping a handkerchief, but it may have looked that way because Jaime Reyes, call him Jim, was handsome. Tall and lean, like an athlete, with the slightest wave in his black hair. Seeing him, Milagros wished she knew more about makeup. She'd kept her hair as short as it had been in high school: wash and go.

Jim stooped to help her with the picket sign and read her Pentel-penned slogan aloud: CITY SHOULD REWARD EXPERTS, NOT EXPAT$. He gave her a look of amusement, or reverence, or both. "EXPAT$," he repeated, tracing the dollar sign in the air with a finger. "That's good." Their palms met as he returned the sign, hers a little damp.

"How did you find out?" Jim asked. "About the wage gap, that is? I can't imagine this was public information."

"A friend in Payroll tipped me off," Milagros said, laughing. "This is my Pentagon Papers, I guess."

That made him smile again, in his amused and reverent way.

If she had ever joined a campus protest, she might have known of him. Jim Reyes had been a fixture at those picket lines, interviewing the long-haired marching children. But because she rarely opened a newspaper, she had never read his stories of the First Quarter Storm or the jeepney workers' strike, his forecasts that the paint bombs and broken car windows and Molotov cocktails would backfire. *Proof of a state of emergency. Exhibits in the President's case for staying on in the palace past his legal term limits.* Martial law—like the word *cancer,* in those days: widely murmured, barely understood. Least of all by someone like Milagros, who would have taken Jim's warnings, if she'd read them, as just another reason to skip the campus picket lines altogether.

Her ignorance made the other nurses giggle. "*I* called him here," Janice Mendoza, fresh out of college, admitted. She'd met Jim at a rally on Mendiola Bridge the year before, when students tried to storm Malacañang Palace. "I was just swept up in what my friends were doing. But I kept his card. *In case anything else should happen,* he told us. Anything that he should know about." Other nurses recognized him from TV. *Movers and Shakers,* a weekly who's-who program not unlike a cockfight or a beauty pageant (Manila and its obsession with crowning champions, and ranking the Best and First and Most) had featured Jim one Sunday. Youngest Staff Writer ever at the *Metro Manila Herald* (Oldest, Most Prestigious daily in the city). "He skipped two grades," said Yvette Locsin, "and finished Ateneo at eighteen." "He's from up north, an Ilocano," said Asuncion Flores. If Milagros watched *Movers and Shakers,* she too would have heard about the first time he'd smelled newspaper ink and decided, at the age of five, that one day he would be a journalist. About the scholarship that brought him to high school in Manila, where he worked his way up from paper route to mail room at the *Herald.* She too might have held her breath when the interviewer asked after Jim's bachelor status, seen Jim shake his head and laugh, embarrassed; maybe at the picket line she'd have checked his left hand, like the other nurses, to see if anything had changed.

Instead, she met him for the first time on the grass in front of City Hospital, where he asked, under the bronze statue, if she'd considered greener pastures. "Saudi Arabia needs nurses," he said. "So does America. It's a booming market abroad. People making three, four times what even Peggy Ryan does here."

But Milagros never wanted to leave Manila. Even as a young girl with no money she had wanted to stay here. In the same way she had ridden out high school calculus and college chemistry: she thought that she could crack Manila, that if she worked at it enough the city would reward her; only sissies quit. She stopped herself from saying this to Jim. Talk of mastery, ambition, had no place on a picket line. A union leader had to talk of solidarity. Everyone rising together, not racing to the top.

"Migration's not for me" is what she said. "And Saudi Arabia's no excuse for shabby treatment at home. 'Love it or leave it' is not a sound workplace policy."

"But don't you think," Jim pressed, "given the chance, that all these nurses would leave City in a heartbeat, for a land of milk and honey? Sidewalks paved with gold or diamonds, depending on whom you ask? The chubby envelopes they could send home?"

"I don't think so," said Milagros, deciding she could speak for them. "Your mother gets sick, you don't leave her for a healthier mother. She's your mother!"

He gave her that amused, reverent look for the third time. It seemed they weren't so much on the same page as in the same paragraph or sentence, even from that first day.

February 6, 1986

Milagros's mother has an idea. "Tell me what you think," she says.

"Let me guess," says Milagros, who hasn't left the house for weeks. "I should go shopping. I should treat myself to a fancy dinner and cocktails with some friends. A massage and a manicure at Aling Betchie's salon. At the very least, get out of bed, go outside, take a walk and get some air. Am I right, Ma?" Tragedy has freed her from good manners; she doesn't care how her words land.

"Those are good ideas too," says Milagros's mother. "But I was thinking something else. And you don't have to lift a finger for it. See, shortly after Jaime . . ."

Milagros lets her stutter. She's through helping people say it.

"Shortly afterwards, you know, I registered to vote."

"You?" It's been three months since the President, feeling heat from both the opposition and Washington, D.C., made his announcement on TV. A snap election. Milagros wouldn't have bet on her mother noticing. Her mother, who has voted as often in her life as she's read Russian novels or listened to Italian opera. "I didn't know you cared, Ma."

"I don't, really." Her mother laughs shyly, touches Milagros on the cheek. "But you do, *iha*. I registered for you. I know it's hard for you to get out of this bed—I can't imagine. For all the bad luck I've had in my life, knock wood, none of my kids . . ."

She still can't say it. Milagros shuts her eyes.

"What I mean is, rest here for as long as you'd like. But I know this matters to you. You haven't missed an election since you married. So tell me who you want, and I'll vote for you. All right? Even better if you remember how the paper looks, and where I should write what."

Milagros imagines her mother, hunched over a booth, arthritic fingers bringing the ballot closer to her cloudy eyes. Casting a vote for the first time in her seventy years, on her daughter's behalf. Once again her own eyes fill. Small, unexpected things set her off now. The name Jaime, on the other hand, the word *death,* leaves her cold and silent. But it doesn't matter. To anyone who sees her crying, she cries only for him.

"You're sweet, Ma," says Milagros. "But voting's dangerous. You check a box on a little card, next thing you know there's a rifle at your head and some thug telling you to try again." From her nightstand radio she knows just how many people want it to be different, this time. An army of poll watchers, thousands strong and still recruiting everywhere from her old college campus to the remotest *bukid*. Senators and congressmen sent over by America to keep an eye on things. But she's seen hope and good intentions spark like this, and sputter out, before.

"I'll take my chances," says her mother. "Thugs won't bother an old woman."

Milagros wouldn't be so sure. "We thought the worst of them wouldn't harm a child."

"Let me do this for you," her mother insists. "Just tell me who you want up there, in Malacañang Palace."

Sweet, too, that her mother, who has shared this house with her for thirteen years now, doesn't know exactly how Milagros— the old Milagros—would have voted. Jackie, with her antenna ears, would have known, at four years old, which box to check.

"Don't bother, Ma. I used to care about these things. But now I don't at all."

1971

"You're famous!" said her brothers, three days into the nurses' strike. A *Herald* had landed at their door in the middle of the night. On page one, instead of a flood or volcano, instead of an election, instead of America: Milagros, in her bandanna, with her sign. CITY SHOULD REWARD EXPERTS, NOT EXPAT$.

In fountain ink, under the headline, Jim had circled the date: June 23. From there Milagros followed his arrow to a tiny margin. *And the rest is history,* he'd written by hand.

The next morning, 160 nurses showed up at the picket line. "Never trusted any union," one of them declared, "but fair is fair." Some came from different hospitals, talking *alliances, community.* Here and there a sympathetic doctor joined. "If we could do our jobs without them," one said into Jim's Dictaphone, "wouldn't we?" *Herald* subscribers read of nursing students, bused in to City Hospital, giving out the wrong drugs in the wrong doses. Saw photos of the elderly with bedsores, waiting hours to be helped to the toilet. "What's lost in all this hoopla," said the chairman, when Jim got him on the phone, "is the City Hospital standard of *patient care,* which ought to be these ladies' first priority. Or what's a nurse for?" A few readers wondered the same in letters to Jim's editor. *The City nurses made their point. At whose expense?* But Manila in 1971 had seen arrests on Burgos Drive, beatings in front of the U.S. embassy, deadly showdowns between students and riot police. Hearts and minds were predisposed to chant along with the young nurses. *Equal pay for equal work.* EXPERTS, NOT EXPAT$. And the chairman of the board of City Hospital hated scenes more than he hated unions. On a rainy day in July, Milagros saw him cross the wet grass toward the picket line, asking for a word with her.

From then on you couldn't separate them with a water cannon. At night, Jim met the City Hospital patients Milagros called her kids. Some still had their hair, the chemo just begun. Others couldn't lift their eyelids. He shook hands with a boy whose tumor had grown into his spine, numbing both his legs. By August all the children in "Pedia-Onco" were playing reporter instead of doctor. Holding blood pressure pumps up to each other's faces for "interviews." Scribbling leads and datelines in the diaries the social workers had left them.

Milagros learned shorthand and how to operate Jim's Dictaphone. During interviews she learned to listen past his subjects' answers, pay attention when they shifted in their seats, cleared their throats, blinked as if the air was dusty. She watched him bring a single pencil to story conferences while his colleagues bumbled with clipboards and fountain pens and briefcases. Jim tented his long fingers, with their trim, clean nails, before his mouth as he listened. He waited to speak, his posture a priest's.

She descended with him into the bowels of the *Herald* headquarters, where massive sheets of newsprint rolled above their heads. The earthy, even fecal smell of ink and wood pulp in her nostrils and her lungs. The presses chugging like a train along its track: a sound that filled her brain and rearranged her heartbeat, till it seemed *she* had become a press, her body printing heds and deks and sentences and stories.

He called her Jo, as if he knew she'd never answer to the likes of *sweetheart*. Who knew where the nickname came from? Maybe Josephine Bracken, José Rizal's Irish muse. Or the toughest of Alcott's Little Women, a tomboy with big plans, who wanted more than what her sisters wanted. *Jo* she didn't mind.

She had another boyfriend at the time: Narciso Beltran, who taught theater where they'd gone to college. The kind of boy who lived at the center of people's attention. Wolfish eyes. Outsize lips. A rasp in his voice that could bring out the nurse or mother in any woman. He never called himself an actor, though; he preferred *performer.* "As are we all," he liked to add. *Life is a performance.*

Naz, as people called him, had been her one link to the campus tribe of long-haired boys and girls. On the same stages where he'd once played Lear and Oedipus and Cyrano de Bergerac, he now coached a new generation of leading men, staging plays Milagros didn't always understand. *Indirection is the only language I trust,* Naz liked to say about his style. Just before she broke it off, Milagros watched his Filipino take on *Jack and the Beanstalk,* set in the foothills of the Mayon volcano. The giant bellowed in military-industrial language; the farmers and the magic soybeans stood for labor and capital. That night she told Naz. *I've decided to focus more on my job than on my social life.*

He wasn't fooled. "There's someone else," he guessed, and Milagros didn't lie. "I see," Naz said, when he asked who Jim Reyes
was. "You want to marry someone with a Serious Career."

Sneering words, that sounded as if purged from his throat
with a finger. The grandson of a sugar baron, Naz could afford
to sneer at institutions. Jim's people in the north had been farmers and servants. Degrees and titles, memberships and mottos,
Jim's press passes and Milagros's City Hospital ID, were false
idols to someone like Naz, knickknacks only squares and parents
worshiped.

"No one's said anything about *marry*," she said. But Naz
wasn't wrong.

Until Jim she hadn't planned it. *I enjoy being* paid *for my
work*, she used to say, against marriage. Throat cultures, spinal
taps—those things compelled her more than caring for a man
did. To the question of children she would say: *No man I know
strikes me as worth repeating.* She had a pocket full of answers
just like that, before she met Jim.

Jim grew up where the President had: on a rice farm up north.
"Back then I called him Manong Freddie," Jim said, of the
plantation owner's eldest grandson. Jim's own grandfather had
plowed the muddy, mosquito-infested paddies in rubber boots
and a *salakot* hat. Jim's father and Jim himself would have been
fated to do the same, until the day Jim's father, as a teenager, long
before Jim was born, saved the infant President from a house
fire. "This *utang na loob* will not be forgotten," Freddie's father
had said at the time, and it wasn't. Jim's father moved up from the
soil to the garage as the family driver, the kind of trusted servant
close enough to live in the family's house, eating at their tables,
washing at their sinks. *Utang na loob:* a debt of the heart, an
unrepayable soul-debt. By Jim's birth and baptism, Freddie had
graduated from law school, and visited home in time to stand as

Jim's godfather. Jim went to school on the family dime, collecting gold stars and 100s while his godfather won a seat in Congress, picking up a paper route in town while other farm children his age were still planting rice seedlings. When their roads improved, the townspeople took it as a personal gift from the new congressman, a wink at the family driver to whom he owed his life.

At the 1961 inaugural, Freddie, now a senator, introduced his godson Jim, now a City Desk reporter at the *Herald,* as "the man whose father saved me." They shared memories of fishing in the Padsan River, village disputes over cattle, *traysikel* rides in town. Catching sight of each other at a "press-con" would yield a nod, a smile, a warm clasp of the shoulder. And even when Jim pressed his godfather on politics—in '65, when he switched parties just in time to run for President; in '66, barely sworn in, when he sent troops into Saigon, a move he'd blocked while he was in the Senate—these challenges felt academic, like staged classroom debates between their younger selves: the lawyer and his journalism-student godson.

Milagros had to doubt Jim's other stories of his first days in Manila: stories of a hayseed struggling to decode restaurant menus and working hard to lose his country accent. What place or language could ever claim Jim? To her he was original as Adam. Near a colony of tin shacks by the Pasig River, she watched him rescue a basketball from mud and shoot hoops with half-naked children. Hours later he stood at an Ateneo podium in his best *barong,* to accept a medal for alumni who had done the school, and the country, proud.

That summer, the *Herald* sent Jim to the "Con-Con," a convention on proposed changes to the 1935 Constitution. One by one, he heard from delegates what they'd received from Malacañang Palace in exchange for what it called "correct" votes. One senator's nephew, guaranteed a spot at the Military Academy. A grant, no strings attached, to a congressman building a bridge in his hometown. And for the others, envelopes of cash. At the palace, beluga caviar and Dom Pérignon and a slideshow of the questions on the table at the Con-Con, and the "best responses."

Yes to a new Parliament, replacing Congress, whereby a former President could come back as Prime Minister.

No to a ban on ex-Presidents running again after two terms.

Yes to the right of any President or Prime Minister to rule by decree.

The story earned Jim his first "love letter" from the Office of the Press Secretary. "I must be doing something right," he told Milagros. *You are therefore urged to adjust your claims against the administration,* she read, *and to issue the proper errata to the* Metro Manila Herald *articles published on the following dates.* Atop the page floated a yolk-yellow sun, borrowed from the country's flag, inside a bright blue wheel: a seal so cheerful she could swear she'd seen something like it on one of her kids' Get Well Soon cards.

Instead of "adjusting," Jim covered the bombings at Plaza Miranda in August. Two hand grenades thrown at a Liberal Party rally, sending that party's senators and Senate hopefuls to City Hospital. In September, he looked into what the palace called an attempt on the new defense minister's life, shots fired at his Ford sedan behind the Wack Wack golf course. A driver whose story didn't match his boss's. Bystanders and a bodyguard, who saw things differently. The President, who blamed Communists—for this as for Plaza Miranda—but didn't, Jim noticed, arrest or even question any.

Later that week, on *Meet the Press,* the President, addressing *Herald* allegations—Con-Con bribery, staged assassinations. "They call us politicians *balimbing,*" he said. "But I think it's the media who are most like star-shaped fruit." Without naming his grown godson, Manong Freddie looked—to Milagros, who watched him on the Pedia-Onco waiting room TV—truly wounded, as by a brother. "No fewer than ten faces," said the President. "And zero loyalty."

February 7, 1986

Vivi, the live-in maid and nanny, wakes her with water. That Vivi can splash water on her *amo*'s face speaks of her particular status in this family. It's how she wakes the kids, also, when they are lazy.

Milagros sits up. The radio's still on. She never turns it off—after thirteen years as a reporter's wife, the instinct to keep up hasn't died. Besides, she can't stand total silence. *The National Movement for Free Elections needs your help,* the announcer urges. *Go now to one of these embattled polling stations. Guard the ballot boxes to make sure everyone who votes is counted.*

"Get up, ma'am," says Vivi. "You can lie down again later, but first take a bath. Ma'am."

Already in the bathroom there's a drum filled with warm water.

"At least don't smell like a sad woman," says Vivi. "Ma'am."

Once Vivi passes the *tabo,* Milagros pours small pailfuls on herself. Her skin feels tender, almost insulted by the water. She takes her time, giving Vivi a chance to change the sheets, open the window, air out the master bedroom. Over a month now she's slept on and off in there, not rising except for the bathroom, changing her clothes only when Vivi (no one else can) makes her.

After she dries off and gets into clean clothes and sheets, back in the bedroom, Milagros waits for the cutoff, for the familiar feedback, snuffing out the radio announcer. One order from the President to his press secretary, one visit from their "muscle," would kill the station's power faster than you could say PLEASE STAND BY. But on the broadcast goes, the Election Day blow-by-blow. As in a regular democracy. Broadcasts and elections a birthright.

Her mother and Vivi have both said, *Why don't you turn it off, if it upsets you?* But Milagros isn't sure it does.

I beg you, if you have the luxury of time and transportation, the announcer says, *stop listening to me. Turn my voice off now. Get to your polling station. You owe it to your country to help out.* A year ago this woman might be dead, or jailed, within the hour. It's like Jim said: the President's gotten too weak to give orders. Or other men, too strong to follow them.

1972

A Friday, near shift's end. Milagros found Jim in the Pedia-Onco lounge, watching *The Porky Pig Show* on TV, waiting for her. Not smiling. Not really watching Porky Pig, either, but leaning forward with his elbows on his knees. Fingers tented at his temples, forcing his head to hold some news it didn't want. A grief-pose. Milagros knew it from the City Hospital fathers. The ones who couldn't always cry at first.

He needed her near him. A friend had died. Once Milagros had handed off her beds to the next nurse, Jim drove her to a subdivision outside Manila proper. "He was my Ateneo brother," he said, as they passed a sign: BATANGLOBO VILLAGE—DRIVE CAREFULLY. "We were the scholarship boys. Me from up north, Billy from just outside the U.S. air base in Tacloban. He taught me Waray-Waray, I taught him Ilocano, so we had each other to speak dialect with when we were homesick."

Through her window Milagros saw dogs on leashes, bikes with training wheels. This was not Forbes Park, where she imagined rich men keeping wives and mistresses in separate wings of their Spanish Colonial mansions. Nor was it the Smokey Mountain landfill, where the poor rummaged for anything to eat or sell. Here, a low wall separated one single-story house from the next. A gate in front kept each yard from the street.

"We want Twenty-six Avalon Row," said Jim. "His mother called me, inconsolable. Can't touch or even look at Billy's things." It fell to Jim to clear out Billy's house and sell it.

Signs: ATLANTIS AVENUE, BRIGADOON ALLEY, EDEN STREET. "An awful lot for streets to live up to," Milagros said. ELYSIUM, NARNIA, OZ, VALHALLA.

"The developer had fun with it, I guess," said Jim. They found 26 Avalon Row: a bungalow with a red-clay roof and cinder-block walls. An L-shaped yard around the front and side. Out back was the *labahan* with its stone sink, drain, and clotheslines. Years ago, Milagros's mother had worked at such a sink, scrubbing at the stains of strangers. Jim let himself in with a key.

"Billy went to college in the States," said Jim. "I used to get postcards from him: Hollywood Boulevard, the Ford Motor factory in Detroit, the NASA space station." Milagros listened— once again, as bereaved parents had trained her to. The stories that they told to bring the dead back. Story after conjuring story, until the raspy voice, the dimpled hands, the child took shape in the room between them and Milagros, as Billy took shape now between her and Jim, and entered 26 Avalon Row with them. "We wrote letters to each other, too. Fighting about Joe McCarthy, the U.S. military bases at Clark and Subic, Nixon. *Communist,* he called me once. I called him Joe 'Kano, like G.I. Joe and *Amerikano* rolled into one."

They brought cardboard boxes from the backseat of Jim's car into the house of a man who lived alone. The master bedroom had only an army cot in it. A smaller bedroom next to this, only a drafting table by the wall. Milagros saw a blueprint on it of some slanted structure, like an escalator. The title block was signed *Guillermo Batanglobo,* ARCHITECT. The smallest room looked out on the *labahan* at the back. A child's trundle bed against the far wall had no toys or books around it.

"Was Billy short for Guillermo?" Milagros asked.

Jim nodded.

"Billy Batanglobo. It was his village."

They went back to the drafting table. "Billy came home with a master's degree and a belief in suburbs. Privacy, the kind you can't get in the city. More home for less money. Grass and fresh air within driving distance of a job in Manila. Batanglobo Village was his lab. He tested all of those ideas here, on his house, first."

"They're nice ideas," Milagros said. "I see why he believed in them."

"But then he went beyond front yards and two-car garages." Jim turned to the blueprint. "The whole time he was living in this house, Billy was testing out another American idea." Milagros looked more closely. A round hatch in the grass, the chute slanting into the earth. She traced the grass with her finger: "Is that—?"

"The yard," said Jim.

"Billy Batanglobo was afraid of a bomb?" she said.

Jim nodded. "If the Americans thought the Soviets would drop one from five thousand miles away, what was to stop Mao or the Vietcong from targeting the U.S. bases here? Or getting what's left of our Huks to do it? He got so paranoid that he decided this one wasn't deep enough or strong enough. One bad typhoon and it'd be an aquarium down there."

Jim turned to the next blueprint, all squares and right angles this time: a forty-foot ladder leading down into a suite with a bathroom, a kitchen sink.

"This one's floodproof," said Jim. "A custom-made Manila shelter."

"Where is it?" Milagros asked, feeling a chill over her skin.

Jim pointed to an inset drawing of the trundle bed, opening onto its side.

"Jim," Milagros whispered, "how did Billy die?" It occurred to her for the first time that Jim hadn't said.

Jim shook his head, over and over. She reached for his hand. "Officially," Jim finally managed to say, "he took his own life."

She waited for the unofficial answer.

When the President sent Philcag, a civilian action group, to

Saigon, Billy had been first in line to volunteer. "No surprise there," said Jim. But the letters he received from Billy just weeks later: *those* were a surprise. Full of news about civilian deaths and crop destruction, POW torture. Then, a phone call from 26 Avalon Row: Billy had gone AWOL. *This village—everything that I've believed—is a complete lie.*

"We talked for a while," said Jim. "I convinced him not to burn this house down." Instead, Billy applied for conscientious objector status. Writing the press, the palace, anyone who'd listen. *Our vain mission in Vietnam. A puppet President who'll keep sending our boys there just to stay in Washington's good graces.*

For all the times he'd wished Billy and he could agree on something, Jim was worried about *this* Billy. This angry, haunted Billy. And for good reason, it turned out. Within two weeks of Billy's call from 26 Avalon Row, he disappeared. Then, just before she found Jim in Pedia-Onco, watching Porky Pig, police found Billy's body in the Pasig River.

"They said suicide." Jim began to shake his head again, bringing his fingers to his temples. "I don't believe it. Billy would have talked to me."

Milagros reached for Jim and kissed him, in the empty bedroom. She was glad to comfort him, if that's what you could call it, to lie down by the drafting table with him, to calm him all the way to sleep after.

At dawn he woke wanting to write, and she took dictation on Billy Batanglobo's vellum sketchpad. He thought Billy deserved a profile in the *Herald*'s Sunday magazine. His arc from Joe 'Kano to paranoid survivalist to conscientious objector to drowning victim in just thirty years. No editor, Milagros still asked Jim why he left out the second bomb shelter. "One shelter gets the point across," Jim said. He wanted to spare Billy's memory, his mind, the judgment of outsiders. Instead, Jim mentioned other "suicides": four Philcag Filipinos, in the last six months, who'd come home questioning their place in Vietnam—no history of suicide attempts between them, not even a tendency to wander.

Between the writing and dictation and typing and editing, he and Milagros came together: in the master bedroom, on the trundle, even on the floor of the basement, that bare, unfurnished safe haven that Billy had created before deciding all his fears had been bogus.

She woke early, before Jim, on Monday and took a last walk through the house—touching the bathroom doorknob, turning on the nursery light, running the kitchen faucet. Despite the grief and loss that hung over it like a net, she liked it here in Billy Batanglobo's house, and would be sad to leave. She imagined the family that would move into it: a lawyer and a teacher, maybe; or a doctor and a housewife. One son, one daughter. What used to be the basement bomb shelter would be their playroom when it rained outside. There was enough yard for a dog to play endless rounds of fetch in, and bury countless bones.

While Jim slept, she began to pack up what was in the kitchen cupboards. All weekend long the favor they had come to do Billy's family had been forgotten. She stacked white bowls, each blue at the rim. Billy must have eaten cornflakes from them, the corn-flakes that still sat in a box on top of the refrigerator, using the single spoon that had long dried on the dish rack.

"We work well together here," Jim said, startling her from the doorway as she unhooked pots and pans, as quietly as she could, from the wall. "Don't we?"

Milagros turned around. "I was thinking the same thing."

They were both wearing a dead man's clothes. She had combed her hair with her fingers; they had used Billy's tooth-paste and soap, and gone into his dresser drawer to replace her uniform and Jim's work shirt. They hadn't planned to spend the weekend there together, away from home.

"What if we *are* home?" said Jim.

February 8, 1986

"I voted for *her*," says Milagros's mother. "The widow."

"What made you decide?" asks Milagros. "Her platform to eliminate crony capitalism and reform the military? Or did you just go with the candidate that has the strongest popular mandate?"

She hasn't been this cruel to her mother since high school.

"I don't know about all that," says her mother. "I just like her face. She has a sweet voice, too."

"And she prays," says Milagros, unable to stop. "Don't forget about that. If not for the five children, she'd practically be a nun."

"You're angry. I don't blame you." Her mother, caught up in the opposition fever, in her own way, has pinned a yellow ribbon to her shirt. *But who's counting?* asks the radio announcer, about the election returns. *I mean this literally. You've got two groups, both calling themselves official.* On one side, the Commission on Elections, hailing the widow "Madam President." On the other, Parliament, appointed by the President himself, has given it to their old boss by a landslide.

"I hope your vote is counted, Ma," Milagros says. "And I hope this person you admire doesn't let you down."

"I doubt I'll live long enough for anyone to let me down anymore," says her mother.

The People and I have won, and we know it, the widow says. *Any victory announced by the palace will be as cooked up as the President's fake war medals.* She vows to get her fans together for street protests if she's cheated.

That night, Milagros tries, for the third time in three weeks, to join Vivi and her mother for dinner. Milagros could get through it if not for her daughter. Jackie clings to information like a dog beside the kitchen table. Any fact you throw her gets sucked dry.

"Jaime Jr. is on vacation," says Milagros, fresh out of answers.

"But school's not over yet," says Jackie.

"So many questions!" snaps Milagros. She who once swore to be the kind of mother who encouraged questions. "Is this what I get for sending you to school like you wanted?"

"But you said before—"

"Forget what I said before," says Milagros. "Jaime's away."

If mothering were an official job, someone would have docked her pay or fired Milagros months ago. She avoids her own daughter—bathes while Jackie's at school, pees while she's asleep—the way a late-arriving worker ducks the boss.

At the hospital, once upon a time, she was the patron saint of siblings. The young survivors—the ones that parents, drowning in their oceanic grief, forgot. "Your brother is dead," Milagros would tell these lost little spares. She stooped to look into their wide dry eyes: "Do you know what *dead* means?" She gave them words their parents couldn't bear to contemplate, not yet.

Who will take up Jackie's cause? Milagros knows how to work hard at a job. But she can't be both grieving parent *and* sensible nurse. *Tama na! Sobra na!* crowds are chanting at the palace. *Enough already! It's too much!* So she feels at home, with Jackie. Enough questions, too many needs. Milagros wants to shake the girl by her small shoulders. She can't forgive her for being so young and knowing so little. The only words Milagros wants to say would harm her:

Mama doesn't want to see you.

I can't be your mother right now.

You don't understand! Come back when you are older, and finally intelligent.

1972–1973

In Batanglobo Village lived doctors and lawyers, teachers and engineers. Schooled on the sweat of their parents. Theirs was a poor country, with just a handful of rich people. And less than a handful—a pinch, maybe a sliver—of people neither rich nor poor, who had some talent and a little luck on their side. A tribe of men and women special in their ordinariness. They found their frontier in Batanglobo Village, and settled it as proudly as if no one else had ever attempted mortgages or marriages before them. Their sedans blazed a trail, lined with flower beds. They pushed their strollers as if touching down on the moon.

Around the time Jim and Milagros bought 26 Avalon Row from Billy's family and moved in, the fears of martial law had risen to a fever pitch in Batanglobo Village—what it would mean not just on paper, and in presidential speeches, but in their real and daily lives. Food rationing? A massacre like in Taiwan? They imagined blood and fire in the streets, maybe a famine. In four hundred years their country had been conquered twice—three times if you counted the Japanese. Chaos was part of its mythology. Waves of panic buying swept through the neighborhood. In the supermarket Milagros stocked up on rice, sardines, instant Nescafé. Cans of evaporated milk. Bricks of desiccated glass noodles.

Living with Jim hadn't seemed to Milagros, at the time, like a political decision. Over morning coffee Jim skimmed up to twelve newspapers, at the very least the Spanish- and English-language ones. These were not underground papers. He loved Latin verbs, Associated Press style sheets, the Constitution, phrases like *due process*. He wasn't a man who hoped to bomb or dismantle anything.

For the cinder-block walls, they chose a paint color called Biscuit. They were listening to the news (Milagros understood from the beginning that they would always be listening to, or reading, or talking about the news) of an embassy bombing in London, and painting the cinder blocks Biscuit, when the radio turned to static.

They had purchased rice, sardines, and Nescafé; milk and

desiccated noodles. They'd prepared for an explosion, people screaming in the streets. Not a silence like this. Feedback from the speakers felt, after all the neighborhood whispers, like the first mishap after the broken mirror or the black cat: their bad luck finally begun. Still, Jim came down from his stepladder to adjust the dial and antenna, as if static were the issue. He turned the radio off and on. Finally he stood and looked down, like a City Hospital doctor would when one of her kids had passed.

"That's what martial law sounds like, I guess," he said.

Congress closed; then the printing presses. When they learned this—later, of course; phones were dead that night, and the neighbors knew less than they did—the thought of all those quiet, empty offices depressed them most of all.

That night Milagros felt sick. "I never get sick," she told Jim. "Work in a hospital long enough and you grow strong as a horse." But now there was no denying the fever or fatigue, quivering like egg yolk in her joints. "The smell of paint must be getting to me."

Jim placed a cheek against her forehead, the old wives' way of taking temperature.

"Maybe we should take a vacation," she said. "You know I've never been to Baguio? We could use the fresh air."

"And leave Manila?" He took his face away from hers. "Your mother gets sick, you leave her for a healthier mother?"

Milagros looked down. The floor seemed to wobble underneath her, as if they lived on the sea.

The President broke his silence the next day. *Curfew is established from twelve o'clock midnight to four o'clock in the morning.* "We aren't children, Papa," Milagros told the TV, and that became their code name for him.

If you offend the New Society, you shall be punished like the rest of the offenders.

"I better get to the office," said Jim. But the television answered, *I have also issued general orders for the government in the meantime to control media and other means of dissemination of information as well as all public utilities. And I asked the international and domestic communications, corporations, and carriers to desist from transmitting any messages without the permission of my office through the Office of the Press Secretary.*

"He can't do that," said Milagros. "Can he?"

Two days later, four khaki-uniformed officers led Jim out of 26 Avalon Row to a Metrocom car. *Utang na loob*, it turned out, had its limits. "What's the charge?" Jim asked. He looked Milagros in the eye, as if the question was for her. "Gentlemen? The charge?" The student in her stood upright, understanding she'd been given an assignment. She watched and took note, for him.

"Just come with us, boss," said the officers, in the voice one uses with a senile or demented man. They led him without handcuffs, more like bodyguards than policemen.

"Why can't I go with him?" Milagros said, as a third officer restrained her from following.

Jim shook his head at Milagros. *The assignment*, he seemed to be reminding her. She said no more, just watched him walk to the police car like a man who'd planned on this trip all along. Nothing clumsy or uncertain in him. She could see now why some colleagues jokingly called him *Capitán*. And his certainty—of himself, the course ahead—calmed her too. Milagros had grown up thinking strong, decisive men were a myth, like the mountain fairy Maria Makiling or the magical Adarna bird. Her brothers had never been in charge. Her father couldn't take them down the street without losing his way. But in this moment, with Jim, she felt sure and safe. She didn't worry. As the typhoon of history made landfall on their doorstep, she could train her eyes on this sane man, and follow him.

After the arrest, Jim's breakfast newspapers stopped arriving, as if he'd moved away or never lived there. Milagros checked their names on the mailbox, to make sure. To spook her even more, Billy Batanglobo's mail kept coming, weeks and months after his death. When the papers trickled in again, one by one, weeks later, they were striated with black bars. Sometimes a word was struck out, sometimes an entire graf, as Jim would call it. A *person* did this, Milagros realized, in wonder: these black bars were someone's job. Probably they gave this person a nameplate and a hollow title. *Media Verification Officer.* Someone's child had grown into a bureaucrat with a necktie, squeaking Pentel pens across newsprint.

She had reason to consider people's children and what they grew into. Milagros was pregnant. That fevered ache, the egg yolk in her joints, were signals from a child, about to make Milagros its mother.

She picked up twelve- and sixteen-hour shifts at the hospital, afraid to be alone at home too long. When Alicia and Cesar Resurreccion, her neighbors on Neverland Street, packed off for America, she bought their Yamaha piano, its black lacquered case scratched only a little. A piano was heavy and took up space. A piano meant lessons for their child, scheduled on the same day of every week in the same corner of the living room. Her own father had played a guitar, her brother a horn—self-taught dabblers, their instruments like snails, housed in form-fitting shells. Built to be packed up and lifted at a moment's notice, surviving eviction and transit. But a piano stayed put. She ran her fingertips across the keyboard, warming the notes. She pressed them one by one, left to right and back again. The evenings were still too quiet.

At a pet store near City Hospital she bought a Japanese spitz whose eyes shone like vinyl. Soba was the name she gave it. Pet stores too flew in the face of her childhood: the only pets she'd ever known were accidental, temporary. Strays that wandered in off the street, the pig she suspected her brothers had stolen—all were sold or killed as the family needed.

At "Camp," as she and Jim called the military prison where he ended up, Jim had a private cell. A strange concession, like the cops who called their suspect Boss and skipped the hand-cuffs. They even let him write letters. These were "checked for errors" before posting from Camp, but their code names for mar-tial law—Marsha Ley, Alex Marshall, Maria Lopez—somehow escaped notice. In her letters back to Jim she made jokes at her own expense. *The panic buying has spun out of control,* she wrote, regarding Soba and the piano. *Maria Lopez is a husband's worst nightmare.*

In the middle bedroom, she replaced Billy Batanglobo's drafting table with a writing desk for Jim. She found lithographs of Marcelo H. del Pilar and Thomas Jefferson and hung them on opposite walls, facing off as for a debate. Between the door and the desk, she hammered a row of iron nails, hooking on the last one a hundred and some odd press passes he'd kept. She imag-ined the umbrella and the suit jacket that would join them one day soon, again.

As she worked and shopped, drove and planned, she started to suspect that she, in all of this, was being watched. Which car it was she couldn't say; and when she turned, she saw no one behind her. But some mist of surveillance hung over Avalon Row. She feared not danger but judgment: the invisible officer laughing at her housekeeping skills. Would the Metrocom have left Jim alone if they'd seen lace curtains in the windows, or *gumamela* in the garden? She scrubbed the sinks at demon speed and buffed the floors with halved coconut shells. *I'm a better housewife than I'll ever be,* she wrote Jim, *and you're not here to benefit.*

Near the end of her first trimester, Milagros's own mother took pity on her and moved in, to keep Milagros company and help with the chores.

Visiting hours were from eleven to six on Sundays, in the prison amphitheater. The theater, they came to call it—like any other place a family might spend its weekend afternoon. Milagros cooked him pork rolls, *pancit,* milkfish stuffed with vegetables: painstaking dishes worthy of a baptismal party or Christmas. "Enjoy it while you can," she said. "I'd never cook like this for a man outside of prison." A radio was allowed, so long as they tuned it to music and not the news. She brought her mother and her brothers, who excelled at feasting in a dark hour. They sang songs, played Pik Pak Boom—anything but silence. And the guards couldn't resist a party any more than her brothers could. As soon as they inspected the Tupperware boxes and bamboo steamers, they accepted plates of their own, chowing down on dumplings right alongside the Sandovals and Reyeses. Over the next few weeks, they went from greeting Milagros with a nod to saluting her, as a joke.

Caught up in that carnival atmosphere, tinged as it was with an End of Days feeling, Milagros and Jim decided to make it official. Milagros's brother read aloud about Adam and Eve in the garden. "Isn't that bad luck," said her mother, "the way that story ends?" But Milagros liked the word *helpmeet* and pictured herself with Jim in the L-shaped yard, tagging every tree and flower and insect together. Father Duncan, a priest who'd taught Jim Latin at Ateneo, married them in the theater.

While the family danced around them, Jim stood behind her and measured her growing girth with his hands. "I have a plan," he said. Milagros closed her eyes. On their wedding day, couldn't the plan wait? She wanted to stand there, with her new husband's palms on her belly, thinking of Adam and Eve on Avalon Row. Jim's plans, she knew, would yank her back here, to this prison, amid khaki uniforms and black bars. Then she opened her eyes, ashamed to be thinking so small.

He'd been writing in his cell. Short pieces, which he'd need her help getting into print and to the right readers. She should expect deliveries, over the next few days, at 26 Avalon Row.

Until the arrest, Jim and Milagros had never really meant to keep the second bomb shelter a secret. They'd planned to host a housewarming, maybe: unveil it for the neighbors, repurpose it as a guest or play or storage room. But now it was clear Billy Batanglobo had left Jim more than a subject and a house. Milagros went home and studied the blueprints. She pulled the nested bed out on its wheels. Then she flipped a lever underneath the outer bed to hinge it open like a lid off the floor. She practiced descending the steel rungs of the chute, and reaching for the switch that closed the hatch and bed above her, until she could do it with her eyes closed, in five seconds flat. And one night, when her mother fried milkfish out in the yard, she added Billy's blueprints to the open flame.

Code sentences began to surface in Jim's letters. He would drop them, oddly worded, apropos of nothing, into otherwise plain paragraphs. *According to Maria Lopez, duck eggs are good for pregnant women. When the duck-egg vendor comes, buy at least a dozen.* And so the duck-egg vendor came, with pulleys and ink rollers in his cart. Milagros led him underground, where he began to build a mimeograph. She felt a guilty craving, then, for real duck eggs.

Soon she could locate those sentences in Jim's letters as expertly as she could find, in the crease of a sick child's arm, the one vein that rebounded to her touch. She palpated her way through each letter until the code rose from the page. An answer to a question she had never asked. Advice toward repairs the house didn't need.

I won't have you finishing the walls all on your own, in

your delicate condition. The walls had been done, all Biscuit-colored, for months. The painter who arrived had ink and rubber blankets inside his tin cans.

Ask the Mercados next door to recommend a piano tuner. She and the so-called piano tuner had a close call. Not fifteen minutes after he'd arrived, a khaki officer came to the door. "Sorry to disturb, ma'am. We're looking for a male suspect, about five-seven. Have you seen this man?"

Milagros shook her head at the police sketch of a stranger. "Not him, or anyone. It's been quiet here."

The khaki, looking past her head into the living room, asked if he could trouble her for a glass of water—*It's so hot outside*—and a moment on her sofa.

Just as she had seated him and turned on the electric fan, out came the "piano tuner," asking if she knew where Jim kept a wrench. "Of course when I say *quiet* I am not counting Tony," said Milagros. "Tony is part of the furniture. Is there hope for the piano, Tony? Can you fix it in time?" She placed a hand on her belly.

Tony opened the lid of the instrument and toyed with a few strings. He pressed a key, with a thinking frown on his face, pressed another. Pure luck that the khaki had no clue about pianos. Pure luck that he stood and thanked Milagros for the water, without peering into the nursery, where the trundle bed lay on its side, the basement shelter open.

After that Jim canceled the deliveries. Too risky. Milagros had to pick up the parts herself.

If Soba's loss of appetite is keeping you awake at night, then take her to the vet. My colleague used to rave about his golden retriever's doctor in Makati. In Makati men loaded the trunk of her Ford Escort with stencils and paper, while Soba's body throbbed lightly in her arms.

Piece by piece a crib came together in the nursery, while the mimeograph was assembled underground.

How Jim reached these men, Milagros didn't know. But all

of them held bits of what he planned to say. Their shorthand filled the backs of invoices, receipts, Soba's prescription. At night, Milagros waited till her mother was asleep. When it was quiet, except for the patrol cars and the geckos, she went into Jim's study. Typing by candlelight at first, then—having memorized the text beforehand—in the dark. She came to know the keys by heart, down to the distance between *R* and *E*, the way the space bar jammed with too much pressure. The dark brought back her mornings as a schoolgirl, waking before her brothers and dressing at dawn. How many breakfasts had she eaten, how many books packed, in the dark, by sense and muscle memory? How many evenings had the lights gone out over her homework, because no one had bothered with the bill? So many that in time her body memorized a link between homework and electricity themselves: if the teenage Milagros rested or stopped working some vast and complex circuit outside of her would die too. She was the conduit. And so she worked until the lights flickered back on. She kept reading, kept studying, kept dreaming of a home where the power never went out, not for that reason. That home was hers now, yet on nights like this, there seemed to have been no break at all between Avalon Row and girlhood.

As she clicked the keys she sometimes set a stopwatch, the one she used at City Hospital, to test her speed, make a game of it. It was silence she couldn't stand. Silence like a radio in September. When she had finished, she went underground and fed the stencils to the mimeo, which churned out one sheet at a time—forty-six copies of Jim's opinions a minute. But still, it chugged like a train; her heartbeat caught up to its rumble, as it had when Jim first brought her to the *Herald* headquarters. To replace the ink, she slid a barrel, heavier than her brother's old guitar, across the grooved belly of the machine until it clicked with satisfying decision into place. She shivered in the basement, cold and gray as a stone church, and warmed her fingers on the finished copies that came out.

In the theater and in letters, Milagros and Jim hoped that *Papa* would sound, to the untrained ear, like just another member of their family. Back in September, Milagros had had no idea just how much the President would live up to his code title. Papa watched over them always, everywhere: from the avenues and highways that now bore his name, to the mountain where his face was carved, Rushmore-style. *The OmniPresident*—as Jim said, and as Milagros later typed. She thought of her own papa, living in the provinces with his second family, missing all her birthdays and graduations. She could see it then. The constabulary thugs, the teenage Barangay Youth: the hole in their lives had been the hole in hers. Who could blame them for wanting the discipline, an ever-present guardian? She had longed for one too.

And this child, growing in her now: how long would he go without one?

For symmetry's sake, they called the First Lady *Mama*.

At Camp, Jim jogged in the mornings. He played chess against himself in the afternoons. Seeing his old Latin professor had him rereading Catullus, translating Horace again. *This will sound odd,* he wrote Milagros, *but Camp does have its moments.* There was, on the inside, all the time you could want, for things life and work outside didn't allow. No ringing phones at Camp, no meetings, no deadlines. Nothing to sign and nothing to complete. "Don't get me wrong," he clarified, in person. "It *is* a military jail." But at dusk sometimes the calm and quiet took on shades of Eden.

February 9, 1986

Gloria, her old friend from the picket line, smuggles in the pamphlets and the application forms. Keeping any kind of text from Jim pains Milagros, a little. Once upon a time she smuggled papers in the waistband of her skirt, for him.

These pamphlets are the second-ever secret she has kept from Jim. The first happened only last month, when she drove day and night, trying to find Jaime. She talked to khaki after khaki, even the most thuggish and intimidating: she had nothing, in her search, to lose. It came to her on one of those drives to open a checking account Jim didn't know about, socking away for bribes she might need, that might save Jaime. She'll need that money now.

YOUR CAP IS A PASSPORT! sings the front of one brochure. In the photo, a brown nurse takes a white man's blood pressure. Otherwise, the brochure is dry, plainspoken. No real sparkle or romance to the Visiting Nurse Exchange Program. Nurses, having slogged their way through chemistry and pharmacology, know how to tear through tiny black print for the main idea. Colors or pictures—who needs them? Who, besides diehards like Milagros and Jim, wouldn't go to the States in a heartbeat? That shiny, organized place where buses run on schedule and bosses pay you well? Who would pass that up for this corrupt and sloppy zoo, where—as the radio reports now—three million ballots have vanished, despite a record turnout at the polls? *Vote counters have walked out on the Commission on Elections,* the announcer says, *claiming they've been bullied to cook the returns.* Milagros dials down the volume and flips the brochure.

Bullet points lay out the perks. A work visa and help getting a green card. Housing placement, community resources. Advice on graduate school and "professional development." A one-time stipend to cover moving expenses. One-way airfare.

What are you waiting for? she seems to be reading, over and over again. *What in the world is keeping you here?*

1973

Jim wrote letters, but only on Camp paper, with Camp pens. Guards held on to Milagros's bag—and any pens or paper in it—

on their Sunday visits. Not for her, then, the soft, so-called pregnancy brain that struggled with facts and figures. Her memory, that deep-sea trawl she had perfected in algebra and Spanish and human anatomy, through exams and interviews and board certifications, stayed sharp. Also she had learned from the best, shadowing Jim at *Herald* meetings, armed only with a pencil.

Outside, she ingested all the news she could—even the candy-coated praise releases, as Jim called them, from the press secretary himself. She who once never had time for headlines and broadcasts now craved them like an addict. She worked at City Hospital until her due date, her legs swollen as she waited at security checkpoints throughout Manila. Some khakis eyed her belly as if she might be smuggling a bomb in there. And some waved her through without laying a hand on even her bag, as if she might faint or bleed or go into labor on their watch.

In May, Milagros gave birth to a son, Jaime Reyes, Jr., an epic butterball at nine pounds, ten ounces. Numbers that made friends and colleagues clench their faces in sympathy. The neighbors came and filled the nursery with Pepe and Pilar books, a wooden abacus, shape sorters and stacking rings, a foam floor puzzle of the alphabet. *Never too early.* Like Milagros, they'd all gotten where they were by worshiping the god of Education. *They can torch your house and rob you blind,* went the saying, *but they can't take Education from you.* Education made the rough places plain, as Horace Mann had promised, as the Thomasites had preached. Never mind that Education didn't always save them all. When Billy Batanglobo, the scholarship boy who'd dreamed up their little village in American graduate school, drowned; when the body of a student activist turned up not far from Diliman, her fingernails removed and skin checkered with ice-pick wounds, Milagros and her neighbors still kept the faith.

Not a day in his life did Jaime Jr. ever sleep in the crib that had been finished in the nursery. She put him there only when she heard an unexpected knock at the door and thought a khaki might be coming to inspect the house. Once the threat had passed, she brought her son back to the master bed, where as a rule he slept, between Milagros and her mother. "Just until he sleeps through the night," she said, but her new son's heat and heft against her body became a sedative she needed. He was too small and soft to live above the railroad tracks.

Once the swelling in her ankles had gone down, Milagros returned to work. Just in time to attend the annual nurses' conference at City Hospital. This year's theme: "talent export." Talent—sweeter than cane, lighter than timber, and cheaper than gold. "And on top of talent," raved an undersecretary from the Department of Labor, in his speech to all the City nurses, "you speak English." This gift from Uncle Sam was now theirs to offer the world: Filipino nurses could empty bedpans and run IVs anywhere on earth. Women Milagros had known in school and internship, at City Hospital and throughout the subdivision, had already scattered to Amsterdam and Los Angeles. Recruiters held special breakout sessions on the Middle East. The labor undersecretary quoted Papa himself, to big applause. "He says, and I quote, *We encourage the migration. I repeat, this is a market we should take advantage of.*" What was good for Melbourne and Dubai was good for Manila. "*Instead of stopping them from going abroad, why don't we produce more? I repeat, if they want one thousand nurses, we produce a thousand more.*"

"*I repeat, I repeat,*" Milagros ranted to Jim, in jail. "What are we—deaf, his people, or a nation of idiots? *Produce more?* Were we built on an assembly line?"

"Every good dictator loves a brain drain," Jim said.

"*I'm* not going anywhere," said Milagros. Ever since Papa had splashed his slogan on billboards all over the city—NO PROGRESS WITHOUT DISCIPLINE!—Milagros really had become the angry daughter.

February 14, 1986

"Will Jaime come back for Valentine's Day?" Jackie asks.

At four years old, Jackie expects the kind of Valentine's Day she had last year. Cousins from as far away as Davao came to their party. In the yard, Vivi had spread bright green *pandan* leaves on tables. They'd feasted on fried rice and barbecue with their hands. Each child had a heart-shaped paper mailbox for cards and sweets. Milagros's brother dressed as Elvis and crooned love songs at all the girls.

This year, Milagros wishes she could boycott Valentine's Day. Protest's all the rage now—not just for the ballot counters. Fifty opposition members have walked out of Parliament, not buying the sitting President's self-proclaimed victory. The widow's called a boycott of all banks and TV channels owned by loyalists. No more shopping at Rustan's. No more drinking San Miguel beer, Coca-Cola, Sprite, Royal Tru-Orange. The archbishop himself won't eat until the President steps down.

Milagros remembers her own strike in front of City Hospital. Is it possible, she wants to know, to picket one's own life? If mothering's a full-time job, as all her neighbors love to say, can't she walk out on it too?

"No," Milagros says to Jackie. "Valentine's will be quiet this year. It wouldn't be fair to have a party without him."

In other countries, there are special ceremonies for guilt. Milagros wants to zigzag a sword through her bowels. To be a dark young bride and set herself aflame. *There's* a tradition she'd uphold, this year. Jackie brings a valentine from school, made of red construction paper. Milagros tapes it to Jackie's bedroom door. She remembered to ask Vivi to buy some candy and bubble gum this morning, but now Milagros can't find it. She corners the gardener. "Did you eat Jackie's gum?" She's become someone who spits out questions and does not wait for answers.

She understands a bit of Papa's paranoia now. Betrayal needs to happen only once to cloud your vision. After that, there could be poison in each cup, a bomb in every drawer. And it's those closest to her who seem most suspect. Vivi. Gloria. Her own mother, who disappears each day to church. (So she says.) When Milagros pulls herself from bed, she walks sideways, her back against the wall.

1975

Milagros would have liked to hire a maid. Almost every house in Batanglobo Village had one. Young *dalaga* saving up for school, or old spinsters sending their siblings or nieces through it. "Tessie's like my second pair of hands and eyes," a neighbor would say. They slept on mats under mosquito nets on their employers' living room floors. *I couldn't do it without her.*

But Milagros had to watch every centavo. She swept her own floor, washed her own dishes, unclogged her own toilet. Jaime went through formula, then jars of pureed Gerber vegetables, like a high-powered vacuum, and outgrew toys and T-shirts faster than she could wash them. There was the mortgage, lawyers' fees. A refrigerator that kept guests in sandwiches and beer. A husband out of work. Soba, no longer a puppy, needed fancier kibbles, a longer leash, a stronger flea shampoo. The mimeo ink. Paper. Repairs. She paid black-market prices for the foreign newspapers, magazines, and journals that no longer came through their mailbox. Above all, she tipped.

From the time of Jim's arrest, Milagros had tipped deliverymen (those duck-egg vendors, painters, piano tuners), security guards, police officers, soldiers, librarians, bus drivers, taxi drivers, wives estranged from powerful men, black sheep disowned by blue-blood families, children. *Tips* was what she and Jim called these bribes, in the Camp theater. *Did you remember to tip that bellhop yesterday?* The same word Jim and his colleagues had once used for leads and clues. "A tip for a tip," said Milagros, thanking a source as they touched palms. She tipped people for addresses, locations, directions. She tipped drivers to bypass their appointed routes and wait while she completed her errands to take her home. She tipped secretaries for their bosses' files; she tipped interns for footage, for cassettes, for transcripts; she tipped phone operators for records; she tipped cashiers for receipts. The price tag varied. A few shiny centavos or *sari-sari* candies for the child who might point her to the right house. Upward of fifty thousand pesos to the khaki who looked the other way on a shipment of black-market ink. Tips were a line item in the household budget.

Her mother had now lived longer in their house than Jim ever had. The woman Milagros thought she'd rescued, when she pinned on her first nursing cap, from a lifetime of laundry tubs and ironing boards, came out of retirement to work for her daughter. She rocked Jaime Jr., who tipped the scales at over thirty pounds now, to sleep; or chased him as he learned to crawl and walk. It gnawed at Milagros to watch her mother's aging back bend to the kitchen sink and stove, to see her raw fingers grip a broom. The only payment she could offer was to bear, without a fight, the things her mother had to say about her husband.

Her mother doubted Jim, was harder on Milagros's man than she had ever been on her own. All the things she might have said about Milagros's father reared up belatedly, against Jim. She didn't read Jim's articles. It was enough to know that they had cost him a job and landed him in jail. Her daughter may as well have taken up with any common criminal off the street.

"You worked how hard on your degree, only to become his secretary?" said her mother, seeing Milagros stay up after her night shift to type.

"There was a time you'd have been glad," Milagros said, "for any of your children to wind up a secretary."

"I was thinking then of secretaries who get paid for their work," said her mother.

Another time she pointed to the bags under Milagros's eyes. *Even housemaids and hospitality girls take a day off once in a while.* It was true Milagros had worked a double at the hospital, then hosted friends of Jim's for dinner.

Milagros needed her mother to wash her uniform at night and starch it in the morning. To feed Jaime while she worked at the hospital. So she held her tongue.

"Don't worry about me," Milagros said. "Helping you with laundry and then waking up early to study trained me well. I don't get tired easily."

"You worked late and studied early," said her mother, "so you wouldn't spend your life doing this."

February 19, 1986

Jim visits their room more often than you would think. He's been sleeping on a cot in the basement, though everyone pretends it's the long news days making him do that. They don't say much to one another. At most, Milagros asks him what's new, and he does for her what he does best: report.

"Jackie's had her bath," says Jim. "Vivi's winding her down for bed."

"Did people come through for Ma's candidate?" she asks. "I can't see the beer boycotters lasting more than a day."

"They did, and how. There's been a run on all those banks. No one's buying copies of the *Bulletin*. Rustan's is so empty you could hear a pin drop."

"Still," she says, "I can't see him just stepping down. Can you?"

"We'll see if he has any choice. He's losing hearts and minds in D.C. fast. Although the Gipper still won't come out and tell his old friend to resign."

These are safe subjects. They don't fight; they have fought enough. Some days, Jim offers a hand, and usually, Milagros takes it. But the old sympathies that used to course between them don't return. Her hand turns limp. She absents herself from her own flesh, the way the infant Jaime Jr.'s weight would slacken in her arms as she rocked him asleep.

1976

Jaime Jr. grew upward and out, with an appetite to match his size. Sweets would be his downfall—so Milagros thought. Pocky biscuit sticks, White Rabbit candies, whose rice-paper wrapping you could also eat, Sarsi cola. He loved all of it; spent, promiscuously, his pocket change. In a year or two, she'd have to rein it in. Before the fat jokes began, or the diabetes or the rotten teeth. One day the knuckle dimples and the wrist folds would not be cute. "Jaime can wait," she sang, like a broken record. *Jaime knows how to wait.*

At his third birthday party Jaime reached for a Shakey's pizza that had not yet cooled, giving himself second-degree burns. *Jaime! What did Mama say about waiting?* She started him at Ateneo preschool with two bandaged hands. Other parents threw them side stares: what child burns both hands on a Shakey's pizza? How much, exactly, was known about Jaime Reyes, Jr.'s *life at home?* Milagros couldn't blame them. She would have thought the same. *Impulse control,* she noted in her mind. *Teach him impulse control.*

These were her worries then, at the age of twenty-seven: rotten teeth, pudgy fingers, shiny wrappers, caps of soda bottles. She taught Jaime to chew on fluoride tablets that foamed red in his mouth. She set rules: milk and vegetables before cake and candy. Inside the walls of 26 Avalon Row, teaching Jaime the Lord's Prayer and marking his height on the doorjamb of the nursery every six months kept her calm enough to face that other world, whose rules and routines weren't hers to make. Camp, where her husband lived, indefinitely; where neighbors landed every day; where guards frisked all thirty-seven, thirty-eight, then thirty-nine inches of her son for contraband pens and paper.

Almost four years after his arrest, Jim finally found out what he had done to get there.

"They call it rumormongering," one of the lawyers said, meeting with Jim and Milagros in the theater. A new charge for a New Society.

Jim tented his fingers. Milagros imagined them cupping around someone's ear, Jim whispering as in a game of telephone. *Rumormongering*. Four years came down to this cooked-up, girlie-sounding crime.

"It's a capital offense now," said the second lawyer. "But we think we can talk the press secretary down to ten years. That is, unless you're willing . . ."

She knew what *unless* meant, and wished the lawyers would leave while she and Jim conferred. But Jim did not send anyone away.

". . . to publish a correction."

"Ten years is a decade," she said to Jim, like an idiot.

"So by my math," said Jim, "I've got six left." She'd heard that prison aged a man, but by some miracle her husband looked the same. His face hadn't weathered like an old shoe, as some husbands' in the subdivision were starting to. He'd lost a little weight perhaps, a few pounds, which on his frame looked like more. Every day, next to a guard who took the blade back after, he still shaved his face clean.

"That's if you trust them," she said.

"Your wife makes a good point," said Lawyer Number Three.

It was the lawyers who were growing old, the shadows darkening under their eyes. "It took this long to get a charge. Do you expect them to keep their word, when ten years are up?"

"Thank you," said Jim. "You've explained the alternative."

"*Jim,*" she said. "Are you sure?"

He gave her the look he'd given in the yard when the khakis took him away. But they had a son now, didn't they? They'd lived apart longer than they'd lived together.

No matter; the discussion had ended. The lawyers looked at her with pity, so she tried a joke. "Rumormongering!" she cried. "*Tsismis,* in other words. If gossip is a crime now, they should arrest half of Manila. Why isn't my mother in jail?"

The first of the three lawyers resigned that day. A few weeks later, the second left for America. The third said, "I'll stay and fight for you," but looked like all he wanted was a nap. Milagros understood they were alone now, in this life of theirs. Every Sunday, while her mother was at church near Batanglobo Village, Milagros and Jaime Jr. went to the theater.

"Hello there, little man," was how Jim often greeted their son.

"No" was what Jaime had to say to his father. He hid behind Milagros's leg.

"Jaime, that's your papa. Say hello."

"That's all right," said Jim. He gave Jaime a smile. "We can dispense with the formalities."

Jaime slowly yielded handshakes, hugs, high fives. Just before they left, maybe a kiss. Father Duncan said a quick-and-dirty Mass, with SkyFlakes and a gallon drum of Welch's grape juice. But Jaime never liked the theater, preferred the courtyard where the other prisoners' children played. Which was just as well. Jim had business to attend to with Milagros.

His sentences came out whole—forged, as she had also seen during the Billy Batanglobo project, in the calm factory of Jim's mind—and punctuated. Along with code names, Jim spoke in a full-body sign language that escaped the guards. For each paragraph break, he leaned back or forward in his chair. She had an excuse now to stare at the tented fingers she had always loved: a tap of his left fingertips to his right meant a comma. Right index fingertip to left was a colon; pinkie to pinkie a semi. He bent his knuckles and locked his fingers together for a period.

"I don't know how you do it," a neighbor in the subdivision said. "What's a marriage, if you can't wake up next to each other in the morning?" But Milagros felt no woman ever knew her husband as well as she knew Jim, watching and reading him as she did.

Watching his hands move, she'd remember how they'd moved on her. She was in trouble when, in need of other signals, he actually did touch her. To open a set of quotation marks, his right hand took Milagros's left; to close them, his left her right. Now and then he traced his fingertips along her brow, tucking a strand of hair behind her ear and finishing along her jaw and at her chin, the approximate shape of a question mark. She closed her eyes then, the signal for him to repeat what he had said, more slowly; she would concentrate on getting it this time. Very rarely did he flick the end of her nose with his fingertip, in exclamation, and when he did he almost always shook his head no, the signal to erase. By the time he crossed his leg under the table, making sure he brushed Milagros's shin along the way, to say the piece was finished, *she* was finished too.

She stood on clumsy knees, sometimes skipping the good-bye embrace, afraid that would undo her altogether. She rushed out of the theater, grabbed their son from the courtyard, and drove home, shaking all the way. After depositing Jaime with her mother, she made it to the study Jim had yet to use, the only room at 26 Avalon Row that had a lock. In private, she wept. Once she recovered, remembering her task, she unlocked the door and washed her face in the hall.

It was her professional self who returned to his study after that, to feed the stencil sheets into the typewriter and tap out his new byline, Mia E. Jersey. An anagram, easy enough to unscramble. He did nothing, either, to disguise the style familiar to any of his onetime *Herald* readers. Taunting the regime, currying disfavor. It shocked her how short the pieces turned out to be, on paper. Her hours in the theater with Jim felt so much fuller than the palm-size square of text she'd later type onto the page (single-spaced, and framed by thick white margins, as Jim liked it); and clone on the mimeograph; and pass on to the neighbors, who passed them on in turn, to people headed for America or elsewhere, who sometimes brought them to Jim's friends at foreign papers, some of whom reprinted them.

These days Jim was paying close attention to a Camp inmate who slept ten cells away from him. They'd crossed paths years before at the Congress Building. A senator who never met a camera or mic he didn't love: Jim had taped him calling the regime *a garrison state,* the First Lady *our latter-day Eva Perón.* A presidential hopeful (any fool who followed politics in Manila knew it), dropping chestnuts for voters to repeat at dinner and remember at the polls. The 1973 election would have been his big chance, but for the Proclamation and arrest that landed him at Camp, with Jim, who could not convince the guards to allow a private interview. And so the Reyeses could only watch the former senator and his wife from a distance in the theater on Sundays, praying at Mass, talking. They code-named him Kuya, or big brother; and his wife Ate, big sister, for symmetry's sake. *At least I didn't marry a politician,* Milagros thought. Kuya had refused a trial—*kangaroo court* was his chestnut now, and *trumped-up charges*—and taken solitary confinement, a hunger strike, and finally a death sentence, instead. *There but for the grace of . . .* For all the trouble Jim was in, Milagros thought, another woman's husband had it worse.

February 22, 1986

The first time Billy Batanglobo—the dead man who designed this house—appears to her, she senses him in her skin, the spread of cold pinpricks along her back. From her bed, facing the wall, she hears a dripping sound, smells fetid Pasig River water. And when she turns he's standing in her doorway: the bloated, water-rotted version of the man she's seen in Ateneo yearbooks, whose name still surfaces now and then inside their mailbox.

"We threw all your mail away," she says. She's not afraid of ghosts. Especially not one in soaked Levi's, his muddy Adidas leaving puddles on the floor as he approaches, his polo shirt clinging to his swollen gut.

Nineteen men have been arrested and detained at Fort Boni-facio for an attempted coup and an assassination plot against the President and First Lady.

"I swam ashore while it was still dark," Billy Batanglobo tells her, the water leaking from his ears and nose. "And there were navy boats already parked from the bay to Guadalupe, guarding the palace."

"You were well out of it," Milagros says, meaning Manila.

"And now you want out too," says Billy. "You'd like America. I stayed for seven years, and only left so I could re-create it here." He sits on the edge of the bed, close to her knees, but Milagros doesn't shift away from him. "But I should warn you. You can leave a place, but places have a way of not leaving you. I learned that after Vietnam. You won't forget what happened here, no matter where you go or how you try." His body makes a damp print in the sheets, and still she doesn't move. Something about him, foul and decaying as he is, attracts her.

"Jim and I defiled your house," she says, again to prove she's not afraid. "We weren't even married yet. Your body wasn't cold. We christened every room in your precious little model home."

Billy Batanglobo laughs, also unafraid. "And that's the kind of memory I mean," he says. "The kind that will hit you, on a sidewalk in New York or wherever, so hard you have to sit down on the curb to catch your breath. And who's to say you deserve to forget? You, about to leave your daughter, in a country that still doesn't know its own fate?" Billy leans over, seizes her wrists with sopping, pruned fingers, bringing his face so close she smells his gassy river breath and sees the veins through his stretched, almost translucent skin; and then, as the cold water drips from his face onto hers, she *is* afraid. She closes her eyes. "There *is* one way to forget—*truly* forget—everything."

"Jim doesn't believe you drowned yourself," Milagros whispers, without opening her eyes.

"Does it matter? I'm gone, aren't I? You can come with me."

He repeats the invitation twice, three times, lying beside her in the master bed and holding her until the words sound like a lullaby, a consolation. She dreams of forgetting as Billy forgot: by floating, and then sinking. She wakes alone. The sheets are dry. She checks the living room: Billy's not there; no one is. All she hears is Jim, on the phone in his study, with the door open. "Asylum in the States," he says. "That's what I'm hearing."

She walks the corridor, expecting a puddle any second. But the floor is dry too. She knows then Billy Batanglobo's hers alone; no one else invited to his world.

"You can drive out there and see it for yourself," she hears Jim saying. "Marines at the gates. Water cannon trucks and Scorpion tanks, on every road that could possibly lead to the palace."

1979

Sunday after Sunday they met in the theater, where wives wept and husbands spoke low, and families sang to drown out their fear. They went to Father Duncan's makeshift Mass, exchanged code words. Before sunset Milagros would collect her son from the playground and leave.

But once a month, in a cabin on the other side of Camp, they let Jim's wife stay overnight. These visits flew. In the dark, Milagros and Jim shed the slow careful pace of theater Sundays along with their clothes. Codes and signs had no place in that cell. They did not talk politics. If they spoke, they did so in rough commands, single syllables, cries or grunts or sighs that were not words at all. On the first of these visits, she'd brought towels to drape over the surveillance camera and to line the doorjamb. But once she knew how fast the time went, she did not care what anyone saw or heard.

They talked about Being Careful. She was already raising a child alone.

"No," said Milagros. "I want one place in our life where we can act free."

But she didn't get pregnant. She came home to only one child waiting at the door. The child who followed her around like a lamb and bleated sadly when she had to go to work. The child who never questioned why the room that held his toys was not the room he slept in at night. All he wanted was to be near her. As well as she came to know her husband at Camp, she was convinced no son and mother ever were as close as she and Jaime were. She knew she'd have to cut the strings someday. But for now, Milagros held tight.

She did attempt to drill him for grade one as all the other mothers would. Jaime would look up from the flash card or the workbook, his puppy eyes pleading. *Let's ditch this boring busi-*

ness and play hide-and-seek. Now and then she put her foot down. Some things he simply had to learn. But most times she relented. *We'll try again tomorrow.* When they went outside to walk Soba together, Milagros held the leash. As newlyweds Milagros and Jim had agreed: no chores until the age of six. *Play is the work of the child,* a schoolteacher-neighbor was fond of saying, and the Montessori slogan felt as powerful to them as *Makibaka!* or Fight the Power.

"Mama," Jaime would say at bedtime, "you know everything, don't you?"

"Mama, I wish we could stay home from school and work tomorrow."

"Mama, you're my best friend."

He didn't care about politics. Life with Jaime Jr. was all cuddles, all games, all splashing Soba with the garden hose. The dummy shelter under the yard was his playground, the chute leading down from its round hatch his slide. It smelled like mold down there, and runoff from monsoons sometimes inched up from the dirt floor to Jaime's calves, but he loved it. And when the khakis came sniffing, Jaime showed them how his voice bounced off the round steel tunnel and the cot that he believed was there for him. When she had to cut off his cartoons to watch the news, she could send him down to entertain himself for ages with the walkie-talkies, the first-aid kit, the yellow Geiger counter Billy Batanglobo had left behind.

These days, watching the news was not so different from doing rounds at City Hospital. "Papa's fat," Milagros told Jim. "Red patches all across his face. They're calling it an allergy." In her living room, Milagros and the neighbors floated their own diagnoses during every speech and proclamation. Stabbing his swollen fingers into the air, the President reminded her of Vienna sausages, all the cans of food they'd panic-hoarded in the days leading to martial law.

The city, too, showed symptoms, flaring up. After seven years of DISCIPLINE and PROGRESS, Manila was bursting into flames: at the Sulo Hotel, in the floating casino on Manila Bay, at Rustan's department store. With the Partido Komunista grown thousands strong since 1972, Jim wrote that the Philippines had finally become the country—dangerous, divided, terror-prone—that Papa claimed it was, back when he'd cried state of emergency. The fears of bombs and chaos, a city on fire, come to pass.

A bad heart saved their Kuya from the firing squad, for now. He flew to Dallas for surgery, then on to teach in Boston. The Church of Best and Youngest, First and Most, prayed for him. Another wonder boy in exile.

February 22, 1986

What is it like, for Papa—the OmniPresident, as Jim has written—to learn his own men have been plotting against him?

Milagros hears reports from Camp Aguinaldo, the army head-quarters where the defense minister is holed up, surrounded by sympathetic troops. Then the chief of the armed forces lands in a helicopter, to join him.

Ideas of betrayal—in here, out there—bleed into each other.

Between long naps she can hear Vivi's voice. *Your mother says,* she's telling Jackie, *your father says.* What little seeds is she planting? Milagros has inklings all the time now, has grown a detective's gut. She opens a drawer and rummages through the pink plastic rollers. When was the last time she used rollers? But now there are strands of hair stuck inside, curlier than her own, a tinge of fake auburn. Vivi's hair.

When the defense minister and army chief take the mic themselves, it's to declare war on the palace.

He is not the President to whom we pledged our service.

We appeal to the Armed Forces and National Police to join us in this crusade for better government.

Reports have circulated of our impending arrest. We plan to die here fighting.

"If you can deceive me like this, what else are you capable of!" Milagros holds the roller out to show Vivi the kink in the strand, the faint smell of coconut oil.

At nine o'clock, the archbishop is on the air. *I ask all my brothers and sisters listening to go to Camp Crame and Camp Aguinaldo to support our two good friends. Leave your homes now. Bring food if you can.*

Our two good friends.

They're all friends, aren't they? Milagros thinks.

After you pray tonight, start fasting, says the archbishop. *Don't eat until I tell you. We're at war here, and you the soldiers.*

1981

Two weeks after New Year's firecrackers blazed across Manila, Milagros and her neighbors watched the President on TV, reciting Proclamation 2045.

A sound economy.

A secure nation.

The end of martial law.

Afterward, the First Lady sobbing into a white handkerchief and singing to the crowd. "Why's she crying?" asked Jaime.

A neighbor said, "Her happy days are over."

An anticlimax, nothing like the spine-chilling beginning, nine years before. Milagros now took presidential words for what they were. Shapes on paper, sounds on a screen. The gaps between *sound economy* and the unemployment lines stretching to Saudi Arabia and America; between *secure nation* and the bombs that seemed to go off every other day in Manila—these were the spaces she and her neighbors lived in.

So when the lawyer called to say Jim's name was on a list, she wrote off the words—*pardon, release*—as only words. She had a job to go to, and a superstitious streak. Her mother shopped and cleaned as for a party—but with the neighbors, Milagros hedged. *They say I'll have my husband back on the thirty-first. I'll believe it when I see it.* When the day came, she picked Jaime up from school and came home to a crowded living room, the neighbors toasting with beer and *pulutan*, and Jim, holding court among them. The room quieted and Jim turned with a smile, raising his bottle.

"You're back" was all she could say.

Jaime did not let go of her hand as Jim embraced her and she wept. Years ago she'd have felt shy, reuniting before other people, but conjugal visits with guards outside the door had cured that. Her neighbors cheered.

"Why are you crying?" Jaime asked.

"Because I'm *happy*," sobbed Milagros, and she was. Happy. Overwhelmed. "Say welcome home, Papa."

"Welcome home, Papa." Sideways, Jaime eyed the man who'd just, as far as he was concerned, made his mother cry. The man who'd never, in his almost eight years, driven him to school or played catch in the yard with him as other fathers did.

Somehow she forgot to plan for Jim's first night in the master bedroom since 1972. Without waiting to be asked, her mother brought a straw mat and mosquito net into the living room to sleep there. But Jaime, before the last of the neighbors left, tucked himself in where he'd always slept, his whole life: in the master bed.

Jim and Milagros stood at the foot of the bed, looking at him.

"He's old enough to sleep on his own," Jim whispered.

"I don't disagree. But where?"

"We've got an extra room."

"You mean the nursery?"

"Yes." He laughed. "The room where children sleep."

"The room with a bomb shelter underneath the bed?"

"Former bomb shelter. Now an office."

Milagros shook her head. "How will that work? Reporters waking him at night to pop open the trundle bed?"

"We can put another bed in there. And nine is old enough to know what kind of work his father does."

"He'll be eight in May." She wondered, without asking, how old that was in fatherless years. Rather than argue, she picked Jaime up. Walking him into the nursery did confirm how big he'd grown, how heavy: too old for his parents' bed, too old to be carried, really. She put him in the trundle, with misgivings.

In the master bedroom, they undressed. Only they had spent eight years in confined spaces, desire scheduled to one day a month. Now the space they had to move and stretch and wrap around each other felt extravagant and awkward. Inhibitions she had shed so quickly in the prison guards' presence returned, with her mother and son nearby. They went about it silently: her body in a bed with Jim, her mind in the nursery, where her son was sleeping alone for the first time, without knowing it. When they fell asleep, she dreamed of the trundle bed collapsing hellward, Jaime swallowed by a pit of flames. She woke, sat up, could hear Jaime bawling in the next room, as if they'd shared the nightmare. Without rousing Jim for permission, she rushed to the nursery and brought her son back to the master bed. Throughout the night she tossed and turned, first facing her husband, then her son, one's snores and then the other's kicks keeping her up.

For weeks she struggled to fit the two halves of her life back together. Separating Jim and their marriage from all she had to do at home and at the hospital was how she'd managed not to break down at the nurses' station, or lie awake all night in their bed. She'd lived her life with him only in designated rooms, boxes of time: the Sunday theater, the conjugal cabins, the basement where she printed all his work. Now here he was, colliding into everything she didn't know she'd been protecting from him.

She didn't budge on Jaime in the master bedroom. *All right, Jo. I work better at night anyway.* Instead, she and Jim stole mornings in the basement, Jaime still asleep, before Milagros's early shifts at the hospital. The basement felt familiar to their bodies. Slowly, then, he clicked back into place at 26 Avalon Row.

The *Metro Manila Herald* invited Jim back, but not into his old post. They could only offer him something in Entertainment. "And so the charge comes true," he said. "Jim Reyes, gossipmonger." Reporters at the City Desk, meanwhile, passed their time on praise releases from Malacañang Palace. *Might as well try writing with their hands tied behind their office chairs.* But he—still the scholarship boy, the company man, after all—held on to his job, and waited for the dead *Herald*'s resurrection.

For the first time in their marriage they were both working outside the house again. If she closed her eyes and just breathed in the normal-seeming air, she could believe no time at all had passed. They were the newlyweds they might have been years ago, if history had been different.

What her mother had to say about Jim and his work took on a different flavor. Every time Jim stayed up or out late—to toast a colleague, see a source, pore over public records with a young and eager journalism student—the innuendo from her mother would begin. *"Journalism student—*is that the code these days? And what's he teaching her?" Or "All that time out in the world, and in his study. How much could that leave for a wife and son?" She found gaps in Jim's stories, reminding Milagros when he'd said nine o'clock and didn't pull into the garage till eleven.

Milagros knew all about looking the other way. But only when it came to Jim's work. At home, after his day at the *Herald,* he kept writing. His first piece, dictated to her in the transformed study that once held Billy Batanglobo's drafting table, took a microscope to Proclamation 2045. The fine print, where the old rules all hid, in effect: the President's emergency powers, the right to redeclare martial law as he saw fit. Why the pomp and trouble, then, of setting men like Jim free? The Pope, said Jim. The Pope, who'd gotten cold feet about visiting Manila, on account of what he called the regime's unchristian human-rights record. A big gesture had been needed to change the Pope's mind back.

The *Herald* wouldn't print this. And when a smaller paper, with braver editors, would, its offices were raided and shut down before press time. So Milagros mimeo'd and mailed it out, like the ones before. Still under the name Mia E. Jersey, like a double-living comic-book superhero.

To silence her mother, Milagros gave her a retirement gift. "You're free, Ma," she said. "You deserve it." And so, to 26 Avalon Row, came Vivi, a small woman ill-fitted with big features. Barely taller than the broom they gave her, most of her face taken up by eyes and teeth. Delicate wrists, a man's hands. On her first day, a mouse darted out from under the refrigerator, and without pause or fumble Vivi struck it with the stick end of the broom: one blow, dead.

They had only a vague sense of where Vivi was from: *the provinces,* as city people said. Inherited from an *amo* who had fled the country in the last year of martial law. In all tasks, Vivi's mouth helped Vivi's hands. A front tooth hinged out farther than the rest, most likely from this habit of using her teeth as fingers: gripping the clothespins, folding the dish towels, struggling with stubborn plastic packaging.

"After eight years of marriage," joked Milagros, "you finally have a wife!"

Now there was garlic rice with fried eggs and sweet pork sausage every morning. Vivi washed the dishes after every meal, so that Milagros could help Jaime with his homework. Vivi kept the house so they could live in it. Vivi used the newspapers, once shredded, to line Soba's dog kennel.

By late August, Milagros was pregnant again. Two children, bracketing martial law like bookends.

February 22, 1986

Milagros catches some television on her way from the bed to the bathroom and back. City Hospital has already accepted her letter of resignation. This is her only commute now: between the radio in the bedroom, patching straight in to the rebels' camp, and the TV in the living room, still run by the President.

On Channel Four, he tells the rebels to surrender. That, or face artillery attacks, from troops already parked outside their camp.

Milagros avoids the kitchen table, where flowers, cards, and pastries still arrive every day, and returns to her bedroom. She has banned all guests, other than Gloria.

But her mother can't say no to a priest. She knocks and swings open the bedroom door. Pale, lanky Father Duncan stands beside her.

"What if I weren't decent, Ma?"

"I'm sorry, *iha*." Her mother dips her head to the priest. "Father," she says, meaning, *She's all yours*. Then she leaves.

"They've called in the big guns," says Milagros. "I'm that hopeless."

"They didn't call. I wanted to come."

"But who's at Ateneo, teaching the boys Latin?"

"It's Saturday." He sees a chair against the wall. "May I?"

Milagros motions to it and turns up the radio. "Were you there?"

Father Duncan nods, raises his voice over the volume. "Nothing there yet but a few sandbags. They wouldn't stand up to little Jackie's toy wheelbarrow. I did see one boy holding up a sign that said, MAKE LABAN NOT WAR. That made me smile."

Laban: to fight, resist. And LABAN: *Lakas ng Bayan,* or "Strength of the Nation," the widow's opposition party. She's heard it translated on the radio as "People Power," but likes it better in Tagalog. More muscular, more like a fist. "LABAN NOT WAR?" she repeats. "That's good." She does not ask, *How old was the kid, and who gave him that sign? His parents?*

Father Duncan lays a warm, pastoral hand on hers. On the radio, a rebel's wife asks for the people's prayers. *And if possible send bread, not sacks of* bigas. *There's really no way to cook rice at Camp.*

Milagros winces. She remembers this. How your thoughts get smaller the more scared you are. "When Jaime went missing," she tells Father Duncan, "I kept wondering if there was anyone to remind him to cut his fingernails. My son was kind of a slob, you know. His nails grew fast and got so dirty." Now the Marines might execute her husband, and Mrs. Rebel wants to talk about rice.

"He was a good boy," says the priest.

Milagros almost says, *Not a star student like Jim, your favorite,* then stops herself. "What can I do for you, Father?"

"I came because I saw Jim at EDSA," says Father Duncan. "In his element, somewhat. You can imagine. Interviewing the crowds, trying to sneak into Camp. But something struck me as . . . lonely about him, today. I've never seen that, not even when we were both locked up."

At the mention of her husband, Milagros takes her hand away.

"Of course I thought of Jaime, but not just Jaime. I also thought of you. How his work depends on you, your life together."

So the priest has come to recommend his former student, urge his wife to join Team Jim again. With that old behind-every-great-man rigmarole. They're all the same to her now, this fraternity of men, who televise their hunger strikes, print articles after they're told to stop. They prize their causes and their names, their principles and legacies, above all. They eat the rice without wondering how it got cooked and to their table. They name sons after themselves and never once worry about those sons' fingernails.

"His grief may not look like yours," says Father Duncan. "But you'd know, if you talked to him, that he's grieving too. Sharing grief helps dissipate it—you know that, from where you've worked. The more you hoard a grief, the bigger it grows."

She says nothing, doesn't even remember falling asleep. The priest has left by the time she wakes to more voices on the radio—politicians, "concerned citizens"—all saying *get to EDSA now.* What exactly will they do, Milagros wonders, when the tanks come? Will the rebel soldiers give them guns?

The more you hoard a grief.

Why should she share? The world has not been generous with her.

1982

Jacqueline Reyes arrived two months early. Under local anesthesia, Milagros felt the doctor's scalpel zip her open layer by layer, like a silk purse. Gloved hands swimming busily inside her. A four-pound, three-ounce creature needing two sound smacks before wailing. Her undergrown lungs went straight into distress. The doctor put her—purple, sputtering—into an incubator. In poor shape herself, Milagros needed a blood transfusion. Only a week later did she get to the NICU to reach her own glove through the incubator hatch and feel Jackie's tiny digits wrap around her index finger.

That was the most contact they had. None of the brass-band fanfare that had greeted Jaime Jr.'s birth.

After Jackie came home, Milagros's milk broke her out in hives. Only a lactose-free formula agreed with her. Jackie had finicky tastes, like the princess in the pea-and-mattress story, thin-skinned to anything common. She cried if the person holding the bottle adjusted his arm. She cried when she startled herself awake at night. Once old enough to sit upright, she'd stamp her palms against a grown-up's shoulders and push back to examine his or her face. *Prove yourself,* her scowl seemed to demand.

With Jaime Jr., Milagros feared excess. Raising a soft sort of man who couldn't waddle up stairs without wheezing. With Jackie, she feared deficiencies. The wispy appetite that made her spit after every nibble. Disorders like anemia and jaundice.

Milagros tried to call her Jacqueline, but the world insisted on Jackie, or in some cases even Jacks, like the common street game, rubber balls and plastic stars hanging in net bags at every *sari-sari* store. And for all her littleness, her refusal to eat, her rashes and her weak lungs, Jackie did have something of the gutter rat about her: the wiry alertness, the stops and starts and darting side glances. In this way Milagros should have known that Jackie'd be the one to survive, the way a rodent could swim through pipes and chew through steel.

February 23, 1986

By some miracle Gloria makes it through the traffic to see her again. "I ran into your husband at the gate," says Gloria. She doesn't touch the canvas tote strapped to her shoulder. "We talked for a while."

"Oh?" says Milagros. No use changing the subject; experience has taught her that when people say they talked for a while with Jim, armored tanks won't stop them from saying more.

"He asked me if I'd gone to the barricades yet," Gloria says. "'Yet?' I said. 'You talk like it's a given.' My husband would kill me! Jim said he couldn't understand that. He'd seen me right there, at City Hospital, when we went on strike. Remember?"

"That was a long time ago."

"Right. The stakes are higher now, I told Jim. Back then I

could have lost my job. Now I could die, or my children could."
Gloria, hearing herself, panics. "I mean—"

"Did you bring them?" says Milagros. "The application forms?"

Gloria takes a folder from her bag and sets it on the nightstand, right beside the radio. "He said that wouldn't happen. He said, what's more likely is that you'll live another fifty years or so. Your children will grow up to ask you where you were on February twenty-third, nineteen eighty-six. What will you tell them? That you played it safe? That history was happening, and all you wanted was to save your hide? They'll ask, *What was it like?* And you will have to say, *Go read a book on it,* because you weren't there."

"He says a lot of things." Milagros's heart clenches, fist-like. "He has a way with words. But guess who'll *never* ask where we were February twenty-third, nineteen eighty-six?"

That shuts Gloria up for a while. Then she says, "My mother told me life doesn't happen to men the same way that it happens to a woman. *It's a mistake to think that,* she said. A woman has her child, and she becomes a mother first. A man stays first a man. Especially a man like Jim."

Turns out Manila people still do what their archbishop tells them, says the radio. They've flocked to the rebels with batteries, cigarettes, and flashlights. Colgate has sent toothpaste; Palmolive, soap. *And food, of course! We are Pinoys, aren't we?*

"Sounds like you've made up your mind," says Milagros, seeing an older Gloria, in the future, telling her children, *We were too excited to be scared.* "Have fun at EDSA."

"It is a nice night to be out." Gloria shrugs. Through the sheer curtain Milagros sees the almost full moon, its light landing on the folder on the nightstand by the radio.

1983

Within Jackie's first year, routine ruled the weekday afternoons. Milagros rose before dawn for the early shift at City Hospital: a way to reunite with Jackie by afternoon and be with both her children until bedtime. At seven-thirty the school bus came for Jaime. Vivi attended to the clothes and meals and dust and baby. Milagros was home before the bus brought Jaime back at four o'clock. Bedtime was at ten, after prayers and two or three storybooks.

Bedtime for a young Milagros had varied with the moods of the man next door, who liked to hit his wife when drunk and make loud love to her when sober. The one routine she'd ever witnessed was that man's son, Boyet, coming outside every morning to do what he called his Exercise. Slow, drooling, soft-in-the-brain Boyet. Neighbors liked to whisper that his father, convinced the unborn Boyet wasn't his, had been extra heavy with his hands throughout the pregnancy. That she had tried and failed to get rid of Boyet. That Boyet had these reasons to thank for his large, lopsided head, the mouth that could barely cry *Ma!* and *Pa!* Boyet did his Exercise by the gutter in their *barangay*. Milagros could see him from her window: bending to the side, the front, the back. Arms up to the sky, fingertips down to the ground. Twist left, twist right. She heard him wailing sometimes through the wall they shared.

Now Jim and Milagros shared walls with no one, and Avalon Row was not the world of their parents. There were pet vaccines here, and the cinder blocks stood up against typhoons.

That same year, their Kuya was rumored to be coming home, after three years abroad. All over Manila people tied yellow ribbons around trees, after the song. Hoping the exiled former senator might run for President, at last.

The day of his return, Milagros had a typical shift at City Hospital, no busier than any other. At quitting time, she saw nurses, parents, doctors, and sick children's siblings packed into the waiting room. A room that saw its share of grief, for sure. Milagros heard the muffled cries of one mother against one nurse's shoulder, figuring another child—not one of hers—had died.

Which child was it? A favorite among the staff, judging by the crowd. The nurses wept so openly it embarrassed Milagros a little. *Pull yourself together, Alma! Effie, that's enough!* These parents and doctors still had to trust them with IVs and dosage charts, after all. But a certain Dr. Tuazon was crying too. She neared the room: some parents were consoling nurses, not the other way around; some parents whose children were doing better, consoled each other. All of them repeating facts, phrases they couldn't bring themselves to believe yet. *Shot dead. Broad daylight. Cold blood.* She understood, finally, when one of the nurses turned to her at the doorway, shaking her head and holding out her hand, inviting Milagros to share in the shock. Those not crying or embracing watched the black-and-white TV on the wall. Kuya, the former senator, facedown on the airport tarmac, steps from the plane that had flown him home.

When the screen blanked—multicolored bars, PLEASE STAND BY—Milagros called Jim from the nurses' station. But he wasn't at the *Herald,* of course. He'd planned to be at the airport. He'd been invited. Shoulder to shoulder, Milagros imagined him, with the photographers who'd captured Kuya on the ground.

That night, in his study, Jim played back a tape from Kuya's Hong Kong "press-con," just before he boarded for Manila. *I am wearing a bulletproof vest, but if they shoot me in the head, I'm a goner.* Instructions to his entourage to think fast with their cameras and mics. *In three–four minutes it could all be over.*

I may not be able to talk to you again after this.

"We weren't quick enough," Jim said. No capture of the death itself, the shooting. Only the lifeless bodies afterward: Kuya's, and nearby the man gunned down seconds after him, pegged as his murderer.

The Betamax tape they got hold of later that week said DUPLICATE COPY. A label, a command. Just before they pressed play, the children came into the living room. Jaime holding Jackie, new to walking, by the wrists, stooping to help her toddle forward. "Can we watch too?" he asked.

Milagros and Jim exchanged a look. Agreed without words, as they often had at Camp. The newspapers had been there at breakfast: Kuya's body on the tarmac, at the kitchen table in between the white cheese and warm *pan de sal*. No doubt the Ateneo priests at Jaime's school would say something, if they had not already, about their fallen Eagle, at morning chapel or assembly. And whatever parents said on phones and in kitchens in Batanglobo Village would be overheard and then repeated on playgrounds and at recess. Far better for the Reyeses to get ahead of what the kids would learn by accident.

Besides, children were also citizens.

"This is not a movie," Milagros began, in her hospital voice. "It's real, and might upset you. Do you understand?" She'd seen enough needles at City give the lie to *This won't hurt a bit.* "A man has died," Milagros said. "Someone shot him with a gun at the airport last Sunday."

Jaime recognized his name from lawn signs and the news and Ateneo. "Who shot him? Why?"

"We don't know." Jaime sat beside his mother, latching on to her elbow with both his hands, as frightened at age ten of the TV as he'd been at three of underbed monsters. His scalp, to Milagros, smelled innocent. "There were many people in this country who liked him. Some liked him so much they wanted him to run for President. But not everybody did."

These were the euphemism years, when the dead had *dis-*

appeared or been *salvaged,* when Presidents had *allergies,* not autoimmune diseases; when people were in *safe houses,* not *prisons.* Papa's habit of renaming was the one issue on which she'd seen Jim lose his cool. *Words have* meanings, she had heard him say, his voice almost cracking. *You can't just slap a sign on hell and call it paradise.* Between their parents' lottery-ticket dreams and the First Lady's poetry about *the Good, the True, and the Beautiful,* frankly, the Reyeses were down on euphemism.

The four of them watched Kuya rise from his plane seat, shake hands with khakis who had come aboard to greet him. Jovial as before, perhaps a little rounder in the cheeks. (Did three years of American food do that to him?) *Hi, boss,* you could make him out saying to one of the soldiers. The khakis braced him on either side and led him to the exit.

The door shut behind him, on the other passengers. A perfect ending, in a way. Shadows of his entourage banged on the exit. Weak, wifely voices. *Hoy!* After that, nothing. Only the disembodied shouts, and shots, outside. Only his body on the tarmac afterward.

Jim was rewinding the tape and pressing play again. Jackie had planted herself on the floor in front of the TV, the silhouette of her thin pigtail straight as an antenna against the screen. *"Hoy!"* she shouted with the entourage, pointing at the exit door closing behind Kuya.

"Can we watch something else?" asked Jaime.

They changed the channel. *The Greatest American Hero,* Jaime's favorite. A clumsy superhero, another crash landing.

"It's a hell of a strategy," Milagros said.

"Every Catholic loves a martyr," said Jim.

Their Kuya had studied his nation's history, the lives and deaths of Lapu-Lapu and José Rizal and Christ himself. He smiled and strolled exitward, as though accompanied by old drinking buddies. As if he knew his fate, and the country's future. That he would die. That afterward, people would untie the yellow ribbons from their trees and tie them around their heads, warrior-style. That they'd take to the streets.

She smuggled transcripts, copied tapes. As a family they followed Kuya's funeral cortege along Times Street, with two million others, in time to military drum taps. Jackie threw a bitter tantrum, wailing and kicking Milagros in the ribs, when Jaime and her father went forward to view the coffin without her. Kuya's body still dressed in his bloodstained shirt. Jaime, for his part, fainted.

At home, Milagros went back to managing the Little Golden Books and puppy kennel, while Jim traveled to Bulacan to visit with the alleged murderer's family. They'd watched in August as military men took him—son and father, petty criminal—four days before Kuya's homecoming. Milagros should have known then that she and Jim had seen, in the same tape, two different stories. They both saw Kuya leave the plane. They both saw his body splayed across the tarmac. But only she was haunted by the weak wifely voices in between, crying out *Hoy!* Only she had imagined her own fist banging against the exit.

February 23, 1986

Naz, her old college boyfriend, of all people, arrives at the house. So her mother's taking all comers now.

"I meant to visit much sooner," he says. "The traffic—it's like Christmas Eve out there. Everybody wants to get to EDSA."

Milagros doesn't raise her head from the pillow. "You'll forgive me, Naz, for not playing hostess."

"Of course," he says.

"I'm surprised you're here and not there."

"I just came to pay my respects. I have a son too."

A refrain, from so many well-wishers: *I have a son too.* This time she doesn't change the subject. "About that son, Naz. What's his name?"

"Oscar."

"Let me ask you something. If you were made to choose between Oscar—"

"Don't do that."

"I want to know. Someone told me men stay men while women become mothers first. Is that true?"

"I suppose it depends on the man. And woman, for that matter."

"Gun to your head, what would you choose?"

He shakes his head, lets out a puff of air. "My son. I'd choose my son."

What had she hoped to hear? "So you'd stop," she confirms. "If they threatened you. You'd quit the lightning protests. No more street theater."

"Gun to my head, yes." Naz crouches at the bedside. "But there is no gun to my head. And you didn't marry me, Milagros."

He says this so gently she knows he means well. They're not backstage at their college theater, Naz spitting out the words *Serious Career.* He's older now. They all are.

"Most of the people out at EDSA aren't activists, or revolutionaries," says Naz. "They just don't want to miss a party. But there'd be no party without Jim. People like him made it happen."

In an instant Milagros sees her house from the outside, her family all aglow with Historical Significance. From far away it is still a beautiful thing. Her younger self would approve: Milagros hasn't lived a small life, not since the nurses' strike. She felt important then, at twenty-two. A human chain, they called her and her friends, at the doors of City Hospital. Small potatoes compared to what's happening now. A barricade, they're calling this sea stretching from Camp Crame to Camp Aguinaldo. Not just bodies but cars, buses, felled trees, streetlamps. Even garbage—that perennial Manila problem—conspiring in the movement.

Still. "I don't want a hero," says Milagros, closing her eyes. "I want a son."

"Fair enough." Naz gets up to leave her be. "I didn't bring a card, or sweets," he says. "Here's what I'm good for. I'm just a dirty aging hippie, but I want to help." A scattering, like beads, on the nightstand; she remembers the magic soybeans from his play so many years ago. She thinks of rosaries, the hippie turned religious in his old age.

When she opens her eyes, there's a mound of small bright pills on the nightstand. *Nothing to lose.* She swallows them down with a glass of water Vivi must have left for her. It tastes like river murk, as if Billy Batanglobo has been here again. She drifts awhile, staring at the ceiling. Then the sky. Her son dancing on the clothesline outside. *Jaime!* She swoops him up and they fly high above the house until the town and then the country is a speck, one in a swirl of a million carnival colors.

There is only one other way—short of Billy's solution—for Avalon Row and Jim and all these years to grow so small and far. She reaches under the mattress. She pauses over the forms before writing—in pencil, in case of mistakes—her first, her maiden/middle, her last name. Later she'll confirm the right answers in ink, erase the rest.

.

1984

After they had parted ways in their twenties, Milagros saw Naz only once. He didn't see her. She'd taken the children shoe shopping, in Quezon City, before the school year started; then to the Social Security building, where their father was covering the assassination hearings. Before they reached the steps, Jackie on Milagros's hip and Jaime walking ahead, carrying his own new shoes, they heard a sound to chill the blood. One scream, and then another—wracked with torment, like a demon being dragged from its host. She clutched her children close and folded to the ground. By then the news had trained her for shootings and bombs, spontaneous fires.

Jaime pointed at the foot of the steps. It was only a show. A papier-mâché vampire—with a familiar chignon and butterfly sleeves—was drinking the People's blood. There was no mistaking Naz even in a dress, his face painted all white. He'd moved his plays off campus and onto the street, she later read. Lightning dramas, so called for all the time they took. By the time the Metrocom cars arrived, the actors had dispersed, and the water cannons' afterspray soaked her children instead.

"I don't get it," said Jaime (as lots of viewers said regarding Naz's plays, if she remembered right). "Why would the police stop a show?" He tried to rescue his new shoe box from a hole in the drenched paper bag while Milagros pat-dried Jackie—who was squealing with delight, no less than if they'd stumbled on an open fire hydrant on a humid day—with her own shirt. When Jim came down the steps, she felt glad to have chosen him, again, over someone like Naz. No mistaking Jim's prose for poetry, whether he wrote it under his own name or not. Code names like Mama and Papa, Ate and Kuya, were the closest he came to metaphor. Day after day this past year he'd sat in on these hearings, listening to experts and eyewitnesses, studying bullet trajectory and blood samples so that his readers wouldn't have to. Tomorrow, he'd cover the parliamentary campaigns, interview candidates and voters, report the final tallies. When he wrote it all down, he would call it copy, nothing more.

February 24, 1986

Billy Batanglobo's at her window when the radio signal goes out. Feedback and static. He looks her way, tries to fiddle with the dial. "You'll make it worse," Milagros tells him, as he drips water on the speakers. She can't hear radio static and feedback without remembering September in this house, 1972, the smell of Biscuit-colored paint making her dizzy. *The more things change,* she thinks. *The party's over.* She imagines the President, back on their TV tonight. What proclamation number are they up to now?

"We don't need it," Billy Batanglobo says, turning the radio off. "I'll tell you what I saw. Thousands camped outside the rebel gates, ready to block the army tanks when they come." Billy goes on: buses parked crosswise in the street, tires set ablaze, make-shift altars. As if any one of them could stop a tank, or a gun-ship raining missiles from the air. Yet colonel after sergeant has defected to the rebel side. Billy lulls Milagros to sleep listing their names and ranks, accompanied by trickling river water and radio static.

By morning her neighbors have gathered in the living room again. Her mother worries her way through the rosary while Jackie plays with her jackstones. On TV, the President looks to be sweating. *Complete control of the situation.* As for his former defense minister and army chief, the constitution will deal with them. *The law of the land does not allow rebellion.*

The jaunty horns of "Mambo Magsaysay." Milagros rushes back into the bedroom. Billy Batanglobo looks up from her bed, its sheets soaked through.

We need more people at the barricades, the radio announcer says. *Our brothers and sisters have been teargassed around Camp Crame.*

"Can you believe these army boys?" says Billy. "For years

they marched in loyalty parades and shoved civilians around. Now they have the nerve to ask us to protect them."

Billy's the first, since Jaime's been gone, who seems to need her consolation, rather than the other way around. She reaches for his cold, prune-wrinkled hand.

Helicopters descend toward Camp, the rebels braced for rocket fire. But the airmen come out waving white flags, their fingers flashing L-for-LABAN. Civilians cheer. The rebel leaders come out for a hug. Then the chief commodore of the navy defects. On the Pasig River a boat about-faces its guns onto Malacañang Palace.

If you're listening, and healthy, we want you at EDSA.

I have a personal message from the general: you are needed at the barricades.

"Part of me does want to be there," she tells Billy—something she would not admit to anyone else. "I started a union once, you know. Yelled into a megaphone, all that. I don't mind marching for the right cause. I could be one of those people at the barricades, easy."

"I see you more as one of the rebels," Billy says. "Sergeant Major Milagros Reyes, defecting to the U.S.A. You just haven't told your commander yet. Or, like these guys, you're planning to surprise him."

"It's not defecting. I just can't live here, and stay alive. What other way is there?"

He grips her hand and pulls her to her knees at the bedside. He glares, through river silt and seeping water.

"I can't do that," she says. "I have a daughter."

"What good will you do her, abroad? We still have no idea what kind of country you're leaving her in. EDSA could turn bloody any minute. But the generals will probably get off without a scratch. Like you. They don't care what happens to the sheep, as long as their own hides are saved. The lambs, I should say."

"You're wrong about me," says Milagros, and to prove it she stands, pulling away from Billy Batanglobo. But his grip is tight, his eyes and the soaked bed, standing in a pool of water on the floor, compelling her to join him. She pries off his fingers, soily around the nails and cuticles, and goes to the living room.

"Jackie." Milagros crouches beside her daughter.

Jackie looks up from her rubber balls and plastic stars, a game she still is young enough to think was named for her. The TV's still on, but Vivi's in the kitchen now, her mother doing laundry out back, the neighbors gone.

"Your brother isn't coming back," says Milagros.

Jackie spins one of the stars on its short axis. It whirls before rattling to a stop.

"Jaime is dead," says Milagros.

Jackie raises her arms in the air, bounces one ball and then the other as hard and high as she can.

"Do you know what *dead* means?" Milagros shouts over the TV, catching both balls and holding them aside, out of Jackie's reach. It looks as though the President has lost at least one channel. On screen, a policeman lays down his badge and billy club, stands on the hood of his car, and plays the national anthem on his whistle. Students and nuns cheer.

Jackie's finger presses on the knobbed end of a single jack, flipping it over. It lands, again and again, with a series of clicks, always at an angle. *Click. Click-click. Click-click-click. Clickety-click.*

"Jackie!" Milagros grabs her daughter's hands, holds them to the floor. She has read Kübler-Ross, a gift among the cards and pastries. She will deliver this lesson whether Jackie wants to hear it or not. Stumbling through a speech about things that look like endings but are beginnings in disguise, Milagros asks if Jackie knows how a caterpillar makes a cocoon, then turns into a butterfly. "Does that make sense, Jackie?"

"Yes," says Jackie, nodding and nodding. She is frightened and wants to get back to her game.

She hugs her daughter with such clumsy force that Jackie tumbles backward to the floor when she lets go.

From the bedroom she can hear Jackie start up again, flipping the jackstone. *Click-click, clickety-click.*

Jacks, they all call her. Maybe the name will self-fulfill. Maybe she will land like this—right side up, no matter which way she tumbles.

1985

They enrolled twelve-year-old Jaime at Ateneo, alma mater to Jim and Billy Batanglobo, to their dead Kuya and every other husband or father in the village. One day, Milagros realized, Father Duncan might even teach him Latin. But was he ready, her sweet soft boy, for high school at a place like that? Alumni bragged about the days they had to copy pages from the unabridged Webster's or kneel on rock salt in the school yard, punishments that toughened boys into men. Jaime still woke with a start sometimes, reaching for his little sister's cheek, then his mother's. *I had a bad dream and just wanted to make sure of you.* His own cheeks had retained the baby fat that, for most, melted away in grade school. He never met an ice milk or *turon* he didn't love. *Please, Ma, just a half slice more?*

Milagros thought of the Americans and their whole business with *junior* high. Could the American school in Taguig City be better, for Jaime? She went as far as sending for a brochure. Jaime could take his time, through sixth and seventh and eighth grades, with boys *and* girls. But she knew better than to expect a debate. One night her mother fried milkfish in the front yard, and Milagros threw the forms into the fire. She did not bring up Taguig City with Jim that day, or any other. Jaime, like his father, would be an Ateneo boy.

He started getting stomachaches—right after breakfast, just

before the school bus. "Can Soba come with me to Ateneo?" he asked, knowing the answer. "What about Jackie?" He stared down at their smiles, waved from the bus window, looking bound for prison Camp.

Well, he did have to grow up, didn't he? Milagros came down hard to help him. If he threw up after breakfast on a school day, she made him brush his teeth again, while Vivi ironed a new uniform. She peered into the chaos of his canvas knapsack every night. *You can do better than that.* She watched him sort by size—textbook, notebook, pencil case, calculator—and timed him, like a sergeant. She should have taken greater care with him in grade school, motivated him with more gold stars. *So sloppy,* wrote his teacher in the margin of one notebook. Much of the hassle of bringing up Jaime could be summed up by *So sloppy.*

Once her son was sorted, late at night, Milagros helped her husband, typing Jim's latest reports on a movement that called itself RAM. Reform the Armed Forces. Outside his Entertainment beat, Jim had visited with the vice chief of the army. Between movie-star interviews, Jim talked to junior officers who complained about the flimsy shorts and rubber slippers they were sent to squelch insurgencies in, while aging bureaucrats who outranked them got rich behind desks. In a *barong,* Jim snuck out of red-carpet premieres to buy drinks for American diplomats, who were using the word *coup.* Jim brought home copies of undated warrants to arrest RAM leaders, CIA briefs on how useful RAM could be at the U.S. bases.

It didn't occur to Milagros, as she typed and transcribed and copied, that Jim's reports on RAM could offend the palace any more than other things he'd written. Already he'd done disappearances and killings, Parliament's motion to impeach the President for padding his Swiss bank accounts with treasury pesos. She'd expected trouble then, those stories landing in the wrong hands. Khakis at her door again, taking Jim's elbows. *Follow us, boss.* Sunday visits, with two kids in tow this time, back in the cold stone theater. But for a good five months no khakis came. Maybe that Bastille-style spectacle had been real after all. Maybe they'd been freer than she thought.

Looking back, she'd say she should have known. That RAM would be the last straw. That the OmniPresident would object most to a story where his name hardly appeared, that already counted him out. That the man they called Papa would punish them, above all, for giving his most wayward, disobedient children the spotlight.

"Walking Soba is your job," she told Jaime, speaking as she would to a grown man. That afternoon, he'd begged her to come along on the errand. But Milagros had been doubling down on this, as on the knapsack, wanting to grow her son up a little. "Look around. Everyone in this house has a job to do, and everyone's doing it." She was in Jim's study, balancing the checkbook; Vivi in the kitchen, prepping dinner.

"Jackie isn't," said Jaime.

"Jackie's three. To play is her work. You are twelve years old, and responsible for Soba."

And you need the exercise, she didn't add.

Off he lumbered: first into the nursery, where she could hear Jackie refusing. Then he was outside, with a grumble, Soba's bell tinkling. The dog came back an hour later, without her leash or collar, without Jaime.

She called Ruel, Jaime's best friend. But Jaime hadn't stopped at his house, hadn't seen or spoken to Ruel since lunch. She called Oliver Castro, who walked his own cocker spaniel every day around the village too. She called Jim. She left Vivi with Jackie and got into the brown Ford Escort, driving past the church, the playground, out of Batanglobo Village and all the way to the school. But the school had sent her son home on the bus hours before. The school had done its job.

It made Milagros ill to think someone had watched her son and memorized his afternoons. Back at Avalon Row her eyes and throat burned. Vivi brewed soup. Jackie sat in Milagros's lap as she dialed mother after mother. Had they seen Jaime? Did he by chance stop to play with Kokoy or Eddie or Paolo on his walk, and forget to call home? *You know how selfish kids can be!* Surely she had met these other mothers at school plays or parent-teacher meetings, but she knew their names and numbers only from the Xeroxed class directory. *Who's selfish now?* Snips of strangers' conversations—weekend beach plans, debt collections—kept cutting into the Manila party line. Vivi found Milagros banging the receiver against the table. In her gentle business manner, as if nothing in this crazy world could surprise her, Vivi took the phone from her and hung it up. *You could use some soup, ma'am.* Vivi was right. The ginger and the garlic soothed her throat. *Thank God,* Milagros would think many times throughout, *for Vivi.* By the time Jim came home, she'd drunk three cups of Vivi's soup and was bouncing her knee so hard that Jackie had scrambled off it into Vivi's arms.

Imagining Jaime's captor was so easy it hurt. Over the years Milagros's own brothers, strapped for cash, had accepted every kind of odd job on earth. What threats or offers had been made in exchange for Jaime? His captor might have been a father too, thinking only of *his* sons, their mouths to feed.

After they drove together a second time through the city, she came home with Jim's gray suit jacket over her own clothes, exhausted. Beside her Jim gave off the oily smell of someone up all night. Jackie was at the door. Milagros looked away from her and went to bed.

"Jaime is in the country, visiting relatives," she could hear Jim saying. "Don't ask your mother about it."

In the days after, Milagros kept hearing things. A scratch at the door, a footfall on the grass. The gate would rattle, setting her on her feet; in seconds she'd unlatched it and swept her head left and right along Avalon Row. Nothing. Back inside she'd think: *Jaime could be anywhere.* One last sweep through the house might even turn him up. She sat beside Jackie and her alphabet, leaving her mind at the gate. When she looked down, she saw that her writing was a mad stranger's: *k*'s and *v*'s deteriorating, across the page, into squiggles.

Visitors, the village that had once calmed her by filling the house in Jim's absence, now threatened to drive her insane. Her family came, of course. Khakis, who claimed to be filing reports. Friends, with food. How to sort the real news from the noise? And the gate! What a fumble to unlatch it! By the time she got it open, the sound in the street was always gone.

They kept Jackie indoors for weeks. *No, you cannot help Vivi hang the clothes. It's more fun in here anyway! The TV's here, and all your toys.* "To play is your work," Milagros said absently. Jackie couldn't wait to work for real: she gazed at maids and street sweepers the way her parents had worshiped their professors. She loved laundry, her grandmother's career: the soap-and-lemon smell, the cold, wet cotton on her cheek. But keeping Jackie indoors, now, was not an idea, not a slogan. "Outside is dangerous," Milagros said. "Outside is just for grown-ups now."

"But how come Jaime was allowed?"—Jackie obsessed, at that young age, with justice.

"In the country things are different," said Milagros. "Here in the city there's a giant lady who eats children for dinner. You just look at her the wrong way," she said, "or laugh too loudly and *poof!* no more Jackie."

Hadn't she and Jim discussed, and sworn off, talking such

nonsense to children? Children deserve the truth, not some mysterious code language: didn't she believe that, still? "Go inside, Jackie. Now!"

After dark, in bed, she tossed like a new mother, waking to every fuss and startle.

They searched in shifts: Jim drove while she sat phoneside, or vice versa. One night, after another useless drive, she stepped over Jackie in the living room and walked past Vivi in the kitchen. There was no news, again. Tonight only Jim's voice could keep her from crying. She approached the study door and heard him at his desk.

"I see," he was saying into the phone. "Understood."

He hung up and sat with tented fingers. On the wall hung his press passes. Jefferson and del Pilar stared across the room at one another.

What did Jim see? What did he understand? She, too, would have liked to see something, understand anything, in those dark days.

She pushed the door open; he turned. "No news," she reported, flatly.

After that phone call, ending just as she walked in, she asked about his afternoons, made him explain his evenings. Could you blame her, tense and tired as she was, for worrying, as wives had worried since the dawn of husbands, that there might be Someone Else? Her mother, after all, had planted the idea for years. And once this Other Woman entered Milagros's mind, she never left. Her son was gone; a stranger took his place. Milagros listened both for Jaime and for Her.

One day, after the sound of Jim's engine had faded from the garage, she opened his top desk drawer. He'd left the key in the lock. They were not a husband and wife who locked each other out of desk drawers. Her fingers grazed the watermark of some letterhead, trifolded, off-white. *Biscuit.* She took the papers out, and yes: they matched the walls. She squinted at the seal on top. These couldn't be school notices from Ateneo; Vivi would have handed those to her. Slowly she recognized the blue wheel. The yolk-yellow sun. THE OFFICE OF THE PRESS SECRETARY. Another love letter, like the kind Jim used to receive long ago. She turned the pages: more than one. Same seal, many dates. A long courtship.

They'd wept together over the torment of *not knowing*. Closed offices, tied hands, phones that rang and rang. Men at the Metrocom station who said, *We're doing all we can*, while paring their nails, flagrantly, in front of her. For all Jim and Milagros knew, some ordinary nut job had kidnapped their son. They had no proof of more. *For all I know*, they'd both said, again and again. *For all we know.* At least they lived in the dark together. But here in this desk were letters, addressed to Jim, dated since Jaime had disappeared.

She shook her head, which made the spinning worse. She made bargain after swift bargain: she'd take an Other Woman, she'd accept receipts for dinners and lingerie, late nights and lipstick on his collar, over this. She flipped faster, reading words she promptly wanted to unread. No use: scholarship girls knew how to scan and skim for meaning.

> . . . *illegal press activity at 26 Avalon Row and the distribution of printed material without the proper media licenses.*
> . . . *specific terms, as follows. You shall (1) cease and desist all printing at 26 Avalon Row; (2) submit to the conditions of house arrest as outlined in our previous memorandum dated 7 October 1985, including the surveillance of all incoming and outgoing communications; and (3) craft a letter of retraction to be printed in the* Metro Manila Herald, *and other outlets as necessary, discrediting all claims listed by date on the following page . . .*

. . . under orders to enforce such consequences as the
administration deems fit, for the failure to abide by said
terms.

There may as well have been an Other Woman. Milagros
felt every pang her poor, scorned friends had described. Their
stomachs, too, had sunk to the floor. And then that floor had disappeared beneath them. Like her, they forgot how to breathe.
When Jim came to the doorway, Milagros was caught, like any
jealous wife, sniffing and rifling around.

To his credit, he didn't insult her with denials. He looked at
the letters and said, "I thought it premature to tell you."

Of course he'd planned to tell her, sometime. Was there reason not to believe that? Because her hands were shaking, the
edge of one page sliced into her thumb, which she brought,
bleeding, to her mouth, dropping the papers.

"The regime is all but over," Jim explained. But anyone could
lose a job. For this country, after twenty years, Jim did not believe
that was enough. After twenty years, a dictator didn't simply get
to be *fired*. Or worse, get to resign. Papa had to be called to
account.

"And unlike him," Jim said, "we'll have the decency to do it
right. With a trial. And with evidence like this. What *hasn't* he
done to stay in power? We're far from the only ones, you know."

"I never said we were the only ones," Milagros said.

"The paper trail itself tells you a lot about his state." Jim
pointed to his brain.

"And *Jaime's* state?" Milagros squeaked, like someone not all
there herself.

"Is safe. This"—Jim pointed at the papers on the floor—"is
theater, that's all. Intimidation tactics. Some goons were told to
shake me up a bit, and this was their interpretation. He's lost
control of his men, along with his mind."

The room tilted around Milagros. *If Papa's lost so much con-*

trol, she would have said, if she could find the words, *how can anyone be safe?*

"My father saved this man's life," Jim said. "He's not about to trifle with my son's. In all my years at Camp, why do you think I had a private cell to read and think in? All the others, even some women, were shoved around, at least. My term was study leave, compared to theirs. Did you ever see a scratch on me? A dubious advantage, I know—I wasn't proud of it, but I'll be damned if I don't use it now."

Milagros knelt to leaf again through the pages on the floor, hoping to see something new.

"You can fill in the blanks," said Jim, as if to save her trouble. "Stop the presses, take it all back, get my son."

"Your son," said Milagros. (*I repeat,* she thought, as in one of those presidential speeches.) "*Your* son?"

"*Our* son, Milagros, of course. And we will. It's just a matter of time. We'll get him back without kowtowing to a dictator. You've always trusted me. On this I need you to trust me more than ever."

There was nothing for her to do but to repeat. "I've always trusted you," she said, her voice so faint she may as well have mouthed the words.

Jaime would escape, she fantasized. This was, Milagros knew, a stretch. Her pudgy boy, so easy to bribe with snacks and candy. She'd sooner believe that Jackie had broken out of her nursery lockdown. But he would miss her, Milagros knew that too; he'd miss Jackie and Soba and want to come home. People talked of how prison had changed them. They came out of Camp Crame or Fort Bonifacio stronger, out for blood. Could this be the thing, at last, that manned up Jaime Jr.? At City Hospital, she'd seen pain turn children bionic. A bone marrow biopsy so painful that a boy bent the steel rail of his bed. A girl whose high, shrill weeping could have shattered the windows. So she had to imagine Jaime in pain to imagine him free. What twisted fantasy was this? From what kind of mother?

In the morning Jim was at the kitchen table with his coffee and newspapers. A stranger. She could hear, in the nursery, his men unlatching the trundle bed from its hatch.

Now she'd found the words in her throat. "Where is he?" she said, sending Vivi and Jackie out into the yard. "You're so convinced that he's safe. How do you know? I want proof."

Jim sighed, as if he'd wished to spare her these details but now had no choice. "A source inside the Metrocom, someone I trust," he said, "told me he's in a safe house outside Santa Clara."

"A source," Milagros repeated. "A safe house?" She imagined a windowless cabin, an armed khaki guarding it—the kind of man who had never, in thirteen years, made her feel *safe*. Her husband, a man who'd always despised euphemisms—why would he accept this one? "Ask your source for an address," she said.

"I'm trying," said Jim. "He walks a fine line too—working for them, and with me."

"You care more about your sources," Milagros said, "than about him. You never cared for Jaime. He was never tough enough for you. You're happy he's in danger. You don't care if it's Ateneo or a 'safe house' that mans him up."

"I care what country he grows up in," Jim replied. "What kind of man he emulates."

"He can't emulate you if he's not here," Milagros said. "Just stop the presses! Where's the fun in being a newsman if you can't, at least once in your life, say *Stop the presses*?"

He looked up from his *Bangkok Post* at her, but didn't close it.

"They will win," she said, "if they have to drag you out kicking and screaming."

Jim shook his head. "I can't fear a weak man. If there's anything emptier than his promises, it's his threats. His own kidneys are in revolt against him, at this point."

"Organs don't get into politics," Milagros said. "Trust me, I'm a nurse."

When he didn't answer, she snatched the *Bangkok Post* from him and tore it, clumsily, to bits. "We are talking about your children here!"

"Yes, Milagros." He stood and left the newspapers splayed on the oilcloth. Before going into his study, he turned to her. "And how do you want our children to remember us?"

February 25, 1986

At midnight she wakes up to fireworks. Or is it gunfire? Even the radio can't tell. But that must be the thrill of EDSA: partying like it's your last night on earth, because it might be. In her suburban bed Milagros closes her eyes and sees Jaime Jr. on an ordinary New Year's Eve, scraping watusi sticks along the ground, the phosphorus sparking under his rubber slippers.

By the time she wakes again, the party has reached her living room. Her mother on the sofa, Jackie on Vivi's lap, and neighbors—mostly wives, Milagros notes, whose husbands must have gone into the city—in front of the TV. Someone has printed yellow T-shirts for the children: with Kuya's face on them, for the boys; and his widow's, for the girls. On-screen, helicopters swarm the country club in Greenhills, where the rebel leaders wait for her. A brass band plays "Bayan Ko" (My Country), "Tie a Yellow Ribbon," and, as if remembering who's watching, "Dixie."

Cheers and yellow banners as the widow steps out of a van. The mothers on the sofa chant her name, teaching their children how to flash L-for-LABAN with their thumbs and forefingers. In Vivi's lap, Jackie's all but trembling with excitement, her quiet, serious house transformed as in some Christmases and New

Years past. But when Vivi sees Milagros headed to the kitchen, Jackie's handed off again, demoted to a neighbor's lap. *Something to eat, ma'am?* All Milagros wants is water; Naz's magic beans have dried her mouth out.

Back in the bedroom, on the radio, the widow takes her oath of office, gives her speech. *Shattering the dictatorship. Grateful to the military. Rights and liberties. National reconciliation.* Her first executive order. Her cabinet. Jim must be there for all of it. Milagros can imagine him, standing in but not of the crowd, as they recite the Our Father and sing the national anthem.

And so he is, sardined in the Club Filipino, watching the people watch their new President. A members-only country club, where all those 1898 heroes are said to have dreamed the nation up. Now it's bigwigs in *barong,* the foreign press. Following the rebels' lead, they've signed the so-called Citizens' Resolution: out with Papa, long live Madam President. The signatures read like a page out of *Manila's 400.*

Rich-People Power. Martial law, to some, was a rude interruption: now their fancy dinner party can resume.

Afterward, he rushes from the club to Malacañang Palace, where—*only in Manila,* says his taxi driver—the stubborn sitting President has booked his own oath and inauguration. A flash of Jim's press pass, a pat-down at the palace gates. In the ceremonial hall, a few cabinet ministers—tourism, agriculture, public works—some soldiers, a New Society youth group. Not a *barong* or butterfly sleeve between them—a first, in all Jim's visits to this palace. Entering to watery applause and out-of-sync chants of his name, the President slurs through his speech. The First Lady, in white, paces behind the podium. It's over within twenty minutes. The room clears quickly. As Jim leaves, soldiers with rifles guard the lawns, between tanks and battle buses, all their engines running.

At home, in Batanglobo Village, the radio and TV blink off the air just as the President appears. His fifth inauguration in

twenty years, silenced by static. A rebel sniper has hit three stations with one shot at a single transmitter. PLEASE STAND BY.

At the *Herald* offices, Jim fires off his tale of two inaugura-
tions. A chaotic week: no one there to police Jim, to send him
back to Entertainment where he belongs. (All the movie stars
are at EDSA anyway, he's noticed.) Not that it's a free-for-all:
there are new rules now. An editor has scrubbed his piece about
the new President: striking out all mention of her inexperience,
or her family fortune, playing up *slain martyr's widow, pious
Catholic,* and *housewife* instead. The same editor would like Jim
to tone down what he's said about the Club Filipino elite. The
piece will end on feel-good lines from the widow's inauguration
speech, not on Jim's wet-blanket questions about the country's
future.

Jim's on hold with a friend from the *Washington Post* when
he hears that helicopters have banked on the Pasig River. By the
time he reaches the palace again, they've lifted off. With the
First Family inside, people are saying, bound for Honolulu. How
has all this happened in one day? After his years at Camp, where
one minute looked so much like the next Jim could lose track of
how many days or nights had passed, a short, full day is still a
shock to him.

On Laurel Street, ribbon after yellow ribbon waves and waves.
Jeepneys, with nowhere to move, have become snack bars, blaring music, offering shade. The archbishop has ended his hunger
strike; his devoted nuns cut cake and scoop ice cream at the palace gates.

A *good old-fashioned fiesta,* the radio tells Milagros. She
thinks of Jaime's first birthday: the single dancing candle flame,
ten chubby fingers in the frosting. The phone off its cradle so Jim
could hear, and sing along from Camp.

With no one left there to protect, the Marines have left the
palace grounds. Jim sees people cutting away at the barbed-wire
fence, fiddling with the intercom and walkie-talkies in the guard

tower. He walks into the mansion freely, no press pass or pat-down this time.

A typhoon couldn't have left more wreckage. Capsized tables, scattered papers, curry gone cold in foil trays on the dining table. He passes the door of the chapel, where servants huddle in prayer. A wardrobe filled with slippery silk gowns and bullet-proof brassieres tough and reptilian to his touch. A frigid meat locker whose shelves of beef are stamped STATESIDE.

Beside the king-size master bed, there's a hospital gurney, an oxygen tank, and an IV stand, its bag three-quarters full. Adult diapers on the bathroom floor, soiled.

On the twenty-fifth of February 1986, thinks Jim, who can't resist a juicy lede, *sometime between his oath of office and his helicopter ride out of the country, the tenth President of the Republic of the Philippines shat himself.* He shakes his head. It's the kind of showy, self-satisfied hook Jim would have produced at fifteen, for his high school newspaper. *Herald* editors won't go for it any more than the Jesuit priests did.

Within an hour, Jim's quiet tour has ended. It seems like half of Manila has stormed the palace. Cries of *Soubenir! Soube-nir!* bounce off the mahogany-paneled walls. Those who can't make off with a military helmet or a high-heeled shoe settle for a radio, a plant. Jim threads his way against the stampede. Outside, people smile for pictures against streetlamps, under trees. He reaches for his Dictaphone, but when he bothers to stop someone for an interview—*Who are you? Were you at EDSA, too? What brought you to the palace?*—he feels like a Camp interrogator, and his subject's in a rush to get inside.

Back at the *Herald* offices, the photo department is shredding pictures of the stampede, and filing others away. "While we're at it," he can hear the harried City Desk editor suggesting, "let's brainstorm some other words? *Stampede* sounds so . . . negative." Jim can hear the former President, his onetime godfather, call them all *balimbing*, ten-sided as star fruit. Wetting their fingertips to gauge the wind's direction. No better than the politicians.

We are talking about your children here.

He stands abruptly—turning all his colleagues' heads, never his style. Without saying good-bye he leaves the *Herald* newsroom.

At home, the door of the master bedroom is open, Milagros sitting on the edge of the bed. "Is it all true?" she asks, as Jim walks in. "We have a new President, and the old one's in Hawaii?"

Jim nods.

She says, "I have something to tell you."

"So do I."

She waits for him to go first, so he does. No time to change their habits all at once.

"I love my work," Jim says. "It was my life."

But she already knows that part.

"So I mistook it for my whole life."

She looks up.

"They say prison does something to you. And I do wonder. If I'd have made the same decisions, living in this house with you—with him—all these years."

Milagros, now and forever the good student, takes a moment to review. The man she never questioned till a year ago, admitting to an error.

"Today was big—the biggest news day of my life. But I'm not going to write about the President. All I plan to write, when I go into that study tonight, is my resignation letter."

She sees he means it. An offer that the Jim she married years ago would never have extended.

Recant. Stop the presses. Cease and desist. He'll do it all, and more. She watches his mouth move. She even hears some words from it. Something about not expecting forgiveness, or even a response.

She doesn't tell him it's too late. They've fought enough already. After she found the letters, all they did was fight. She's out of stones to throw at him. And yet.

A shred of her, still young and hopeful and capable of being inspired, considers it.

What could that life look like? She'd find work at another hospital, if City wouldn't take her back. He'd learn, like anyone changing his field, new skills: write in other, safer genres; teach. Together they'd raise Jackie as their only child—and who's to say there wouldn't, after they had patched things up, be more? On paper, it seems possible.

But no.

This house would still be this house, Manila still the city where she had her son, this country still the country that took everything away. You couldn't erase history, but you could close up chapters of it, just as in a textbook.

"Jim," she says. Carefully, as if to an employer. *I am leaving the country.* A serious answer to a serious offer.

Jim nods, the fingers tenting at his forehead once again.

As with an employer—one who taught her things, one she's sad to leave—Milagros goes on. About green cards and graduate school. She even shows him the pamphlets and the forms. Brown nurses smiling at the bedside of white patients who look to be better already.

And he responds in kind. *Of course* and *opportunity.*

Her eyes turn red. She senses there is more. In its effort not to cry her face looks like a young girl's. But he must continue.

"I remember when I first met you."

She hears only some of the rest—how smart she was, how glad he felt getting to know her. Her passion and her point of view. But his words do take her back, all the way to June 1971, on the lawn outside of City Hospital. The girl with the bandanna and the picket sign, who must have seemed like someone who'd do anything to prove a point. And didn't that girl marry him?

And take dictation, type, and print for him? As if it were her life's mission, to tend the flame of his work like a priestess at some temple. That girl lived in this house, where a man had died; that girl married Jim inside a prison; that girl let her children play, sometimes, above a shelter where objects no safer than bombs were made. And now that girl's son, her only son, is gone. But Jim is not the one—at least, he's not primarily the one—Milagros blames.

1985

Some say a phone never rings in Manila before breakfast, unless it's an emergency. But given Jim's work, all his sources and contacts abroad, theirs rang in the early morning all the time. When it happened that December, Milagros let herself hope it was D.C. or Berlin calling. Then Vivi answered, and Milagros watched her shoulders sink before she passed the phone to Jim. And to Milagros, Vivi whispered, "They found our boy." A sentence like that had no room for good news. It never went, *they found our boy and he is fine* or *he's alive.* Jim took the phone, listened, and let it go. The receiver struck the floor. "Oh no," he said, shaking his head, bringing his fingers to his temples. "No." Milagros watched her husband cover his face and fall to his knees before the kitchen sink, as if the time for praying, or begging, had not yet passed.

Acknowledgments

This book wouldn't exist without my family. Along with the beloved cousins, aunts, uncles, nephews, nieces, in-laws, and honoraries who inspired and cheered on its creation, I especially thank my parents, Concepcion and Jose Alvar, and Josefina and Gerard Couture; and my sister, Anna Newsom.

Deep thanks to Julie Barer, my agent and early adopter, whose faith in these stories made a lifelong dream come true. And to the Barer Literary team, past and present, for being so kind and so good at what they do: William Boggess, Gemma Purdy, Anna Wiener, and Anna Geller.

I couldn't be more grateful to everyone at Knopf for their enthusiasm and hard work—in particular, Oliver Munday, Jaclyn Whalen, Susan Brown, Maria Massey, Helen Tobin, the wonderful and heroically patient Tom Pold, and of course my editor, Lexy Bloom. Thank you, Lexy, for taking on my work with such care and imagination, for asking the smartest questions, and for leaving the collection so much better than you found it.

Columbia University, SLS, the Blue Mountain Center, the Corporation of Yaddo, Sarah Lawrence College, the Lower Manhattan Cultural Council, the Djerassi Resident Artists Program, and the Sirenland Writers Conference generously provided the time, space, and support I needed to finish this thing, as well as the fantastic company of other writers and artists.

Thank you to the editors who found space for me in their magazines, and made these stories better in the process: Brock Clarke and Nicola Mason; Speer Morgan, Evelyn Somers, and Michael Nye; David Daley; Adina Talve-Goodman, Maribeth Batcha, and especially Hannah Tinti.

ACKNOWLEDGMENTS

For their wisdom, encouragement, and example, I thank my teachers Cathy Blackburn, Patricia Powell, Binnie Kirshenbaum, Jaime Manrique, Nathan Englander, Sigrid Nunez, Mark Slouka, and Joan Silber. And all my workshop-mates, from St. Petersburg to Cambridge to the Upper West Side, who taught me too.

Thank you to the friends I laughed with and leaned on at various times while writing this book, and whose domain expertise I occasionally abused for story "research," including Joy Somberg, Misha Wright, Ammie Hwang, Maya Rock, Jonathan Tze, Nina Hein, Ana Martínez, David Petersen, and Pia Wilson.

And to bring it back around to family, my last and deepest thanks go to the king of husbands, Glenn Nano, whose excellent love makes life and work worthwhile.

A Note About the Author

Mia Alvar was born in Manila and grew up in Bahrain and New York City. Her work has appeared in *One Story, The Missouri Review, FiveChapters, The Cincinnati Review,* and elsewhere. She has received fellowships from the Lower Manhattan Cultural Council, Yaddo, and the Djerassi Resident Artists Program. A graduate of Harvard College and the School of the Arts at Columbia University, she lives in New York City.

A Note on the Type

This book was set in Caledonia, a typeface designed by W. A. Dwiggins (1880–1956). It belongs to the family of printing types called "modern face" by printers—a term used to mark the change in style of the type letters that occurred around 1800. Caledonia borders on the general design of Scotch Roman but it is more freely drawn than that letter. This version of Caledonia was adapted by David Berlow in 1979.

Typeset by Scribe, Philadelphia, Pennsylvania
Printed and bound by RR Donnelley,
Harrisonburg, Virginia
Designed by Jaclyn Whalen

1-15

F   Alvar, Mia
          In the country.